PRAISE FOR MALU HALASA

"Malu Halasa has a mind like an octopus. She reaches in all directions and in *Mother of All Pigs*, her first novel, she pulls together more characters and plotlines than most writers would dream of. You could say *Mother of All Pigs* is a novel about defiance, or innovation, or emigration, or family. You could say it's about Christianity or Islam or the Syrian civil war. You could say it's about feminism. You could say it's about a pig. No matter what, you'd be right. It's an ambitious novel, and a fun one. Halasa's got a great sense of humor to go with her wide-ranging interests and expertise, and the combination makes *Mother of All Pigs* a delight to read."

— Lily Meyer, Politics & Prose

"*Mother of All Pigs* is the book that western readers have been waiting for: a novel about ordinary people in the Middle East told with deep, sympathetic, understanding of the region. Halasa tells the stories of Middle Eastern women and men with rare familiarity. An enjoyable book about a fascinating set of characters, this is essential reading for anyone who wants to know more about the Middle East."

— Maziar Bahari, author of *And Then They Came for Me: A Family's Story of Love, Captivity and Survival* (now the feature film *Rosewater*)

"Malu Halasa's richly woven tale of family duty and private love, of loss and repossession, is quietly subversive. Lamentations follow the birth of girls, she tells us, and helps us to understand the psychological hardships of womanhood in modern Arab culture. Halasa's novel reveals in moving and warmly human ways the effects of large events and complex histories on everyday life."

— Darryl Pinckney, author of the novels, *High Cotton* and *Black Deutschland*, and two works of nonfiction, *Blackballed: The Black Vote and US Democracy* and *Out There: Mavericks of Black Literature*

MOTHER OF ALL PIGS

A Novel

Malu Halasa

The Unnamed Press
Los Angeles, CA

The Unnamed Press
P.O. Box 411272
Los Angeles, CA 90041

Published in North America by The Unnamed Press.

1 3 5 7 9 10 8 6 4 2

Copyright © 2017 by Malu Halasa
By Agreement with Pontas Literary & Film Agency

ISBN: 978-1-944700-34-8

Library of Congress Control Number: 2017952070

This book is distributed by Publishers Group West

Cover design & typeset by Jaya Nicely
Cover Artwork: Haphazard Synchronizations: Majd Masri, YAYA2016

For Andy

MOTHER OF ALL PIGS

1

Disappointment burns like desertification. It smells of old socks and leaches through the crevices and cracks of the new house. The odor, familiar and unchanging, greets Hussein every morning. Equally persistent is the dull heaviness in his brain, today the result of too much Johnnie Walker Red at last night's welcome dinner for his American niece Muna. It is her first time in her father's homeland, and Hussein thought he was lifting the mood of the family gathering when in fact he was just being selfish and getting drunk. As he slowly dresses, he hopes that the fog in his head will clear once he splashes water on his face. But after he turns the faucet in the bathroom sink, not even a trickle emerges. He suddenly recalls the empty and creaking tanks on the roof and the water truck three weeks late. Guided as much by the smell, he gropes for the tins his stepmother usually reserves for such occasions. After tap water runs low, Mother Fadhma fills containers at the town's communal cistern. Her health is poor so she brings it home by taxi. Because he is too lazy to help, he never complains about the expense.

This water is leaden, elemental like the smell that finds him in bed. The same taste pervades the glass of tea waiting for him on the kitchen table. His greedy first sip both scalds and steadies him, but the taste, so raw, repels him. It's like eating dirt. When he bends to kiss his stepmother good morning he nearly loses his balance. He coughs, sags down into a convenient seat, and dismisses the prepared food in front of him with a barely perceptible shake of his head. He clutches the hot glass of tea to his chest like a life preserver.

"*Khubz?*" The old woman offers a piece torn from a piping hot pita. Mother Fadhma has arranged his tea and breakfast dishes with care as if the world revolved around his every want and need. Wrapped in a new blue polyester robe—a gift from her grand-daughter from America—she is prepared to wait on him, but he only shakes his head again, so she takes a bite of bread herself.

"Such a party last night." The words come out long and heavy like a sigh, but the inflection rises. She is soliciting his opinion.

Hussein sits utterly still. He knows she would appreciate a conversation about the party, about Muna, about anything, but he needs to save the already depleted energy he has for the long day ahead.

When she receives absolutely no acknowledgment Mother Fadhma's small eyes narrow. She wants to scold him for eating too little and drinking too much; however, her silence was secured long ago. Even when he makes a fool of himself, as he did last night, she forgives him. On the rare occasion that she does summon the courage to rebuke him, her admonitions are gentle and consoling.

Hussein is still considered the most handsome of his six brothers. He even managed to look good in the plain khaki uniform, identical to thousands of others, that he wore during his military service. Something about the worn red beret enhanced his boyish features. The combination of his lieutenant's star and the discreet embroidered eagle of his elite brigade produced a subtle magic that more than one woman had found irresistible. Now, as he takes a grubby butcher's overall from the rack behind the front door and leaves the house, it is clear that this once dashing effect has been lost entirely. The intervening years have engraved crow's-feet across his formerly smooth and attractive features.

The cracked stone staircase outside tells a similar story. The house is the newest of the buildings lining the rough dirt track. The neighboring dwellings are made from mud brick or stone; irregular, stunted, and worn, their walls conceal rooms like cavities in a row of rotting teeth. Despite its modern construction, Hussein's home already exhibits the telltale signs of decay.

Immediately beyond the fence, sparse scrubby fields stretch into a misty distance. The haze isn't his hangover; heat is rising quickly again. In the dirt track, two or three stray dogs skulk listlessly. They are there every morning, attracted by the unmistakable smell of blood emanating from the battered van that occupies most of Hussein's truncated, sparsely graveled driveway. Usually he pretends to pick up a stone. It's not necessary to throw it; just stooping is enough to send the dogs, conditioned since puppyhood to expect cruelty, scattering down the street. He enjoys this small victory, but today he feels too queasy to bend down. Instead he half-heartedly kicks some dust at the nearest mutt and runs his finger along a fresh scratch that starts near the taillight and ends just in front of the driver's-side door. It was not there the previous morning. Several similar scratches, not caused by the normal wear and tear of unpaved streets, disfigure the paintwork. The latest addition is longer and deeper than the rest. Either things are getting worse or stones are getting sharper. Hussein sighs and squeezes into the driver's seat. The van was designed for someone much smaller. With the seat pushed fully back, his knees nearly touch the steering wheel. In the rearview mirror he catches a glimpse of a face disappearing behind a curtain in a window across the street. He has grown accustomed to being watched, but in a futile gesture of defiance he revs the engine higher than necessary, throws the van into gear, and reverses violently out of the driveway. Lurching to a halt, he immediately regrets his rash exhibition. His stomach catches up with the rest of his body and churns unpleasantly. A clammy sweat spreads across his shoulders and forehead. His hands feel light and clumsy, and he slumps back in the seat, breathing heavily. A black-and-brown dog gets up from the gutter, regards him apathetically, and trots away.

"Wine is a mocker, strong drink is raging: whoever is deceived by it is not wise." Jaber Ahmed Sabas was fond of quoting Scripture to his children. But Hussein remembers his father's words only when they can do him the least good—after the fact rather than before. It is easy for him to imagine how his father would have assessed the current situation. Jaber Ahmed Sabas, a Christian, always sought to reconcile the various faiths he lived among, not estrange them. To

Hussein, this willingness to avoid conflict sometimes bordered on weakness. If the old man had not been so constrained by respect for his neighbors, the family would not have waited so long to reap the benefits Hussein has been able to provide. But it is impossible for Hussein to think about his father without feeling uncomfortable, as though he has somehow failed him. When the town was still a village, Jaber Ahmed had emerged as a natural unassuming leader, a man of worth. He was a humble and tenacious farmer known for his love of history and storytelling. His reputation as a thinker and generous host became so well established that the whole community—even his immediate family—called the old man Al Jid—"Grandfather."

The dual specters of Al Jid and Johnnie Walker are dispelled by a loud burst of static and the cry of the muezzin cackling from the mosque's loudspeaker. For an instant, Hussein is completely still; then as fast as his fragile condition allows, he starts off down the hill toward town. He knows he will have to hurry if he wants to avoid trouble.

The livestock pens are clustered next to an open space that functions as an impromptu abattoir at the back of the market on the other side of town. Hussein glumly surveys the animals crowded into small stalls. Today is Friday, the day he will sell nothing unacceptable, nothing to affront his Muslim friends and neighbors. It is a pledge he made to himself early on in the business and one he is determined to keep. A dirty white sheep, a little larger than the rest, catches his eye, and he gestures to the young boy who sits chewing gum in the corner of the stall to bring it out for inspection. Hussein looks deeply into its eyes and ears, opens its mouth to see the teeth. The animal appears healthy. He lifts its back leg, trying to gauge the proportion of fat to meat. Satisfied, he hands the rope tied around its neck back to the boy. Hussein selects a goat and again examines it thoroughly. Of course the asking price is too high and his offer too low. The bargaining continues for several minutes until he agrees to pay slightly more than the true value. He simply cannot be bothered to argue anymore. Besides, the sheep is for a special order. He will pass on the loss to his customer.

Sometimes the animals come meekly, but when one decides to go north and the other south, they become difficult to handle. Hussein roughly jerks the struggling beasts to where he parked. He ties the sheep to the rear bumper, then, with a series of practiced, determined moves, throws the goat onto the ground, binds its feet together, and slides it into the back of the van. The sheep quickly follows. He locks the doors and pauses to wipe his brow. Already he feels as if he has done a full day's work. He squeezes into the driver's seat, starts the engine, and glances back to check the animals. Their eyes are glazed, muted, expecting death.

Past the old communal cistern the road narrows, then forks. Usually Hussein takes the left-hand track, which skirts the eastern part of town, before doubling back to the main road: five or ten minutes out of his way, nothing more. But the special order for tonight's wedding feast is due before nine, and a dull pain has been growing in the middle of his forehead. Also, he resents being made to feel like a criminal who has to sneak around. Recklessly, he turns right onto the shorter route.

Abruptly, a man riding a horse bursts out of a narrow side alley, and Hussein is forced to swerve, swearing, to the left. Up ahead, men and boys spill out of the mosque. Hussein feels a flutter of nervousness in his chest and thinks about turning around, but there is no room. The crowded mean little street refuses to give way. He rolls up the window and tightens his grip on the steering wheel.

Angry hands slap the van. People shout abuse. Their voices rouse the goat, which bleats mournfully for its all-too-short life. Hussein, hunched over the wheel that pushes into his gut, refuses to let himself be intimidated. His body seems to be swelling with indignation, but his mind becomes clear for the first time that morning. He keeps the van moving steadily forward. The hostile faces pressed up against the window meet his steely gaze. He is not prepared to satisfy them by showing either anger or fear.

Just beyond the mosque the road widens and turns. The crowd parts slightly and the van inches through, throwing up a small staccato hail of gravel. Then something shatters. In the rearview mirror Hussein catches sight of his teenage assailant. The boy, with a smattering of facial hair, isn't even old enough to grow a beard. In retaliation for his smashed taillight, Hussein slams the horn down hard. Alarmed, the stragglers scatter and the butcher's van shoots through to freedom in a cloud of sand and dust.

2

Laila peers past the cologne bottles and carefully checks the mirror for any evidence of strain on her face. Gently massaging the tender spot above her right ear, she wonders how it is that whenever her husband drinks alcohol she gets the headache. She is oblivious to the acidic smell of the toddler's soiled diapers rising from the hamper or her older sons in their bedroom. There is only one thing she demands and fusses about each and every morning. She doesn't care how much water is left or where it comes from—the farm, one of those pirate tankers, or a damn hole in the ground—only that there is an ample supply available for her sole and immediate use. On days when she has to remind Mother Fadhma that the tins in the bathroom are nearly empty, she can become loud and abusive.

Using almost all of what's left in the largest remaining container, she washes her face, then brushes her medium-length brown hair before applying makeup. Behind a cigarette taken from a pack on the windowsill, she examines her reflection again, nodding in pained appreciation. She looks good, despite everything that conspires against her. Some women are physically drained from having too many children and never fully recover. But after each birth Laila took rigorous precautions: the correct diet, makeup and clothes. Her nails are manicured, her skin supple and soft.

Discipline has always formed the core of her character. Her normally unbending demeanor gives the impression of someone firmly in control no matter how she may actually be feeling. Turning from the mirror, she experiences a flash of pain, bright and sharp. A reminder or a warning? She opens a bottle of extra-strength aspirin, swallows three tablets with the last of the water from the container, and takes a final drag from the half-finished cigarette before grinding it into a smoldering ashtray.

Mother Fadhma has had years of practice and is attuned to her daughter-in-law's nuanced expressions. She can tell if Laila desires solitude at the breakfast table and will retreat from the kitchen without a word of greeting or a second thought. Fadhma stays out of her daughter-in-law's way. It's bad enough living in Laila's house, but her stepson Hussein has to support Fadhma and her youngest daughter, Samira.

This morning Laila is apparently making an effort. She refills the old woman's tea glass before pouring one for herself and sitting down on the other side of an impressive spread of boiled eggs, *lebne* yogurt, sliced tomatoes, scallions, green and black olives, dried *za'atar* thyme, olive oil, and bread.

"So what did you think?" Fadhma rarely initiates conversations with her daughter-in-law, but she has been feeling unsettled since the arrival of their twenty-two-year-old visitor. Muna's father, Abd, is the second son of Fadhma's sister, Najla. Fadhma raised him and his five brothers with her five girls and two boys, after she married Al Jid following her sister's death. Abd's departure from Jordan twenty-five years ago accelerated the decline of her immediate family, but the old mother doesn't blame him for that. He was the first of Al Jid's thirteen kids to challenge a thousand years of tradition by marrying an *'ajnabi*, a foreigner.

"She certainly doesn't resemble our side of the family," Laila observes drily.

Yesterday evening, when Fadhma met Muna for the first time, she blurted out, "Like Chinese," which made everyone, including Laila, laugh nervously. The vast stretches of land and ocean separating the two countries have not prevented unpleasant stories from arriving by mail, telephone, and, worst of all, word of mouth. The ugly temper of Muna's foreign mother, who slashed her husband's suits and smashed a kitchen's worth of dishes, entered Sabas family legend long ago. The accounts only confirm the uncertainty of marriages to unknown, unscreened outsiders.

"Imagine," the old woman snorts, "the girl could have come with her father. Instead she insists on traveling alone when the Crushers are smashing their way across Syria and Iraq."

Laila is frustrated that Mother Fadhma insists on calling the jihadists the "Crushers,"—from the word *deas*—seemingly just to annoy her, but she refuses to be drawn in. She's rarely interested in her husband's family. She finds the young woman by herself fascinating.

"When I asked Muna if she has a boyfriend or if her family has plans for her to marry, do you know what she told me?" Laila picks at the food on the table and doesn't wait for her mother-in-law's reply. "She said, 'You've got to be kidding.'"

Last night Laila felt such a mixture of disapproval and jealousy that she was unable to continue the conversation. Going over it again this morning, she still finds it hard to believe and adds aloud as an afterthought, "Such confidence—freedom." As soon as the words leave her lips she can tell she has said something wrong.

"We've had too much of that around here. It's contagious, don't you think?"

The malice in Fadhma's voice is unmistakable. But Laila wasn't referring to the unpleasant subject the two of them have been avoiding, although she admits to herself she has been bothered by it for quite a while.

"You need to talk to Samira," Laila states matter-of-factly. "After all, you are her mother."

"Yes, the mother is the first to be blamed." The old lady makes a desultory motion with her hand under her chin as though slashing her own throat. "But I tell you now," she adds testily, "I am not the only person at fault in this family."

Laila, expecting the worst, steels herself for a first-thing-in-the-morning fight. Instead her mother-in-law begins to openly despair, which strikes Laila as out of character, for Fadhma usually shows no emotion other than stubbornness.

"I've begged Hussein to remind Samira of her duty—to counsel her. It is her reputation and ours at stake." Straightaway Fadhma's mood changes and her words come out as though forged in molten lead: "But his attention has been elsewhere."

Suddenly one of the English idioms Laila teaches in level two at school comes to mind: there is an animal in the room more unpredictable than an elephant—dirtier and smellier too. It is rampaging through their lives... However aren't all their disagreements like this? Fadhma always tries to deflect any criticism. This morning Laila refuses to be dissuaded.

"When I've questioned Samira she always has perfectly good excuses for going out," Unperturbed, Fadhma sips her tea.

"The new headmistress said she saw Samira in the capital," Laila responds. "Imagine, the girl drops out of teacher training college, has nothing to do, and ends up among strangers when it's so dangerous! Of course Mrs. Salwa only thought she recognized someone who *looked* like Samira."

The two women huddle together in strained silence. Laila doesn't exactly remember when she began to suspect that Samira was acting carelessly. It hadn't been during the big upheavals during the Arab Awakening; she and her teenage friends were too young to go to the demonstrations. But something's turned toxic. Laila isn't sure why that is—the political uncertainty all around them or the company Hussein's half sister is keeping.

Although Laila harbors many doubts about the society in which she lives, she meticulously stays within conventional boundaries, and she expects those she lives with to do the same. Samira, her husband's unmarried half sister, is particularly vulnerable since relatively little is needed—perhaps only a rumor of a girl's indiscretion—for the entire town to become inflamed and a family ostracized forever. In a culture where a woman's virtue is paramount, any defense of it is a sign of its erosion. Better to avoid scrutiny. The women of the Sabas family have to protect one another because no one else will.

Rising slowly from her seat, Mother Fadhma smirks triumphantly and says, "At least with our guest, my girl won't be out by herself, will she?"

The old woman draws the new robe around her like a protective shield. Its thick material will make her sweat like a pig. Forgetting herself, Laila almost laughs out loud. It is the English idioms about animals she finds useful inside and outside the classroom.

Her thoughts are interrupted by seven-year-old Salem bounding into the kitchen. Relieved, the two women turn from each other. Laila takes her son's perfectly formed face and squeezes it between her hands. She admits that despite everything she has cause to be thankful. Her eldest is a great source of comfort to her, and seeing him fresh and alert immediately improves her mood. He was born exactly nine months after her marriage, and with Hussein still living full-time in the army, her firstborn became the love of her life.

In the doorway, a second, smaller boy waits quietly. Dark like his father, Mansoor also inherited his father's disposition and tends to be reserved and moody. Sometimes the most trivial things overwhelm him and his asthma flairs. Laila instantly notices his furrowed brow. He finds it hard keeping up with a brother who, though a year older, is much more self-assured.

She beckons to her second son, calling softly, "*Habibi*, darling, come here," and pats him on the back as he climbs onto the chair beside hers.

Both children still in their pajamas have washed their faces. Salem stuffs bread and yogurt into his mouth, while Mansoor begs Laila to feed him.

"You're a big boy now," Salem sneers.

"Am not..." Mansoor's voice trails off into wheezing.

Laila, shushing him, cuts up a boiled egg with a spoon and slips it into an unreceptive mouth. Before the taunts start again she warns, "Your new aunt is sleeping!"

The boys lower their voices. Her sons like their visitor. They tore open the gifts she delivered from their overseas relatives and were impressed to meet a real live American, like Abby on *CSI*. Moments later Salem forgets his mother's warning and waves a fork under his brother's nose. The squabbling brings Fadhma immediately to the table. She envelops Mansoor in her arms while at the same time cajoling Salem until both brothers promise to behave themselves. As they bask in her affection, Laila momentarily reflects on why her children never share their troubles with her. She suspects they are closer to Fadhma because she panders to them. The feeling they have for their mother—which Laila actively cultivates—is respect, fashioned more from fear than love.

"See the trouble you're causing your *jadda!*" she tells her sons. She doesn't care if the boys torment their grandmother. However, some display of formal courtesy, no matter how empty, is necessary.

"I am not worthy, Umm Salem," Fadhma answers. Her simple statement is a two-pronged assault in the understated conflict between them. She knows that Laila finds false humility irritating, and by calling her "Mother of Salem," she effectively reduces her daughter-in-law from a person to a function.

Laila imperiously looks through Fadhma to the repurposed five-gallon clarified butter tin waiting on the sideboard near the sink. Filled with the last of the precious washing water for dishes, it has been standing there for the past three weeks. "That truck better come today," she complains, disgusted at the chaos all around her. It doesn't have to be like this.

Last week the boys didn't require such supervision; they ate quickly, dressed, and went outside to play with their friends before the walk to school with their mother. Now the two of them bicker and play with their food. Laila has also noticed that when it is time to leave they become unusually quiet. She wonders if she hadn't spied on them would she have been able to determine the cause of their unhappiness.

After Muna's arrival yesterday evening, Laila was in the kitchen when she heard Mansoor's whine from the back terrace: "Those boys don't like me anymore." Instead of going and asking what was the matter, she hid behind the thick curtains over the terrace door.

Salem put down a shiny new toy gun, a gift from one of his American aunts, and said, "So what? They told me they hate me too."

As Laila watched, she knew her younger son would not be able to understand how anyone could feel anything other than admiration for his older brother.

"What?" Mansoor asked incredulously.

Salem, wiser than his years, took a tissue from a box among the cushions, wiped his brother's nose, and gently placed his arm around the six-year-old's shoulders. Laila's sorrow at that moment was outweighed only by the rage she still feels toward her husband.

She suddenly rises from the table. "Hurry up!" she orders the boys, and leaves the kitchen. Her steps soften once she opens her bedroom door. Behind it, in a wooden crib, sleeps Fuad, the youngest of her three sons. She pushes a damp curl from his forehead. The toddler, not yet two, spent most of the previous night awake with a sour stomach; he had gotten too excited at the family dinner for Muna. Laila gets ready. She glances at the sleeping child one last time before pulling the door behind her.

The hallway is deathly quiet. Samira's bedroom door is also closed, its occupants still asleep. Laila can just about make out someone moving around the living room—Fadhma, no doubt, complaining to that dead husband of hers. She finds the boys in their bedroom, waiting silently, prepared for school. Salem and Mansoor stare up at her.

"*Yalla,*" she whispers, "let's go."

3

At the butcher shop, Hussein is scrupulous when it comes to the storing of meat. He keeps two refrigerators, one for meat that is permitted and another, much larger, to accommodate forbidden flesh. They are not labeled halal and haram. While he observes no particular dietary restrictions because of religion, he wants to act responsibly—even if he is the only one conscious of the precautions. The halal box is almost empty except for a few pieces of offal. He sells all the freshly slaughtered mutton and goat from the hooks displayed in the window. The other box is filled to capacity, ready for the weekend. He will bring even more ham and sausages under the cover of darkness later tonight, but by the close of business on Sunday, every bit will be gone.

The premises of the dingy butcher shop are washed down daily, water permitting, but the drains are often clogged with fatty grease and give off an unpleasantly pervasive, putrid smell. Hussein lights the gas burner and puts a pan of water on to boil. He can hear his assistant, Khaled, at work in the back. The boy mutters a prayer. This is followed by a frantic scrabbling of hooves against the tile floor, then a spattering that dissolves into a barely audible gurgle as the blood, rich and soupy, drains into an old galvanized bucket. Several muffled thumps—the head and hooves being removed—then a sound like an old oily carpet being torn in half as Khaled peels off the skin. With a liquid slap the entrails pour out, silken and milky.

Hussein pictures his assistant rummaging through the pile, like a sorcerer searching for auguries, and picking out the delicacies: the liver, kidneys, and small intestine. The boy inflates the lungs with a series of quick, hard breaths, the time-honored way of testing an animal's health. He returns to the front of the shop, lays the sheep's cadaver on the long wooden counter, and, wiping his bloody fingers on his grimy apron, grins stupidly at his boss.

Hussein ignores him and takes a cleaver from the extensive array of well-used hardware that hangs on the wall. There is something deeply satisfying about dismembering a carcass, something irrevocably final about each bone-crushing blow. With each swing of the cleaver Hussein feels his mood improving. *Bam!* This shows the young delinquent the error of his taillight-smashing ways. *Whack!* That is for the water truck. *Crack!* Laila. The next crunch is going to be for Samira and all the trouble she's been causing them, but at the last moment Hussein changes his mind and once again delivers it as his personal contribution to the struggle against juvenile crime. He works methodically, separating leg from loin, shank from breast, rib from shoulder, venting his frustrations with every stroke.

From his handiwork, he selects two handsome joints and hangs them in the window. Already flies are beginning to gather over the piles of meat, which ooze fat, soft as jelly, onto the counter. The bell over the screen door suddenly rings, announcing the first customer of the day. Hussein forces a welcoming smile.

"Mrs. Habash, good to see you. What will it be today? We have delicious lamb."

The mayor's wife is one of the town's most prominent citizens. She married her cousin and belongs to an ancient tribe, which, like the Sabas lineage, traces its ancestry back to a fortress settlement in the country's south. Over a hundred years ago their families, and other Christians, were forced to flee northward—the result of a misunderstanding that turned into a sectarian conflict. Eventually they came to a Byzantine city destroyed by earthquakes and established a village that grew into a town. This historic connection is useful to Hussein. It makes it easier to stop by the mayor's office every couple of weeks with what he calls "a little bite" that is bigger than the crumbs the mayor usually receives. Hussein considers the expense of these friendly consultations another indispensable operating cost. Why should he and his uncle Abu Za'atar be the only ones with their noses in the trough? It is only fair, and no one asks him to do it, but it doesn't make dealing with the mayor's wife any easier.

Mrs. Habash dismisses his offer. "I was thinking Issa would like chicken for lunch. You don't have one in the back, do you?"

Hussein began keeping a few birds in a small coop in the yard after Mrs. Habash told him that she didn't like going to the market. She feels it's beneath her dignity to bargain like a *falah*, a peasant. She prefers to come to Hussein instead and is prepared to pay for the privilege. He calls out, "Khaled, *jajeh*!" and the boy appears clutching a robust, speckled fowl in his arms.

Hussein is puzzled. Khaled is fond of this particular bird. It is the pick of the flock and the boy gives it special treatment and feeds it extra food. But he can't say anything in front of Mrs. Habash, so he takes the plump chicken and turns it around for her benefit. She nods in approval. Hussein hands the bird back to Khaled and tells him to prepare it. He urges the boy to hurry—"*Assre'!*"—more for his sake than for the customer, whom he regards as intrusive. She has probably ordered chicken only so she can gossip while it's being plucked.

"How's the family?" She inspects the meat on the counter. "I hear your niece has arrived. I hope she's not like one of those Arab hip-hoppers."

"Not at all. Muna is a well-mannered young woman," he replies, although from what he remembers from last night, he cannot be sure.

"I look forward to meeting her. I would be happy to show her the mosaics after service on Sunday."

"I'm sure she will enjoy that." He can already anticipate what's coming next.

"Perhaps you will join us?"

Long ago Hussein abandoned whatever religious convictions he held. Experience made it impossible for him to carry on believing.

Nevertheless, in the past he went to church for the sake of form. As his drinking, disillusionment, and shame increased, he gradually stopped going. Those had been his reasons. His wife insists on attending for the children's sake, even though it has become difficult. Sometimes people whisper and stare.

Hussein doesn't want to offend such an important customer. He usually compliments Mrs. Habash's good taste and even agrees with her when he thinks her opinions are ill judged. His uncle stupidly recommends this as sound business practice.

Hussein instead opts for evasiveness: "Sundays are my busiest days, Mrs. Habash." It was hard to miss the cars that blocked the main street during the weekend. "All of my customers are Christians anyway. And when I can, I take a moment alone to..." He can't bring himself to lie outright, so he swallows the word "pray."

"That's all well and good," she sighs, "but commerce is no substitute for worship. Religion anchors our way of life."

At any moment she is going to remind him that their town was mentioned in the Bible. The Byzantine ruins their families settled on had been an ancient Moabite town where Musa walked and Isaiah prophesized. Like the writing on the side of the tour buses said, VISIT THE LAND OF THE PROPHETS. His father would not have agreed more.

Hussein throws up his hands and wearily concedes, "Can't argue with that."

Ignoring him, Mrs. Habash presses on: "I was just telling Issa this morning, even a woman of my considerable years feels the strain whenever I'm near the Eastern Quarter. Mark my words, in a year's time all us ladies will be wearing hijabs."

Hussein knows how he is expected to react, but his customers from the Eastern Quarter have been thoroughly decent to him. His van may have been assaulted outside the mosque, but he cannot bring himself to hold a grudge against a religion and all who follow it. His eighteen years in the army taught him to be extremely wary of organized bigotry, and even his two-year special assignment didn't dissuade him.

Hypocrisy, he reminds himself, is not the exclusive preserve of the pampered and protected who rarely venture beyond family and home. He encountered it in his commanding officers and the secret police, men far more devious than Mrs. Habash. Yet he finds her attitude disquieting. When the numbers of Syrian refugees were low and they were housed with relatives and sympathetic friends in the country, she talked about the importance of solidarity and initiated a few desultory charitable collections. The homeless and bereft who wandered through were nothing more than annoying nuisances, to be pitied rather than feared. Once hundreds of thousands fled over the border and the Eastern Quarter filled with refugees and other migrants, the town's demographics started changing and Christians, historically the majority, were being outnumbered. Those with the most to lose—people like Mrs. Habash—responded by locking their gates, building their walls higher, and closing their minds.

"Laila hasn't mentioned any trouble to me," he admits slowly.

"She will," intones the mayor's wife, before complaining, "I just don't know when the country will return to normal and our town will belong to us."

Hussein finds Mrs. Habash's memory highly selective. The town has never been theirs. When their grandfathers and their uncles and fathers—then small boys—first settled, they fought side by side against local nomads over a watering hole. Go back a few generations and someone somewhere is always fleeing or seeking sanctuary with strangers. The entire region has a long history of forced migration. The Syrians are not the first refugees, nor will they be the last.

To divert Mrs. Habash's attention, he remarks blandly, "I sell so much goat these days—"

"I suppose it's cheap meat they want for all those children," she declares. "You can see why they have no money."

Hussein suddenly feels drained. The morning has already taken its toll. There are too many lines of division between those who have money and those who do not. Hussein sees himself scrabbling in the middle, attempting to grab whatever he can for his family but feeling like a failure most of the time.

Tiredness overrides his better judgment. "All of us like a lot of children, Mrs. Habash, whatever our religion, don't you agree?"

The mayor's wife has no offspring; it is the one weakness in her social armor. Hussein doesn't care that he is being reckless. Lower than refugees are barren women. Everyone agrees: they are without purpose. Christian, Muslim, and Jew alike, they have failed their families and their gods.

Mrs. Habash's composure instantaneously toughens, as she aims for Hussein's most vulnerable spot: "By the way, how's business?"

Before he can answer, Khaled appears behind the counter, his clothes flecked with chicken feathers. He proudly holds up a freshly plucked chicken.

"Wonderful." Hussein slaps the boy on the back with more enthusiasm than is necessary. He wraps it up, saying, "Fine, Mrs. Habash, just fine," and hands it to her.

She has already counted out the change. "I only ask because there are rumors, you know."

As she leaves she holds the butcher's door wide open. Hussein is sure she is going to remark on the sorry state of the van. So to save himself the embarrassment, he turns his back toward her. Without a ready audience, the screen door slams shut. The sound brings Khaled in from the back with the speckled bird he loves clucking in his arms.

The boy might not be so dumb, Hussein thinks, but his satisfaction doesn't last long. "Put it back. We've wasted too much time."

Together they pack the mutton into clear plastic bags. The meat is destined for the kitchen of Hussein's friend Matroub and tonight's feast celebrating his eldest daughter's wedding.

Normally Hussein reminds Khaled not to stray on his errands. Today Hussein promises more kindly, "If you hurry they'll give you *ma'amoul.*" Khaled's face lights up at the prospect of semolina cookies. Hussein follows the boy out of the shop and stands on the main street.

The other stores and stalls have opened, as a queue forms outside the bakery. Down the street in front of the pilgrims' hotel, baseball caps and sun visors board one of the Holy Land tour buses. In front of him, on the other side of the street's only asphalted section, looms the Marvellous Emporium, a storehouse of untold proportions owned and operated by Abu Za'atar. Hussein wants to go over immediately, to demand his uncle's attention and pour out his troubles, but the sight of a large truck from Iraq parked beneath the emporium's neon display stops him. He is all too familiar with Abu Za'atar's priorities. Drivers bringing loads of potentially profitable goods take precedence over family matters. This truck has an added bonus. It comes from a place known for its American swag—recycled military attire, packaged food beyond its sell-by date, even spare parts from defunct air-conditioning units—which is highly coveted and requires Abu Za'atar's undivided attention. For it is in the few minutes between refreshment and unloading that a deal is struck. "What a hungry man clings to a full belly gives away" is another of his uncle's cherished aphorisms.

In the past, Hussein would have been amused. However, since their business venture has become troublesome, he finds himself wondering whether he is just another victim of Abu Za'atar's avarice. In any commercial transaction his uncle always takes more than his fair share of the profits—that is to be expected. In this one he has managed to avoid both the inconvenience and the social stigma enveloping Hussein. The butcher purses his lips in disgust, mainly with himself. He knows there is no point in being annoyed by Abu Za'atar's behavior. The new uneasiness in their relationship is not his uncle's fault. He's always acted exactly the same way. The problem is that Hussein is finding it harder to accept his relation's philosophy of profit above all else. Sighing, he retreats back into the shop.

Alone before the morning crush, he crouches down behind the counter and reaches behind one of the refrigerators. Making sure that no one sees him, he surreptitiously extracts an ordinary jar, unscrews the lid, and drinks, long and slow. The neat *arak* is like fire in his throat, but with the burning comes the savage calm he always finds, temporarily, at the bottom of a bottle. People like Abu Za'atar and Mrs. Habash shouldn't have a monopoly on a decent future. He wants the same opportunities not so much for himself—it is too late for that—but for his sons. So he did what many would have found inconceivable: he sold his father's land. Through his own initiative his family resides in a new house. But no amount of money, as his uncle continually reminds him, is ever enough. Hussein glances around again before quickly reaching for the jar and taking one more potent swallow.

From the moment Abu Za'atar showed him the pig, Hussein knew it was not going to be an easy road to riches. He had not really thought any further than the first litter and assumed the piglets would be fattened up for a one-off bonanza sale. Then the business would end. He had not reckoned on the pigs' natural behavior. No sooner were the young boars weaned than they acquired the mounting reflex. First they tried their mother, then each other, and finally turned their attention to their own sisters. Hussein watched them and began to wonder whether there might be more to the project than he thought.

He knew castration was the best way to ensure that the boars fattened up properly, but he decided to spare two of them from the knife. He left them with their mother and five of their sisters and moved the other thirteen piglets into different pens. The males mated with an uninhibited, libidinous indulgence, reveling in their thirteen-minute orgasms. Fascinated, Hussein timed them on a fancy Taiwanese stopwatch (accurate to one-tenth of a second) borrowed from the Marvellous Emporium. The experiment paid off. At the end of the fifth month, the mother and three of her daughters were pregnant. The rest of the litter was ready for market, but Hussein made a peculiar discovery: he did not have the heart to kill them. It was strange that the son of a farmer, accustomed from an early age to the necessities of slaughtering animals, should be so squeamish; stranger still that a former soldier schooled in the accoutrements of death, from small arms to switchblades, would be incapable of cutting a pig's throat. Irrationally, he had developed affection for the creatures, born out of respect for their intelligence. There was no question of going to Abu Za'atar; his uncle would not have understood.

Hussein wondered whom he could safely approach with his problem. Then he hit upon the idea of asking the head of the family who rented his father's mud brick house. Hussein had overridden

strenuous objections from Laila when he originally leased the building to one of the oldest Palestinian refugee families, who had arrived
in the town during Al Jid's lifetime. His wife could not understand
why he charged so little rent or why, when there was a surplus at the
shop, he took gifts of meat to his tenants. It was more than welfare
relief on Hussein's part. By using his father's house to benefit the
less fortunate, he hoped to atone for selling off Al Jid's beloved land.

Whatever the reason, the family was grateful for his kindness
and the husband, a man of about sixty, was more than willing to
care for the pigs and get one of his sons to slaughter them for a small
remuneration. In this way Hussein took on his first employees, and
Ahmad proved to be a capable worker. Nine months and a hundred
piglets later, there was more to do than ever before. The retail side
of the business was growing, and it looked as though Abu Za'atar's
prediction of easy wealth had not been unfounded.

There remained, however, one apparently insurmountable problem. Hussein scrupulously examined each new litter. He measured
each piglet's weight and size, inspected hooves and tails, and checked
eyes, looking for signs. So far he had been lucky, but he knew that
his chances of producing another generation without some evidence
of inbreeding were very slight. As Laila put it: "Who would want to
eat a two-headed beast with six legs?" The gold mine would have
closed prematurely if not for Abu Za'atar's intervention.

The wily emporium proprietor had already made numerous contributions. He provided, at only a fraction above cost, feed, antibi-
otics, a large and rather noisy freezer, and even an electric prod that
Hussein didn't have the heart to use; but the solution he devised totally eclipsed his previous efforts: through his cross-border contacts
Abu Za'atar managed to discover a supply of frozen boar semen.
Hussein had not been too keen on the idea—there was something
unnatural about it that made him feel queasy.

When the first consignment arrived aboard a Damascus-bound
truck, Hussein's misgivings multiplied. Both the label on the box,
which contained the vials of sperm, and the instruction booklet that
accompanied it were written in Hebrew. Although there was also
a religious prohibition of pork on the other side of the river, it was

marketed as *basar lavon*—"white meat." At first pork was sold secretly in butcher shops, but when eight hundred thousand Russian immigrants arrived in Israel after 1989, pork was practically on every
street corner. To many in Hussein's town, the very idea of artificial
insemination was outrageous enough, but Hussein knew that if the
origin of his latest secret were to become public knowledge, then
everything he had worked for would go up in smoke.

Abu Za'atar was, of course, thrilled by the prospect of such technological innovation. With his good eye and magnifying glass, he
studied the thermometer and other equipment with giddy enthusiasm. Poring over the instructions, he displayed a knowledge of Hebrew that shocked Hussein. As Abu Za'atar assembled the catheter,
he airily explained that when no one in the wider Middle East was
allowed to say the word "Israel" in public without being arrested,
he wanted to learn the country's language as an act of youthful rebellion. His dream was realized after peace was made between Jordan and Israel in 1994 and cheap Hebrew correspondence courses
became available from the Knesset in Jerusalem. Then he brushed
aside his nephew's fears once and for all by declaring, "What's good
for pigs is good for politics."

Bolstered by his uncle's confidence, Hussein reluctantly agreed
to give the procedure a try. They restricted themselves to working on the big pig until the method was perfected. The first two
attempts were not successful, but by carefully monitoring the
signs—a certain redness around the genitals in the presence of
one of the boars, a rise in body temperature—Hussein was able
to choose the opportune time for the third attempt. The resulting
litter was small—eight piglets—but it was clear that the benefits
of introducing new blood far outweighed a temporary slowdown.
As the litters grew in number and frequency, it was Ahmad who
christened Abu Za'atar's pig. When he groomed her, he whispered
to Umm al-Khanaazeer, Mother of All Pigs, how she alone had
brought them good fortune.

In any event, there had been a period during the early days when
production outpaced demand. This troubled Abu Za'atar, who hated to see waste, particularly if there was a way of turning it into

profit. The freezer he supplied was not large enough to contain the surplus, and the fuel costs of running the generator proved to be unnervingly high. So the old man urged his nephew to find some other way of preserving the meat.

Hussein started visiting culinary websites at the town's relatively new Internet café and found one that detailed various methods of producing ham. He arrived at the farm with two aluminum pots. To ensure against trichinosis, an incomprehensible but nevertheless unpleasant-sounding condition, the meat had to be treated at high temperatures. Hussein was by no means confident in the small fire Ahmad had built, so he compensated by insisting that the meat be steeped in a brine solution and then subjected to several prolonged applications of salt, sugar, potassium nitrate, pepper, and spices, all of which was supplied from the emporium. The result was then dried in the sun. These hams were hard and waxy; Abu Za'atar was not persuaded.

Next, Hussein scoured the Internet for smoking techniques. He left instructions for Ahmad to build a small hut out of corrugated iron while he set about finding the right fuel himself. One site called for oak and beech, woods guaranteed to give the meat a golden hue, but not only were these particular species unavailable, Hussein lived in an area where it was hard to find any wood at all. So he sent Ahmad's sons to comb the countryside. The assortment of zizphus scrub they managed to collect gave the meat an unhealthy blue-gray tinge and made it smell rank and bitter. "No wonder these bushes produced the thorns in Christ's crown," Hussein said, disgusted. He was prepared to give up the project altogether but Abu Za'atar urged him on. Through his infinite contacts, the old man learned of an olive grove in the occupied territories that was about to be destroyed to make way for a new settlement. He procured a truckload of olive wood and, at his own expense, arranged for it to be transported to the farm. Hussein protested about the political implications, but his uncle was unimpressed.

"Surely Al Jid told you the story about the sacred olive," his uncle explained. "Each leaf bears the words '*Bismillah al-rahman al-rahim*,' 'In the name of Allah, the Beneficent, the Merciful.' If a tree does not pray five times a day, God forsakes it and its fate is to be cut down. Is it my fault the Israelis find every Palestinian olive grove impious?"

Hussein let the gnarled branches weather outdoors to reduce the tannin in the bark and then carefully built a fire in his smokehouse. At last, he was rewarded. The meat, everyone agreed, gave off the aroma of bitter olive, a rich mellow flavor that became instantly popular with the customers. However, consignments of wood arrived too infrequently for smoking to be economically viable. Apart from one man who provided his own juniper twigs and berries—he had a cousin who sent them from Germany, which enabled Hussein to produce a perfectly acceptable Westphalian ham—he was forced to go back to boiling his commercial product. After much trial and error he hit upon the method of coating the cooked hams with honey, anise, and dried *nana* mint. The real breakthrough came when he made a thick coating of Mother Fadhma's *za'atar* spice mixture and a very Arab ham was born.

This required time and space and necessitated the construction of a processing house to keep the meat out of the sun and away from flies. Although Hussein scrupulously never tasted the meat himself, judging only from its density and feel, he was not as satisfied with the texture of the boiled hams as he had been with the smoked variety. So he was pleased that Abu Za'atar was able to arrange for most of the farm's processed meat output to be exported. Hussein made a point of never asking its destination. If frozen boar sperm and olive wood were easily smuggled across the river, there was no reason a cargo of hams couldn't go the other way. He just didn't want to know.

Anything that was not made into processed meat was taken to the sausage machine in the other part of the processing block. Even before the arrival of the machine, Abu Za'atar had insisted that any leftovers too unappetizing to sell be partially cooked, minced with stale bread, and stuffed into intestines. He reasoned that the sheer novelty would ensure sales, and he was right. It was a labor-intensive process by hand. Ahmad's sons helped out, but it was still too much work. Hussein complained to Abu Za'atar, who responded by turning to his mysterious friend Hani, a former Palestinian fixer and purveyor of the improbable. He had managed to smuggle Umm al-Khanaazeer across four hostile borders, the first of his magic tricks. The second was the unexpected delivery to the farm of an ancient German Wurstmeister.

The sausage machine was a thing of baroque beauty. Pipes, bowls, pistons, mixers, drums, shakers, grips, and pots exuded a futuristic, functional elegance. The power unit looked like it could drive an ocean liner, and when the machine was working it rattled alarmingly. But it performed its task with flawless efficiency. Brain and brawn, ears and jowls, lungs and trimmings, and Hussein's failed hams were placed in a large hopper above the primary grinding assembly. Once ground, they were mixed in a moving bowl by a rotary knife blade and then transferred to the emulsifier, a large drum where bread, cooked grain, herbs, and spices could be added gradually from their own separate hoppers. When the mixture reached the required consistency, it was forced by a screw mechanism through a small opening into the casings. The skins were washed, scraped, and treated with hydrogen peroxide and vinegar in a different part of the machine. An automatic tying arm twisted the links into two sizes, breakfast or cocktail.

The sausages were more popular than the hams. In fact the only by-product that met with outright consumer resistance was the blood pudding. It simply would not move until Ahmad came up with the novel idea of dyeing the casing turquoise, a color that traditionally warded off the evil eye. After that, it sold steadily. The processing building was a monument to Abu Za'atar's cheerful dictum that there was a use for "every part of the little piggy."

Swept along by his uncle's enthusiasm and seduced by the money he was making, Hussein focused on the positive benefits and suppressed his apprehensions. The morning's incident outside the mosque caused all the old anxieties to resurface. He would have liked to think of it as an isolated occurrence, but it was clearly more serious than that.

4

Before crashing into the bedroom door, little Fuad grabs hold of the handle and pushes hard. The slow gliding motion is deeply satisfying; it is the toddler's first triumph of an otherwise unexceptional morning. Tentatively he enters a silent room. Muna, in one of the single beds, gives the impression of being fast asleep.

Tiny juddering steps take him to an opened suitcase in front of a table between the beds. For someone still honing his rudimentary motor skills, stepping over something no matter how sleight is akin to scaling a mountain. He crouches beside the suitcase, then without warning hurls himself into it face-first. He uses a tartan miniskirt to pull the rest of himself inside. Muna, amused, raises herself on her elbows and watches.

Meddlesome fingers trawl buttons and zippers. Unable to find anything suitable to suck in his mouth, the child considers his options. Ignoring a natural inclination to pull a strand of Samira's long dark hair escaping from a nearby pillow, he grabs a convenient table leg and pulls himself upright. He's still not tall enough. An erratic sweep of a small hand brings that which glitters enticingly on the surface within reach. Plopping down, he prepares to taste each contact lens package and family snapshot, when he is inexplicably removed from his heart's desire. The intrusion is so rude and unexpected that he falls backward into Muna's arms and screams. The more she soothes him, the louder he becomes. Once he sees that

Auntie Samira is awake, he insists on going to her, bawling and kicking. An indifferent shake of her head sparks another outburst.

The aroma of coffee and cardamom signals his imminent rescue.

Mother Fadhma had left Fuad for only a moment. As quickly as her ailing physical condition allows, she enters Samira's room and places a steaming tray of Arabic coffee on the table. "Shame on these girls for treating you badly," she scolds, and takes the little boy in her arms. Safe with his *jadda*, Fuad swallows deep, long gulps.

"Mamma is his favorite," Samira says, and yawns. "The rest of us are fed up with babies."

Sitting next to Muna on her bed, Fadhma retrieves a handkerchief from her apron pocket and wipes the tears from the child's blotchy face.

"I didn't mean to..." Muna is embarrassed but her grandmother raises a hand.

"Nobody can be held responsible for a tantrum." As she rocks baby Fuad, she remembers Muna's father, Abd. Her special affection for him began the instant she saw him, seconds after a difficult premature birth. Fadhma had been a teenager at the time—probably a decade younger than Muna now. She took the tiny dark baby from her fifteen-year-old sister, Najla, and fell in love. It was Fadhma who had given him his nickname. In any other mouth Abd, which means "servant" or "slave," would have been derogatory, but in those few moments she could tell his future: he would be dedicated in the service of his family. Although she couldn't foretell her own: after her sister's death and Fadhma's marriage to Al Jid, she would raise thirteen children.

After the inappropriate playthings have been safely retrieved, the suitcase shut and Fuad prowling with a newfound swagger on all fours, Mother Fadhma takes the photos Muna brought from America and looks through them again. She'd glanced at them last night, but in the harsh morning light they tell a different story. The sons of her sister dominate the pictures as they do the family. There are no proper images of Mother Fadhma's beloved daughters—Magda, Loulwa, and Hind—even though they too live in Cleveland. Sometimes the camera catches a shoulder, back, or side view showing more hair than face, as they cook and clean in the houses of their half brothers and husbands. Her fourth daughter, Katrina, and her two sons, Abdul and Sharif, don't appear at all: they settled in Chile with Najla's eldest, Yusef.

In the United States, her sister's boys have grown old. Mother Fadhma looks twice to pick out Farouk in his businessman's suit and tie. Qassim lost all his hair, but he remains the comedian, still joking with the others outside one of the garages he owns. Boutros, a medical technician, appears quietly content as the father of four girls. Abd has an even darker complexion now that his hair has grayed. Mother Fadhma wonders whether it is his scientific career or his stormy marriage that is to blame.

The men stand beside cars or in stiff family groups, or play ball with their sons and daughters. Everyone looks smug and overfed, even the children. "Like fattened calves," Mother Fadhma whispers to herself. In their rush to assimilate, her stepgrandsons in their Cleveland Cavaliers jerseys seem to have lost any connection to Jordan.

Normally the old mother would not have expected gratitude. She has long been accustomed to unrewarded work. She was the one who scrimped and saved; she had even sold her few pieces of gold jewelry to pay for their travel. While they didn't have to constantly thank her, she wouldn't mind being remembered once in a while. Mother Fadhma becomes aware of Muna's eyes on her. The girl had been remarking on one of the pictures, but the old woman had been far too engrossed in her own thoughts and hadn't paid attention. It occurs to her now that Abd's daughter shouldn't be blamed for her father's and uncles' apathy, just like she cannot be faulted for a toddler's tears. It really is time, Fadhma thinks, to rid herself of this burden of resentment. Ever since Muna's arrival the Jordanian family has been too preoccupied with their own troubles to be truly hospitable. Leaning over, Mother Fadhma wipes the sleep from her granddaughter's foreign eyes—her first act of intimacy toward the girl—then returns the stack of pictures to the table. She pours out two demitasse cups of Arabic coffee and tells

Muna and Samira to start without her, as she gets up, albeit painful-ly, from the bed and moves slowly from the room.

She returns with a battered cardboard box and declares proudly, "Every piece of correspondence the family sent over the years." In-side, neat bundles of papers and letters are tied with brown string. At the bottom lies a faded powder-blue airmail envelope, as dry as onionskin. It contains extra passport photographs taken before each of Al Jid's children—her sister's and her own—left the country. Fadhma wants her granddaughter to see her aunts and uncles when they were young and starting out in life, full of hope.

At first Muna doesn't recognize the two yellowed snapshots of Magda and Loulwa. "Look at them!" she exclaims, somewhat baffled. The middle-aged, overweight women in Ohio bear little resemblance to these two rouged, willowy girls. The next picture is easier to identify: "It's Hind," she cries out. Muna knows Moth-er Fadhma's second-youngest daughter well. At age sixteen, Hind was sent to live with Muna's family in Cleveland. She was only two years older than Muna. It took a while, but eventually the two girls became close, Fadhma knows through Hind's letters home. She also wonders if Muna agrees with her daughter's assessment that it was during this period that Abd and his foreign wife fought most bitterly.

As Muna leafs through the old photos, Fadhma unties the string around Abd's correspondence. "The freak pockets of snow at home did not prepare your father for the severity of American winters," she tells her. In Greenville, Illinois, his German landlady, Mrs Schneider, had given Abd the clothes that belonged to her deceased husband, a man who had been over six feet four inches. "'Not all the loaves of Wonder Bread and peanut butter and jelly I eat during the night shift at the town's cafeteria,'" Fadhma starts reading, "'are ever going to make me taller.'

"Then he found work in an extremely dirty kitchen," she says, grimacing at the next letter. "'I got rid of ten-day-old pork chops—eight big bags of stinking garbage!' But your father wrote that this job was not without its benefits. The owner, it seemed, sewed better

than she cooked and cut down the dead man's clothes to fit him."
When Abd was hired as a hospital ward orderly, he paid his landlady for his new wardrobe and sent home to the family whatever cash
he could spare.

He had also written about a very shocking incident. One evening, after he left work and went to a bar. Mother Fadhma's voice
rises in excitement. Her eyes still grow wide with the horror she felt
all those years ago. Fadhma still can't imagine the dens of iniquity
that are American bars—do the women walk around naked? Is this
how all the young Arab men become ensnared, end up forgetting
their families and staying abroad? Pushing aside her fears for the
sake of her guest, she says brightly, "After your father ordered a
beer, your grandfather appeared to him: 'As real to me as the bottle
in my hand, and all Al Jid kept saying: "So I've sent you all the way
to America to drink alcohol?"'"

Feeling as though she is holding a precious time in all of their
lives, Mother Fadhma smiles gratefully at Muna for allowing her to
share it. "I can't tell you the excitement these letters caused when we
first received them."

Samira, who has been watching quietly and listening all along,
interjects, "Whenever an airplane passed in the sky, all us kids used
to point up and call out, 'Abd! Abd!'"

"And one by one," Muna inquires, "all of them left home?"

"Yes," Fadhma affirms. Why pretend otherwise? In the beginning she thought of her husband's children, both home and abroad,
as two equal halves of the same whole. But as one place claimed
more than the other, it simply wasn't true anymore. Apart from the
letters and the funds that were sent home, they disappeared. By the
time her own children were old enough to travel, Fadhma understood she was losing them for good.

"Their lives are better there," she sighs. What she wasn't going
to say was that during those days she still clung to an unreasonable
belief that Abd, the son who was destined to care for them, would
not desert her and Al Jid completely. She continued feeling that way
even when her stepson's financial contributions began to arrive less
frequently and his letters exhibited a marked change in tone. Instead

of reporting minute details of his day-to-day life as a way of including his parents, he seemed to be building up defenses. Occupied by his intense studies for a college degree in chemistry, he had little to write about. The personal news he included was ominous. He was becoming friendly with another foreign student, a young woman and fellow immigrant to the United States from the Philippines. Then, without warning, they married.

It was a blow to the family. No one in the Sabas family married a stranger. Abd had not only wedded outside his tribe but outside his culture. And who could predict the consequences of such reckless behavior? Fadhma feared the worst, but it was Al Jid who took the news particularly badly. He had already mapped out his son's life. He had chosen a suitable woman to be Abd's wife and even made the initial approaches. The young couple would have probably ended up in the Gulf, where his son, the chemist, would have worked to support the rest of his siblings. When that was no longer feasible, Al Jid accepted the inevitable and sent his blessing... even though it was not asked for.

The second eldest's brazen independence humiliated his parents, but there was worse to come. Another letter in Fadhma's box, one that had been folded many times and shoved to the bottom—never referred to but never forgotten—had been written in English. It arrived after Abd's wedding. But with no English speakers in the village, it remained unopened until business called Al Jid to the capital. That night he returned home clearly depressed. Mother Fadhma thought it was the low price for barley, but when she inquired, he pulled from his pocket the letter with a translation written in Arabic. In an expressionless voice, he read, "'All you do is write and ask for money. How dare you bastards keep bothering us! I'm pregnant, and your son wants me to give you the little money my family sends to me. Go to hell.'"

Not even this message completely destroyed Mother Fadhma's confidence in Abd. Her illusions were finally shattered a few years later, when a snapshot arrived in the mail. The picture was of a little girl in a grass skirt and Hawaiian halter top, with an orange lei around her neck. Her hands were held to one side and a bare foot pointed forward. It was Muna, aged three and a half, poised to dance the hula. The accompanying letter was simple and direct. Fadhma recites it as though it arrived yesterday:

"'My dear family, I am writing to you from my lab, the only place I can find peace. I have a good job with a big company that makes plastics. My wife and daughter are well. As you can see, the child does not look Arab. This is the problem of a mixed marriage. Neither she nor her mother would be accepted in Jordan, and all of our lives would be miserable. So I think it's best for us to remain here. God bless you.'"

Saying nothing, Fadhma hands Muna the picture of herself when she was small. "I don't remember this," her granddaughter grins uncomfortably. After a long, hard stare, she passes it to Samira before asking Fadhma, "Why did you give your children Muslim names, Jadda?"

The old grandmother again regards the girl in a new light. At least Muna isn't unintelligent. Fadhma smiles proudly. "It was your grandfather's idea."

In the hopes that Muna's interest in family history is greater than Samira's or Laila's, she begins slowly. "Hundred of years ago, Christians dedicated to Sabas, the patron saint of our family, waged war against the pagan gods of the desert. After those battles, they settled in the Crusader fortress in the country's south and would have gladly stayed there, if not for a dispute over a local woman—"

"There's always a woman," interrupts Samira with a laugh. "Someone looks at someone. Someone's father gets upset. So-and-so's brothers become involved, which pretty much all the time leads to murder."

Fadhma refuses to acknowledge her daughter's comments and continues: "It would have ended in a sectarian war, but the church leaders in Jerusalem petitioned the Turkish governor in charge of the region and the Christians were given permission to come to the mountains here"—Fadhma twirls a finger in the air—"and settle in the ruins of an abandoned Byzantine city that had been destroyed seven times by earthquakes. When the tribes arrived, they took shelter in a cave by a spring, which they thought was God's gift to them. It belonged to someone else. Inadvertently our relatives traded one fight for another, and your great-grandfather was killed in a battle. It was devastating for the family. But at the young age of ten, Al Jid made a solemn vow not to avenge his father's murder, something remarkable considering the code of honor among the tribes. Once he married and had children of his own, he called them not by Christian names but ones that were either Muslim or considered neutral. That way they could live unmolested among strangers."

She pours herself a second cup of coffee. "Your grandfather believed Islam and Orthodox Christendom were a large and small tree that had grown into one. The leaves were different but the shade the same. He also taught himself to read and write." She could see him now, spending hours in the window alcove at the front of the old house, where he sat in the natural light with his books. "He was in love with the history of Arabia. Our daughters were named after great Islamic women, some of them warriors. Would you like to hear his favorite poem? It was their bedtime story."

Mother Fadhma sits up and recites a little self-consciously:

We are daughters of the morning star,
We tread on pillows underfoot,
Pearls adorn our necks.
Musk perfumes our hair.
If you fight, we will embrace you,
If you retreat, we will abandon you.
And say farewell to love.

"This was the song of Hind and other rebellious Meccan women on the field of battle," she goes on explaining. "They banged their drums and urged their men to kill Muslims who had come from Medina to steal Mecca's profitable pilgrim and caravan trade."

Finally Mother Fadhma feels like she is enjoying herself. Since Hussein's troubles, she has been denied a favorite pastime, taking morning coffee with the elderly women of the town and telling stories. Neither Muna nor Samira displays the wit or feistiness of her old friends, but the young women are a reasonable audience. Fadhma would have told them all she knew about the bravery and savagery of Hind on the battlefield and her run-in with the Prophet Muhammad; the conversion of the pagans who first fought the Christian saints and the brutal dawning of a new era belonging to the One God. It would have been a history lesson that her husband would have been proud of, but he was oftentimes oblivious to the repetitive nature of his stories. Already Fadhma can sense the tedium rising from Samira's side of the room, so she leaves her tales for another time and asks, "What are your plans for today?"

Muna eagerly nods at Samira's reply: "We might go to Amman and come back early for the wedding feast tonight. Or we can spend the afternoon at the Internet café. I'm sure something will come up. We haven't decided yet."

"Don't go far," her mother warns. "Guests are expected this afternoon."

"Guests?" Samira echoes incredulously.

"Some of the townspeople are coming to meet Muna," her mother proudly exclaims.

"Well, maybe we should try to get a SIM card for my phone," suggests Muna evenly, "but it probably won't work. I'm told the town has bad reception"—she sounds almost apologetic—"because of Jebel Musa, but the mountain isn't the problem. It's me. I'm addicted to the Internet."

Samira appears sympathetic, although Fadhma doesn't know why she should be. The young speak a different language and Fadhma can't ignore the feeling in her tired old bones that her daughter is hiding something. Where has she been going these past few months? Whom is she spending time with? A man? Just because Muna is visiting, Samira shouldn't think she can take advantage. Fadhma is keenly aware this is not the right time. She would rather sew her lips together with coarse straw than cause a scene and create a trail of speculation that finds its way back to Cleveland, Ohio. Suddenly the room feels hot and claustrophobic. Wordlessly, Fadhma packs the letters back into their box.

5

Two men haggle loudly by a truck. "You must make up your mind," bullies the taller of the pair, a much older balding, beak-nosed man. His shoulders droop winglike and his arms flap excitedly. Thin, wiry, ornery—more scavenger than songbird—he bobs up and down in barely suppressed excitement. Blood rising, talons at the ready, he is about to land a decisive blow. But mid-swoop he flutters impotently back to earth, acutely aware of being watched. *Not every rabbit needs to know when the hawk strikes*, Abu Za'atar thinks, and ushers his prey into the Marvellous Emporium. Fresh kill is always needed to line his nest. He hasn't earned the nickname ar-Rish Ajjanah, the Featherer, for nothing.

Once the transaction is completed, the driver summarily dispatched, and the precious boxes of junk, really—electrical parts and secondhand US Army T-shirts—dumped in a storeroom, Abu Za'atar berates himself for getting overexcited. Some men his age wind down with backgammon or crossword puzzles. Armed with only a feather duster and microfiber cloth, he often takes these forays through the canyons of his empire, a momentary respite from life's duller pleasures. These expeditions also serve as a stark reminder that his most prized possessions, many hidden away from public view, have a value beyond money.

The accumulated layers of kitchenware; exotic imported foodstuffs (mainly Asian); sports, casual, and ready-to-wear—men's, women's, children's, toddlers', and newborns'; absurdly high high heels and flat, sole-destroying trainers; festive decorations for all holidays, including those Islamic (Shia, Sunni, Druze, Alawi, and Ismaili), Christian (Syriac Christian and Catholic, Greek Orthodox, Armenian, Maronite, and Phalange), and pagan (Yazidi, Zoroastrianism, and Druidic), and the big names in between (Buddha and the Maharishi); syncopated doorbells; Chinese paper cuts; hotel-standard pants presses; analog telephones; electric shoeshine machines; and haute couture nail polish, among thousands of other remarkable products and gadgets, are more than just a jumble of unrelated artifacts. A passerby glancing in through the window would be forgiven for mistaking the Marvellous Emporium for a postmodern aberration of outsider art. Abu Za'atar keenly insists to first-time customers that no one but he alone can prize an object from its exhibition place, citing avalanches as a clear and present danger.

In the past he considered the emporium a fixed monument to his life on earth, to be dismantled when the appropriate time comes, buried in a landfill, and forgotten. But Umm al-Khanaazeer has made him appreciate its finer aspects. He now considers the Marvellous Emporium a work in progress not necessarily about himself, but one that has been growing organically, with a universally generous purpose. The Featherer vociferously argues with his imaginary critics as he dusts among the shelves. If anyone were to ask him, he would insist he means advancement in the greater sense. No one in the town has been as devoted as he is to improving the public good, even if that means shoving a superstitious people into the present. Right or wrong, politically correct or deeply insulting, he remains an APC—Agent of Progressive Change—the letters of which should appear like a degree from the university of life after his name on the emporium's neon frontage.

That is when he is not misled, waylaid, or kneecapped by nostalgia. It is no accident that his inventory through the winding aisles deposits him in a very private place. He takes the tiny key he religiously keeps in his pocket and unlocks the aptly named "booty nest," a secure, glass-fronted case stuffed with jewelry. Since the

Syrian conflict, many more beautiful refugee women have been bombarding the Marvellous Emporium, desperate to sell their gold. But the acquisition of these pieces no longer contains the emotional frisson that once excited him. His current business venture with his nephew pretty much consumes his every want and need. Now he realizes, not without a tinge of bittersweet regret, he has no desire to dose himself with herbal Viagra.

Despite his apparent disinterest, women have been doubly persistent in their desperation to sell jewelry, and he has been acquiring quite heavy pieces for a song. He casts his eyes over the substantial fortune represented by a deluge of bracelets, brooches, necklaces, hatpins, camel cuff links, stray antique beads, and a fine array of filigree silver and gold in the booty nest. He scrutinizes the mound of glittery, lurid stuff, and still what he so desperately wants eludes him. Roughly yanking the magnifying glass on a chain around his neck and holding it up, he peers cockeyed and peevish through it. An incessant forefinger pecks at the stash and impatiently flips over the only business card kept there to reveal any hidden pieces underneath.

By the time he excavates a broken pair of tarnished earrings, embossed with a cursive design, he feels feverish. He repositions a more solid, crass gold collar with pink rubies to camouflage and protect the inconspicuous bits of metal, which have an unearthly glow, like the dim recollection he has of a slender Palestinian refugee girl. She sold the cheap earrings to him and he extracted a high price from her for the privilege. It was the first of those kinds of bargains he ever made, all the more satisfying because of his innocence and hers too, although that has never once crossed his mind.

Abu Za'atar lowers the magnifying glass and carefully closes and locks the glass-fronted chest. He pauses and takes in the Marvellous Emporium rising around him. Despite his hard work and lifelong dedication, even he has difficulty believing how it all began—as a board under a sheltering cloth tied to four poles. The stall back then had but a single purpose: selling the dried thyme-and-sumac mixture sprinkled with sesame dust that gave the family a purpose and a name: *za'atar*. From a few brittle leaves, seeds, and a secret magic ingredient—*onboz* seeds from the marijuana plant, to which Abu Za'atar attributes his own predisposition toward flights of fantasy—the tent eventually grew into a short, squat structure along what was becoming a well-used pathway.

Under his father, the village shop was never much of a money-spinner. Occasionally the wooden shelves overflowed with bags of coffee from Yemen or cotton thread carried along the Silk Road by itinerant salesmen. More often than not the only goods on display were several nondescript, crumpled packages, which remained unopened on an upper shelf, and a large drum of cooking oil. It was simply a question of limited supply and even lower demand. There was very little money to spend on nonessentials; what the farmers could not produce in the fields, they generally did without.

For his father's generation, three qualities were held to be far more important than the number of sheep and goats a man owned. First and foremost came respectability. In this regard the storekeeper had been handicapped by his profession, which ranked low in a strict social hierarchy. At the top were nomads, nobly roaming the country in the time-honored way. Next came those who cultivated the fields and herded animals. They represented the bottom line of acceptability. Beneath the farmers were *madaniyeen*, or city people, who had been lured by modern invention and severed their ties to the land. Then, only one step above soothsayers, prostitutes, and thieves, came the merchants, a class blighted by popular suspicions of *nasabeen*, or shiftiness.

Despite society's inclination to dismiss him altogether, the elder Abu Za'atar transformed a place of minimal commerce into a community center. He wrote letters on the side and kept the coffeepot and the *arghileh* handy. When none of the men was around to avail themselves of the water pipe, he invited in the village youngsters. There was a whole generation for whom childhood was defined by the sweet taste of *fustokiye* candy and the tinny orchestra of Tahia Carioca playing on an old gramophone. This ended abruptly when the father died in 1947, and the shop passed to his teenage son.

Za'atar ibn Za'atar had been named after his father, and he, in turn, named his firstborn son after himself. Social custom dictated that he therefore should be known as Abu Za'atar—Father of Za'atar. The term demonstrated the importance attached to the provision of male heirs and was supposed to confer dignity and a sense of responsibility, but Fadhma's brother treated it like a joke. He was fond of saying that he was the father of himself—self-made and determined. He had time for many things, but not for his father's social niceties. In the beginning when he took over the store, he dedicated himself wholeheartedly to the pursuit of profit. Given the circumstances, this was something more easily desired than achieved, but he was not discouraged. He canceled the informal credit system his father operated and energetically set about collecting outstanding accounts, some of which had remained unpaid for decades. None of this endeared him to his neighbors.

It was not a question of blind faith. Abu Za'atar was a fellow of wide-ranging interests. He studied the newspapers that came into the shop wrapped around other goods. Although they were six months out of date, he carefully flattened out each sheet and pored over it for hours. The knowledge of current affairs he gained confirmed that his task was not impossible. Success in the world hinged on attitude. All he had to do was take advantage of whatever came his way.

He did not have to wait long. It all started a lifetime ago during a virginal encounter with Palestinian innocence. Once the refugees inundated the isolated mountain village and the camps were set up, the international aid caravan that supplied them encouraged local businesses to get involved, and more than the odd bag of cornmeal was contributed to the store. Ten years later in 1958, everything was turned upside down again when King Faisal II of Iraq was executed. Lebanon was in the throes of its first civil conflict, and Egypt's charismatic Abdel Nasser formed the United Arab Republic with the Ba'athists of Syria. Abu Za'atar was just the kind of hot-tempered young man that pan-Arab nationalism should have appealed to, but the free market economy had already stolen his heart. The first time he saw refrigerators with automatic interior lighting in black-and-white Hollywood movies, he was forever smitten. When the British backed the teenage King Hussein after the assassination of his grandfather King Abdullah, Abu Za'atar showed his appreciation by hanging Union Jack KEEP CALM—HAVE A CUPPA flags throughout the shop. It was not long before he was the beneficiary of another unexpected reward: a significant investment in Jordan's infrastructure by the Western countries vilified during the Suez Canal debacle. Their capitalization of Arab countries that were not Egypt resulted in the building of new roads, which connected the village to the rest of the country and allowed access to increased trade all the way down to the Gulf of Aqaba and the Red Sea. So began Abu Za'atar's network of cross-border contacts and the future foundations for a dream still to be conceived, the Marvellous Emporium.

Every ten years a new political upheaval set Abu Za'atar's cash register ringing. For many, the an-Naksah, the "Setback" of the disastrous 1967 war, was an abject failure. But for the ever-watchful proprietor it provided an unexpected boost. Undoubtedly his country had been fooled into joining that colossal misadventure. The jets a gullible king saw over the West Bank were not Egypt's, as promised by the irascible Nasser. In 144 hours, Jordan lost the West Bank and East Jerusalem. But whether through victory or defeat, any changeover of government on that scale meant an assembly line of contraband. Even when it arrived soggy and snail infested from the other side of the river, everything was upcycled and put on display. To handle the tonnage, Abu Za'atar constructed a labyrinthine annex to the store. However, the country's political defeat extracted its own price.

In 1970 the buildup of militarism in Jordan exploded like a pressure cooker, and twenty thousand Palestinian *fedayeen* were ousted from the country during Black September, another euphemism for an attempted coup and civil war, while their families stayed behind. There was suspicion of spies everywhere and a surge of arms next door in Syria, a few choice samples of which made their way to the emporium. The next conflict came along three years later and was named after the religious holidays of Ramadan —Tishrin—or Yom Kippur, depending on one's affiliation. When the Gulf States invested in the front line countries against Israel, which didn't include Jordan, the only benefit Abu Za'atar saw were oversize Syrian cotton underwear and ill-fitting T-shirts.

He returns to his cleaning duties, dusting energetically among the clothes racks, and finds himself in front of an Yves Saint Laurent midi-rain mac near a pyramid of Charles Jourdan shoes in their original boxes. If war made the emporium the best it could be, then the one that contributed the most was Lebanon's.

"Some quarrel," the proprietor says to himself, grinning. He isn't sure when he came up with his observation about nationality and conflict, but it must have been sometime during the country's fifteen-year-long civil war. It was true then and remains so today: you can take the mettle of a people not by why they fight but what they must sell to continue fighting. Daesh may be oil-rich and fanatically violent, but the detritus of its caliphate cannot rival that of a world-class capital like Beirut, whose castoffs alone effectively fueled the lesser economies of other Arab nations for decades to come.

Rearranging the plastic covering on a nearby clothes rack, Abu Za'atar suddenly feels a surge of affection for his best mate, Hani. They have known each other since the Palestinian refugee camps. Hani was an adolescent when he followed the fighters out of Jordan, and then a decade later he showed up in Abu Za'atar's store covered head to toe in bling. As the goods and services procurer for an al-Fatah general, he had access to a Mercedes, a chauffeur, and a Romanian mistress.

More crucially, Hani offloaded black-market merchandise hot from Hamra Street in exchange for hard currency. As a deal sweetener, he often threw in a consignment of faux Louis XIV furniture. The profits generated from the enlarged stock enabled Abu Za'atar to make impressive changes to the store. He moved his family from behind the curtain in the store and installed them in splendid isolation on the edge of the growing town. But the real bonus was a massive electric generator, another backhander from his best pal. It encouraged Abu Za'atar to rebrand and power up the newly christened Marvellous Emporium, the flashing neon of which can been seen from space.

After the Lebanese civil war ended, Abu Za'atar felt lethargic and depressed. He thought the emporium had seen better days. Then out of the blue Saddam Hussein did him an enormous favor by invading Kuwait. The international coalition of countries that banded together to punish the Iraqi dictator thankfully did not include his own.

"A smart king is first and foremost entrepreneurial," Abu Za'atar proclaims to nobody, and waves the microfiber cloth in tremendous appreciation. During the more than decade-long UN sanctions against Iraq, oil tankers filled with Iraqi black gold made their way across Jordan's eastern border, hung a left, and traveled straight down the King's Highway past Abu Za'atar's small town to the Gulf of Aqaba and the sanction-busting world beyond. Everyone within a twenty-mile radius of the illicit trade grew fat.

Peace is rarely as lucrative as war, but it would be foolhardy to overlook the underpublicized shipments from Israel after the 1994 Camp David Accords. Whenever there is any excitement in the region and someone needs a hard-to-source item, he has become the go-to guy. In 2003, after Saddam was discovered in a hole, Abu Za'atar found himself in a quandary. He didn't like feeling remorseful—after all, the man and his son Uday were brutal murderers. But to his mind and, more important, his balance sheet, the invading US Army was just as bad, and to add salt to the wound, they were too damn self-sufficient. "Prefab this, prefab that!" he tut-tuts to himself. During their long involvement in Iraq, the Americans flew in, assembled, killed, murdered, raped, and then dismantled, packed up, and flew off again, answerable to no one except their contractors. Only clutter and chemical dumps remained. The renewed American engagement in Iraq against Daesh promises the Marvellous Emporium some paltry but at least easy pickings.

He can't complain. Sometimes a lucky dip presents itself, like last month, when a clean-shaven stranger, sporting a neat military-precision haircut, stalked the town. It was obvious he wasn't just looking around. From across the paved part of the main street, Abu Za'atar watched him spend an inordinate amount of time with Hussein at the butcher's. Then the fellow in question entered the Marvellous

Emporium without a by-your leave, ignored everything on its loving-ly arranged shelves, and plunked himself down in the only available comfy chair. *The nerve!* Abu Za'atar thought. He was not used to such forward behavior.

However, the stranger had an air of propriety that Abu Za'atar im-mediately responded to. In an instant he was no longer a purveyor of rare goods but an Armenian tailor. First meetings are often like that— to take the measure of a man. The mysterious stranger soon made his requirements known. He was in the market for information and he heard that Abu Za'atar was well placed to help. Surely he must have been aware that jihadists were using the town as a rat-run?

The proprietor didn't confirm, deny, or contradict. If the Jordani-ans were the paymasters, the bounty would be insignificant. To con-vince him, the mysterious stranger strongly intimated that "once the Americans are involved, the sky's the limit"—and Abu Za'atar always appreciated finer distinctions between like-minded business partners to be.

Emboldened, Abu Za'atar inquired, "And the Israelis?"

"Their skies watch over us." The stranger placed his hands side by side and rubbed his forefingers together. "We've heard of a cache of weapons," he went on to say. "We don't know if they're for sale or..."

Abu Za'atar, smarmily polite, corrects him: "From my understand-ing, sir, it is an antique collection, I hear, of little value. And I am told it rarely sees the light of day."

His visitor only grunted.

Deferentially the Featherer accepted the man's business card and locked it in his booty nest for safekeeping. Despite the open-ended-ness of the exchange, Abu Za'atar took heart that his modest patriotic efforts were being recognized, and his resolve grew to the strength of ten M1 Abram tanks the Americans used to level Iraq. Whenever any occasion appeared, whether orchestrated by a *mukhabarat* agent, undercover policeman, informant, or con man, he promised himself to squeeze every drop of goodness from it.

Throughout everything, only Hani, dear Hani, understood the grandiose nature of Abu Za'atar's plans. His friend had an eye for the imminently advantageous, despite falling from the great heights of civil war profiteering and spending it all on Eastern European prostitutes. It was during a late-night phone conversation when Abu Za'atar started riffing on a heartfelt but unrealized ambition of his: to popularize an internationally known foodstuff for a prickly domestic market.

"Like opening the first Chinese restaurant in Bethlehem?" Hani asked, exploring the concept.

"Cold." Abu Za'atar sometimes played this game with him.

Hani tried again: "Like baking gluten-free pita bread in Beirut?"

The Featherer wasn't quite convinced; in his mind there weren't enough Arab celiacs to constitute a consumer revolution. "Aim higher."

"Ah!" exclaimed his friend. "Like bringing McDonald's to Afghanistan."

That's what Abu Za'atar appreciated, Hani's ability to think outside the box. He alone presented Abu Za'atar with the opportunity of a lifetime, this time arriving with a health certificate. It too was a refugee of sorts, escaping hardship and crossing borders illegally: from the Zabbaleen in Greater Cairo to the Sinai and through the tunnels of Gaza, under the noses of Hamas, and then over the wall—a nursing home hoist, Hani said, was used—past illegal West Bank Jewish settlements, and finally not over but under the Allenby Bridge on a raft across the Jordan River.

Whenever Abu Za'atar remembers his own contribution to international cuisine, dusting becomes reverential. It's rare for him to find someone he truly likes and trusts. His friendship with Hani is like spontaneous combustion, while with Hussein it has taken years, even decades, of grooming before the flames of mutual profiteering could be ignited.

The Featherer had been dusting the morning his nephew returned to their town. Carrying a clipboard, Abu Za'atar was also noting down inventory and paid little attention to the uniformed man loitering by the counterfeit designer timepieces. The increasingly troublesome border in the valley below made the town a regular stop for soldiers on their way to the various outposts. On the whole, none of them had any money and was therefore of no interest. So when the mustached young man greeted him politely, Abu Za'atar's reply was offhand

and distracted. The shopkeeper was certain that any conversation would lead to the inevitable inquiries into the whereabouts of the only available local girl.

The soldier continued to entertain himself among the watches. When at last Abu Za'atar glanced up, he was stunned to encounter the broad smile of his favorite nephew. He kissed him on both cheeks and then gripped his shoulders at arm's length, trying to assess what changes had taken place since they last met. The slender, uninspiring boy who had run away into military service had returned, in his uncle's estimation, a man.

"What was it like, eh?" Surely such a handsome lad must have had many adventures. Tied to the small town, the shopkeeper lived vicariously through the travel stories of wayward traders and truck drivers. In his excitement, he asked question after question, but Hussein's elusive replies suggested that his experiences were not altogether satisfactory. Finally the young and old sat in silence over *arak* and the *arghileh*.

"Amo," Hussein began shyly, as he would have done in the old days, for he had always found Abu Za'atar's company fascinating, "did you keep the magazine?"

He was referring to an old copy of *Good Housekeeping* his brother Abd had sent from America. In the past Hussein and Abu Za'atar spent hours poring over its pages, working on their English and wondering about the purpose of so many colorful and unusual household goods.

Abu Za'atar immediately retrieved the issue from its original hiding place in a drawer under the cash register. He had placed it there on the day of Hussein's departure, as a token of their shared interests. Taking the magazine, Hussein turned to the double-page spread of a supermarket. He had recently returned from a US military training program for overseas officers at Fort Knox in Tennessee and was able to name and classify all the foodstuffs from peanut butter to wieners, which he himself had purchased from an all-purpose superstore as tall as Jebel Musa, the mountain known to the Christian tourist hordes as Mount Nebo.

The older man became solemn. "Puppy Chow?"

Hussein hesitated. To tell the truth would only make him look foolish, but who else could he confess to, if not his favorite uncle? It was embarrassing to be sure, but if he was going to become an officer, he would have to learn to readily admit his stupidity. Fooled by the supermarket's generic brand, he bought several cans and enjoyed some tasty curries before realizing his mistake.

As a point of honor, Abu Za'atar never ridicules a heartfelt blunder. "Your father once told me a story about a Bedouin tribe." He tugged thoughtfully at his receding hairline. "At certain times of the year, on the rising of the morning star, they cut a camel to pieces and ate the raw beating heart before dawn. In this way the tribesmen ensured that they absorbed the animal's spirit. They wanted the camel's endurance and vitality to enter into their own lives."

He peered at his nephew.

"So what did you get?"

"Knowledge that depressed me every time I walked down an American street."

Hussein had also visited his brothers and their families in Ohio and had been surprised.

"My nieces care for their pets as we do for people. They talk lovingly to them, hug and comb them—" His voice choked with bewilderment. "I'm telling you, man, their dogs live better than we do."

Abu Za'atar exhaled the dense rich smoke and muttered, "Sometimes it's best not to know the world."

Since that time, Abu Za'atar vowed to help this sensitive young relative who showed such initiative and promise. After Hussein retired from the army, it was the proprietor who guided him through the intricacies of selling his father's land. Even when Hussein insisted on keeping a last piece of Al Jid's legacy, his uncle bowed to his wishes, although he would have preferred a clean final break; his commission would have been higher. Also, farming was never going to be Hussein's future. When he ended up in the butcher shop across the street, Abu Za'atar racked his brain to come up with schemes to liberate him. He knew the young man was destined for better things—although it took Hussein a while to fully embrace the unique form his uncle's aid took.

After Hussein settled in at his new job, Abu Za'atar sent his youngest son, Sammy, to fetch him whenever something really interesting came into the Marvellous Emporium. The quick-witted, weedy fourteen-year-old was instructed to never ever run but stroll casually over to the butcher's. There was no point in attracting unnecessary attention. However, the tremendousness of Abu Za'atar's latest prize could be gauged by the boy's insistent cries of *"Ibn ammee"*—"my uncle"—heard reverberating down the main street.

After Abu Za'atar received Hani's gift of natural wonder, he ushered Hussein quickly into the warren of rooms in the back of the Marvellous Emporium, where the floor and tables were littered with crates of Johnnie Walker Red, the latest contraband in the thriving underground economy.

Setting the stage, he ordered Sammy to prepare drinks for the two men and stand at attention for further orders, as Abu Za'atar disappeared behind a closed door. He had the air of a magician about to produce the truly spectacular. Neither the whining from what sounded like a baby coming from inside nor the impassive face of his son was going to give the game away. Little Sammy, Abu Za'atar appreciated, was well trained. He was adept at making frozen margaritas and telling off-color jokes. More important, he had been schooled in keeping secrets. So Abu Za'atar had no doubts that the boy standing motionless by Hussein's side would remain there for hours if need be.

After a series of loud thuds, followed by Abu Za'atar's muffled cursing, the door behind the proprietor opened ever so slightly. In the half-light, only his pointy yellow leather Moroccan slippers were visible. The rest of his body was submerged in straw and grabbing at something unseen. An acrid odor exploded from the room, and Hussein fell back coughing.

"Shut the door!" bellowed Abu Za'atar, but it was too late. Hussein spilled his drink and crashed into Sammy, still standing at attention, as a creature with black, tan, and ginger fur, remarkably agile for its size, slid past the whisky crates and fled squealing through the curtained partition. It vanished beneath a rack of faux DKNY chased by a straw-covered Abu Za'atar. He understood if any of his customers caught so much of a glimpse of this special commodity, he would lose them forever. With an athleticism that belied his age, he dived into the dresses and began searching wildly, but he emerged empty-handed, pressing his fingers to his lips before his nephew had a chance to speak.

Sammy, alert and focused, took his place beside his father, straining to hear the tiniest sound that would give him some clue as to the whereabouts of their quarry. A tinkling in the corner made his father jump, but the boy held up his hand and whispered sagely, "Balinese wind chimes." Another noise came from the far end of the shop, but before they made a move the boy quietly cautioned them again: "Windup toy robots."

Then with poise and skill, Sammy reached for an old CD / cassette player—something he was rarely without—and switched on the Emir of Kuwait's marching band starting its medley from *Fiddler on the Roof*. He had played this rousing selection to the closed door and knew it was a favorite of this creature, which sometimes responded by throwing itself against the door. Sammy had experimented with everything, from love songs to Fairouz, but only martial brass elicited a sure reaction. After a few bars, the animal stepped out from behind some bolts of cloth, its impressive bulk swaying to the music.

Abu Za'atar grabbed the beast's leg and snarled, "Ten-hut!" and juvenile Sammy straightened like a board again. The marching band's closing musical signatures from "If I Were a Rich Man" were impatiently switched off. Abu Za'atar retreated behind a curtain, dragging the animal behind him. Once he regained his breath, he invited Hussein to join him. After they settled down with fresh drinks from Sammy, he petted the prominent snout of the sleekly furred sow that lay placidly at his feet and told Hussein, "This, my friend, is the future."

6

"What a nest of scorpions you've dropped us in!" Mother Fadhma scolds the photograph on the living room wall. "And you're supposed to be watching over us!"

With the acute sensitivities of a divining rod, her feelings would be able to discern any sort of change taking place in the room, from temperature to mood to lighting. But everything remains as it is, a clear indication that Al Jid is not paying her the least bit of attention. His picture projects only the special vanity that belongs to Arab men. A carefully arranged keffiyeh and agal headdress give him the appearance of a Bedouin chieftain.

"I only have myself to blame." Her disgust turns inward. She always spoiled him. His floor-length djellaba robe, like his pride, is starched and unyielding; she ironed it thread by thread to make it so. When the shutter snapped he was leaning forward, his left forefinger pointing accusingly, caught halfway between a frown and penetrating stare. In the photograph, as in life, he had been every inch the classic patriarch.

"You said you loved all your children, but you only loved the large numbers of them," she rails at the portrait again. "And as soon as they left the country they forgot about us, so you were wrong about that too."

Al Jid had assured her that a quantity was more advantageous than a few; he often referred to all his children as insurance. Remembering his words, she loudly slaps her hands against each other in rapid succession, in effect eliminating both of them for good. If they can't rely on their own sons, surely they are the ones at fault. Too many children emigrated, when keeping large numbers at home would have kept Al Jid and Fadhma protected and safe. A rising hollowness aches in her chest. She desperately needs some kind of assurance, a minuscule sign from the man in the picture, yet all he does is stare.

In frustration she moans. Her husband has been either derelict in his duty or just doesn't care, like his son. As the head of the family in Jordan, Hussein should have control over Samira. Instead, dominated by an awful wife, Hussein has lost the ability to think straight. And now because of his suffering, a bad situation is getting worse. He is not the only one in the family who has perfected the art of seeing everything while pretending to know nothing. Fadhma too has watched him stagger into the house late at night and smelled the odor of defeat, stale and putrid, on his breath the next morning. Despite her unhappiness, her heart begins to soften. On closer inspection Najla's son isn't a thoroughly bad man. His one failing is that he is weak and easily led. Fadhma is prepared to indulge his mistakes and excesses, as she would any of the children, but she refuses to do the same for the man responsible for corrupting Hussein. Behind his misfortunes lurks the specter of her malevolent brother. Abu Za'atar has been greedy and untrustworthy for as long as she can remember, although she never expected him to destroy her family. The hatred she feels for him cuts across her ribs like a knife.

As his older sister, she unquestioningly accepted his behavior when they lived together. On the day of their father's burial Abu Za'atar announced that henceforth she was to be confined to the house. No family honor was worth protecting if women roamed freely in the wider world. Since there was no one to appeal to, she reluctantly complied.

With everything she possibly needed in her brother's store, she effectively became his prisoner. Only Abu Za'atar's business acquaintances were admitted to the house, and in time nobody in the village bothered to ask after her. When his wife belittled her,

Fadhma promised to do better. As the brunt of his children's jokes, she was the one who laughed the loudest. Once she overheard her brother discussing the purpose of women with a business associate. They were good for cooking and cleaning, plus one other function, he said, lowering his voice. His remarks sent his companion into raucous howls of laughter. Fadhma's self-esteem sank so low she wasn't sure whether she disagreed with him. She knew what to expect from him and his family. Her life was completely restricted, but at least she was cared for. In time she yielded to what she perceived as unalterable fate.

After Najla's death, the marriage proposal from Al Jid upset the equilibrium, and it loomed like a precipice before her. After years of despondency, happiness was something that belonged to those who were never in the way. The prospect of the unfamiliar terrorized Fadhma. There was no guarantee she would be treated well. Worst of all, she knew this was her last chance. If the marriage proved to be a sham she doubted whether she would survive. She tried to discuss her anxieties with her brother, who told her, "I've done my duty. Do yours."

With each passing day, she became more agitated. Najla had given Al Jid six healthy sons one right after the other. Whenever Fadhma glimpsed the brood from her hiding place behind the curtain in the store, her eyes filled with tears; she could never replace their dead mother, her beloved sister. Fadhma sank deeper into depression. Even in marriage, all she could expect were the morsels from someone else's table. Debilitated and listless, she moped around her brother's house.

One day a troupe of clowns in faded Harlequin costumes invaded the village and advertised their one and only performance with the nasal whine of a zurna pipe. The whole village was entranced. Abu Za'atar, who had never taken a day's vacation in his life, closed the store and rounded up his family. As they were leaving, his wife stopped Fadhma from crossing the threshold and then locked the door without bothering to say good-bye.

It was the kind of petty cruelty Fadhma had grown accustomed to, but alone in the house it seemed to penetrate to the very core of her dilemma. In the past she would have accepted her lot and climbed to the roof, where she worked among the herbs drying for *za'atar*. She had always taken solace in handling the leaves and flowers of the thyme plant known to the ancient Greeks for stimulating inner strength and courage. However, not even an herbaceous recipe, laced with the magic properties of hemp, could heal such a troubled soul. She was afraid of leaving the life she knew, no matter how often she was mistreated. At the same time the possibility of a better life, however faint, made her present situation unbearable. Her mind was a churning waterwheel in motion.

As soon as her brother and his family were out of sight, she adjusted her scarf and unceremoniously climbed out a back window. The path that confronted her led away from the village to an unbroken, undulating expanse of rock and sand. An inky blue-gray bruise of a sky pressed down onto the horizon. A storm was fast approaching. She didn't have the faintest idea where she was going nor did she care. For the first time she was totally alone in the world, responsible for herself.

A torrential rain started lashing down. The imminent threat of flash flooding quickened her pace. As she passed through a gap between some boulders, she almost ran into a black *beit al-sha'ar*, a Bedouin tent woven from animal hair. Unwilling to retrace her steps but unsure of going forward, she stood beside a damp, smoldering campfire, soaked to the skin, cold and panting hard.

Fadhma knew the old stories. There were some places where you did not venture, some people who should never be approached. Certain women were powerful enough to curse life and turn it into barren solitude. Fadhma didn't give much thought as to why she had not yet married, although her sister-in-law never stopped warning her against sleeping on the wrong side of the bed or in the light of a full moon. But Fadhma understood ruggedness on a man's face translates differently on a woman, so she rejected superstition, preferring to believe that it was the will of God, which she had no choice but to obey. The storm was reaching its height. Each raindrop, the size and weight of a small stone, was a physical force that urged her forward.

Cautiously peering inside the tent, Fadhma adjusted to the gloom and saw a home much like those in the village, with cushions, water jugs, a trunk, and a rifle. She had heard rumors about the sisters of soothsayers who lived there. They did the jobs nobody else dared to do: abortions, exorcisms, and séances. They could make the unseen visible and they could change the present. Under their tutelage, an experienced girl bled like an *a'thra*, a virgin, on her wedding night or a mature woman could be given a vagina as succulent as an over-ripe fig. To the sisters who lived completely outside society, Fadhma was just another silly village girl unable to distinguish good fortune from bad.

Inside the tent she expected someone to appear. When nobody did she sat down and squinted into the dark corners before blurting out her innermost fears: "I am to marry a man who I am told is good. But my sister, his first wife, is already in her grave. Shouldn't I stay where I am?"

Gathering a small heap of pebbles and bones on the rug beside her, she thoroughly examined each one, running her fingers over their pitted surfaces, feeling their weight and shape. Then in cupped hands she shook them, like dice, and threw them. They fell clattering to the ground against the noise of the wind and rain outside.

From one angle the pebbles and bones appeared to form a question mark, from another, a broken line of mountains in the shape of a heavily pregnant woman. It was not the answer Fadhma expected, but it was the one she deserved. When she climbed out the window, the decision had been made. She would go because she wanted to and leave if it turned bad, an act that would result in the irrevocable dishonoring of her family and her own death for sure. At least she might get to experience a life that would be truly her own, and any power she exerted over it would be better than the existence forced upon her. Fadhma marveled how things of the heart could be decided in a moment.

After a small family gathering and a blessing by the priest at the Church of the Mosaic, she moved her box of belongings from Abu Za'atar's to the ramshackle mud-brick-and-stone home belonging to Al Jid. She took care of her sister's six sons out of a sense of duty.

Fadhma approached the mysteries of sex in the same spirit. When she first saw her husband naked, she told him that he reminded her of a strutting rooster, and Al Jid was pleased by her inexperience. She had no understanding of pleasure, but she was not too old to learn. Late at night as they lay side by side, she wondered if Najla had also experienced such unequivocal joy.

They didn't possess much, but Fadhma felt wanted and needed. However, there was one aspect of her husband's behavior that baffled her. He was the most proud and attentive when she resembled the woman in the shape of the mountains—always pregnant. In time, she had her own seven children to care for, as well as her sister's six sons. After the birth of so many, it seemed curious that the villagers occupied more of Al Jid's time than his own burgeoning family.

If someone came to the door—no matter day or night—he was ready to be of assistance, and he expected her to extend the same courtesy. After the emptiness of life at her brother's, the constant stream of visitors was unnerving at first. She had to be constantly ready to make tea. So she kept her scarf handy and the water jugs filled. People always seemed to call when the family was about to have a meal, which meant that her husband and the male guests ate first. She and the children made do with anything that remained, which usually wasn't much. Those years of hunger left a lasting mark. Her sister's sons fought over the little that was available and the conflict sowed discord, which took root and grew into a dense, thorny jungle of salt cedar around each of their hearts.

Whether in repayment of an obligation or to secure future favor, Al Jid was often invited to the homes of other villagers and treated to the best that could be offered. Late into the night he told stories or related the news he picked up on his market trips. Fadhma never knew where he was or when he was likely to return. The only clue to his whereabouts was if a neighbor reported seeing her stepsons hanging around outside somebody's window. The only time they stopped fighting was to eavesdrop on their father's tales.

"Toil and you serve God and yourself," Al Jid lectured his family. Mostly Fadhma worked among the poor, people like herself. She boiled *meramiyeh*, the bitter sage cure for dysentery and night sweats; prepared *isbet il-gizha*, a Bedouin recipe made from honey; or administered *habbat al barakah*, the Prophet's "blessed" *Nigella sativa* seed, known for soothing broken hearts and laryngitis. However it was the family's signature dried herbal mixture that was most sought after. Their *za'atar*'s health benefits were incalculable: it was an antidote for whooping cough and menstrual cramps; it stimulated memory and enlivened the brain. Most of all it smelled and tasted of home. The simplest of foods, it was mixed with olive oil, spread or baked on bread or used as a condiment. Even if the land was barren, it still produced aromatic scrub and bushes on little water, a sign from nature that people had not been entirely forgotten—yet. With the scant resources they did have, Fadhma served her husband and the many men who came to consult him without complaint. At the same time she started to build an independent network of her own. In the neighboring Muslim households, where wives and womenfolk were not usually allowed out unchaperoned, Fadhma visited unannounced and she was always welcomed.

Fadhma could not help comparing her husband's generosity and high moral standards with those of her unscrupulous brother. Abu Za'atar was a man who profited from the despair of others. He lived off war and corruption. His increasing wealth made him mercurial and pleasure seeking. He collected cuckoo clocks one week and cheap calculators and wide white ties the next. Fadhma grudgingly accepted his deals and gambling, but he had developed an unhealthy malicious streak.

He could not resist tormenting his sister about her spartan existence. Knowing full well that Fadhma, her newborn daughters and sons, Al Jid, and Najla's boys all slept on the floor in one room, he invited her to test his latest acquisition. Alone together, he encouraged her to sit beside him on his new brass bed.

"See what you are missing." He fingered the soft sheets and appraised his older sister. She had suddenly blossomed into a mature woman of confidence and experience. "Come, sister," he suggested slyly, "a little closer..."

Alarmed, Fadhma made her excuses and left quickly. If she lived with him long enough she might have been provided with her own brass bed, and it would have been a cage of shame. With an intensity equal to her love for her husband, she began hating her brother.

When her stepson Hussein fell under Abu Za'atar's spell, Fadhma begged Al Jid to take quick action, and the boy was bundled off to the army. Both parents were relieved, thinking the matter was at an end. Only Fadhma lived long enough to see that another road to ruin had been inadvertently taken.

The night their lives irrevocably changed for the worse, Mother Fadhma had been getting into bed when she heard the butcher's van crunching onto the gravel driveway, followed by hushed voices trying without success to enter the house undetected. On the evenings her stepson was drinking, he took to creeping in past midnight and sleeping, fully clothed, on the cold tile floor in the one place in the new house that required furnishing, the empty reception room. While this was uncomfortable, it had an advantage. He did not risk disturbing Laila by going to bed and, as he always left home before she rose in the morning, he sometimes escaped the tongue-lashing she customarily administered when she caught him drunk. Aware of this routine, Fadhma would have ignored everything and gone back to sleep, except the sounds of struggling were growing louder. So she crept to her bedroom door, opened it a crack, and peeped into the hallway.

Initially, her suspicions appeared to be correct. Red-faced and staggering, Hussein and her reprehensible brother, Abu Za'atar, were having considerable difficulty coping with a large burlap sack they were carrying between them. Intrigued, Mother Fadhma stepped out of her room. The men, however, were so engrossed in their task that they were completely oblivious to her presence. Then she realized that their inability to control their burden had less to do with alcohol than the fact that the sack was twisting and heaving, as though alive. Keeping her distance, she followed them.

Roused from sleep by their yelling, Laila, Samira, Salem, and Mansoor rushed into the reception room to find Hussein breathing heavily in one corner and an enormous black-, tan-, and ginger-speckled pig—tired and disoriented from a clandestine trip across town—sitting on its haunches in the other. The arrival of so many strangers unsettled the animal, and when Mansoor ran forward to take a closer look, it made a desperate bid for freedom that was thwarted only by some neat footwork on the part of Abu Za'atar. In the ensuing confusion, Mansoor was thrown to the floor, prompting Samira to join Laila in a fresh outburst of screaming. Fearing that the situation was about to degenerate into panic, in which some disaster might befall his porcine passport to wealth or, at the very least, attract the unwanted attention of the neighbors, Abu Za'atar shooed the family out of the room, leaving the pig to regain its composure alone. Samira was ordered to take the far too excited children to bed. The four adults sat down at the kitchen table, where, over tea, Hussein explained Abu Za'atar's proposals.

To Mother Fadhma's surprise, it was Laila who coolly assessed the situation. Granted, all of them had been shocked by the way the pig bolted at Mansoor. As with a mouse, the sudden unpredictable movements were far more frightening than the thing itself. Now listening to Hussein outline the potential profits, her impossibly arrogant daughter-in-law appeared to warm to the animal, which could be heard scuffling in the empty reception room down the hall. Mother Fadhma, fascinated and horrified, watched Laila closely. There was only one part of the plan Hussein's wife found hard to accept. Until suitable accommodations were arranged, the pig would stay in her shiny new house.

For the first and last time—Mother Fadhma could tell—Laila saw the value of their old house of mud brick and stone, where she lived as a new bride. She once said she hated it, but under these unusual circumstances she had come to instantly appreciate its unique qualities. For deep in the house, away from prying eyes, there had been a *zariba*, an inner courtyard for livestock. When the household was run entirely by women, before Hussein's retirement from the army, Laila intimated that she felt agriculture was beneath her. She had absolutely no interest in keeping animals and regarded the *zariba*, which after Al Jid's death accommodated only a few scrawny chickens, as outmoded and embarrassing.

When the new house was under construction, she insisted it be thoroughly modern—no *zaribas*, no storage bins. Laila told her mother-in-law it was a fresh start for all of them to demonstrate they were people of respectable status. The centerpiece of her reinvention was to be the reception room, which would be outfitted to her exact specifications as a showplace for entertaining and impressing guests. Now Hussein was determined to turn it at least temporarily into a pigsty.

Although the prospect remained extremely distasteful to Mother Fadhma, she was intrigued that her daughter-in-law had not dismissed it out of hand. She was aware that Laila's meager teaching salary, combined with what her stepson brought home from the butcher shop, was not enough to fulfill such wide-ranging ambitions. With no more of Al Jid's land left to sell, barring the final piece Hussein refused to part with, the family was again in financial straits. What husband doesn't know how to bribe his wife? Fadhma was disgusted as she watched Hussein appeal to Laila's greed. The first profits from the obviously pregnant pig would be spent on furnishing the reception room. "Besides," he announced, "it will only be for a few days. A week at most." He looked to Abu Za'atar for confirmation. Afterward Laila needed no persuading, and soon only Fadhma was opposed to the scheme.

She knew that her opinion carried no weight, yet she felt compelled to express her husband's views. Al Jid had always argued that the teachings of the Prophet, Peace Be upon Him, offered guidance not only to the followers of Islam but also to people of common sense. "The animal is delusion and ignorance. These are grave sins. Pig is *muharram*," she pronounced sternly. "It is also forbidden by God to consume hyena, fox, weasel, birds of prey, or elephants." Before she could add crocodiles, otters, and wasps, her despicable brother cut her short.

"We're not talking about religion, woman. This is *commerce*!" Abu Za'atar turned to his nephew and modified his tone, saying seductively, "A farm of these tucked away on what's left of your father's land—you will be the only butcher in the whole of the Levant to sell specialty meat. People will travel for miles to see... Hussein Sabas, King of the Pork Chop!" He moved his hands manically through the air as though he were designing another elaborate neon sign for the Marvellous Emporium.

As his pudgy fingers flitted in front of her face, Fadhma stood up from the table and put more water on to boil. Of the four, she was the only one who, as a farmer's wife, had any real experience raising animals. Hussein played on the farm when he was a boy, but Al Jid never allowed any of his sons to follow in his footsteps and sent all of them away as soon as possible. Laila, who had never dirtied her pretty manicured nails, exhibited all the prejudices of someone from town, while all that Abu Za'atar consistently ever managed to do was erase his sister's voice and presence, an accomplishment he spent a lifetime perfecting. Fadhma made the tea and kept quiet. It didn't take a genius to know that since everybody else in the household would be out for most of the time, the day-to-day care of the pig would fall to her.

Abu Za'atar gave Fadhma detailed instructions on catering for the new houseguest. Until a supply of corncobs could be secured with no questions asked, Fadhma was to use a special blend of dried grains and soybeans that he ordered from Slovakia. There were also several large jars of vitamin and mineral supplements from the Marvellous Emporium. Abu Za'atar had obtained them some years earlier under the mistaken impression that a fitness boom was about to take place in the town. He had been unable to dispose of them so he contributed them to the pig's welfare.

Mother Fadhma was to measure out precise amounts of feed and mix it in one of the two large metal bowls provided by her brother. The other bowl was to be kept constantly full of water. When she protested that there wasn't enough for the growing family, much less a pregnant sow, Abu Za'atar shook his head in disappointment. "Honestly, *ukhti*, if the family fortune depended on you..." He did not bother to complete the sentence, as though words were inadequate to describe the fate that would befall them.

She hated it when he called her "my sister." Some men used the term as one of endearment, but on her brother's tongue it carried a sardonic tone that emphasized the power he had over her. They were standing by the double doors of the reception room, observing the pacing animal inside. She could not bring herself to approve of the pig, but she was beginning to feel a certain sympathy for it. Their fates had been directed by Abu Za'atar's arbitrary will. He had been more concerned with his standing in the village than her happiness when he married her off to her dead 'sister's husband. Likewise, placing the pig in her care was only a matter of expediency. In light of their shared experience, she resolved to do her best.

In addition to the dry feed, Abu Za'atar told her to augment the pig's diet with anything she could find: leftovers from the table, even offal from the butcher shop. Abu Za'atar, no dainty eater himself, was filled with admiration for an appetite so prodigious that nothing was excluded. He had been going to the Internet café and reading Porcine Truths, a website "devoted to all things piggy." Much of it, he thought, was simply too fanciful to be true and purposely overlooked the etymological implications of *porcello* from Italian and *choiros* from Greek, both slang words for "vulva."

Abu Za'atar's attention was taken up with practicalities. "See if you can feed it spiders," he told his sister. Then, making sure no one else was listening, he stressed: "Keep the baby away." Fadhma couldn't tell if he was being serious or just tormenting her. With a certain amount of trepidation, she prepared to feed the beast for the first time.

She entered the reception room warily, holding the bowl in front of her like a peace offering. Drunk with hunger, the sow, which had been lying in the corner chewing straw, scrambled up and lurched snorting toward her. It was a big animal, with muscular shoulders and a powerfully broad back. Before she could place the bowl on the floor it knocked against her, spilling some of the food. She stepped back hurriedly, clutching the bowl for protection, while the pig—incensed by the smell of food—tried jumping up to get at its meal.

Weighed down by its prodigious pregnancy, it could not get high enough. Frustrated and angry, it circled, pawing the ground as if getting ready to attack. Frightened, Fadhma backed against the wall and slowly inched toward the double doors. The sow, grunting loudly, was not going to be denied. It rushed sideways, blocking her only means of escape. Staring straight at her, it stalked dangerously close.

Fear settled in Fadhma's stomach like something disagreeable she had eaten. She shut her eyes and prayed for her husband's protection. A soft, wet snout timidly poking her leg caught her off guard. Like a damp human hand, it caressed her knee with a tender, insistent urgency. Astonished to discover gentleness disguised in such a fearsome form, she put the bowl down quickly.

As the pig buried its snout in the grain and ate voraciously, Mother Fadhma watched, entranced. Unlike the sheep, goats, and chickens she once tended for Al Jid, this animal seemed almost intelligent. She reached over and scratched the spiky ginger-colored bristles that ran down the pig's spine. Absorbed in its meal, it paid absolutely no attention to her.

If the pig had been forced to rely solely on scraps from Mother Fadhma's plate for variety, its diet would have remained bland. The old woman's life experience had left a mark on her eating habits. At mealtimes, whether hungry or not, she always cleaned her plate. She never felt confident that supplies would not run out and leave her wanting.

The rest of the family rarely thought about waste. The amount they consumed was determined by preference rather than availability. When bread, salad, or pieces of fat were shoved to one side, Fadhma eyed them greedily and devoured them in secret while she did the dishes. After the pig came into the house, she collected the leftovers with great restraint and took pleasure in feeding them to her charge.

Besides Mother Fadhma, the family member most involved with the pig was little Mansoor. He had been by his grandmother's side when Abu Za'atar told her to feed it as much as it could eat. The statement astonished the boy. Sheep grazed, but not all the time. Camels drank, but certainly not forever. Everything had a stomach.

He did himself, and when it was full, he wasn't hungry anymore. This animal was the glorious exception. The more it was fed, the more it wanted. When the metal bowls were licked clean, a quick, sure kick sent them flying across the floor tiles. The clattering echoed throughout the house, a signal for more food.

When Mansoor heard the sound he ran excitedly to his grandmother and hung on her apron. "She's still hungry, Jadda." Together, in the kitchen, they measured feed and stirred it carefully. Mansoor fetched the bowl of water and they went into the reception room. Half hidden behind his grandmother's legs, the child watched wide-eyed as the pig sloppily demolished yet another enormous meal. Sometimes the pig fell asleep with its head in a metal bowl, but it seemed to the boy as though the animal kept a half-opened eye on the reception room's doors in anticipation of its next meal.

Of course, the more the pig took in at one end, the more it expelled at the other. To Mother Fadhma, the relationship was completely disproportionate. Although she cleaned out the room every morning and again at night, gathering up the soiled straw into large plastic bags and spreading out the fresh supplies that Abu Za'atar brought under cover of darkness each evening, she was unable to keep up. Even in the most remote area of the house the smell would engulf her, and she would rush for the squeegee-mop and ammonia. After a couple of days, however much she worked and meticulously checked her slippers, the smell clung to her clothes and followed her everywhere. Embarrassed and fearful that the secret guest would be discovered, she stopped going out.

This provided a convenient excuse to put off friends who were accustomed to visiting for morning coffee. They were told that Mother Fadhma was ill and in need of peaceful recuperation. If they commented on the pungent odor, it was passed off as an unfortunate problem with the new house's drainage system. No amount of explanation would make the smell go away, and when the wind blew in from the river in the west, instead of the crisp, clean air that normally filled the town, a rankness that defied description emanated from the Sabas home. Strongmen acted like girls and drew their keffiyeh headdresses over their faces and fled the dreadful stench.

The constant cleaning and feeding disrupted Mother Fadhma's routine, and she became forgetful. Laundry ended up in the wrong drawers; food was burned. By the end of the week, she forgot to lock the reception room doors. She had been drying herbs on the back kitchen terrace and needed something from her room, when she noticed that the reception room doors were open. She was confused. Even unlocked, they should have remained closed. Then she realized: the pig had used its precocious snout to press down on one of the handles. It had been watching her all the while, biding its time until she made a mistake.

In a panic, she retrieved a broom from the kitchen and began to search the house. Samira had taken baby Fuad out for a walk, so Mother Fadhma faced the crisis on her own. Stealthily, the old woman entered the living room. With nowhere for a pig to hide, everything was as it should be. Her husband's stern expression from his frame urged her on. She checked the front door. Fortunately it had been locked, or by now most of the town would have gathered to admire the bizarre apparition in the Sabas yard. Hearing a noise, she rushed into the kitchen, but there was nothing; the door to the yard was closed. The back terrace was another potential worry. When she looked all she saw were the herbs she was drying outside in the sun. She shut the door to the terrace, locked it, and returned to the hall.

One bedroom door waited like a sentry. She was reminded of one of Al Jid's apocryphal stories. A pagan envoy went to Mecca to pray for rain. He came out of the desert at exactly the wrong moment, during the twilight transitional period between the many gods of old and the solitary God of Muhammad. After the envoy prostrated himself, a voice ordered him to pick from the white, red, or black clouds on the horizon. Associating the darkest cloud with a heavy storm, he chose wrong and inadvertently condemned his idolatrous race to death. Mother Fadhma understood the story's real-life applications. With the breakdown of accepted codes, a bad choice was as easy to make as a good one, and usually it was irreversible.

She made the Orthodox sign of the cross over her chest and, clutching the broom, entered her daughter's room. Bright light streamed in through the window. Against the walls, two single beds were neatly made up. Samira's nightgown was folded on the pillow at the head of one of them. On a table, a single red plastic rose stood in a cheap brass Indian vase. There was nothing out of place in her room or the bathroom. In Mansoor and Salem's room, Fadhma made a thorough examination underneath the bed, in the closet, and inside the toy chest. There was only one place left. She gently pushed open the door to Laila and Hussein's bedroom.

Because of the baby and Laila's migraines, the curtains were always drawn. Mother Fadhma switched on the light and nearly fainted. Fuad's clean clothes, kept on top of the chest of drawers, lay in a mess on the floor. Laila's jewelry box had been overturned, the contents scattered among the broken fragments of two china figurines of braying camels she received as a wedding present. On the carpet in the middle of the room, a large red stain oozed like blood from a trampled tube of makeup. Nearby was a crumpled silk blouse that Fadhma, trembling, held up. One arm had been completely bitten off. She folded it neatly and put it away. Maneuvering cautiously around the baby's crib, she opened closet doors and thrust the broom into corners, discovering nothing. Only the bed was left. She lifted the skirting at the edge of the bed frame. Underneath in a nest of clothes and torn children's books, their animal guest from hell was nibbling on a baby's rubber bib.

Mother Fadhma knew she would have to account for the destruction of the room, and she was fearful of the consequences and annoyed with herself for allowing it to happen. She was so upset that, for once, her passivity disappeared and she brought the broom down hard on the bed, over and over again. When she stopped, the room was utterly quiet except for her rasping breath. Unsatisfied, she hit the bed again and again, and still there was nothing. She crouched down and craned her neck to get a better view. Undisturbed, the pig was sniffing one of her daughter-in-law's sandals.

Fadhma wondered why whenever her brother was involved, she was the one who suffered. Using her full weight, she pushed the bed away from the wall. The legs scraped against the tile floor, but the sound was nothing compared with the pig's high-pitched squeal as the broom came down hard on its backside. It rose up, shaking free bits of torn paper and cloth, and squared off against its assailant. Mother Fadhma was sure it barked like a dog before it charged. With the agility of a woman twenty years younger she vaulted up onto the bed.

When Laila and the boys came in from school, they found an old lady with a broom acting as the last line of defense between a prowling pig and the vegetable cupboard. Red in the face, Mother Fadhma was sweating profusely. "This one," she wheezed, "is ruled by gut alone."

After that, the pig was moved to the farm and the operation became more professional. Instead of allaying her fears, the meat's popularity only made her apprehensive. Now, in front of Al Jid's portrait, she closes her eyes and calls out to him, "Do not forsake us. Do not forsake us. Do not forsake us. Do not forsake us."

The words are a mantra. In an intensity of belief that burns white hot, all she can hear is her beloved's voice: "Eat meat and drink wine rather than partake of the evil of your brother's flesh. If you meet the evil of the world with good, then your own passions will not devour you."

She perceives him quoting, as he often did, their mystical ancestor, the starving desert hermit Saint Sabas, whose arcane pronouncements were always filled with references to food. If she applied this advice to her relationship with her brother or Laila, life would be easier. But her dead husband still hasn't told her how the family might escape the envoy's fate and the approaching devastating storm.

7

No matter how often the businesses on either side of the butcher shop have been painted, the cracking asphalt, gravel, dirt, and garbage give the cramped parade of single-story buildings a uniformly grubby appearance. From his stool behind the counter, Hussein gazes onto the street. With the busiest period of his day over, he's glad to be sitting down. In the morning, the wives of farmers and tradesmen who prepare substantial midafternoon meals come in early, and the cheaper meat sells quickly. They are an unpretentious bunch, loud and chatty. When he first started the job, Hussein exhibited the suspicion of a man who spent a limited amount of time among women. The army had not prepared him for his female customers' ribald jokes and vigorous haggling; but in time they wore down his natural reticence.

As he got to know them better, the women confided in him and he kept abreast of anniversaries, engagements, and baptisms, any occasion that could bring additional revenue to the shop. He also found himself becoming more sympathetic to the needs of the community and charged less or sometimes not at all. "He has a sixth sense," remarked the poorer women of the town.

But Hussein has no special talent for divination. He guesses rising or falling family fortunes from individual purchases and offers assistance if necessary. In this he resembles his father, except that he gives freely without sermons or proverbs. More important, he assists the less fortunate without starving his own.

He is about to reach for a cigarette when the arrival of a veiled woman outside the store stops him. Hussein knows she is still deciding on whether to come in and won't do so until he's alone, so he orders Khaled to leave his comic book and clean the yard. Still, the woman hesitates outside. Rising from the stool, Hussein goes to the door.

"Please, the lamb is gone," he says, "but we have goat."

She is not a regular customer. Many Muslim women use the butcher's, and although they are veiled and say little, he recognizes them, sometimes by a piece of jewelry or simply by the way they drape their robes. From her manner, the woman is clearly nervous. Among the stricter Muslim families it is customary for the men to do the shopping. Religious rules, however, rarely apply to the poor, widowed, or abandoned. Hussein doesn't bother with which category the woman belongs to. The scarf obscuring her face doesn't disguise her need. She motions at the joint that she would like to purchase.

When he gives her the parcel she pays in piastres, which he doesn't bother to count. "This is too much," he says, and deposits most of it back into a hesitantly outstretched palm. He would have charged nothing, but then she, beholden to him, would never return to the shop. In this way embarrassment is avoided and a way left open.

The woman speaks in a near whisper, "*Shukran jazeelan.* Thank you very much." A feeling of sadness lingers in the shop after her departure.

Hussein sighs. He relies on his Fridays to be smooth and uneventful before a hectic weekend of selling pork. But today hasn't been like any other. With Khaled in the back, Hussein thinks about the jar, but the sound of the bell jerks his hand away and he wipes the counter instead.

A friend, Nabil, steps inside. He is around Hussein's age and works on one of the larger farms that grow herbs for Western supermarkets. At one time many of the men in the town would have stopped at the butcher's on their way home from praying at the mosque. Their numbers have all but dwindled except for Nabil, who regularly visits. Hussein doesn't feel like smiling, but for Nabil's sake he makes an effort. "Come in, come in."

"Word travels fast. Teenagers get excited," Nabil says, and takes a cigarette from the pack Hussein proffers. "And there are fanatics among us, asking questions. This morning's khutbah was particularly vitriolic. The sheikh is again calling for the town to be cleansed of un-Islamic elements. Although you were not personally named, many people thought of you."

After the two men light their cigarettes, Nabil speaks first: "They say the meat is succulent. Have you tasted it?"

"It's similar to human flesh." Hussein is deadpan, then grins. "To be honest, I've not tried it."

"Truly?" Nabil leans closer, surprised.

Hussein feels ashamed. He shouldn't have tried to fool a friend and weighs more than a half kilo of chopped meat and refuses to accept any extra payment from Nabil. The two men argue back and forth, Nabil insisting and Hussein pushing money away. The laborer finally acquiesces when Hussein says, "Because you are my friend."

"And as your friend I tell you, Hussein Sabas, today might be your last chance to listen. I don't know what's planned but I thought I should warn you."

Hussein feigns indifference as he shakes Nabil's hand and says, "Tomorrow's another day." After Nabil leaves, he suddenly becomes aware of the smell of meat emanating from the corners of the butcher shop, unremarkable in every respect, but tomorrow it will be transformed into a specialty deli—all because of a single pig. Gone are the days when a few pork cutlets were sold discreetly from under the counter. Now orders are filled, hams wrapped, and sausages stuffed for the weekend. Much of the work that he and Ahmad and his sons accomplish at the farm is done almost mechanically, with little physical and emotional effort on Hussein's part. It is the passions running high in the town he finds difficult and draining. He sinks back down on his stool and stares at his hands and then at the floor.

The discordant jangling of the shop bell rouses Hussein from his torpor. His first reaction is to tell the sheikh and three of his followers that they've come to the wrong premises; he never sells pork on Friday. However, the old sheikh's steely countenance kills the whimper of sarcasm in his throat. The man refuses to look Hussein in the eye and speaks loudly, forcefully, as though preaching to a multitude.

"It is time for you to consider the effects of your sins." His booming voice shakes the narrow confines of the butcher shop. "Every one of them moves us further from the greatness that should be ours. Instead of walking the path of righteousness, we are victims of your decadence. Don't confuse material advancement with moral good. I tell you now, what you are doing threatens our survival and yours."

He raises his walking stick to prevent interruptions, but it's not necessary. Hussein couldn't have spoken even if he wanted to. Despite the sheikh's robes and scowling companions, he is struck by the similarity between the religious leader and his father. Certainly Al Jid was rarely bombastic. But the sheikh's arrogance, the bullying of Hussein, makes the two men similar. Hussein intuitively knows that like his father, the sheikh believes that with the passing of the prophets, ordinary men can no longer be innocent bystanders in their own fate, reliant on soothsayers, gypsies, and fakirs. Abandoned on the earth, alone by themselves, they must act as agents of God's righteousness, with every individual having a duty of faith and conscience, and if they failed, there would be inescapable ramifications—eternal and earthly.

"Why have our people been forced into exile? Why are we the ones attacked?" despairs the sheikh. "From Syria to Iraq, Afghanistan to Chechnya, innocent Muslims are being slaughtered—entire families destroyed, homes and lands lost forever. We wander through the winter of our existence. *Laish?* Why? For what reason? What have we done?"

He thunders again: "We live in the end of days predicted by the prophets. There is no turning back. As believers, we stand unafraid. We do what Allah demands because if we forgo the one true path, we remain miserable, mired in failure, because He has forsaken us. Allah has willed our misfortune, our suffering, our backwardness."

His words hang oppressively in the air—it is a grave accusation against all who call themselves Arab.

"Think carefully on what I've said." The stick again admonishes the butcher. "The time will come when actions will demonstrate the truth of my words. If you block our way, then you and your family must accept the consequences. What is the saying of the People of the Book? 'You reap what you sow'?" It is a not so veiled threat against the once mainly Christian town. "No cult, no worm, not even the president of the United States, obstructs the will of Allah."

As quickly as they arrived, the sheikh and his followers file out of a shop that doesn't even belong to Hussein. The owner, Khaled's father, is so advanced in years that he is unable to take an active role in the enterprise. In fact, he had been obliged to continue long after he should have retired. His eldest son, after attending the university in Cairo, refused to take over the family business, and Khaled, his youngest, was regarded as too slow-witted to be responsible. It was with some happiness, therefore, that the elderly butcher offered the job to Hussein, who was in desperate need of one.

"A man is lucky if his sons appreciate his handiwork," the old butcher complained as he showed his new manager around for the first time. Hussein, reminded of Al Jid, agreed. The arrangement worked well. The butcher secured retirement and enhanced his status by doing a favor for a member of such a prominent family. When Hussein decided to sell pork and went to consult him, the old butcher said, "Strip the meat from the bone and the starving won't be able to tell the difference." Except for the new fridges, the shop hadn't changed much since the old man's day.

Looking around, Hussein is gripped by conflicting emotions. He resents the sheikh's officious manner and is so angry that his face has turned red. But his blush also contains an element of embarrassment and guilt. He does not want to be pressured into doing something he does not believe in; at the same time, his own conscience will not allow him to feel at ease with what he has done.

He also wonders why they bother with him at all—and there it is again: that niggling suspicion that never really leaves him, that somehow they have found out about his military past. But he shrugs off these thoughts as he always does. If they did know they would come after him—not in broad daylight with rocks and a walking stick, but under the shield of night with a knife. No, Umm al-Khaana-zeer, Mother of All Pigs, is responsible for the passion infesting the town, where pork is being sold and eaten, although never in his own home. Hussein is sure about that.

So deep is his self-absorption that he does not immediately notice a man waiting by the shop's screen door. And when he finally comes in, Hussein sees at once he's not a customer, although he doesn't recognize who it is straightaway. The bearded man, unkempt and dirty, wears old fatigues and heavy well-worn boots. After a curt nod he places two bulky, makeshift bags under the counter out of sight. Their shapes remind Hussein of the long distances he and his men covered by foot in the army, and the complicated weaponry they used under extreme conditions, which they learned to assemble wearing blindfolds.

The man in the butcher shop has the appearance of someone who has been on the road for months. His eyes are animated but some-how vacant. He keeps glancing from side to side as though search-ing for a hidden threat. Hussein knows the expression. It belongs to someone who has seen action.

As a rule, Hussein thinks about the army only when he's forced to. There were men who believed in what they were doing and em-braced the experience wholeheartedly. It was as though they were able to inhabit different personalities. They could change who they were depending on the company they were keeping. It was a kind of dissembling of which even Allah approved, in the doctrine of *taqi-yyah*. With civilians these men were civil, with their enemies they were harsh and cruel, and if they lived among their own kind had a disagreement and broke with them, God forbid, they became mur-derous. Hussein knew he was not talented in that respect. His fa-ther's opinions, although he did not always readily accept them as his own, had penetrated the shreds of what was left of his principles and formed some kind of basis for his behavior. For many of the men he trained, particularly those who came under his command once he was promoted to the antiterrorism platoon, morality was not fixed but porous.

The arrival of the haggard young man in the butcher shop brought back a time that Hussein would have preferred to lock away in the furthest reaches of his consciousness and forget. After he retired, he was secretly relieved his army days were gone for good.

"Mustafa?" he asks carefully, as if peering out of the dark tunnel of his past. "Can it really be you?"

They hug and kiss each other twice on both cheeks. Despite all that had gone on before, Hussein is exhilarated to be once again in the company of one of his men.

"*Ahlan*, Mustafa, what are you doing here? The last I heard, your brother was in"—again it is something Hussein doesn't like to consider too deeply—"Afghanistan."

It was more than just a rumor. Only last month he had come face-to-face with his military past when a mysterious stranger arrived unannounced at the shop. The man, introducing himself first by saying he was grateful for Hussein's contribution in keeping their country safe, identified himself as a concerned individual from one of the ministries. Then without warning he asked what Hussein knew of a breakout from a secret facility. Hussein admitted only what he had gleaned from newspaper reports published outside of Jordan at the time, which he had read at the local Internet café. He was aware that enemy combatants captured in the field were often brought hooded and shackled to Jordan. While the CIA didn't maintain an official presence in the country, Jordanian intelligence, the GID, had proven its usefulness many times over. Not only did the agents speak a difficult language, which the Americans struggled to master, but they were also enmeshed in local religion and culture.

Then the mysterious stranger suddenly asked after one of Hussein's men and received no reaction whatsoever from the former commander. Natural suspicion prevented Hussein from volunteering information that he knew to be true: wherever Sayeed was and in whatever guise, his brother would not be far behind.

"I'm on my way home, Lieutenant," says Mustafa. "I'm tired of journeying," and he touches Hussein's bloodstained butcher's coat. "This is how you're supposed to look in the places I've been, not during peacetime as a civilian." He is attempting to make a joke but his eyes are dead.

Good-naturedly Hussein slaps the young man on the back. He is more than happy to see Mustafa. However, there is a question that dies before it reaches his lips. One brother without the other seems incomplete, like a man with a missing limb. Instead he remarks, "You have come far, Mustafa. You must be hungry. There is a sink in the yard. Wash up and I'll prepare something."

Once the soldier goes out back, Hussein interrupts Khaled sloughed over a comic book in a corner and orders his assistant, "Go and get me a lemon, an onion, and some bread. Take the money from the register. When you get back you can go home." Then he adds, in case the boy doesn't realize it's Friday, "Take more time for lunch today. I will close the shop myself and come back for the evening trade."

After Khaled sets off, Hussein opens the halal refrigerator and removes a plastic bag filled with offal. He selects two kidneys and a liver and washes them in the sink. With a sharp knife he cuts a slit in the membrane around each kidney, peels it away, halves them both lengthwise, and carefully trims off the fat and gristle. He is in the process of arranging them on a cracked plate when the soldier emerges through the back door, drying himself on his shirt, which he'd removed.

A henna tattoo of cursive writing covers the surface of his chest, his shoulders, and his back: "In the name of merciful Allah! We grant you triumphant victory. He will absolve you of all your sins in this life and in the hereafter. The war between the sky and earth belongs to Him!" Hussein has seen such markings on the bodies of nameless men in secret facilities, and the writing reminds him of engraved amulets or prayers concealed in the walls of old houses to protect them against evil. The words are different but the meaning the same.

And the fragile bodies covered by the prayers collapsed even easier under pressure than those ancient structures.

Still, Hussein can't stop himself from staring. He never once suspected Mustafa or Sayeed of piety. Meeting his gaze, Mustafa nonchalantly buttons his shirt but lurches at the sound of the shop bell. Khaled has returned from his errand. Hussein takes the parcels from him and then dismisses the boy with a brusque wave of his hand. He cuts the lemon in half and squeezes it over the kidneys. After making sure that there are no seeds, he pushes the plate across the counter to the soldier and places two slices of pita bread beside it.

"Eat," Hussein instructs. He turns around, slices the liver and sets it to fry on the tiny gas jet in a little olive oil with onion, salt, and pepper, and then places two glasses on the counter. "Did the mujahideen stop you from drinking?" He crouches down behind the refrigerator and brings out the secret jar.

The soldier laughs. "They gave us tea, hot milk, and sugar, but that was only on good days. When the water ran out in the mountains, we drank urine. So I have tasted all manner of refreshment except the one you give me now. Is it as delicious as I remember it?"

His face screws up from the straight *arak*.

"I've been waiting for this, Lieutenant. Some of the places I've been make your town look like paradise. There you could only buy rugs, hashish, and Kalashnikovs; here you can have a drink and eat raw *kalaawi*. To decadence!" he toasts. "May you never grow old," then ends his sentence with a loud and defiant "sir!"

Hussein drinks lustily to his young comrade, but his throat remains dry. The soldier grows serious over his food. He asks, "So what do you know of Sayeed?"

"I heard a few rumors, nothing definite."

"He had been saying things he never thought before," the soldier continues, but talking as though to himself. "I've known him all my life and suddenly he's telling me he rediscovered his faith—not in a mosque, not in the company of our religious uncles, but while a notorious fundamentalist is being tortured?"

The question hangs in the air until Mustafa speaks again. "When Sayeed disappeared, I expected to hear that he had been kidnapped.

But no ransom demand materialized. The very last time Ummi and I saw him, she was fussing over us as mothers do. He kissed her and said, 'Never ever forget me.'"

Hussein can easily picture the scene: a proud mother who won't take no for an answer attended by her two grown sons. She had heard about Hussein from a relative and surprised him by showing up in the army barracks one morning unannounced, demanding that he watch over her boys in another unit. How she made it past the guards remains a mystery.

After her visit, he arranged for Mustafa and Sayeed's transfer into the battalion he was serving in at the time, and his efforts produced an unexpected reward. The brothers were not much to look at; physically, they appeared spindly and small. It was an impression that was exaggerated when they wore full battle dress. However, given the choice between larger, obviously tougher men and these two slight brothers, Hussein always chose the latter. Growing up in one of the poorest, toughest neighborhoods in Amman had given them surprising reserves of resilience and stealth. Their mother could have saved herself the trip, because they knew how to fend for themselves.

Sayeed, two years younger than Mustafa, was the more determined. He set the bar and viewed each exercise or assignment as a test of his ability. His older brother worked hard to keep up with him. To outsiders they seemed in competition with each other; to Hussein they were two sides of the same coin. The brothers thrived in the army. They liked the exercise, put on weight—despite the bad food—and didn't object to being ordered around. Sayeed and Mustafa turned into impeccable soldiers, quick-witted, dependable, and brave. Hussein had almost come to regard them as surrogate sons. If his own boys grew up to be like these two, he would have no reason to complain.

Then, when Hussein's exemplary work became the focus of official attention and he was promoted to the army's elite antiterrorism platoon, he recommended both men. But only Sayeed made the grade. Due to the platoon's relentless schedule of reconnaissance and surveillance, Mustafa faded from Hussein's view. He always managed to drop by, totally relaxed and casual as though it was nothing for him to check on his younger brother, all the while glossing over the fact that news of the platoon's clandestine activities was filtering down to the lower ranks. Of course, after Hussein left anti-terrorism for good, he lost contact with both men, and in the intervening years, Sayeed and Mustafa seemed to have disappeared off the face of the earth. Whenever Hussein allowed his mind to wander, he often found himself turning over one unalterable fact: men of fortitude, no matter their politics or religion, were like gold dust in the region's many wars and conflicts.

Mustafa wrenches Hussein away from his recollections. "Brothers are supposed to have an unspoken bond of trust between them, but I swear I knew nothing of Sayeed's plans. On the day I left the army I vowed to find my brother.

"It was impossible at first. Every door closed," he confesses. "Then slowly, slowly, there was a crack I was able to slip through, which led to a man who knew of another place to go. It almost seemed as if Sayeed left signs. Whenever I faltered, someone inevitably appeared to guide me. Eventually a path presented itself: east into Iraq, through Khuzestan and Fars in southern Iran, and across the badlands of Balochistan into Afghanistan. I made my way slowly, under the radar of those who are supposed to know, stopping in out-of-the-way villages and moving among shepherds and their flocks. When I was asked the purpose of my trip I always told the truth: I was searching for my lost brother. The most unlikely people helped me, Allah be praised for their kindness. I crossed borders late at night or in the early morning. It took me close to a year, but I finally found him in the mountains outside Khost, fighting with the mujahideen near the Afghan border with Pakistan. When he saw me, he fell into my arms and gave thanks to God for my safe delivery. He was crying, begging me for news of our mother. It was deeply emotional..." The soldier's words momentarily trail off before starting again. "Only when we were alone at night, and everyone else was asleep, I whispered to Sayeed that he had damned himself and the rest of our family by running way. But he turned on me, saying only under Islam would the poor, like us, be truly free. At times I thought I was talking to a stranger; but he was my brother."

He composes himself in a moment of silence. "Thirteen-year-old boys fighting under the banner of Islam disemboweled American contractors. If you are attacked often enough, you fight back. Martyrdom was all the mujahideen talked about—but not even hell can be more horrible than jihad."

Hussein has never liked the word. Over the years its once traditional meaning of "striving" for God has become shorthand to mean all-out holy war. It is the justification used not only by the faithful whenever they feel cornered by the powerful—the British, American, Israeli, or Russian armies—but also the powerless: people shopping for vegetables in a market in Baghdad or eating cake in a bakery in Dhaka. Every new group added to the roster of the damned is attacked with a vengeance.

But jihad's ever-widening circle of aggression has also radiated inward, and tensions between the Sunni and Shia have been ignited. Despite the death and destruction, nothing has changed. The corrupt take bribes; guns and drugs are bought and sold; women are raped and suffering continues. To Hussein, jihad signifies ineptitude. It is the last resort of a people who feel so badly done by they eat their young.

"So jihad murdered your brother?" Hussein purposely keeps his voice sounding neutral.

The soldier chews a mouthful of bread. "That depends on your point of view," then he asks, "Have you seen drones in action?" He doesn't wait for Hussein's reply. "I had heard about them, of course, but the first time I *saw* them was in Afghanistan. Suddenly, without warning, Sayeed and the mujahideen started running in circles"— he half smiles, remembering—"like children playing a game." He explained about the time lapse between from what's seen on the ground and the image that appears on a computer monitor, via satellite link, at a military facility thousands of miles away in Oklahoma or Omaha.

Mustafa checks himself and slows down: "Then a Hellfire missile came close. Maybe it wasn't targeting us. In an instant a fireball descended from the sky and blew up the van in front of us on the road, which buckled in half. An old woman and her teenage girl, their burkas shredded, crawled from the wreckage. They were trying to call for help, but the shock and their wounds were so great that no sound came from their mouths. Instead every one of us—on the roadside and in the other cars—were screaming. We stayed frozen to the spot. It was too dangerous to venture any closer. Sayeed knew that. But before I could stop him he ran toward the victims. There's always a second missile—the Americans call it the 'double tap.' Before my eyes, in seconds, my brother and the two women were gone. But I will never forget the way they stared accusingly at me. That's when I knew I could not go on living as I have."

Blood drains from Mustafa's face. "My trip back has been long. I've been drifting, sometimes working as a laborer in places. But whenever I get into a van or on a bus, like last night, the ghosts of those women appear to me."

The soldier's face fills with a mixture of horror and fascination. He continues: "They wear white and sit silently together, watching me. I know my mind is playing tricks but it feels like the women expect something. What, I don't understand." His terrified eyes look up. "See, I am frightened for my mother. She has lost one son, and the other is *majnun*—crazy!" Mustafa can barely pronounce the word without choking. In desperation he drains the glass in front of him.

"I don't have the courage to go home and tell her Sayeed is dead. So I have come to you, Hussein Sabas, because there is nowhere else to go. There is chaos everywhere. At the Jordanian border, hundreds of Syrians were trying to get in, and those who had the bad fortune to be Palestinian or men of a certain age and look were turned back. They'll be slaughtered, but the authorities are frightened of Daesh. With good reason." His laugh rings hollow.

"I had to cross the Jordanian border illegally. I mean, the soldiers were never going to welcome me with open arms, not with..." His eyes wander in the direction of his stashed bags.

"Late at night I started heading west by foot and came across some poor farmers and boys, Syrians again, this time traveling northward. I could tell by the way they were covering ground they had few guns between them. Then several hours later, before dawn, I could sense another group behind me. Then the storm struck. When you're out in the rocky desert of the Badia in the dark, you don't want surprises, but the wind doesn't care. Sand blinded us all and I could hear them shouting."

He tells Hussein, "I nearly ran into one of them. He was so close I could have pulled the scarf from his face. They were experienced, all right—men who had seen time in Syria and Iraq. I didn't have to ask where they came from or their final destination. The Arab Awakening has been a distraction. The Salafis have rallied and regrouped, and they are much more determined this time."

Listening to Mustafa, Hussein wonders if anything has changed at all. The present conflicts—Alawi vs. Sunni; Salifi vs. the Jordanian intelligence; Saudi Arabia vs. Iran—may appear localized, but they have been shaped by Western invasion and interference. Granted it wasn't the barefaced colonialism of his father's day. Now a sleight of hand was at play, due in part to the availability of more sophisticated long-range weaponry. But whether you're murdered close up or from far away, the message for subjugated peoples is the same: toe the fucking line. All the wars that have been started and withdrawn from, or dragged out as long-simmering territorial occupations, have left a legacy of bloodshed. Every country has been affected... or, as Hussein corrects himself, *infected.* So many lives wasted and for nothing.

He fills the young soldier's glass again and signals for the both of them to drink. The two men stand bound in the knowledge that one of their own has fallen. Others can decide the value of Sayeed's life and death. He and Mustafa commemorate his passing. In the chasm of silence between them, Hussein casts his mind back to his last mission with Mustafa's brother. They had been tracking jihadists through arid mountainous terrain in Jordan's south, where a report had come in about human trafficking and the illicit movement of weapons.

In the desert between Jordan, Saudi Arabia, and Egypt, nomadic tribesmen or Bedouin traveled freely. In Hussein's country, the

Bedu were considered upright and honorable. Those of significantly less valor bombed tourist resorts in the Sinai, left mutilated Muslim Brotherhood corpses on the border to the Gaza Strip, and attacked military outposts in their way. The Bedu had become guns for hire and acted as guides to anyone who needed to make their way unseen through the barrenness. Women desperate for a better existence outside Eritrea were often enslaved or murdered during the crossing.

The antiterrorism platoon spent the night marching up a rough spur. As dawn rose, Hussein recognized the landscape of his father's stories. The Dead Sea to the north reflected the sun's rays like a great bronze plate cradled between the mountains of Moab and Judah. Reading the landscape, Hussein was sure that the very spot his unit had drawn up to was in the shadow of Jebel Nebi Harun, where Musa's brother Harun was killed and buried during the great exodus of the Israelites. Behind the platoon lay the Nabataean city of Petra, the site of many great biblical prophecies. It was hard for Hussein to be lulled by a vista that was in many ways familiar, because he understood the dangers of relaxing his guard. The Bedu inhabited the land's hidden nooks and crannies, while the Salafis who followed them were known for their mercilessness.

It was midmorning when Hussein's squad emerged from the low cliffs and thorn bushes of the mountains onto the undulating dunes of desert scrubland. Hussein would not have ordinarily stopped there, but the mission's commander ordered them to halt for twenty minutes. Suddenly several sharp cracks punctuated the air, and without warning the man next to Hussein was lying on his back, arms thrown wide embracing the sky. Blood welled from the corner of his mouth, and a red patch spread across his chest. He was twenty-three.

Twenty yards away Hussein could see the unit's communications officer, either unconscious or dead, clutching a handheld radio. If there was any chance of saving his men, Hussein knew he had to take it. He got up and ran, crouched over, to call for help. But as he did so he realized that even if he reached his goal, the line was not secure—the Americans had not yet given the Jordanians the technology—and his actions would probably alert more of the enemy to where they were. He was reaching for the radio when something as heavy as the hand of God hit him in the back, and he fell among the rocks.

He stayed in the hospital for three months. During the first few days as he hovered between darkness and light, the war on terror worsened, but Hussein was not aware of it. He drifted in and out of consciousness, oscillating between pain when he was awake and morphine-drenched nightmares when asleep.

Al Jid had told his son the story of Enoch and the ring of fire. A group of angels came down to earth, succumbed to temptation and mated with human women. The resulting offspring was a race of voracious monsters that copulated with everything in sight. Outraged, the rest of creation—animal, vegetable, and mineral—appealed to God for salvation. The Almighty responded by creating a hole ringed with fire into which the sinning angels and their appalling progeny were dumped for all eternity.

One day, the prophet Enoch was walking where water is borne on Jebel ash-Sheikh and heard voices bemoaning their everlasting punishment. They begged him to mediate on their behalf. Only a holy prophet had the ear of the Lord. Touched by their suffering, Enoch agreed to plead for them, but the Almighty was unimpressed by his servant's ignorance: "Angels intercede for man. A worm cannot plead for the divine." A terrible thundering raged in the landscape of fire, "When your time comes, which invertebrate will speak for you?" As Hussein lay in his hospital bed, the tale ran around a fevered imagination. Occasionally he was Enoch, but more often than not he was one of the damned.

He was lucky. Some of the shrapnel was removed from his back and the bone in his shoulder healed well enough. He left the hospital wearing a sling. The doctor advised him that given time his left arm would improve, but there would be residual shaking in the hand because of injury to the nerve. However, it was not only his body that had been damaged. When he returned to his hometown for three weeks' convalescent leave and his neighbors welcomed him as a hero, all he answered was "You're mistaken." He closed the curtain of his father's house and sat in the cramped space between the *zariba* animal pen and storage bins, hardly acknowledging the greetings of his stepmother or youngest half sister. He made up his mind to leave the army, but the decision only made him feel worse. All day he sat by himself, speaking to no one, lost in thought.

When Al Jid came in from the fields one night, he came to Hussein carrying a pot of Arabic coffee and the *arghileh*. "We should talk," the old man said.

Haltingly at first, then with growing emotion, Hussein told his father about the broken promises and his disillusionment. It was the terrible futility that bothered him the most, the killing of Arabs by Arabs. When he finished, the old man nodded. "If any one people needed a sign or a miracle, God knows it is us."

It was completely dark. Al Jid reached for a candle and lit it. The globe of light encircled father and son, insulating them from the outside world. Even the rustle of the penned-up animals in the *zariba* seemed hushed and far away. In the years that had passed, Al Jid had grown wizened and bloated. He had trouble breathing and moved slowly, but he still insisted on tending the land. Lighting the water pipe, he inhaled deeply.

"In al-Abbasiyah, the third dynasty after the Prophet's death, there were two poets."

Hussein was in no mood for his father's stories, but in the depths of his despair he felt compelled to listen.

The old man settled into his tale: "Khalaf al-Ahmar was a known prankster with a talent for joking. He wrote many beautiful ballads that are recited to this day. He taught composition and philology to a young Abu Nuwas, still a novice in the craft of poetry.

"One day Abu Nuwas asked for his master's blessing so he could compose and recite his own poems in public. The experienced Khalaf al-Ahmar said that he would gladly do that, but first Abu Nuwas needed to undergo a trial by words and memorize one thousand verses. The undertaking was long and difficult, but Abu Nuwas was eventually successful. To celebrate, he honored his master by giving him a lavish feast over the course of several evenings, during which the younger poet recited the verses he learned by heart.

After Abu Nuwas declaimed the last triumphant couplet, he again asked his master for his blessing. Khalaf al-Ahmar was undoubtedly impressed, but before he could agree, one more small task was required of the poet-to-be, whose life and career would eclipse that of his master's. He had to forget each and every one of the verses he committed to memory."

Al Jid fanned the hot bowl of the water pipe with his open hand until the embers glowed.

"In his great wisdom, Khalaf al-Ahmar explained that for immortal composition, one needed to know everything and to forget everything." The old man regarded his wounded son. "Memory and forgetfulness will enable you to live your life. Then you too will find a way in your heart to continue. If you give up, your time on this earth will truly be over, and you will never be at peace with yourself again."

At the end of his convalescent leave, Hussein went back to the army. He resigned his commission from the antiterrorism platoon and transferred to a desk job, where he watched the war from afar and concentrated on following his father's advice. The combination of repetitious bureaucratic duties and liberal doses of alcohol resulted in a trancelike state of amnesia, which, while not exactly contentment, was at least not too hard to endure. In his darker moments he blearily toasted Abu Nuwas. Hussein was only following in his venerable footsteps. The poet had gone off to a monastery, where he had drunk his thousand verses into oblivion.

Mustafa's return stirs up emotions Hussein had long put to rest. Only a day before he had come across a book of Iraqi antiwar poetry. He assumed that it was Samira's since nobody else would have brought it into the house. He leafed through it, not really paying proper attention. Now one of the verses comes back to him:

Abdullah liked cars.
He drove them around the town.
He was sent to the front.
Afterward, the hand he steered with was sent home in a box to his mom.

Noon brightness pierces the shutters of the butcher shop, casting an ornate pattern of darkness and light over the soldier who has nothing to show for his brother, no box, not so much as a fingernail.

"There is someplace you can stay." It is a tentative offer. "But you should see it first. If it offends your sensibilities we'll make other arrangements."

Hussein slips the jar into its hiding place and washes and dries the glasses as the tense young man waits, with his bags, by the door.

8

It is unusual for Samira to have a late start to her day. Normally by this time she would have been finishing her housework. She makes her bed, then straightens out Muna's, dreaming of the perfect afternoon. Ideally she would like to slip away to the capital, but under the circumstances that's impossible. Her mother said they are expecting company. Samira thinks Fadhma's plans border on the fanciful. After all, the townspeople have been staying away. Surely the arrival of a cousin from America is not enough to lure them back.

Yesterday evening Samira peered over her oversize bifocals at Muna and felt that apart from their blood connection the two of them had little in common. She expected her to make a mistake. In the morning she didn't have to wait long. Muna's outfit, a pair of above-the-knee culottes and an identical sleeveless blouse—a different color from the one that she brought Samira from a stylish New York boutique—shows Samira that there's no way of ignoring it now.

"That's okay for inside the house, if we're alone," she begins slowly, "but you won't be able to go outside or meet company dressed like that."

"There's a problem?"

Samira had assumed Muna would have figured it out by herself; after all, she is the one who's college educated. Last night when everyone opened their gifts, Samira held up her present of the blouse, and both her mother and Laila looked askance. It was obvious that something was wrong, but no one passed comment and Muna appeared clueless. The awkwardness was finally dispelled when Samira's girlfriends came over. Yvette and Gigi, a pair of cheerful fraternal twins whose names were inspired by their parents' honeymoon in Paris, worked in Amman as secretaries. Their good humor was infectious.

"Come to Samira's room." Gigi winked conspiratorially as she led Muna by the hand. "We have lots to talk about."

After the four of them were alone, the twins quizzed Muna about New York and boyfriends.

Once Hussein arrived home from work and Laila retrieved their guest, Samira noiselessly shut the bedroom door and showed Muna's gift to her friends. She admitted somewhat sheepishly that she preferred to let Muna find out about the inappropriateness of the blouse by herself. Samira had, to her mind, a perfectly good excuse: her older sisters always resented being told what to do whenever they came home to visit. She cocked her head in the direction of the living room. "Why should Muna be different?"

Yvette was the first to disagree. Of late she had been arguing with Samira. Earlier that week she accused her of putting politics before her family and friends, because Samira supported the rebel opposition in Syria, even if it meant the destruction of the Christian minority there. "You no longer know when to act in your own best interests," Yvette told her.

Yesterday evening the twin was again unimpressed. "If your American cousin finds out from a sharp stone in the back, what does that say about women's solidarity and standing up for what's right?"

Her question has been haunting Samira this morning.

She breaks the news gently to Muna but is fully prepared for a fight. "There is a problem. I couldn't go out dressed like that. That blouse you gave me is really lovely. But it would have to be worn hidden underneath a sweater or a jacket but never by itself. Now the shorts..."

Muna looks down. "These aren't really shorts. Short shorts are in fashion but I never wear them. This is more like a skirt—"

"That's what it is to me and you, but for some people the idea that women have legs and show them off cause problems." The inflection in her voice is rising; it is not something she agrees with.

"It's not legs," Muna mutters under her breath. "It's *kuss*."

Samira is not sure that she heard her cousin correctly.

Muna is the picture of innocence as her mouth fills with filth: "*Kuss umek! Kuss ukht elee nafadak aars!* Who would have guessed you could learn to say 'Fuck your mother's vagina' *and* 'Your aunt's vagina is a slut' from the Internet?" she observes. "Come to think of it, a lot of Arabic cursing—and thinking—seems to focus on that one word: *kuss*."

Samira laughs out loud; her American relations don't usually behave like this. Al Jid and Fadhma had their last child in the old world shortly before Muna was born in the new. Muna strictly speaking isn't a cousin. A year older than her, Samira is in fact her aunt. Timing had made Samira the brunt of her siblings' jokes—"Look at the old goat!" they scoffed among themselves. Still the closeness in the young women's ages makes "aunt" inapproprately old, so both of them unthinkingly adopted "cousin." Samira giggles again.

"What?" Muna, annoyed, sits down on a single bed. "I guess I was being foolish," she continues more seriously. "After Tahrir Square I thought women's clothing wouldn't be such an issue anymore—all those girls there in skimpy T-shirts and tight jeans. Teenage boys from the Muslim Brotherhood said that the women were owed an apology; no matter how they dressed they cared about Egypt. I was hoping there were more important issues at stake than a blouse."

Disappointed, she turns to the opened suitcase on the floor. "Is there anything you'd prefer instead?"

Samira, not as clothes obsessed as Yvette and Gigi, shakes her head. Because Muna has been honest with her, she returns the favor. What is it that Zeinab from the women's committee told her? The goal isn't to end a disagreement nicely. A clear, well-reasoned argument will have a longer-lasting effect and might actually end in mutual friendship and respect.

"There has been a change but not like you think. There are still too many 'red lines,'" Samira explains, also frustrated.

After a pause Muna confesses, "In 2011, Dad stopped me from coming to Jordan. For this trip I didn't bother to ask his permission, I just booked my ticket. I don't care about Daesh. Auntie Magda and Hind believe the region is doomed, but they've been saying that for years. Watching the Arab Awakening from afar made me feel ashamed I didn't have more faith."

"When the first demonstrations broke out it was exciting," agrees Samira, "but with wholesale slaughter going on next door in Syria, no one in Jordan talks about the need for a democratic government. I saw Facebook posts of demonstrators being beaten up by the police in Amman. And Jordanians—you could tell by their names—were clicking 'like.' They believed the protestors should be arrested *and tortured.* And there's something else." Samira isn't sure how far to go. "Daesh, Muslim Brotherhood, Hizbullah, and Hamas are all in competition with each other. Who is more Islamic? Who's more in charge? And so a revolution about freedom and dignity has been hijacked by armed men. Arabs never learn. 'Disagree with me or look at my sister, I'll kill you.'"

Samira usually doesn't get a chance to talk about such matters inside the family, she presses on. "So what is the difference between a 'secular' state and a Muslim one? Both use violence against the political opposition. Both torture in prison. They are as incompetent and corrupt as each other. The only real difference is the extent to which they control women and their bodies."

The reason Samira doesn't want to tell Muna what to wear is because it makes her sound like an advocate of the conservative religious forces she despises. Covering up is loathsome to her. However, since becoming politically active, she has started to appreciate—albeit grudgingly—the value of a good disguise. Yvette is right: better safe than sorry—or at least under the radar. Samira's approach softens. "Nowadays it's important to blend in and not call too much attention to yourself."

While the situation in Jordan is not as bad as the neighboring countries, caution is still advisable. In isolation, the preaching of the town's new sheikh would be ignored; he is a blowhard. However, with Daesh gaining ground beyond the border and an upsurge in local militancy, Samira and her friends were among the first to notice the differences. In a town previously characterized by a degree of tolerance, 1970s posters of belly-dancing singers, which adorned the walls of the music store, were torn down overnight. Nasty stone-throwing teenagers chased a friend of the twins' who had been wearing a T-shirt, vest, and baggy jeans. Suddenly the right clothes seem important. Young women out of step with the increasingly strident social order are only bound to suffer.

Samira adds as an afterthought, "On my better days, I like to consider it a question of fashion. Remember, in Egypt in the sixties, women wore miniskirts." She doesn't want their lives to sound all doom and gloom, although she knows that her political mentor, Zeinab, who escaped the ongoing "starve or kneel" siege of the Palestinian refugee camp Yarmouk in Damascus, would have scolded her for reverting to type: good Arab girl trying to make everyone feel a little bit better. She corrects herself: "Even in miniskirts, the women in Egypt were not as sexually harassed as the women wearing veils and robes today. So what's going on?"

Muna doesn't have an answer. "I just don't believe the lives of women or families should be controlled and programmed by mullahs, priests, or rabbis."

During their conversation, she holds up a skirt or a top, and her cousin either nods or points to the pile of haram clothes multiplying in the suitcase.

Samira charts Muna's progress with growing admiration. "My brothers and sisters believe the old country has stayed exactly how they left it when the opposite is true. Wars and revolutions have altered everything. This broken promise of the Arab Awakening will only leave another deep scar on a people who have a long history of self-harm." She reveals, "People like me long for something different, but until that happens, the men are firmly in control." There is something brittle and apologetic in her manner, as though she is not entirely convinced by what she's saying.

"That's what the aunties have always told me," Muna admits. "I just didn't expect it to be confirmed so soon after my arrival."

Over her bifocals, Samira takes a closer look at her cousin as though seeing her for the first time. She might have been too hasty in her assessment. In an effort to make amends she confides, "It's something I've always been aware of but never discussed until I started working with a group of Syrian women activists."

Muna is genuinely surprised. "What kind of work?"

"Pickup and delivery; I help out."

Samira doesn't add anything more than that, and Muna, she notices, has the good manners not to pry. Instead her cousin returns to the clothing and says distractedly, "Honestly, Samira, I don't know what I was thinking."

By the time the unsuitable items are sorted, Samira actually likes her American relation. She does not have to be in competition with her, and they could even become friends.

"This afternoon we'll be entertaining old people, but if no one shows up we'll escape. With the wedding feast tonight at least we're going out," Samira says. She buttons the back of a dress Muna has borrowed from her. With its high neck and three-quarter-length sleeves, her cousin finally looks respectable, although Samira prefers the culottes and the beautiful blouse from New York.

Alone afterward in the kitchen, Samira steps through the heavy curtains onto the back terrace. The view, which once induced such emotional turmoil in her, seems ugly and ordinary in daylight. There is no romance in the rough concrete walls and spare struggling trees. Fifty yards away stands the flat-topped house that belongs to the family of Walid, the boy who broke Samira's heart. Their meetings were brief stolen moments, intensified by the fear of discovery. It was a clandestine courtship, filled with intrigue and concealment, but for Samira it had been true love. Because she believed Walid felt the same way, she agreed to meet him on the back terrace late one night regardless of the risk.

When Mother Fadhma discovered them among the cushions, Walid jumped over the ledge into the darkness and fled out of Samira's life forever. She waited for him but he never contacted her again.

Then she heard he had taken a job in Dubai, and the long, painful process of accepting her loss began. As the aching, raw sore of rejection healed, another worry festered. A disastrous scandal could erupt if any of Walid's family or friends found out. Her guilt expanded until she imagined that people were talking about her indiscretions even when they were not. Without a word of explanation to her family, she quit teacher training college, avoided contact with anyone who might know about her relationship, and stayed at home. However, it was stifling to remain in the new house with her mother. So despite their arguments about what she was doing with her life, she began to take trips to Amman by minibus. There, wandering the wide boulevards, utterly dejected and alone, she at least felt free from scrutiny.

Samira smiles to herself when she considers how mistaken identity and a glass of sweet tea began a new important chapter in her life. On one of her excursions to the capital, she had been in one of the alleyways and saw a small teahouse that went against all she knew. Instead of being filled with only men or hipsters, it had been taken over entirely by women. Curious, she stepped inside, found an empty seat, and ordered a refreshment. As she was about to leave, a slim girl with a moon face and big dark eyes, wearing a hijab, rose from a nearby table, sat down without being invited, and immediately inquired why Samira looked sad. Samira didn't mean to tell the story of her broken romance, the abandonment of her studies, and, worst of all, the loss of her mother's respect, but like a torrent everything poured out of her.

The young woman was Zeinab. "You feel as if you don't belong," she told Samira. "Fate brought you here."

She placed a warm, soft hand on Samira's arm and motioned to the women at the other tables, who rearranged their chairs loosely around the two of them. Samira was at first intimidated by the commotion but also intrigued. Some of the women reminded Samira of herself and the twins—with or without headscarves. Others were obviously working mothers Laila's age and elderly grandmothers who, upon reflection, should have been watching the door more closely and stopped Samira from entering in the first place. Once the women realized she didn't pose a threat, they continued where they left off. It was a meeting of Syrian refugee women, including Palestinians and Kurds, now living in Amman and the surrounding towns and villages. Before Samira's arrival they had been listening to a report on the conditions in al-Zaatari refugee camp, which was growing at an unprecedented rate.

"Sometimes two thousand or more men, women, and children arrive daily and after being admitted to the camp they are not allowed out."

Afterwards another woman stood and read from her notes. "'Life in the camps,'" she said, "'is brutal. In the heat or extreme cold, the UNRWA tents are unbearable. Large extended families survive on a minimum of necessities and the children, the majority less than eleven years old, are not going to school. Instead some are working to support their families. The camp is rife with criminal gangs.

"'Nearly everyone there,'" the woman continued reading, "'has lost someone near to them. The threat of rape by both the regime and opposition fighters made many women flee; and just when they feel a degree of safety for themselves and their daughters, the girls are being married off by their fathers or uncles to wealthy Arabs who come to the camp, looking for a beautiful and young third or fourth wife.'" She sat down.

A heated discussion followed. The women wanted to do as much as they could for the people inside the camp, but as refugees themselves, their lives were also constricted. Another woman raised her hand and started complaining how difficult it was for her to get away because her relatives were always questioning her. "One of my brothers has even started following me," she admitted. "He hasn't confronted me because he's only seen me in the company of women, never men."

From the other murmurs of assent, apparently it was increasingly hard for young and old women to get away. Preparing for all eventualities, the leader of the women's committee had already formulated a plan.

Raising her voice to reestablish order, Zeinab explained, "Suspicious parents, husbands, and brothers should be visited by Umm Ghaliyah. She's our cover."

The moonfaced Zeinab in her hijab held one hand over her mouth like a niqab and with the other pointed to a heavyset, sturdy woman in her late sixties standing by the door. Umm Ghaliyah's floor-length dress and shawl were obviously homemade. With a twinkle in her eye and big, rough hands accustomed to manual labor, she was larger than life—beguiling and indomitable at the same time.

"Any trouble, *yani*, let me talk to your menfolk." Her voice was shrill and forthright. "Times like these require extraordinary measures. I'll explain about our meetings and study sessions. It is a chance for Syrian women to remember who they are and where they come from." Umm Ghaliyah moved her large shoulders with pride and added, "My sisters and I convince even the most suspicious. Few say no to witches like us."

Laughter rippled through the crowd. Her generous hands opened to include two elderly women seated beside her. Protected by their guardian angels, the activists forgot the dangers lurking beyond the teahouse door.

"Consider my situation," offered Zeinab. "As a Palestinian and a Syrian, I lost my home twice. Because of the Israelis, my family fled the catastrophe of 1967, and now only a few of us have escaped the violence by the regime and its supporters. Our first home is under occupation; our second one has not been given much of a choice, join Assad or burn. In Syria, there have been 400,000 people murdered, half the population of a country of 22 million displaced, and 117,000 detained and tortured in jail—and still there are those among us who believe women are not responsible adults able to decide or fend for ourselves!"

Sensing the restive mood of her listeners, she became conciliatory. "Of course I understand. You are not fanatics. You are God-fearing women who pray, work hard, and raise families, but where are the people who will wrench the Syrian and the Palestinian nations from their collective tragedies? I'll tell you where! Locked inside the refugee camps of our minds. We are not fighting for the future of one or two countries. We are fighting for the survival of us all."

Throughout Samira's lifetime, regional war and politics were a natural phenomenon, like a rock or a tree. In the past they were seemingly as unconnected to her life as a desert to a department store. Yet even then she wasn't entirely immune. Like many others of her generation, she was observant and critical, although without an outlet it was an anger that often turned against oneself or, if private finances allowed, found expression in unbridled consumerism. Under the spell of her new activist friends, Samira was beginning to see that everyone met on a common ground of unhappiness, bitterness, and betrayal. All of them had been forgotten: the refugees by an apathetic world, Arabs by their own corrupt governments, Muslims by jihadists, and, at the end of a very long funnel of diminishing proportions, Samira by Walid. Each and every one of them had been spurned, and the result was a world filled with anguish and pain.

Samira never worried that some members of the women's committee professed a different religion from her own. She felt that, at last, she was among people who understood and did not judge her. Her father would have been pleased that his daughter displayed such tolerance. Whereas Al Jid hoped that integration would promote understanding, for Samira it provided an opportunity for rebellion and conflict.

As her preoccupation with the group grew, she began to borrow reading material, much of which she didn't understand. Later when she admitted her shortcomings in understanding the assigned postcolonial readings, Zeinab said, "All you need to know is that there are many refugees in the world, people used as cheap labor, living in unimaginable conditions of poverty and oppression. Their lives will never change except through revolution, and sometimes that requires violence."

During meetings the women voiced their resentment about how their uprising had been hijacked by Daesh. Through their relations, some still inside ar-Raqqa, they heard about foreign fighters who had come from as far as Chechnya and Malaysia to join the jihadi free-for-all. And in the brutal caliphate that had been established, they took out their insecurities against the modern world on women, who were expected to marry between the ages of nine and seventeen, tend homes for their fighter-husbands, and be ready to marry a second, third, or fourth time once those men took their own lives as suicide bombers. People of the Book, like the Christians, endured sexual and menial enslavement, meaning they served as concubines to the man of the house and maids to his many wives. Women not of the Book, followers of so-called pagan religions like the Yazidis, were condemned to sexual servitude by men who believed intercourse with virgins an ecstatic religious experience and raped girls as young as twelve.

Still, existence continued in rebel-controlled areas. With the men away fighting or killed, it fell to the women to hunt for food, firewood, and water, as they cared for the young. Despite the conditions, that wasn't all that they did. Those women caught inside communicated with the refugee activists in Jordan, who followed their reports on Internet radio and raised funds to support local initiatives, like a new generator for a newspaper.

Among the activists, inside and outside, there were disagreements. Some desperately argued for surrender to the regime and a return to the life that had been destroyed. Others, like Zeinab, felt that the growing savagery on the part of both the jihadists and the government must be met with brute force as a form of self-defense. She made little distinction between the two, calling them "a snake with two heads."

She reminded the women of the first year of the Syrian uprising: "You remember when everything changed. Everyone wanted a nonviolent revolution and people were starting to wake up after forty years of fear. New civil society groups were forming and there were workshops on nonviolence and citizen journalism. This stopped once the government erected checkpoints and we could no longer move freely inside Syria. By December 2011, soldiers entering towns and villages raped women as a matter of government policy, in front of fathers, husbands, brothers, and sons. If there is a sniper on your street, or the house where you live is constantly shelled, or pro-regime *shabeeha* militias slaughter your children, can you really stand idly by? No one is such a saint! Anger is natural; revenge is not. The real question is: How do we stop ourselves from becoming as bloodthirsty as they are?"

These talks had a tendency to become heated. During one meeting Zeinab made an impassioned plea: "Women are a bridge to the future. Women are the donkeys of tradition. Women are caregivers and self-obsessed. They suffocate and love. They abuse and they suffer. The killer or the victim, which one are you?"

Samira wrote her words down in a notebook she started keeping.

Zeinab's cry for action caused such consternation that even proud Umm Ghaliyah shouted out: "It's not this *or* that; it's this and *more*." In the excitement, someone ululated as the women's protector and guardian angel sounded her own call to arms: "Drip by drip, like water, we melt stone!"

Phrases like this also appeared in Samira's notebook, which she scrupulously hid under her mattress at home. Other reading material, like the book of Iraqi antiwar poems, was left out in the open. She expected her mother to ask where it came from, but Fadhma made no comment. Samira knew that her mother was in some ways relieved that she was no longer moping around the house.

Zeinab's tutorials, combined with a late-night regimen of secret reading and studying, had the desired effect. Samira slowly became conversant with the theorists of the Syrian nonviolent uprising, like Gene Sharp, as well as Palestinian and Kurdish history. But her favorite times were when she and Zeinab stole a moment together and her friend took out her phone and scrolled through her personal photographs, telling Samira about her family and friends in the Yarmouk refugee camp and their lives during better days. Over time Samira learned what happened to every one of them: Zeinab's boyfriend had been imprisoned and died under torture; her uncle was shot leaving a bread shop. And then there was her first cousin. A mother of three darling little girls, she fled Syria on one of the boats bound for Egypt and her daughters, all under eight, drowned when the boat capsized. Zeinab had the good fortune to be smuggled out of the camp. Those of her extended family who remained during the ongoing siege were being picked off one by one—by hunger, barrel bombs, or snipers. Samira came to the conclusion that the Arab regimes and Daesh both considered all life cheap.

It was the photo of the three little girls with their big brown eyes that followed Samira as she did her political work. Identically dressed in their mother's hand-knitted sweaters and leggings, they stood shyly together, proud of getting their picture taken. They could have been any of the children from the town or her brother Boutros's daughters when they were small. The demise of Zeinab's little cousins was terribly cruel. But realpolitik was indifferent to death, injury, or injustice. Samira felt an urgency to pick sides. She thought she had a better chance of helping the activists and other children than arguing for herself or her neighbors. She was disappointed that the Arab Awakening faltered in the other countries before it had a chance to take root in her own.

Although she yearned to take a more active role, she was unsure how to do it. Then after one meeting, Zeinab asked her to remain behind. She had a request to make of Samira. A comrade's mother needed to go to the medical clinic, and Zeinab wondered if the newcomer to the women's committee would accompany her. A Jordanian national might come in handy. The committee was becoming more active among the wider Syrian refugee population, and Samira was in a position to help them. Eager to please, she agreed to go.

After that Samira was regularly called upon. Traveling alone by bus or shared taxi, she ferried money, messages, or reading material among the various Syrian political groups. The opposition movement was fractured, and it seemed groups were unnecessarily isolated or in disagreement. Sometimes, because she was an outsider, she moved easier between them as she picked up and delivered envelopes and packages unaware of their contents. All she did know was that her actions were a tiny link in a long chain that extended both ways: across Jordan's border toward Damascus, Homs, Hama, Idlib, and Aleppo, through to Lebanon and the Syrian activists working there, and back again. It was a trail that was becoming increasingly fraught—and not only because of the enemy but also because of so-called friends. The Arab governments wanted to corral the refugees in the camps, which were tinderboxes waiting to be ignited.

On one trip, the thin brown paper over the parcel split ever so slightly and Samira saw she was carrying opposition newspapers.

If she was caught, it could mean trouble or, worse, a jail sentence. While the Jordanian government didn't prevent hotheaded Sunnis from crossing the frontier and fighting for Syria, upon their return they were arrested and charged. Periodically a father made a public appeal, in the hopes that his son fighting a few hundred miles away was watching the news and would come home. However, the Jordanians weren't going to tolerate cross-border traffic of any kind, including incendiary political material. On one bus she had a close call: two policemen came on board and began searching refugees. She slipped off before her stop. When she voiced her fears to the man she handed the parcel to, he informed her, "Don't worry. Tell the policeman your brother is a retired army lieutenant; he won't bother you."

She was surprised that an absolute stranger knew about Hussein, and her first thought was to sever her associations with Revolutionary Change in Syria, the umbrella group that included the women's committee and other small initiatives. However, the political officer, who identified himself as Mr. Ammar, patently ignored the alarm on Samira's face and ushered her into an office filled with old computers, typewriters, books, and papers. Paint was peeling off the walls, and in the middle a cluster of twenty or more wooden chairs encircled a battered table. Samira took a far seat, but it didn't matter where she sat. Mr. Ammar towered over her. It seemed unlikely that this balding, mustached man was one of the handsome Free Syrian fighters whom Zeinab talked about. She promised Samira that there were many and suggested that the two of them take a trip to northern Syria—only four or five hours away by car from Amman—for a visit. Needless to say the overweight Mr. Ammar in his checkered shirt and frayed sweater vest wasn't one of them.

He explained to Samira that the office, which produced nature magazines for children, was a cover for group activities. He was impressed by the work of Zeinab and the women's committee, and had become their most vocal supporter inside the group, which had many small units and cells spread across Syria and in the countries hosting the refugees. Mr. Ammar, pleased with himself, explained that for strategic purposes, the left side didn't know what those on the right were doing. This prompt delivery of Samira's parcel gained her entry close to those operating at the top.

"Don't be surprised if we are familiar with you and your family," he added, "including your brother's, let us say, *unconventional* business. From our perspective we need to take precautions and know our friends and enemies alike."

He went on to discuss the decision-making process at the beginning of the uprising, when everyone in the front had a say. If one person disagreed, the group was paralyzed. "This changed once the fighting became more intense and we were forced to respond more quickly. When you live for so long under a dictatorship you become suspicious of anyone making a decision for you, no matter how pure his or her motives might first appear."

Unsure of how to respond, Samira surveyed the view from a grubby window: parched urban grayness interrupted by shiny glass-and-steel skyscrapers. In times of wars, preferably those taking place in other countries, Jordan always enjoyed a building boom. As quickly and politely as she arrived, she took her leave. The next time she and Zeinab were alone by themselves, Samira broached the subject of Mr. Ammar. If she was expecting an explanation, she was disappointed. All Zeinab said was "He has a tendency to crop up unexpectedly. You never know where he'll be. I rely on him, and you should too."

So Samira suppressed her misgivings and continued her involvement. Over the course of the last several weeks, she came to realize that Zeinab was busy with assignments more advanced than her own. She once gave Samira a clue when she explained that the modest scarf was the best form of camouflage: "Everyone thinks I'm quiet and submissive—nicely nicely Muslim girl." Samira knew that they made an odd couple, herself always heavily made up and the intense barefaced Zeinab in somber black. Through her, Samira learned to appreciate the deceptive nature of first impressions.

The most difficult part of the enterprise was not being able to confide in someone. Her family was out of the question, and although she loved the twins like sisters and from time to time discussed politics with them, she could only go so far. She never told them or anyone else about the women's committee or her work. When Samira first heard about Muna's trip, she considered her cousin as solely a means to an end, a new way of getting out of the house. After so many months, she was running out of excuses. Her family, while not as strict as many others, was starting to press her about where she was going and whom she was spending time with. Surely her mother or Laila wouldn't object to her showing Muna various historical sites, and on the way Samira could easily run her political errands as well.

She surveys the view from the terrace once more. In the past the sight of Walid's house would have caused her pain; now her mind glances over it as though it doesn't exist.

Last night's storm gathered sand and grit in the desert, fields, rough tracks, and town streets, depositing a fine film of dust over the furniture and floors, even in the rooms where the windows and doors were shut. Whether visitors are coming or not, Samira has to clean. Before she began working politically, she tended to start her housework slowly, lose interest in the middle, and finish only before Laila scolded her. These days she cleans energetically; her services may be required later on. Although the women's committee views domestic work as another form of enslavement, Zeinab's observations are never far from Samira's mind: "A maid is as important as a politician. In most countries, they get more work done."

Humming distractedly, Samira fetches a broom and duster from the cupboard in the hallway. Laila and her mother are both naturally fastidious and tidy up after themselves, so their rooms are the easiest to do. Her nephews' shared bedroom is not so neat. She collects the dirty socks and arranges the toys on top of the chest of drawers, out of the way of her dust cloth and broom. She decides to leave her own room. It seems somehow discourteous to disturb Muna's things since Samira feels she has interfered enough. After clearing away the previous evening's wrapping paper and the bows from the living room, the floors are ready to be washed.

No matter how much water remains in the house, this is something Laila always insists on and can become particularly nasty if it isn't done thoroughly. Samira has become adept at carrying out the task with minimum wastage. She fetches about a pint of water from a container in the bathroom, goes to Laila's room, sprinkles a small amount on the floor, and then spreads it around with a squeegee-mop, picking up any of the grimy excess with an old towel. When she finishes the other bedrooms, she steals more water from the supply under the bathtub and starts on the living room.

She has just finished wetting the floor when a loud crunching of gears and the rattling of an impossibly antiquated engine resound through an open window. The noise brings baby Fuad crawling excitedly into the room, closely followed by Muna, who doesn't realize that the floor is damp until it's too late. She stops midstep as Samira scoops the toddler into her arms, removes his sticky hands from her hair, and gives him to Muna, calling out, "*Ta'ale*, Mamma, come quickly!"

Pushing back her glasses, Samira goes to the window, throws open the shutters, and leans all the way out. "Where have you been all these weeks? What did you expect us to do, drink dirt?"

The driver climbs out of the water tanker and shrugs apathetically, which only exasperates her more. Before she has a chance to cuss him out, Mother Fadhma appears at her shoulder and pulls her inside.

Roughly handled and trussed up, the tiniest exertion on her part—even a breath—nearly suffocates. Flat on her back, she's engulfed again, her engorged belly moving, as she relives trauma: the searing and bruising of delicate skin, her imprisonment and fear. It is not loss of control but none whatsoever: soiling herself in the heat and a deep, abiding shame as diarrhea swills between her legs, rises beneath her belly, and fills a crate she's been stuffed into. Filthy, twisted rags have been pulled tight over her head. Impossible to move, bloated, disgusting—all she can do is hate, hate, hate herself.

Umm al-Khanaazeer remembers everything: her kidnapping and containment; each quivering turn in the road; the jolt of the rickety pickup truck grinding to a halt, followed by the wheezing inky exhaust of an uncooperative engine.

Erratic stops make up the first leg of the journey, as larger pieces of recyclable electrical waste are summarily dispatched before the truck moves on. As the stench of her beloved Zabbaleen recedes, she leaves behind an extended family fattened by Cairo's mega-waste, from the raw—the skins and seeds of tropical fruits—to cooked leftovers of grains and pastas made with the baharat medley of cloves and cardamom pods, coriander seeds, cinnamon, black pepper, smoked paprika, nutmeg and cumin. The lack of smell tells her of lessening human habitation as she and the truck trundle southward. She is utterly alone, the only one of her kind for miles around, a novel experience for a young sow who has spent every waking moment running in a pack of inquisitive pigs.

Without warning, another stop in a way station reeking of diesel, rancid old falafel, and human piss. A rapid changeover of vehicles takes place. Squeezed this time on the floor of a speeding station wagon, hidden beneath heavy boxes and overfilled bags, she feels the ground taking off all around her like sickening g-force. Half curses and unfinished sentences uttered by the man who stole her drift toward the back and get lost in the road's thunder—sounds that might as well be coming from the moon.

She loses track of time. After hours of forever, and stationary again at last, she is extracted from the crate. Her hood is wrenched free and an entire bottle of water is shoved down her throat. Coughing, choking, and dry heaving, she nearly drowns. Shitting herself, she manages to break free and crawls as far as her shackles allow before passing out. When she comes to, she is starving, unable to move inside the crate.

At another rest stop, guttural Arabic bursts in through an open window like a knife, a reminder of a bad end drawing near. No matter her agony, bribes are taken, a forward route planned. There'll be no going back.

Ear-splitting music from Radio Tel Aviv beats in her brain until a dial is flicked and classical quarter notes of infinite sadness fill the air. The prisoner is transported to a kinder, gentler time, when a woman singing melancholy love songs fed food sifted from trash to the beasts in her care.

On one occasion she's left behind—there's business that doesn't involve her—and is tied to a pen of camels, cousins of sorts due to an evolutionary glitch. Both are even-toed ungulates, but here the similarity between them ends. Pigs are naturally empathetic, while camels, resentful of their long-standing servitude to man, barely acknowledge each other, let alone a poor relation in their midst. Their disdain only confirms her own feelings of inferiority, enforced by a watery gruel left beyond her reach no matter how hard she strains at her ropes.

Sweltering sun barbecues tender flesh behind her ears. Dehydration makes the steps she is still able to take slow and deathlike. When the driver returns and finds her gasping, he scolds the camel keepers for their ineptitude. With bottled water, he pours a puddle so she can wash herself, and when she doesn't move to do so he wets a rag and pats the blisters on her skin. Afterward he applies sunblock to the most affected parts. After being mistreated for so long, she can no longer tell if the hand of the abuser offers salvation or is just pretending to. Either way, they have reached an understanding. She struggles no longer when rags are secured around her head and she is folded like a pillow back inside the crate.

In the dark, beyond the watchtowers, a floating bridge has been surreptitiously erected, one from a raft and ropes that will be dismantled before first light. Money always exchanges hands. Crossing of the Jordan River, her handler has been informed, should never be hurried—noise travels far in the dead of night. After the cargo is secured, her crate is separated from the rest, its top prized off. Head freed, she is encouraged to look around.

"It won't be long now," her torturer promises.

As the raft pulled by the ropes glides across water, she nearly starts to cry. The ordeals of travel and changes to her body have taken their toil. Along the way she doubted whether she and her children would ever find a home, yet despite all that has been done to her and to them, inexplicably she feels they may be getting closer to one.

She can almost taste it in the sweet grasses along the banks and in the swell of the current, the man by her side as quiet and watchful as she is. Together they share a moment of the essential timelessness under the stars. She had forgotten of their existence. When she wakes, she feels rested and at peace.

9

In school, Laila passes rows of students and a few teachers on their knees, praying, in one of the larger classrooms. Instead of lessons continuing with a percentage of the pupils absent, she and most of the teachers take a lunch break in the staff room, where a single ceiling fan clatters overhead.

Usually Laila sits by herself, but today she feels isolated despite making little effort to socialize herself. Longing for a kind word or trivial exchange, she settles in an empty corner chair among her colleagues, and she is reminded that the new headmistress expects the staff to be above reproach. So far Hussein's name has not yet been mentioned.

She rests her eyes. While some of her coworkers bring a sandwich from home or buy a snack from the school canteen, Laila avoids eating in public. Successive small cups of industrial-strength Arabic coffee from Amina, who's in charge of the teachers' hot drinks, will hold her until she returns home. She takes out student exercises from the folders she's been carrying and starts to grade. When the hubbub of voices around her diminishes she knows, without looking, that the headmistress Mrs. Salwa has entered the staff room. As she gazes up from the exercises in her lap, Laila feels the slow, dull breeze from the overhead fan on her face and sees the headmistress coming straight toward her.

Laila immediately stands, papers in hand. She is convinced this is the moment she has been dreading. "Mrs. Salwa." Laila glances at her watch but the numbers blur.

The headmistress, a stout woman in her fifties, smiles pleasantly, which only confuses the teacher. "I've only come to say that I'm off to the Matroubs this afternoon to greet the bride."

Laila, recovering herself, smiles. "Of course." She can't stop her eyes from straying to her wrist. It's easier to look down than at Mrs. Salwa. This time the numbers appear stark and vivid. She would like to emulate the headmistress's easygoing manner but blurts out instead, "I have a few things to do after school and probably won't be able to stay long. I hope I don't miss you."

"Looking forward to it." The headmistress stops and talks to other teachers on her way out.

In a daze Laila returns to her grading. She would like to go to the Matroubs, if only to show her face for a few minutes, while the neighboring women offer advice to the new wife-to-be. Perversely she enjoys those sorts of outings, but one obstacle prevents her: she was not invited. In any other circumstances this might have been an oversight, for Laila and the bride's mother, Warda Matroub, are close friends. Everyone knows that, even the headmistress, who has been invited to the Matroubs as a matter of form.

Although Warda is nine years older than Laila, she and her family moved to the town the year Hussein brought his new wife home. Warda's husband had been working as a structural engineer in Jeddah and took the unusual course of taking his wife with him to live there rather than leaving her in Jordan. She therefore spent most of her marriage in seclusion. Women aren't permitted to drive cars in a country as religiously observant as Saudi Arabia. So Warda—from a large, boisterous Muslim family in Amman—occupied herself by reading romance novels published in English. She attributes her survival in the cultural wilderness to the potboilers of Jackie Collins and Barbara Cartland, supplemented by countless afternoon teas taken in the hermetically sealed, marble-encrusted reception rooms of other women living in purdah. By the time she, her husband, and three daughters returned to the town of his birth, she told Laila she was set in her ways and planned to spend her afternoons receiving guests. However, she found her husband's female relations as tedious as the townswomen. So when she was introduced to Laila, she latched on to the modern Christian teacher who taught English at the government school. She told Laila they had much in common, and not just their love of *Wuthering Heights*.

The basis of their friendship was the shared alienation they felt in the small, conservative town. Laila has always talked openly with Warda, even when Hussein's growing business venture was not to the liking of some members of her friend's community. Warda vowed to be "unadulterated and completely honest" with Laila, borrowing a cover line from one of the romance novels. Despite the pact between them, Laila is sure that Umm al-Khanaazeer has something to do with her exclusion from the women's get-together.

Warda's daughter Anna, the bride-to-be, had overheard the two of them talking about the pig's fecundity, and she became so physically ill that she began retching in the toilet. As they ministered to her, Warda made light of the situation: "Honestly, Laila, many women would be thrilled if their daughters-in-law were as productive and gave birth to eight or twelve children at a time—preferably all boys!"

Anna, objecting, cried out in pain, "Ya, Mamma!"

Warda had sympathetically glanced down at her daughter and then rolled her eyes at her friend, who was laughing so hard she hid her face in a towel.

Laila hopes that Anna—and not her mother—was responsible for the lack of invitation. Warda would never succumb to the growing climate of suspicion in the town. Whatever the reason, Laila knows that by not attending the get-together her social standing will be further eroded among people like Mrs. Habash—the type of tired, blind minds Laila is constantly warning her students and their parents about. She has too much consideration for Warda to arrive unannounced. That would be too embarrassing. Proud and unbending, Laila finishes grading, then flicks through the plans for the next lesson, the composition of an English letter. Once midday prayers are finished, she heads into the maelstrom of the hallways.

Maps, photographs, and school projects cover the walls of a room duplicated throughout the school. Behind thirty desks wait fourteen-year-old girls. School has changed since Laila was a student. Teaching no longer involves a brisk rap across the knuckles—punishment for a wrong answer. Laila is strict, but she would never hit her pupils. She finds a sharp word or disapproving gaze adequate enough. Sometimes she wonders whether her students have grown more docile or she has become more intolerant.

She is writing "dear" on the chalkboard in English and Arabic when a hand shoots up. Reema is one of Laila's more precocious students. Lately she has become outspoken. "Miss, in our letters we open with 'Thanks be to God,'" she says. "Don't the English or Americans have a similar greeting?"

The atmosphere in the classroom is suddenly charged. Reema's friends who pray and study together are not the only ones listening closely to their teacher's reaction. Girls who aren't necessarily religious but feel the pressure to conform to the sheikh's teachings are also curious.

"Some people, no matter their religion, begin letters with '*Al-hamdu lillah*' and others don't," Laila explains. "In the UK and US, they normally start with 'dear.' This has to do with the culture of letter writing and social convention, just like the beginnings of letters here. Today's topic is English composition, not religion."

Reema raises her hand again. "Miss, why do we study a decadent culture?"

"Learning and mastering English will enable you to get a better job," Laila counters patiently. "I believe God matters in those countries but as a rule not at the start of their letters."

These kinds of exchanges have become a regular feature of this English class, and Reema is the instigator. But she is not the only student who has become energized by faith. Other normally reticent girls have become more forthright too. They brim over with—Laila hesitates to describe—a newfound confidence, through which students' questions can often degenerate into outright disagreements with their teachers. Laila believes that Reema and others like her state their views so forcibly because they feel obliged to lecture an older generation who, they feel, has failed them. It is this moral righteousness that, for Laila's mainly Christian colleagues, borders on rudeness, although she makes a point of not taking it personally. Encounters like these are a welcome change from the usual apathy that accompanies learning by rote. This is, Laila thinks, a chance to cultivate inquiring minds. There will come a time, and she understands this implicitly, when Reema and other students will turn against her. Until then, the girl is allowed to ask her questions. When she does Laila manages to deflect her criticisms in hopes of providing an alternative view for the class's consideration.

In only a few years, Laila's students will come face-to-face with the meager prospects for their future. Reema's precociousness will not shield her from being married off to someone she doesn't know or like, or being treated as a second-class citizen in her wider community, the result of religious conservatism in both Islam and Christianity. But that is a discussion for another time that will probably never take place. For now, the excitement is over, and Laila returns to the mechanics of paragraphing and punctuation. As she watches her students take meticulous notes—something she taught them and insists upon—she paces between the aisles of desks, gazing through the windows at the back.

The school, built to stay cool, now houses three times the number of students and staff it was constructed for. As the lesson continues, the air grows stale, and Laila feels herself becoming sluggish. She nearly yawns but catches herself—like a contagion it would travel up and down the aisles. By insisting they review the lesson again, she wills herself into a state of alert wakefulness. Some of her best teaching is through example. If she is fully engaged, her students will be too.

They answer her questions about composition. However, they are less successful in the spelling of simple words they were supposed to have memorized. Laila doesn't want to lose her temper, but when the smartest girl in the class misspells "sincerely," she slams a ruler down on a desk. It cracks as sharply as her disappointment. She is tired of feeling bad about herself, her family, and her students. Irritated, she orders them to pay attention as she decodes the English words on the blackboard for them again. She is still assigning homework when the bell rings, and she gathers up her papers and books for her next lesson to a roomful of eighth graders on the school's other side.

A strict timetable has been imposed on pupils. After intensive study periods, they are allowed an elective: art, music, or gym. Whenever parents seek Laila's opinion on which is appropriate for their daughters, she always makes a point of urging physical education for those not artistically or musically inclined. She has noticed that the girls who take the opportunity to play volleyball return to the classroom with renewed vigor. Physically they have settled down and mentally they are pliant. Sometimes, traditional parents find exercise unbecoming. There is an unspoken fear that a daughter's innocence, hence marriageability, would somehow be threatened. To convince them, Laila usually quotes a Hadith, or saying attributed to the Prophet Muhammad: "Refresh your mind from time to time, for a tired mind becomes blind." By using this as her guide, the teacher impresses Muslim parents with her wide-ranging knowledge and reminds Christian ones of the importance of an inclusive education within a government-run school. Today she feels she would do well to heed her own advice, shaking off stupefaction and moving energetically toward her next classroom assignment.

10

Outside the butcher shop, Hussein opens the rear double doors of the van and checks the interior. Khaled removed the straw after the morning market, but the vehicle parked in the sun still carries the stink of animal fear. As Hussein reaches to pack Mustafa's bags away, the soldier keeps hold of them, saying, "Let me take care of them, Lieutenant." A withering glance from Hussein tells him that he has no choice.

The older man gauges the weight of the large rough canvas duffel in his hands before sliding it as far back in the van as it will go. Its contents, he can tell, include a barrel and a butt of some sort. The other bag, squatter in size, is heavier than Hussein expects, its bulk coming from clothes or soft wadding wrapped around other metallic pieces—another dismantled weapon. As the soldier wedges his knapsack carefully between the bags, his former commanding officer comments drily, "Souvenirs from your travels?"

Both men climb into the van's tiny front cab. Squashed together in the minuscule space that is no bigger than a rendition cage, Hussein starts the engine. "No wonder you moved cautiously through borders. How did you cross? Leave the bags, scout out a route, double back and pick them up?"

Mustafa's gaze is fixed out the window. "I didn't want to travel without protection. A wrong move in a Shia or Sunni district in Iraq, no one comes to your aid. I stayed away from Daesh and the Pesh-merga. It's a quagmire of angry religion."

"Like everywhere else."

Hussein prepares to drive off but not before a shadow flits across the window of the Marvellous Emporium. In seconds, Abu Za'atar is hurrying across the asphalted patch of the main street faster than an attack falcon on a pair of mourning doves. The Featherer, craning his neck to get a better view of the bearded stranger in the passenger seat, is gesticulating frantically at the butcher's van. Before he reaches them Hussein leans out his window and waves him off with a forced smile: "Amo, we catch up later."

The van pulls away. Now isn't the time for introductions. Hussein still has a few questions of his own for Mustafa.

Keeping his eyes on the road, he casually remarks, "We were told that the Taliban were using whatever the Soviets left behind from the war in the 1980s, in addition to the antique rifles of the British and the Russians when they fought over the Khyber Pass in the 1800s. Any gaps were filled by replica 'made in Peshawar' automatic rifles and grenade launchers." It's amazing how much information he retains from those antiterrorism briefings.

"Afghanistan is awash with guns," confirms Mustafa. "The situation is seriously dangerous but funny too. During every government amnesty for weapons, clan lords collect rifles old, new, and automatic from their men and sell them to the Taliban. The weapons bazaars are flooded with equipment from Serbia and Croatia. But the Americans are in a class by themselves."

"How so?" asks Hussein.

"Imagine, they buy modern Russian-made ammunitions with US tax dollars and give them to their allies. The Afghan army and the police then sell these weapons to the Taliban." The soldier can hardly believe it himself. "Everything goes full circle. There's a joke among the fighters. Need or want anything? Buy it online. It can be delivered wherever you want, like ordering pizza. They don't have Amazon there yet, but they will. It is a country where middlemen do very well."

"The reason war lasts so long is because of the profiteering." Hussein is reminded of Abu Za'atar and his trucks.

"But not everyone is making money," points out Mustafa. "Afghan askar privates paid poorly by their allied keepers have to support large families—small armies themselves. So askar and police sell all sorts of things: ammunition, gasoline, and damn good boots." He glances down, but the confines of the tight van restrict his view of the sturdy footwear that his commanding officer secretly admires and that covered the five thousand miles to the butcher shop. "Probably off a dead US serviceman."

For someone so long on the road, Hussein assumes any mode of transport would be welcomed. But the soldier squirms uneasily in his seat and nearly smashes his head on the van's roof. Hussein realizes he is not used to being so exposed. Mustafa probably did most of his traveling at night and laid low during the day.

Hussein jokes, "I don't know what you're thinking, but I sure as hell know how you're feeling. This van can barely hold a tin of sardines, much less the two of us."

He was never any good at making his men laugh, but in the past they appreciated his efforts. He slaps his hand hard on the dashboard and the sound effectively clears the air. Mustafa leans back, settles in his seat, and starts talking.

"When Sayeed and I were kids, the men of our neighborhood were like giants to us. We lost our father when we were young. And despite every hardship our mother pampered us. We were badly spoiled! Sayeed was selfish. How could he leave us like that without saying a word? I blame it on the men we admired. We wanted to emulate them no matter what. By the time we learned the truth about them it was too late."

"Even if your heroes had been brutally honest about their shortcomings, you and Sayeed wouldn't have paid any attention at all." Hussein remembers the impressionable young men formerly in his charge as he maneuvers the van through narrowing streets. "The values of your childhood are useless today. Look at Afghanistan. The tension between the old and the new is ripping apart a country that never recovered from the last devastation. Add drones to this time bomb and everything goes to shit pretty damn fast.

"But tell me," Hussein continues, genuinely curious, "what good are nineteenth-century bolt-action rifles such as Russian Mosin-Nagants or British Lee-Enfields against an army on the verge of biochips and robots?"

"Everyone thinks war is high tech, but it really is only bodies against sharp objects—bayonets and knives—and IEDs," Mustafa observes. "The Afghans haven't survived too badly off the scrap heap of history. The Taliban still put up a good fight despite ancient weaponry and handmade guns. When they lose, they collect their dead and leave nothing behind. No invader has stopped them."

Time, Hussein agrees, is on their side. Once the Afghan people tire of being fleeced by a corrupt government, they will seek salvation in the arms of those who are equally crooked but pay lip service to God. It will be another way of reclaiming a life that was lost after the British, Russians, and Americans.

But Hussein still feels that Mustafa hasn't been entirely straight with him. Sayeed went off with a known terrorist called Al Bilal, who in the end was obviously playing a double game. After his torture, Al Bilal became an agent for the GID, the Jordanian intelligence service. Hussein remembers reading between the lines of the news reports at the time. Whoever this man pretended to be, he had no difficulty walking into Forward Operating Base Chapman, a heavily secured facility used by the CIA, in Khost. Not even the US soldiers guarding the perimeters stopped and questioned him, because everyone knew he was *their* informant in the area. Once inside, Al Bilal detonated the explosives belt under his clothes and killed his handler, a member of the royal Jordanian family.

The suicide bombing had all the earmarks of an attack by Al-Qaeda, whose members weren't grunts like the Taliban who operated in the field. They had a higher calling; their brains were hot-wired. In groups like Al-Qaeda and Daesh, more effective than a charismatic leader is the bomb maker. But the Taliban fighters are fast learners.

Every spring when they come back after a hard winter of little or no action, there are spectacular bombings against the Americans, IEDs dug into major roads and asphalted over, ready for detonation at the optimum split second when casualties will be at their highest. It's no wonder that the GID is looking for Sayeed.

"So who were you and your brother fighting for?" Hussein finally asks outright.

"I stayed with Sayeed, who was living with Al Bilal's people. But I didn't have the skill set they needed, so after my brother's death I drifted away from them. When I asked the Taliban, '*Akhee*, my brother, can you help me?' good Muslims that they were, they shared all that they had—including their enemies. I should have questioned the high price of their hospitality but I didn't."

As the van keeps to the edges of the Eastern Quarter, the soldier gestures at the heavily veiled women and men in traditional garb. "This looks familiar, poor and pious." Whenever they slow down, bearded men stare in through the windows first at Hussein, then at Mustafa.

"They're shocked by the company you keep," Hussein mutters under his breath. He could have gone directly to the farm, but he wants to talk a little longer to the soldier by himself. So instead of heading toward the mountains, he veers off by the market and takes another route out of the town. The time has come to broach a difficult subject, one that has been on his mind since Mustafa's arrival.

"A man came looking for Sayeed." Although he is concentrating on a road that has shrunk into a winding dirt track in front of them, Hussein can again sense Mustafa's disquiet. "He had some idea as to the whereabouts of your brother and asked me if I knew anything. He wanted me to provide him with some leads."

"What did you say?" the soldier asks.

"Nothing."

"Where was he from?" Mustafa is watching him closely.

"He said one of the ministries, but my guess is the GID. He didn't mention you. He was waiting for me to do that. But I don't discuss the activities of men under my command, especially with strangers. In the same way I don't harbor jihadists."

Hussein had pulled into an empty field abruptly and switched off the van's engine. Despite the awkward space inside, he shifts his weight sideways, his face an inch or two from Mustafa's.

"I've never been much of a killer, Lieutenant," admits the soldier, who stares past him, "but those were my darkest days. It's not easy to kill. Then you are told by the people who feed you and show you kindness that their children are being raped every day by American troops." Mustafa, turning away, continues. "My main concern was for my brother. Once his life ended, so did mine. Much of what I have experienced has convinced me there is nothing left in the world worth fighting—or dying—for."

For the next few minutes the two men sit together quietly. All around them the yellowing fields scorched by heat are as dry as kindling. From their vantage point they can just make out the town below and, to its west, where the ground rises sharply toward Jebel Musa, the prophet's mountain.

Hussein speaks first: "In my childhood, it wasn't the men who were giants. It was this"—he holds his hands aloft—"the land idolized by old and young alike. When I was a boy, we were repeatedly told stories about a remote time in history when the mountains were ringed with pine and spruce; the valleys and the plains filled with carobs, olives, and pistachios. There was even a farmer who, it was said, stumbled into a secluded grove of tropical vines and palms, a jungle filled with trees of frankincense and myrrh. But we never learned the farmer's name or the whereabouts of his fabulous discovery.

"My father and the men like him," he explains, "were so consumed by the potential of the land that every successful harvest took on mythic proportions. The infrequent good years, when a whole herd of camels transported the heavy burlap sacks of wheat, always heralded the start of the long-awaited turnaround. But the next growing season failed to fulfill expectations, and we were lucky to get a few misshapen eggplants and tomatoes for the storage bins. Abundance and wealth were one good harvest or one solid rainfall away. It would have been easy for me to spend my life believing that too."

As a boy Hussein savored the rare times of plenty: when the great mounds of okra were taller than he was, or the summer he ate so much melon he made himself sick. But there was something in him that would not be convinced.

"There are too many parallels in these obsessive love affairs—the farmers with the land and your brother with religion. Both require unwavering faith that one more sacrifice or killing will turn everything around. But where does all the failed harvests of our lives leave us? Only in a dream about life deferred, never in the here and now."

He returns to matters uppermost in his mind. "The travel souvenirs, who are they for?"

Mustafa adjusts himself in his seat and says, "Prepare for all contingencies." He is once again a soldier and Hussein his commanding officer. He adds soberly, "Surely all the antiterrorism training taught my brother that." Then he lets slip, "I just couldn't abandon the few precious possessions that meant so much to him."

Hussein revs the motor again, checks the rearview mirror, and swings the van around. The only sounds are the low rumbling of the engine and the crunching of the tires as they climb back onto the dirt track, which leads to the mountain and the farm, although they are not so far from the new house.

A thought occurs to Hussein. It is not revolutionary but it could be useful. Despite the fact there isn't much in the containers at home, a man used to drinking his own urine in the mountains could probably shave with a few centimeters of water. Then Mustafa could begin his reintroduction to a semblance of normal life. Rehabilitation can take place only with small, incremental steps—something Hussein learned not in the army but alone by himself. And if the GID is planning to arrest the soldier, it might overlook a clean-shaven young man in a crowd, someone who could have been a protestor in Tahrir Square but has since learned his lesson and now knows his place.

"You might think about losing the beard," Hussein suggests evenly.

11

"How can people survive without *na' bat ma'*?" Mother Fadhma asks the tanker driver, as she unlocks the gate.

She has chosen her words with care. Just as the Bedouins have hundreds of names for the desert, farmers who live and fail by the seasons know the secret syntax of water. If she wanted to be accurate, she shouldn't have said *na' bat ma'*, pure spring water, but *ma' raked*, stagnant water. The liquid from the tankers tastes metallic as though left in an iron pot baked by the sun. For the past few weeks she has been living with even worse ill-smelling water, the dregs from the cistern. Suddenly she recalls water cool, fresh, and running—*ma' jary*—moving in hypnotic rivulets or chains—*salsabeel ma'*. Her memories are so vivid she can almost taste it. She would gladly climb into the undergrowth and search for the mountain path to the old springs. When she was little such a journey took a few good hours. In her current state of health it would probably last longer than a day and a half. During her lifetime the village had grown into a town and with it a demand that neither the springs nor communal cistern could meet. As a result, every house and refugee hovel became prey for the jackals who own the water trucks.

"We have small children," she adds, hoping the driver is listening with his heart. She is keen to avoid sounding critical of his services, but at the same time she needs him to be aware of the stakes involved. In the future she hopes he will remember the Sabases kindly and bring water without delay.

The dirty keffiyeh that the man is wearing has left a grimy oil-colored ring around his neck. He throws his still-burning cigarette butt to the ground and gruffly unhooks the hose from the truck. Dragging it through the front yard toward the side of the house, he informs her, "If you have complaints, call the company. Rely on them and see how long it takes."

Fadhma hides her disappointment. She should have recognized the kind of man he is—more than likely a terror in his own home, a belittler of women. His threat against her own family leaves her cold, and she positions herself on the front terrace of the new house and watches him climb the metal ladder to the roof. Despite his deplorable attitude, the water inconveniences facing Fadhma today are nothing compared with those of the past. She remembers droughts and famines. During her childhood there were times when a mouthful of water would have been the sole contents of the massive earthenware pot that stood, constantly sweating moisture, in the corner of her father's house. Her life had been shaped by the toil and disappointment of trying to keep the pot from drying out completely. Somehow she succeeded, just as other women have done, against all odds, for thousands of years. A trail of water jars could be traced back to the brilliant moment when God told the prophet Musa which rock to strike with his rod, and the children of Israel were saved.

The miraculous Ayun Musa, named for the prophet's springs, was seven kilometers from the village. On one side of the rocky crevices from where groundwater emerged, grape vines grew on terraced plots. On the other was a clear, breathtaking view over the dry brown hills and mountains to the river valley, which stretched past Jericho to the Dead Sea. Fadhma's earliest memories were of waking before light and walking with her mother and aunts to fetch water. Even as a toddler, they made her carry a small goatskin bag that gave off a musty odor and felt rough against her skin. When she cried and begged them to carry her, they laughed: "Only birds fly to the springs."

She no longer complained after her feet became hard. The easy camaraderie of her female relations and friends turned a disagreeable chore into a pleasure. No matter how early they arrived, other women were already there, dark shapes against the gradually brightening sky. It was an unlikely place to be schooled, but in the half-light, soothed by the sound of running water, the women talked freely. Between Fadhma's Christian kinfolk and Muslim neighbors there was universal disagreement on all matters, from the relative powers of Christian saints—because Muslims prayed at certain shrines—to the best methods for baking bread. However, on one point they found consensus: the different standards of behavior expected of men and women. It was a certainty the little girl pondered as she watched her snide younger brother, Za'atar, rule over their father's meager store. Worse yet, he was allowed out whenever he liked, while she, sequestered and protected by her family, was permitted to follow only the one path that led out of the village to the springs, and when she was really lucky, her mother and aunts tarried longer in the mountains, gathering fresh herbs for za'atar.

"To be free!" The lament echoed in the stony clefts of Ayun Musa as women of both faiths adjusted their clothing and headscarves before carrying their heavy loads back to the village.

Years passed, and still the water flowed. The goatskins were replaced by tins and then by plastic buckets. Finally there was a plan to pipe the springs into the village. Many feared that Ayun Musa would dry up when the pipe was laid. Perhaps modern convenience would end that which God provided so abundantly. However, when the final piece of tubing was in place, the water ran as freely as the blood of the sacrificed lambs that consecrated the project. The new water supply was the biggest change the village had ever faced. The women now met around the modern, brick-lined cistern, but they still liked to gauge the day's weather by the feel of the first temperate hours. In the early coolness, there was also time for news.

"Hottest before noon." An old woman sniffed the air and spoke with the confidence of an experienced meteorologist.

Nobody replied, but the water, ropes, buckets, and rustling clothing made noises that Fadhma still hears in her dreams.

Another younger woman spoke. She was frightened: "You heard them in the valley last night?"

There were low murmurs of assent.

Water and food—these were always Fadhma's immediate concerns, not fighting across the river. All of them had seen the refugees and heard their stories, but the village, in the midst of a drought, had its own problems. With no pasture, the sheep and goats starved. After the carcasses were stripped of their hides and the little meat there was, they were burned, and the stench of singed hair and horn hid in the folds of the villagers' garments.

Fortunately, the surrounding hills and mountains were like a sponge. Even in the driest seasons, the little water that was there collected in underground wells. In time, the trickle to the cistern would stop, but the women knew other secret locations. For Fadhma, the natural catastrophe took precedence over the man-made one. The conflict was like a distant storm, an unfulfilled promise that only benefited others. Its consequences arrived in the village indirectly, if at all. Still, the meaning of the woman's words was not lost on her and lingers until today.

"Our only hope is our children." Absentmindedly Mother Fadhma bends down and pats baby Fuad's head. His appearance on the front terrace draws her from her reverie. Straining backward against the railings, she checks the progress of the man on the roof. Then motioning to Muna to watch the little boy, the old mother moves ponderously through the house toward the kitchen. When Samira finds her at the stove, making tea, she pleads, "Mamma, that man doesn't deserve a thing. The water companies make a profit out of something we all need."

Fadhma continues to prepare the traditional glass of compromise and hospitality, which only upsets her daughter more.

"Sooner or later there will be a war over who controls the river, and then that terrible man and his bloodsucking company will cheat us again. Meanwhile everyone dies of thirst. Is that right or just? And"—she can't stop now—"he's been rude at every house up and down this street and at every one he has been given tea. Why not bake him a wedding cake? You reward someone when he comes on time, not when he's holding us ransom."

Mother Fadhma waves her hand as she would at a fly and answers from a store of proverbs she employs on such occasions: "When your hand is floured, don't meddle in men's business."

However, as she sets out the tray her heart bursts with pride. All on her own, with no prompting from anyone else, least of all her mother, Samira has become a true daughter of Ayun Musa. "Maybe I should do us all a favor and use rat poison instead of sugar," Fadhma muses out loud as she stirs the sweet tea with a spoon.

Samira doesn't respond; she has already left the kitchen in a huff.

When the tanks are full and the driver is by the truck winding back the hose, Mother Fadhma appears with the glass on a tray. She makes her request even more deferentially than before: "Do not let us go without for so long again. *Yani*, I am old and unimportant, but think of my grandchildren."

The driver takes the hot drink from her. "You've heard the rumors? If they start fighting over the river, the cost of water is going up! Up! Up! Who knows how often it will be delivered?" Leering at Samira, who watches them from the window, he raises his glass in a toast—"*Al-hamdu lillah*—thanks be to God"—and declares in a voice loud enough for the neighbors to hear, "There was a time when your daughter would have brought me tea herself." He shakes his head. "These young women, so liberated nowadays!"

Wordlessly Mother Fadhma stares past the grubby little man and his godforsaken truck. If the opportunity ever arises she—not Samira—will give this bonehead a sound thrashing.

12

In the labyrinthine Marvellous Emporium, among the aisles, cubby-holes, dressing rooms, and special promotional displays, two places remain off-limits to prying eyes. With a bundle of keys in hand, Abu Za'atar checks that no one is lurking in the shadows before slipping behind a tasseled rope with a red-and-white triangle sign warning of MEN AT WORK. He unlocks a set of heavy doors, steps inside, and then closes them with a reverberating thud. A click of a switch and fluorescent lighting illuminates a well-proportioned room. He takes stock of the tastefully arranged menswear hanging along the walls, on the shelves, and in the glass cabinets, with a freestanding full-length mirror in attendance. It's always the same. If the emporium celebrates unbridled entrepreneurialism with the usual obsessions about acquisition and pricing, across this particular threshold those baser impulses do not apply.

Had he not glimpsed the stranger with his nephew, there would be no need for him to be clawing through a stash of freshly laundered and starched shirts. Khaki and dark brown, anything with epaulettes, are thrown aside: too militaristic. Frivolous checks and stripes send the wrong message, and powder blue is normally reserved for financial undertakings at the bank or in his own capacity as a loan shark. Abu Za'atar melancholically yearns for what could have been. If he respected his customers and suppliers more, he wouldn't disguise his true plumage beneath a dirty shirt and frayed apron. But these are the people he pleases the least. In a lightbulb moment he pulls out fail-safe white. After selecting a pair of neutral brown trousers, he changes. A tie is untangled from an extravagant floor-to-ceiling forest of neckwear trees, and in lieu of a silk pocket handkerchief, which would only mislead, he opts for a pristine white cotton hanky, a never-without, as it has proven time and time again. Other manly adornments crowd a cabinet: rings and necklaces, bottled colognes and aftershaves, cover-up sticks to hide gray, blush for color, and embossed cigarette cases. Under the circumstances these too seem inappropriate. He puts on a medium-grade pair of tarnished gold cuff links and a plain black leather belt—nothing too memorable or in your face. As he dresses, Abu Za'atar can feel himself inhabiting the part.

In the full-length mirror clothes dwarf a body shrunken with age. But leanness too has its advantages; it is something to be pitied rather than envied. A fashionable accessory, instincts tell him, will seal the deal. He kicks off the sandals he's wearing with brightly striped socks. Giving in to temptation and élan, he decides not on a pair of brogues or desert boots, but on a pair of Cuban heels, which will give him an inch of extra height, just in case he has to lord over anybody.

This is, for Abu Za'atar, the litmus test of personal armory. With everything on the shelves and along the walls, so soft and well made, he reassesses his choices. He could have opted for something sleeker. But too much sophistication often ruins a mood. While he is a firm believer that all life is seduction, this time he only has to ingratiate himself, make those around him feel at ease enough to confide in him, even when it goes against their best interests. He inspects his reflection again, this time from the sideways and the rear. The last touch is a large, shapeless jacket, fitted at the back, which suggests ambition beyond the ability of its wearer. His transformation into a benevolent dithering relative is complete. It is an idea so preposterous it makes him sneer.

He takes one last look at himself, transfers his keys to a pocket, and starts feeling underneath the branches of the neckwear forest. Like blindman's bluff, smothered by neckties and scarves, he finally locates a hidden set of panels. When he clicks them open, the neckwear tree becomes a 3-D sculptural construction with a gap large enough for him to enter through. He thinks of it as being waved in by flags. Inside, automatic motion-sensing lighting floods a cavelike space.

Along these walls too, items have been exhibited to their best advantage. Abu Za'atar doesn't have to look at the medallion on a silver chain that he calls the "Arabs' Shame," issued by the Israelis after the Six-Day War. He has already memorized its every detail: Moshe Dayan, with eye patch, in front of the Jaffa Gate in the Old City. On the back in Hebrew, *Im eshkachech Yerushalaim*—"If I forget thee, O Jerusalem"—from Psalm 137, which continues: "let my right hand lose its cunning, let my tongue cleave my palate"—an inscription prescient for its time. Arab cunning and Jerusalem were lost in a matter of a few days. To Dayan's right hangs the Arabs' response, a 1973 ribbon-infested medal released by the Syrian government for the Ramadan/Yom Kippur War. And beside them another rarity, a dog tag showing the Shia martyr Imam Hussain, previously owned by a Persian Basiji who fought the Iraqis in the Iran-Iraq War in the 1980s.

These were the inspired beginnings of a carefully curated collection that includes more than military medals. Abu Za'atar particularly relishes the international associations among his array of pistols; carbines; assault rifles; light, medium, heavy, and general-purpose machine guns; grenades and grenade launchers. Two of the vintage machine guns, the Port Said and the Akaba, manufactured by the Egyptians from Swedish designs, saw action against the British at Suez and the Vietnamese by US Navy SEALs.

A Syrian refugee had approached Abu Za'atar with the sniper rifle, the Yugoslav Zastava M9, employed by Syria's National Defence Forces. Before money was mentioned, the man took out his smartphone and showed Abu Za'atar a YouTube video. During one of the mass demonstrations in Hama, someone filmed a Syrian army sniper with a Zastava M9 on a balcony. The video ended abruptly as the camera recorded its own clattering fall to the floor, after the person holding it was shot dead by the sniper. Abu Za'atar refused to haggle and paid the refugee's asking price. The Zastava was given pride of place in the collection, at least until the man returned to the

Marvellous Emporium; he claimed he could get Gaddhafi's pistol. Abu Za'atar, never one to enjoy being taken for a ride, nearly lost his temper. "That's like promising me Scheherazade's panties. You're going to have to be more imaginative than that."

The Featherer pauses beside a handsomely attired mechanized robot on wheels, aptly named the Eagle's Talon. With the facility to travel in all directions at high speeds, the Eagle's Talon can destroy insurgents' armored cars at the click of a mouse. Before he owned one, Abu Za'atar researched it on the Internet. Once the piece had been acquired he went back to the Internet café to check its serial numbers. The information had been blocked. It was that rare and dangerous.

But was it epoch changing?

One Syrian refugee had placed in Abu Za'atar's hand a small, insignificant piece of metal that had transformed mankind forever. It was a seven-thousand-year-old copper awl or, as the proprietor likes to envision, a mini-spear used for stabbing, gouging, probing, and fixing. Four centimeters long and a millimeter thick at the end, it had been recovered from the grave of a woman during archaeological digs in the country next door that were interrupted by war. Her skeleton, adorned with a belt of beads made from ostrich eggshells, was found in a sixth-century trading city, where metalworking began almost a millennium before historians originally thought. The man might have been a refugee, but he had the mind and eye of a university professor.

In Abu Za'atar's collection, a special shrine in honor of an ancient woman's sophisticated metallurgy had been created for the awl. He could have easily spent the entire afternoon wondering about an era when tools were weapons for survival and women, like the one in the grave, were not chattel. He admired age-old traditions and considered adopting some of their codes of practice, such as respecting women and advancing their opportunities, but the perks of traditional and modern patriarchy were too enticing for one man to resist. Abu Za'atar closes the secret panel and withdraws up a passageway that deposits him outside another locked door behind a carefully curtained-off enclosure inside the Marvellous Emporium.

He picks his way through the aisles, pushing the shoppers, slackers, and kleptomaniacs toward the exit. By the wooden slivers purportedly belonging to either Musa's staff or Christ's cross—made by different manufacturers in Guangzhou—he is pinned down by a group of evangelicals. They have a myriad of questions, but his regal deportment silences them.

"It's true," he says, "we rarely close for lunch. However, my American niece has recently arrived and I must go and welcome her."

They too are moved out the door.

By the register, Abu Za'atar stuffs two insignificant baubles lavishly gift-wrapped into a pocket and avoids an unscheduled detour to the booty nest. At such an early stage in the proceedings, he doesn't want to jinx his plans. Diligently, he hangs the BACK AT... notice facing outward and then, straightening his tie, steps purposely outside to face the dreaded locking up.

There is a terrible finality in the clunk of the five double bolts, a twist of the wrist he tries to avoid whenever he runs to the Rest House and Internet Café for a quick browse on the Web. Once the deadlocks are in place, he feels as though he has slammed the door in his face. Almost mournfully he takes in the huge mass of products, artifacts, and secondhand goods threatening to explode out the windows onto the street. With its miles of snazzy neon signs flashing impotently in the hot afternoon sun, the vulgar attractiveness of the Marvellous Emporium remains a heart-stopper. If he admires it long enough, he will be unable to tear himself away.

Despite his misgivings, he maneuvers himself toward the very last inch of tarmac and gingerly steps off the partially asphalted main street, the first of many small acts of defiance. With each click of a Cuban heel he brightens. The prospect of the chase and the possibilities of a large reward, commingling with the anticipation of new sights and sounds, might even make ar-Rish Ajjanah soar.

Waving down a shared taxi, he breaks his own rule of tightfistedness and barters with the driver to remain the only passenger. His reasoning has less to do with traveling in style: he must work out his next move. Past the town's outlying shops, he nods pleasantly and could have easily started waving to people; they would surely want to acknowledge this rare sighting of him, a thought that only adds to his giddy excitement. By the time the car passes the Eastern Quarter, Abu Za'atar remembers with a jolt, or perhaps it is a pothole, that he isn't out on just any old lark. He feels his mind sharpening once the taxi reaches the vacant land beyond the crumbling houses and farm sheds, which stretches off into the distance and disappears into the bright arc of nothingness. This is how his life could have been—dry and uneventful. His mind darts back to the teeming habitat of his beloved Marvellous Emporium and a very rare collection that appears to be gaining a reputation in all the right places.

Another jolt throws him against the backseat. But self-aggrandizement is not his only purpose. If only people would believe him. He wants to save them from themselves. He smiles beneficently at the driver, who has been so busy watching his passenger's flights of fancy through the rearview mirror that he keeps smashing into craters in the road. At rest with his motivations, Abu Za'atar relaxes in spite of the bumpy ride. If yoga has taught him anything, it is posture is the font of good ideas. All he has to do is breathe deeply and wait for the logistics to come.

Fifteen minutes later Abu Za'atar emerges from the cab discombobulated. The heat doesn't help, and the glint of his smart but tight Cuban heels on the dirt pathway makes him feel only sickly foolish, a novel emotion for someone so self-possessed. Leaning against a crumbling wall, he delicately presses his never-without against a sweat-drenched forehead. He usually doesn't venture to Hussein's side of town. Whenever he and his nephew discuss business, they meet at the Marvellous Emporium, the butcher shop, or, if necessary, the farm.

Off in the distance, a moving dust ball of wheels trundles down one of the dirt tracks. Abu Za'atar doesn't give it much thought until its color—flashes of blue—and then its shape emerge. "Ah, Hussein's van!" He isn't expecting Hussein and his friend quite so quickly. The emotions he's experiencing have little to do with his customary bravado; he hasn't yet generated a plan, plausible or otherwise. He could say he happened to be in the vicinity—a sudden emergency, perhaps, involving Fadhma, but she would give him away. Or he could follow his instincts: steal a few precious minutes more to get a bird's-eye view, as it were, before the inevitable kill. In effect, hide.

The Featherer flies into a nearby garden that has a divan under an effervescent grape vine. Leafiness is always soothing. As his thoughts meander through the greenery, he nearly trips over a stray black-and-brown dog lying on its stomach, enervated by the heat. No friend to the canine, Abu Za'atar is about to kick it when the van zipping past leaves his stylish Cuban heel dangling in midair. After the vehicle pulls into a sparsely graveled driveway twenty feet away, Abu Za'atar, still holding his pose, can't quite make out what Hussein is saying, as the two men retrieve a knapsack from the back and double check that the van is locked before going quickly inside.

A weedy voice shatters Abu Za'atar's illusion of invisibility. "It's been years since you've gone door-to-door. Business must not be good." All along someone has been spying on him from the stone house adjacent to the garden.

Lowering his foot, Abu Za'atar realizes the statement has some basis in reality. The house, the garden, the cur, and the voice—though age has made it less melodious to his ears—are not unfamiliar. When he was young and full of energy, he used to wander the outback before there was a road, offering cloth and sewing needles to lonely women like this one.

"I no longer do rounds, but I am available for free consultations in town, with an appointment," he brags weakly, distracted by the way the mind, foot, and time conspire against the unobservant. He gives a perfunctory wave to the shadowy figure behind the curtains; there is a good chance that they were once close. Back on the dirt road, he can't shake off the sensation that there are many eyes undressing him down to his Calvin Klein boxers.

Behind Hussein's van, he casually crouches down and pretends to tie a lace-less Cuban boot. Standing up slowly, he makes a prolonged appraisal of the contents in the back. Just as he thought, clues abound. Exaggeratedly wiping his brow—aside from its practical uses, the never-without has obvious theatrical applications as well—he climbs the steps to Hussein's new house. Glancing around to make sure everyone has a clear view of him, he enters without knocking, like the old trusted family relation he is.

Inside Abu Za'atar moves past the empty living and reception rooms. He treads lightly on the tile floors, peering into a series of dark and silent bedrooms where curtains have been drawn. By the closed bathroom door he hears the muffled movements of someone inside, but it is the gurgle of water in the pipes that impresses him; no one in the town is inured to the unreliability of the water tankers. Inch by half inch, his Cuban heels tiptoe down the hall toward the sounds of merriment and cooking. With his back pressed against the wall, he stops a few inches before the kitchen door and allows himself a split-second glimpse inside, making doubly sure that none of the inhabitants in the house has seen him.

At the counter Mother Fadhma is dicing tomatoes, cucumbers, and green onions and placing them in a bowl. Beside her, fluffy dark green bundles of parsley wait for the cleaver. Samira rescues a bunch and parades around the kitchen. "Like the wedding party tonight!" She is smiling and about to throw her bouquet to Muna or Fuad, when unexpectedly she cries out, "Amo!" and tosses it in his direction.

An expansive Abu Za'atar steps into the light, burying his nose in the bouquet with a wry grin.

"Our most troublesome relation," Samira calls out to Muna by way of introduction, and then tells him, "I've been wondering when you were going to show up."

"Me, trouble?" A wide, stupid grin, added to his carefully attuned dress-sense, masks his true intentions. "I apologize for missing the family meal yesterday, but, Samira, it is you who has abandoned us. We never see you anymore in the Marvellous Emporium—in and out of town, off on your travels."

The girl winks at him and raises a finger to her lips as she checks on Fadhma, who has been pointedly ignoring the antics of her daughter and brother by hacking at the salad vegetables for tabbouleh.

Oblivious, the Featherer basks in his niece's attention. It is so refreshing; the young accept everything at face value. Samira would never ask him what he's doing here, nor would she care. The two of them have an implicit understanding, like his relationship with Hussein when he was that age.

As Muna shakes his hand, Abu Za'atar hands her the parsley bouquet with one of the small gift-wrapped boxes. "Welcome, my dear, I knew your father." He lowers his voice: "He did well to escape."

He gives the other gift to Samira, whispering, "Peace offering," when he really means "Bribe."

The two young women open their gifts and admire the slender silver necklaces with a single turquoise glass bead.

"To ward off the evil eye," explains Abu Za'atar, before calling gleefully to Fadhma, "*Ukhti*—my sister!"

His arms spread out for an embrace that will never come. Despite her inability to return his affection, he makes a point of never stinting to show how much he cares. It always amazes him: here is a woman with the fortitude and determination of ten men. And she still acts like they don't need each other?

Mother Fadhma eyes her brother warily. Whatever unpleasant comment she is about to make is interrupted by Hussein pushing through the curtains from the back terrace. Smoking a cigarette and carrying an empty tea glass, he nods in disbelief as he clasps his uncle's hand, saying, "Why, you wily old bird."

"You couldn't keep me away." Abu Za'atar appeals to Samira, "We rarely get visitors and now there are so many of them. What's to be done?"

Hussein instructs the girls, "Make your *amo* coffee."

While Muna fusses with the brass pot on the stove, Samira is about to take Abu Za'atar onto the back terrace, but a look from her half brother changes her direction and she suggests briskly, "The living room will be more comfortable for the both of us." They tease each other as they head up the hallway.

Facing Al Jid's photograph, Abu Za'atar settles on the couch. Having had enough of the chase, he begins the next phase: interrogation. "Have you met Hussein's friend? If I'm not mistaken he comes from far away."

Samira doesn't seem to be following his hint. "Muna is the one who's traveled the farthest, from New York," she replies, stating the obvious.

"That's the known world." He speaks patiently as he would to Saleem or Mansoor. "As for our other guest, his origins have not yet been revealed. Did you notice that he carries all that he owns in a few canvas bags? Certainly that should be a tip-off."

Samira still gives nothing away. "He's probably from Amman, so that's not exactly what you would call 'foreign.'"

"Really." Abu Za'atar, unconvinced, is getting a little bored. "Hussein hasn't said anything to you? Where does he know him from, the market or the farm?" He is clutching at straws, hoping that Samira will come to his rescue. When she doesn't, he bluntly states, "There's a chance this person is dangerous. Who knows what he plans to do?"

"Do people shower before they commit a crime? Imagine," says Samira, "the first time we have water in the house in weeks and it's wasted on a stranger. All I can say is Laila better not find out."

When Muna carries a tray of coffee and sweets into the living room, Samira teases him again: "If you ever need anything nobody else has, our favorite relative might be able to find it in that jumbled monstrosity he calls a store." She toys with her uncle's gift, the lucky charm around her neck.

Abu Za'atar would prefer not to change the subject but feels obliged to correct her. He clears his throat and says, "You mean the Marvellous Emporium." Samira feigns disinterest, as he continues: "She only insults me in front of guests... but no matter. I am her best friend and supporter. When everyone fights her, I remain true."

"Yes," says Hussein, following Muna into the living room. "Uncle Abu Za'atar is loyal. Girls, he and I have a few thing to discuss— if you don't mind."

On their way out, Hussein takes Samira's hand in his and squeezes it. Shutting the door gently behind her, he turns to his uncle. "I was going to see you earlier today."

Abu Za'atar is delighted. In the excitement his nephew hasn't forgotten him. There are ties between them that still bind, and who knows the plans that will be hatched in the next few minutes. He feels a rising impatience, like falling in love. But Hussein's words only disappoint.

"I was attacked today, near the mosque."

The old man's eyes grow wide with disbelief. This isn't at all what he expects to hear.

"They were waiting for me, and I was a fool to be there. They are trying to intimidate me."

"No"—Abu Za'atar shakes his head, hoping that this is only a prelude to the main event—"they only want to see how the successful make money." He helps himself to coffee on the tray.

"There's something else."

He looks up at Hussein standing over him. Beneath a placid exterior Abu Za'atar is boiling.

"Special visitors came to the shop today," Hussein reveals.

Finally, something. Abu Za'atar thanks his lucky stars for his patience but deliberately dampens down any eagerness in his voice: "Oh yes, I saw him and want to—"

"Visitors," Hussein interrupts, and goes on to relate the unexpected appearance of the sheikh and his acolytes in the shop. "They feel we've transgressed."

Abu Za'atar notices that he has been included in the damned, although he has always insisted to Hussein that as a silent investor in the enterprise, his reputation and that of the Marvellous Emporium must remain above reproach. However, this might not be the time to argue the finer points of their contractual agreement. He allows his nephew to finish.

"Of course Umm al-Khanaazeer isn't responsible for the violence of the world. But I have been warned there will be serious repercussions."

Abu Za'atar is bored to tears. Why does Hussein waste time worrying about this nonsense when he has the makings for bigger success in his bathroom of all places? The mysterious stranger who left his business card had offered Abu Za'atar a sizable reward. Still, it would be impolite to ignore the topic under discussion. "Same old argument. Let them say something new."

He wants to move on to something pleasant before doubling back to the real reason that brought him here in the first place.

"And Abd's daughter?" asks Abu Za'atar. "I was lucky to get away when I did. You know, trouble brings untold delights..." He rubs his hands, and his face contorts into a tight smile that on anyone else would give the impression of a chronic pain.

"Humpf," utters Hussein.

Now it is Abu Za'atar's turn to be baffled by Hussein's response. If encouraged, the proprietor would have taken the opportunity to announce another moneymaking scheme he has been formulating of late. Instead of pork and beans, he has come up with an interesting fusion dish: pork and *freekeh* wheat topped with Bull-Dog, the Japanese equivalent of Worcester sauce. That would be an international taste sensation. However, Hussein is too preoccupied to talk recipes. There was once a time when, like Samira, he would have hung on Abu Za'atar's every word. The older man irritably returns his empty coffee cup to the tray.

Only after he has situated himself again does Hussein snap, "Well, what are we going to do?"

"About what?" Abu Za'atar is genuinely surprised, then remembers in a flash. "I told you, do not give in, not one inch, or they will take advantage. Better to sell your wares every day of the week, but you insisted on having it your own way. I told you then and I tell you now, give Fridays up for the Muslims, Saturdays for the Jews, and Sundays for the Christians. Be nice to everyone and go bankrupt! Now you come crying to me because a few hotheads and a sheikh have thrown a fit. Honestly, Hussein, for real success you have to put up with a few minor inconveniences!"

It is an all too familiar tactic on his part. In tight situations Abu Za'atar creates a smoke screen behind which his own obligations vanish. Still, he refuses to be blamed for what are essentially Hussein's troubles. Much of what the two of them have accomplished has turned out better than either of them expected. Continuing profits have benefited the entire family. What better yardstick of success could there be?

"I've helped you each step along the way." Abu Za'atar doesn't enjoy rebuking his favorite nephew, yet continues. "Your wife and children eat well. My own sister enjoys a lifestyle that your father"—he derisively gestures at Al Jid's photograph—"never thought of giving her. I risk everything to provide you with this important opportunity, and my reward? Disrespect and ingratitude." He wags his finger. "This reminds me of all the important changes I've made in this town that nobody bothers to acknowledge!"

Recounting the hostility he's faced as an Agent of Progressive Change upsets his sensitive equilibrium. "When I created the Marvellous Emporium I filled it with goods and services the superstitious were frightened of and now can't live without. Granted it's not the trendy treasure trove it once was, compared with the state-of-the-art shopping malls and department stores operated by the Gulf investors in Amman. But our little town offers something no place else has."

The deepening furrows on Hussein's forehead make Abu Za'atar lose his temper.

"Progress, my boy, never comes easily to those who insist on living in the past. If Allah did not want the world to change, all powerful, all knowing that He is, the Internet and satellite TV would never have been invented. The Arabs were once the fathers of science and mathematics. Without their hoarding of ancient texts, nobody would have ever known that a crazy Greek philosopher discovered the atom. We have globalization now? We had it then; it was *our* ideas and systems of distribution and exchange that transformed the world."

He is gesticulating madly. "With the simplest tools of their day —a tent, a spear, a horse—our people conquered lands as far away as Europe. Then what happened? It wasn't original thinking that won the day but religious dogma—the defeated didn't want to pay taxes for worshipping a different system. Instead they learned the beautiful language, memorized the Qur'an, aped their masters, and a religious bureaucracy was born. But bureaucracies don't invigorate the world. Instead of demanding sharia law, why not teach quantum physics? Surely that is another of God's secret languages. Instead of worrying about women's honor, why not harness their minds and forget about their bodies. The Saudis and Qataris combined could give every house in the region a laptop *and* a flush toilet. It wouldn't bankrupt them. Instead the richest and the most devout buy up London's Covent Garden and race Ferraris through the cobbled streets and harass girls on roller blades. Or they're busy exporting religious extremism.

"Life," he intones, "is not a struggle between good and evil. It's a tooth-and-claw fight to the death between enterprise and stagnation." With his ire up, Abu Za'atar is getting ready to argue for hours. His determination to never give in—not one iota—blows everything out of proportion and, like an expanding hot-air balloon, obscures the real reason he snuck into the house in the first place.

13

Samira has never seen her brother take charge. It is as though the drunken fool at last night's dinner has been replaced by someone alert and decisive. He ushered the young man he introduced as Mustafa straight into the house and ordered Samira to retrieve a change of clothes, a fresh razor blade, and scissors from a chest of drawers in the bedroom. Once their guest was installed in the bathroom and his knapsack stowed on the back terrace, Hussein took Samira and Fadhma aside and told them that only their discretion would help a lost soldier reach home.

Samira thinks she has enough time and returns to the terrace but stops short of touching the knapsack. She could understand if this were happening with Syrian activists; strangers were always showing up unexpectedly. But nothing like this ever takes place in her brother's home. She makes sure she is waiting by the door when Mustafa emerges from the bathroom, his face raw from the razor.

"You look good." Samira keeps her voice low.

In Hussein's clean cotton jersey and jeans, Mustafa shyly returns the compliment: "So do you."

It's a throwaway comment that means nothing, but Samira still blushes. Self-consciously she takes his folded old clothes. Carrying his heavy-duty boots, he follows her in socks.

Mother Fadhma welcomes the dazed young man to the kitchen. Samira would have liked to have stayed and listened to them both, but she quickly puts down Mustafa's clothes and retraces her steps. In the bathroom everything is in order. The towel has been hung up to dry, the sink rinsed and wiped. Wherever he's from he has good manners. She almost leaves without taking out the trash, then remembers Zeinab's advice: it is the details she needs to pay attention to. In the kitchen, Samira throws away the evidence. As she places the soldier's old clothes into a black plastic bag, her mother comes in from the terrace and ties back the curtain. Samira soon joins Mustafa outside with a glass of water on a tray.

"Home tastes good," he says quietly, looking up from a plate of tabbouleh in his lap.

"I bet we're a lot like your own family." She wants to draw him out, get him talking more about himself.

Mustafa again regards her intently. He has brown eyes and hair, and his skin is dark from the sun. But his face is open and clear. "Better," he states.

It is that shy smile she ignores as she probes again: "When were you last there?"

"Too long ago."

Samira changes tact. "Hussein didn't say where your family's living. I assumed the capital." she doesn't want him to think she has been considering it too deeply. "You look like you've been traveling for a while." Her reticent brother wouldn't have given so much away, but her nosy uncle had said as much.

"Yes." Mustafa takes the water from her tray.

"You can go as far away as you like, but it's not hard to know what's going on."

"When I crossed the border yesterday, I saw refugees trying to get in." He puts down the glass.

Samira checks the kitchen to see if Fadhma's around; she's not. "I've waited by the fence by al-Zaatari refugee camp. Much of what you hear about the camps is that they are hellholes—and they are—but people survive. They get married, have children, and you know the Syrians; they're good at business. Despite all that's gone wrong, some life continues."

"Syria's a mess—too much fighting for too long."

Clean-shaven, in normal clothes, the soldier's appearance doesn't give much away, but that's the point, isn't it? Samira decides she has no other choice but to rely on what came before. "That certainly doesn't help matters any. Unless you think a sharia state will solve all of our problems."

"I didn't say that."

Loath to waste any more of his time or hers, Samira asks straight out, "Where were you, exactly?"

"Afghanistan," he finally admits quietly. "My brother went to fight there and I went to bring him back, but he didn't make it. You could say he had been brainwashed, and for a time I was too."

"And now?"

When he doesn't answer, Samira tries making light of the situation. "That's what our families have in common: we've all been brainwashed to some extent." Mustafa is staring, not at her but at the floor. She continues, somewhat chastened, "Someone with your experience, working with the right people, could make a difference." She doesn't have to wait long for his response.

"To be honest, I am no longer useful, not even to myself."

His apparent helplessness upsets her. "You mean," she whispers sharply, "it's our duty to fight the Americans and the Israelis, but when Arabs are slaughtering Arabs we stand by and do nothing?"

"Who's fighting? Ugly Americans again?" Muna comes out onto the terrace with a tray of hot tea, which she puts down. From the look on Samira's and Mustafa's faces, she pointedly closes the terrace curtains behind her.

"He has"—Samira motions—"in Afghanistan."

Muna is so astonished she forgets to offer the soldier a glass of tea. "You're really a jihadist?"

"An occasional one," Samira answers for him.

The soldier looks askance at his hosts and says nothing.

"I can be arrested in the US just for talking to you," reveals Muna.

"Doesn't that say something about your country's freedom of speech," observes Mustafa somberly.

Remembering her manners, Muna offers him and Samira tea. "Some people say it's impossible to protect certain freedoms, especially for those intent on murdering you." Then she declares mischievously, "I get it, you want to kill me because I'm American. But we're the good guys now. The US is bombing ISIS in Syria. I mean, it's not like the government ever consults me about US foreign policy. So how can I be held responsible?"

Mustafa grunts. "That's my problem. I don't want to *kill* anyone." He reaches for his boots and puts them on.

"That's what I mean," Samira joins in. "It's all wrong. Why kill Americans when there are those fuckers across the border?"

Mustafa regards Samira again. "And what took you to al-Zaatari? I don't think a refugee camp is a place your brother would want you to go."

Now she is really annoyed. If Samira doesn't allow her own family to dictate her movements, she certainly isn't going to listen to an occasional jihadist. "Going to fight in Afghanistan is probably not something your mother would have wanted you or your brother to do," she lashes out before deeply regretting it. The soldier's grief-stricken face makes her feel immediately sorry and she explains more gently, "I do political work." She is addressing Muna as well. "I'm proud to help people who need me." As a proviso she adds, "I don't believe in slaughtering innocent civilians for religion," then challenges Mustafa again. "What about you?"

It is a question he doesn't answer as Hussein pushes through the curtain. "Mustafa, *imshee*, let's go!" He tells Samira and Muna, "Mother Fadhma needs you. Guests have arrived." He can't believe it himself, "Abu Za'atar is right, we have so many we don't know what to do with them." Something else is on his mind and he instructs his sister, "If anyone asks about the van, say it broke down and the mechanic will pick it up more than likely when the guests are here—so they won't miss it on their way out." He turns to Mustafa: "We leave from the back so the whole town won't know your business." Hussein almost looks as though he is enjoying himself.

As Mustafa collects his knapsack, Muna says in parting, "Don't think so badly of all Americans that you want to kill us." She flashes another brilliant smile and then goes to her grandmother's aid.

In the kitchen Samira is waiting with his bag of clothes, which she presses in his hands as she says good-bye. She doesn't want to pester him but can't stop herself from saying, "Think about it. There are people who demand your help and others too traumatized to ask for it. Where do you stand?"

Her words frighten him off and he follows Hussein out the back door.

At the front door, Abu Za'atar is already greeting two mustached men, one in a suit and tie, the other in farmer's overalls. "Good to see you. Please come in." When the girls join him, he warmly makes the introductions: "This is Abd's daughter. Muna, Abu Omar and Abu Salih are your father's friends from boyhood. Abu Salih went with Abd to America. Abu Omar stayed with us here at home and became like a son to us."

Why does her uncle always exaggerate? Samira leads the visitors through the new house past the living room and into the reception room.

Outside on the steps is a woman in her sixties, Umm Omar, Abu Omar's wife. She has brought along her two grandchildren. Mother Fadhma welcomes them. "Everyone looks well, Umm Omar."

"Our land is not giving us much. But there's gold on Jebel Musa if you know where to look." Umm Omar hands Fadhma a bag of fresh green leaves.

Fadhma crushes the soft leaves and buds of za'atar thyme between her fingers. With a childish delight she deeply inhales, then trails her scented fingertips underneath Abu Za'atar's elegant proboscis. Revelling in this rare example of shared intimacy, he proclaims out loud, "Delicious—reminds us all of home and a certain emporium."

The children are led to the living room, where they can play undisturbed. Samira returns from the reception room, but before she can greet Umm Omar properly, the older woman glowers at her. "Don't say anything bad about Assad."

Her hostility is shocking, but it doesn't prevent Samira from blurting out, "The man's a butcher."

"*Kuss umek*—fuck your mother's cunt," exclaims the farmer's wife out of earshot of the men.

Muna, witnessing the exchange, cocks her head and makes a discreet V sign with her two fingers. "See, no matter war, dictatorship, even food poisoning—really, whose fault is it?" She and her cousin start giggling. One look from Mother Fadhma quiets them.

"Please, brother." Fadhma offers Abu Za'atar a seat.

As he triumphantly settles in, he murmurs to her, "For a long time no one would talk to us. Now look at them, clamoring to get in. My goodness, *ukhti*, you are really something! Turning adversity into a blessing is a family trait you must have learned from me!"

Fadhma raises an eyebrow at her daughter. "This will keep the old feather duster happy. And *our* friend?"

Mother and daughter peer up the hallway and through the still-open front door. Hussein's van, which has rolled quietly away, with its engine off, jerks into gear and starts picking up speed. Despite the intrigue, Samira knows better than to neglect her duties and checks on the water heating on the kitchen stove.

When she returns, Abu Salih is telling Muna about the early days in America with her father. He remembers bringing her milk when she was very tiny and her parents were poor graduate students. Samira places an enormous silver tray laden with Laila's best coffee set, a plate of sweets, and a bowl of fruit onto the long, low marble table and begins pouring the coffee.

Umm Omar has been quizzing Muna. "It must have been difficult for your father to send you to Jordan when everything is so unsettled. This Arab Awakening has been a descent into madness. We should have left the dictators in place."

"Dad didn't send me." Muna stops and begins again, more politely, "Some people think it's not the best time to come but that didn't stop me. The 2011 uprisings were the only worthy political movement to come out of the Middle East for decades."

Abu Za'atar, fanning himself with his hand, apologizes to the guests on her behalf. "You must forgive the young. They think they are the first ones to rebel. But many communists, leftists, socialists, Trotskyites, pan-Arabists, belonging to an assortment of movements named after every day of the week, the Eighth of March, the Fourteenth of March... have been there before. If they didn't die tortured in prison they faced the poverty, depression, and loneliness of exile, all for the sake of a glorious ideal: to change the system. And when this much-vaunted change does take place, the new charismatic leader—no doubt thoroughly dedicated in the service of his people—is worse than the one before. So all we can do is live with the instability, and to be honest"—he regards his audience thoughtfully—"it hasn't been so bad for business."

Samira can tell her uncle is making an effort or he would have droned on. Abu Omar perches stiffly on the edge of Laila's impossibly opulent sofa, ill at ease in the formal setting of the reception room. He had come directly from the fields with bits of plant and dirt still clinging to his overalls. Beside him, his wife has taken enough offense for the both of them.

"In the past," she observes, "we looked to America or Russia as great countries; we respected them. Now we see that they are not only inept but dangerous. Better to make our own way alone without their interference. It's Daesh we should worry about."

"But we have always had marauders who killed and looted. Who are the Crushers," Mother Fadhma says, calling them by her name, "but criminals—plain and simple. This isn't about religion but power. Granted they appear more bloodthirsty—"

"And better at scaring us," the farmer's wife interjects. "The video of the pilot burned alive was horrifying. It's bad enough we have the refugees, but now we have to worry about terrorists hiding among them." She turns to Muna. "I'm sure you weren't thinking about this as you planned your holiday."

Abu Za'atar hasn't been following the conversation and suddenly lurches forward in his seat. "Hussein?" His good eye bounces from face to face in the reception room.

"There, there." Mother Fadhma pats him as she would a startled pygmy parrot. She hushes him by saying, "Abu Salih is telling a story."

"When the refugees first arrived in the town they were selling walnuts; they had carried the harvest with them from home. Another man sold apples, and he told me that even though they were unable to stay in their village because of the shelling, they returned every night and watered their orchards. After the apples and walnuts ran out, the children started begging. The Eastern Quarter has become a Little Damascus. Eventually these people will be forced to go back to Assad."

"I keep asking myself"—it is Umm Omar again—"why Bashar al-Assad spent ten years building his country to destroy it. I blame those dirty Saudis and Qataris who have been paying the Islamic terrorists. Now look at the results."

Samira doesn't need Umm Omar to tell her to look. She has seen the videos of the bombed charred remains of Homs and ancient Aleppo and the wounded children in makeshift field hospitals. While Fadhma's guests drink their coffee, cluster bombs rain down on an opposition village or on starving people waiting for deliveries of UN food aid that never get through. Umm Omar should be ashamed of herself. But Samira knows that any criticism on her part would appall her mother. Instead she offers everyone a napkin, a plate, and a piece of baklava. As she serves Muna, she whispers in a voice that only her cousin can hear, "Blah blah blah."

Of course Samira feels sympathy for those frightened by the conflict. And of course everyone wants things to go back to normal, as though all those hundreds of thousands of people never died. And the nearly five million Syrian refugees in Turkey, Lebanon, Jordan, Egypt, and Iraq, and the more than one million asylum seekers who fled to Europe, of course, they should all be forced back to their country to live with their killers. Arabs always live with their killers and torturers; the Syrian state knows this all to well. Zeinab told Samira about the chilling phone calls she and others like her have already been receiving from the country's secret police. "All is forgiven," a soft-spoken male voice at the end of the line soothingly informs her. "Time to come home and rebuild *your* country."

And Fadhma's guests believe that there's no need for change? If these are the people who have been ostracizing the family because of Umm al-Khanaazeer, better that they stay away. Samira feels nothing but contempt. Luckily the empty coffeepot provides her with the perfect excuse. She gathers up her tray as unobtrusively as possible and withdraws to the kitchen, where she places more water on to boil but keeps the flame deliberately low. She wants to take as long as possible and checks on Fuad, who has followed the older children outside into the backyard. All three are absorbed in a game that involves rolling pebbles into a dip in the ground. Samira stands looking out the back door and watches them play.

Bored, she returns to the back terrace and sits among the cushions. There has been too much excitement as of late: Muna's arrival, a restless night, the water tanker, and the appearance of Mustafa and then her uncle, topped off by her mother's tomfoolery. It is uncharacteristic for Fadhma to do anything deceptive—Samira smiles remembering the two of them watching Hussein and the soldier drive off. If she is being truthful with herself, she could have spent more time with Mustafa. He didn't seem inherently bad, despite the fact he tried to tell her what to do. She yawns and the afternoon heat closes around her like a comforting blanket. As the faintest breath of wind stirs the dust in the yard and causes the wind chimes hanging at the end of the terrace to tinkle softly, she lies back, and her eyes slowly shut.

Nose, brain, belly, and backside—all informed her that a momentous change was taking place the night she was removed from the house and taken away. When the butcher's van finally stopped and its back doors swung open, she didn't wait for the new man in charge, the sad one who smelled of alcohol or bad cologne—she didn't know him well enough to distinguish which. Before she could be stopped, she leaped from the van, squealing, and ran straight into the dark.

She sensed apex predators nearby, but she wasn't afraid. She had survived all manner of dangerous predicaments, including the journey from Egypt and the odd interludes afterward: the labyrinthine store smelling of gunpowder and metal, and an empty room in a house ruled by a grumpy old lady.

This was different. The fresh mountain air was a jolt to her system and her animal instincts took over. Relying on an internal compass, she headed

straight into the old barn and selected suitable surroundings. To the amaze-
ment of her new keeper, she arranged straw and bits of paper apparently
to her liking and nested comfortably. The man too spent that first night
nearby, under a blanket of newspapers. While he snored, the pig emerged
from her bed and continued sniffing, first fully around Hussein and then
a nearby bottle, before exploring the length and breadth of the barn. Fortunately its thin walls were not open to the elements. She lingered by cracks
and corners, looking for field mice or spiders. A leaking hose, which left
pools of water where it snaked under a sliding door, suggested a range of
possible wet spots, but before she allowed herself the pleasure of attending
to herself, she determined that the location of another private space should
be outside, so she could defecate if and when needed.

By dawn she felt herself settle. She had exerted control over her new
surroundings. Her determination surprised the man, who initially left her
alone for long hours but always managed to return for feeding and watering, sometime during the day or late at night. Every time he drove up in
the van that had brought her here, he was distracted, deep in himself—she
recognized the signs—but with just the two of them she realized that his
demeanor improved with time. If clean air and enterprise didn't bring him
out of himself, she found she had the ability to.

She stumbled across her own powers of persuasion by accident. He
didn't keep her in a crate or in the barn and appeared to enjoy walking.
Whenever they went out together he looped a rope around her neck and
held it, trailing far behind to give her enough length to explore at will.
Whenever he stopped for any stretch of time, he left the rope secured under
a rock or attached to a bush, as he prepared the land for the working farm
it was going to become. One afternoon he was busy and she, bored with
ground already picked clean, slipped out of her noose. Pregnant sows insist
on roaming. Hussein meanwhile hadn't noticed the slack rope, and when he
did, he called out sharply. Unseen, she tiptoed silently behind him. When
he turned around and nearly tripped over her, instead of losing his temper
he laughed out loud. Her reward was a lengthy back scratch. There was
nothing better that she liked: building trust.

Once construction work began in earnest, she persisted underfoot, but
only if the two of them were alone. When strangers came to the farm she
didn't have to be told to stay out of the way in the barn until after their

departure. With Hussein, she reveled in her freedom, and she surveyed the new developments, running through or alongside them, smelling, always smelling. If something was particularly ripe, she retraced her steps, punctuated by loud grunts, and spent a few minutes more in rapt investigation. She watched with a mothering pride as small buildings, outhouses, and pens were erected and finalized.

Only when Hussein was completely immersed in his work did she allow herself to wander farther afield. She was naturally suspicious, particularly before dusk. In the lengthening shadows she felt a menacing presence, but she was intrigued too. The more directions a place could be ambushed from, the more ideal for burying and digging. In time, familiarity pacified a nervous disposition and developed into an unhealthy fascination. She was always careful, but there was open ground surrounded by rocks, away from the barn, she couldn't leave alone. Odd visits, which had started as cursory checks once in the morning and again in the afternoon, after her nap, soon turned into long hours searching among clumps of spongy soil and grass around the spring and pump and, farther away, where hardier herbaceous plants sent moisture-seeking roots deep underneath, a microclimate delicate enough for the wild black iris. Where the water never reached was sand and scrub. In a relatively contained area, wetlands, pasture, and desert were at her disposal. Each had its delights. Yet as thorough as her explorations became, she wasn't altogether satisfied. During different times of the day but more noticeably that moment when she should be returning to the barn and turning in for the night, the earth turned pungent and fungal, redolent of flavors she loved.

During her first encounter with the Great Smell, she mistook it for tubers twenty-five feet underground, but hard digging got her nowhere. The source wasn't something rotting deep in the earth. Only when she pressed her mobile nasal disc along the surface did her mouth and brain explode with possibilities. The farm's plain diet and the rococo urban waste of her youth had given her an ultrasensitivity, most noticeably in the realm of olfaction.

More out of inquisitiveness than hunger, she turned over rocks and kicked up soil. Hers was a refined palate formed by experience and travel. Still, of all the foodstuffs she was acquainted with, it was dirt she knew exceedingly well. Generations of swine before her had picked clean the dust of pharaohs, leaving it thin and wanting. In Palestine, despite imprisonment and an upset tummy, she detected a distinct sourness to the soil as though the goodness that had once been there had been leached out. Human density left a trail, much of it unpleasant.

Not here. True, she was temporarily waylaid by a small fiber from an old coat. But her olfactory nerves sensed the most amazing possibilities. Around and around she rolled in the dirt, with all her faculties firing. Ghostly trails at once turned solid, blending into and infusing a sensory onslaught. Inhaling deeply, she was enveloped by the Great Smell and one with the past.

She had tasted pistachios in flakes of baklava and leftover sprinklings in milk puddings gone sour, but petrified pollen from one of its trees was an entirely new experience. Finally she understood viscerally the full import of the messages her most sensitive organ had been telling her. Her eyesight was not the best but her prescience was clear. She was surrounded by what had once been ancient woodlands of cedar, pine, and oak. However, as the tastes of her childhood—cinnamon, carob, and the glorious date—flooded back to her, she understood this was only a part of a larger story. The forest had been cleared. In its place expansive gardens of fruit and nut trees, flowers, and vegetation had been planted and flourished, watered by a spring that ran more forcibly in its youth.

In the instant paradise was revealed, it was gone. Startled, she sniffed at the empty air. Instead of the Great Smell, pheromones of a wolf stretching itself in the caves above drifted past her on the wind.

Afterward she kept close to Hussein like a dog and was not averse to performing tricks. Consciously or not, she made him her own. They had been taking one of their strolls. But when he was staring off into the distance, she turned to face him. As he took a step forward, she laid her hoof gingerly on top of his foot, something the sad man didn't quite believe. He moved his other foot forward, and a corresponding hoof met his. With each step, man and pig progressed. Over time they perfected a private dance of their own.

She needed no prompting and repeated the trick whenever he called to her. Neither was she shy nor stupid whenever the old eccentric from the store came to the farm, demanding amusement at their expense. She didn't *mind in the least because this was her home and she was in charge. If Hussein thought she hadn't noticed the changes on the farm were for her benefit alone, he was wrong.*

Her first litter of eight perfectly formed piglets survived the road trip. Her milk was strong as long as she had the freedom to forage, root, and snuffle. Of course the piglets couldn't be entrusted to stay close, and she never paraded them around the spring. Some tastes came only with maturity. As the babies grew stronger by the day, she felt deep and abiding satisfaction.

Soon the thoughtful Ahmad joined Hussein and took over her and her children's immediate care, but Umm al-Khanaazeer remained unaccountably attached to the sad man. Every three months, three weeks, and three days, she was pregnant again, and the father was Hussein, who kept the spiral-tipped insemination rods at the ready. She was an object of study, a being of great fecundity. She had finally become an exemplary representative of the animal kingdom.

14

Girls spill out of their classrooms, turning the hallway into a noisy flood. From a doorway, Laila plunges into the torrent and is swept along. In theory, teachers take precedence over pupils, but in the school's cramped conditions the rule is hard to enforce. Nevertheless, when two chattering teenagers block her path, she pushes through them.

At the end of another workday she feels relieved to be outside. This afternoon, more than usual, she is looking forward to her sons' company for the walk home and she scours the children's faces for her own. After a few minutes, she impatiently checks her watch and sets off by herself at a brisk pace. She doesn't slow down until the water tanks on the roof of the new house come into view. In her haste to get inside, she skips up the front steps two at a time.

In the living room she kicks off her shoes for slippers and collapses onto the sofa. When baby Fuad appears in the doorway, followed by Muna, Samira, and Mother Fadhma, Laila inquires, "Have the boys arrived?" She was hoping that they were ahead of her.

"Not yet," Fadhma says. Like the morning, after school Laila can be sensitive. So the old woman makes no comment other than what's necessary.

"I waited." Laila helps her youngest son into her lap. "I expect they're off with friends." Then she asks Samira and Muna, "What have you been up to? The house looks spotless!"

It is unusual for her to comment on Samira's cleaning without first checking every corner, but Muna, oblivious to the finer nuances of household relationships, answers for them both. "We stayed at home. Visitors came."

Laila stops hugging Fuad and looks up at Mother Fadhma. It would be bad enough if something happened, but not in front of their American relation. Laila's headache is on the verge of flaring up again.

"They were childhood friends of Abd's." Fadhma's quick response mollifies her daughter-in-law's concerns. The two of them might not be the best of friends, but they rely on each other. Fadhma senses that Laila wants her to continue, so she adds, "We had a good time. That is, when this one is polite"—she eyes Muna—"and that one doesn't fall asleep." She glares at Samira.

Laila takes some perverse satisfaction in imagining the situation before her expression darkens. "Nothing was said?" She still expects trouble. When it does not materialize she never allows herself to feel entirely safe. There was a time when disaster didn't constantly hover over her, but she can't remember how that felt; now any delay in bad news appears more as a cruel trick than a reprieve.

Mother Fadhma nods quickly and changes the subject. "We can wait for the boys or have lunch now. What do you prefer? Hussein won't be joining us—"

"*Naam*, let's eat." Laila carries her son to the kitchen. She senses there is more to be learned about the afternoon but she can't wait.

After securing her son in his highchair, Laila reaches for one of the empty tins by the sink. It is not like her mother-in-law to neglect filling them, but before she loses her temper Fadhma turns on a faucet and water sputters forth. It is a good omen. Laila gratefully washes and dries her hands.

"We're going to eat, Fuad. Look what Jadda made." She spoons tabbouleh into a blue plastic bowl and sets it in front of him. The little boy is ready with a matching spoon.

Mother Fadhma places bread on the table. "I didn't cook much today because we're out tonight."

Normally Laila would have interpreted Mother Fadhma's comment—however innocently intended—to be a gibe; this afternoon it would have been about the women's get-together that Laila was missing. But their American visitor has ameliorated the usual tensions of the household and it is in everyone's interest to avoid discord. Laila asks Muna about her father's friends.

"They were okay, and once we stopped talking about politics, it was all right," the girl assesses. "I shouldn't second-guess people. I kept waiting for Umm Omar to ask the inevitable question that all the old ladies get around to in our church. Why did my father not have sons? Was he upset at having only girls? That's not something he could control."

Another Hadith Laila learned for the school parents comes back to her. "'From what is man created?'" she recites out loud from memory, "'The Messenger of Allah answered... : "Man is created from the union of both the semen of the man and the semen of the woman. The *nutfa* of man is thick and from it the bones and nerves are created. And the woman's *nutfa* is thin and from it flesh and blood are created."'"

She explains, "During medieval Islam, people thought that a baby's gender was determined by the parent with the strongest 'semen' in both men and women. Nobody believes that today, but some people assume if a man doesn't have sons he didn't try hard enough. If he really wanted boys, he should have as many children as possible or marry a new wife ready and willing to try to produce sons. Eventually the odds would be in his favor even when the genetics were not."

Muna isn't convinced. "What about Uncle Boutros? Auntie Dallah couldn't keep having girls forever. What were they going to do if a boy did come along? Get rid of the girls?"

"That's the question," Samira joins in, "that has baffled the Middle East, South Asia, the subcontinent, not to mention the Far East and Central and Latin America. What do you do with all those girls?"

Laila pulls a face. "There isn't one woman in this town who hasn't been told she should have been born a boy."

Despite loud groans and cries of "Oh no!" the women are merry around the table. In the excitement little Fuad rocks side to side in his highchair.

"When I was growing up," Laila says as she helps herself to some salad, "my mother's advice was 'Do not look at, talk to, or go near a boy; never be alone with a man. Be constantly vigilant since your honor and mine are at stake.' Then it was time to get married."

"So why do you think it's like that?" Muna asks. "Because of religion?"

"It's easy to get the impression that religion's at fault," considers Laila. As it has engulfed the town, she has become intrigued not by its expression in women's lives, but by its permutation. Through her friend Warda she was surprised to learn that Islam is forthright about sex and counsels women to enjoy their marriages, to pleasure their husbands and themselves. Laila feels that she and other Christian women are prudish by comparison.

Jesus was too much of a firebrand for a prolonged relationship with a woman. Always a son, never a husband or a father, his experience of women was limited and he never truly understood them. Meanwhile the number of Muhammad's wives, according to scholars, ranged between eleven and thirty-one. During the religion's great conquest of the Middle East many women had been widowed. Out of sympathy and duty the Prophet took them as wives and urged his followers to do the same. Such large households effectively socialized the region. It also made women a topic of study among the Sunni and the Shia. Laila had also been shocked to learn there was a canon of literature that focused entirely on female anatomy, sexuality, and psychology that was sometimes taught in mosques. It showed a lack of squeamishness on the part of Islam toward women, but it also pinned them down: biology as destiny. Marriage is the only relationship between men and women that is sanctioned by both the Qur'an and the Bible.

Yet, it seemed to Laila, Warda's interior life was deeply satisfying, despite her religion's emphasis on submission, first to God and then her husband. Even after death, men are favored in Islam. In Paradise, true believers are promised virginal *houriyat* who regenerate their hymens immediately after having sex. These gazelle-eyed women companions of the faithful are not, as promised, pure and untouched: just recyclable.

"The *houriyat*," Laila tells Muna, "are really no stranger than the virgin birth." She doesn't want to be misunderstood and explains, "The regulation of women's lives by religion and state is nothing new. The empowerment of women is not dangerous. It's the reactions to that by men which are."

She picks a fresh fig from the fruit bowl. "This is the food of Paradise." Her lips cover the soft green skin. "It has always been the same—what men enjoy, women endure. No matter her religion, before a woman marries she must suffer for her husband. You know about sugaring, Muna?"

The girl says she has seen it often enough: her aunts in America boil lemon and sugar together into thick taffy, smear it over their arms and legs, and then yank it off to remove body hair.

"Before her wedding a girl sugars her whole body," divulges Laila.

"The cousins told me," Muna says, grimacing. "I never understood why they don't just shave."

"All except for her eyelashes, eyebrows, and the hair on her head," Samira chimes in, laughing. She finds Muna's reaction humorous. Because her mother is foreign, she probably hasn't been schooled in Arab femininity.

Laila confirms Samira's words as she peels a fig for Fuad. "That way her husband can see she is pure and virginal."

"Just like American teenage boys watching porn over the Internet who have learned to dislike pubic hair," Muna informs the women. "However, that doesn't stop them from having sex with a 'hairy' girl. Afterward they go on Facebook to make fun of her and call her 'dirty.' So when it comes to banning hair from the marital bed, the Arabs were obviously ahead of their times."

"Oh, great," moans Samira.

"Well," counters Laila patiently, "sugaring is the fate of brides. Right now women are toasting the happiness of a young girl getting married tonight. They're filling her head with the same nonsense that my mother told me before my wedding day. 'Be like a jewel in the palm of your master, or perfume, an odor that entices. You are to please but never demand. If you are too eager, he will only be ashamed. Close your eyes and pray to God it will be over quickly.'"

If Laila were to give advice to the bride about her future it wouldn't be about sex. She would have warned her not to give in to social pressures of starting a family too quickly. With the upheaval of getting to know her husband and moving in with her in-laws, a young bride should at least try to enjoy herself. She adds, "It's not the first night's sex that's hard to endure but the rest of your life with your husband."

Despite Mother Fadhma and Samira, Laila's voice is hard and mocking. Quickly diverting attention from herself, she says to Muna, "Your *jadda* knows many traditional proverbs about marriage."

Fadhma, in thought, rubs her chin. "These are old sayings, maybe not good advice for such modern girls."

"Jadda, do tell," begs Muna.

Her grandmother gives in. "'An old man takes a young wife, and the young men of the town rejoice.'" The mood at the table has changed and everyone is smiling.

"'The shorter the woman, the younger she will appear to her betrothed.' Or how about: 'Be good to your own wife'"—Fadhma's small eyes grow wide—"'and you can have your neighbor's.'" She warns the girls, "Don't repeat these in polite company."

"But we're not polite," Samira teases her mother.

Fadhma places a finger to her lips. "There is a proverb for every situation imaginable: 'If you haven't seen the face of your intended, examine her little brother's.' But let me tell you my favorite: 'Marriage is like a watermelon; you don't know what's inside until—" The words die in her throat.

In the doorway Mansoor and Salem stand covered in dirt. Mansoor's nose is bleeding and a blue-black bruise is forming on his face. He has been in a fight. Laila stifles a cry and runs to embrace her second son.

"Mummy, five boys attacked us," he tells her. "They tried to hurt Salem but I wouldn't let them."

She hugs him tighter. "You fought for your brother?" She extends an arm toward Salem, who walks solemnly to her.

Fuad has been watching his mother and brothers from his highchair. When he tries climbing out, Samira frees him and keeps hold of him, as Laila informs her mother-in-law, "I knew something like this would happen."

"That has been my feeling all along, but who could say anything to that brother of mine."

Laila insists that Hussein must be told right away, after Fadhma thrusts a kitchen towel in her hand and she wipes the faces of her sons. The old mother has started filling a carrier bag with food for the trip to the farm. It is amazing that she knows what Laila needs before she does. Perhaps this is the unbroken connection between women who have fought and lived together for so long.

Half an hour later, Laila and her two boys make the short walk from the house to a nearby square, where belching car exhaust and the oily fumes from fetid open-air barbecues hang in the motionless air. Laila wipes the sweat from her brow and switches the bag of food from one arm to the other. A hawker approaches them: "Lighters? Flashlights? Shoelaces?" Laila dismisses him with a curt shake of her head and directs the boys to where they can catch a taxi.

Inside the cars most of the drivers are lounging, half asleep. The ones awake tend to specialize in long distances and travel all over the country. Unlike the locals who doze away the afternoon, these men are gripped by road fever. They are content only when moving, preferably at high speeds. Earning a living is only an excuse, a means to an end.

An unkempt youth leans out of his car and waves: "Where you off to, lady? I give you a good price." She ignores him. The farm is in the mountains outside the town. She and the boys could make the hour-long walk, but the road is straight uphill and none of them is in the mood for hiking. Because of the butcher's van, the family rarely comes to the service square. Laila hopes that the treat of a taxi will cheer up her sons. By now Salem and Mansoor should have been fighting over who gets to pick the best car.

"Which one?" Laila attempts to draw them out, but they, saying nothing, only look at her. So she keeps their usual criteria in mind. In the past they shunned newer vehicles and selected ones that were badly dented, their roadworthiness proven by their battle scars. Some of the cars are unexpectedly luxurious, like a Mercedes-Benz smuggled out of one of the war zones and picked up for a song on the Jordanian-Iraqi border. But not even the best engineering lasts long in the gear-grinding roads of the mountains, and the taxis present a uniformly dilapidated spectacle no matter their age or model.

A teenager washes one that looks like a patchwork quilt. The doors, spoiler, and hood of different makes and colors give the impression that the car has been glued together. "Is Mikhail around?" Laila inquires.

The youth tosses his rag into a bucket and whistles twice through his fingers. A portly man emerges from a cheap eating establishment, brushing crumbs of food from the corner of his mouth.

"The butcher's wife," he says, wiping his hand on his pants before shaking hers. "How often we sing the praises of your husband and his excellent product. Umm Salem"—he notices her sons' faces—"this looks grave indeed." As he bends down, the folds of his stomach nearly burst through the straining buttons that hold his shirt together. "Whoever it was, they fought dirty." He pulls each boy closer to him. "Should we go and find them in the car right now and teach them a lesson?"

Mansoor kicks a pebble into the gutter and says, his voice barely audible, "No, Mr. Mikhail. I will get them myself."

Mikhail asks Laila, "What happened?"

She tries to appear unconcerned, but she can barely look at her sons and the driver without crying. "I'm not sure, a fight after school."

Mikhail opens the back door for the butcher's wife. Before the boys can clamber in after her, the driver directs them to the front seat. "You guys belong with me. My car is yours, but before we leave we must take the necessary precautions," and he walks to a ragged sumac tree and soft drink stall, where he buys four bottles of lime-green soda from an elderly woman who pours the contents of each bottle into a clear plastic pouch, inserts a straw, and ties the neck shut. Mikhail hands everyone a pouch and then takes his place behind the steering wheel. "Everybody ready?"

Salem and Mansoor nod over their straws.

He starts up the car's loud engine and they roar off.

Laila, sinking down into the seat, barely touches her drink. It has taken everything out of her to walk through the streets of the town with her battered sons. She is moved by the driver's kindness and feels anger only with herself, her husband, and the situation.

Mikhail's taxi seems to be the only one on the road. Even the cries of children playing in the streets sound faint, as though coming from afar. In an hour the entire town, even the service square, will be at a complete standstill as everyone, regardless of age, gender, or religion, retreats inside from the afternoon heat to nap or work after lunch.

In the backseat Laila is alone with her thoughts. She and Hussein will have to decide what to do, and it won't be easy. The whole family has been involved, and their reward is the wonderful home they live in. She corrects herself—that hasn't been their reward, but hers. She encouraged Hussein first to build the new house and then to furnish it. The others came along whether they liked it or not.

With clarity, she sees what she has been hiding from herself: she isn't the easiest person to live with. There is something in her that will not leave her husband alone, and she has tested him at every available opportunity. Who does he love more, his wife or his sister? Who runs the house better, his wife or his stepmother? She has been so intent on her petty struggles that she has failed to notice that her husband no longer cares. All she nags him about is whether he has kept his side of the bargain, which he has adhered to scrupulously. She twists uncomfortably in her seat. She had mistaken that for approval, as if only possessions were enough.

While she was obsessed with buying and ordering, he occupied himself by drinking. During one of the family gatherings to celebrate the new house, Laila lost her temper and lashed out at Abu Za'atar. He had taken her husband to too many nightclubs and late-night drinking sessions. But the old vulture refused to be intimidated. "Look around," he said. "You have nothing to complain about. Real luxury requires real sacrifice."

Soon afterward Laila railed against Mother Fadhma and accused her of raising a drunk. The women did not speak for weeks. Now that events are overtaking her, Laila can no longer overlook her culpability for her husband's decline. Disgusted by her anger and greed, she makes a fist and raises it to her mouth. They need a plan. The fist becomes tighter. In all matters she endeavors not to be drawn in or compromised. Indifference and resolution have shielded her; her personal defenses are impenetrable, this much she knows. Her only weak spot is her children. There is nothing she would not do for them.

She attempts to follow the conversation in the front seat. Salem's delicate laughter rings out at one of Mikhail's jokes. They look normal enough, two schoolboys—one of them worse for wear—on a special outing. Laila tugs gently at Mansoor's ear and asks, "Feeling better?"

He turns around, his expression mischievous. "Oh, Mummy, if we meet those boys now, Mr. Mikhail and I would show them a thing or two!"

Laila forces a smile. Mikhail, watching through his rearview mirror, adds soothingly, "They're fine, Umm Salem, don't worry about them."

She leans back and gazes through the window. The passing scenery is like a narcotic. As the car climbs higher she can see out across the desert, where every now and then water unexpectedly nourishes the sand and a patch of green intrudes. The car stops to let a herd of sheep cross the road.

"Why are sheep the dumbest creatures on earth?" the driver asks the boys. It is his turn to laugh out loud when Salem replies, "Because their parents eat grass."

The shepherds come into view in their distinctive rural clothing. A little boy wears a knitted cap and a girl, slightly older, has kohl circles drawn around her big, dark eyes and tiny, delicately hennaed hands. Salem and Mansoor wave to the shy children on the roadside close to the herd, their family's only means of support.

"Let's hear a song!"

Mikhail slips a cassette into a battered player in the dashboard and the car fills with Lebanese folk music: *"Salaam alaikum, salaam alaikum, bahi salaam, mini alaikum..."*

He raises his voice over the music: "If we weren't driving, we'd be dancing the *dabke*. Tonight we'll dance at the wedding feast."

He gets the boys to sing along, their high, soft voices out of key. Laila joins in but can't follow the simple words. They have almost reached the turnoff for the farm.

"Mikhail, if it's not too much trouble, could we stop and admire the view?" She needs a few minutes to gather her thoughts. The taxi pulls into a convenient clearing near the path that leads to Ayun Musa.

Everyone gets out. While Salem and Mansoor practice dancing with the taxi driver to the music, Laila leans against the side of the car and surveys the scene below: the houses and the buildings of the town in miniature surrounded by dry brown fields and steppe, the peaks in the distance falling off into a violent cleft in the landscape and a secretive river glinting like a mirror, revealing itself only here or there. On the other side rise the green hills of the West Bank. With the air smelling of animals and crushed earth, it is so tranquil. She can almost be lulled into believing that everything is all right. Then disgusted, she berates herself. If she can lie so duplicitously to herself she should expect no mercy from others. Done with self-delusion, she gets back into the taxi and waits for the others.

15

Heavy wooden doors open and a stooped figure in a scarf enters the church. At the front, by an altar, an Orthodox priest swings a heavy censer and the air fills with dense, sweet-smelling clouds of frankincense. As the smoke dims the chandeliers and swirls into fantastic shapes in the thick bars of afternoon light, his voice praying for "plentiful solicitude and tenderness" interlocks with that of a chanter singing "Lord have mercy" forty times.

Mother Fadhma has arrived early. Usually she meticulously times her arrival in the dazzling Church of the Mosaic minutes after the Ninth Hour service has finished and evening vespers have begun, so those in attendance will have already settled in their seats. All her life she has prayed in this church that is more than a second home; it is where she is incapable of lying to herself or to others. This is why she is so unwilling to meet her fellow worshippers. God is a minor consideration compared to the town's elderly women. But the attack on her grandsons demands a change in schedule, and it is not only worship that has brought her here.

In pews, those who are hard of hearing lean forward to catch the elusive prayers of the priest. "Thy people despair. O Forbearing One, allow Thy Mother, Theotokos, to intercede for us, and save the unfortunate and undeserving..." One or two members of the aged congregation have given up the struggle, and their heads are bowed in sleep rather than devotion. Others are lost in profane thoughts.

In years gone by, these same women once met at the cistern. Even though they no longer carry water to their families, now in church, every day, they hope to bring back something precious. Many of the women are distantly related and the majority are over seventy. The basis of their fellowship is the shared experience of poverty. In times of want, they pooled everything they owned, and the destitute village eventually flourished and grew into a town. Now all their collective efforts have been overlooked, and they represent the vestiges of a disappearing culture. More out of necessity than spite, they cultivate their memories as stubbornly as their husband-farmers once tended the fields.

Mother Fadhma proceeds along the north aisle. She would like to kneel at the statue of Theotokos, the Birth Giver of God the Creator and Christ, His Son, but the pain in her legs prevents her. Woodenly she clings on to a convenient railing. Unlike the icon on the *templon* showing the Annunciation, the first meeting between a willowy young Mary and an archangel, this figure of Christ's mother is in the prime of womanhood. With arms outstretched in benediction, her painted face exudes sober serenity. However great Fadhma's own distress may be, it can never match the suffering of the cherished Birth Giver who witnessed the crucifixion and resurrection. Fadhma crosses herself and prays, "Oh, Mother, how I need you."

The adjacent candle stand is nearly full. The town's elderly have their own burdens to bear. Fadhma takes candles from a nearby box and lights one against another's flame before scraping its waxen stem and securing it in a metal holder. Every important event in her life has been illuminated by light. Candles were exchanged at the baptisms of all her children; now they are prayed over to comfort the torments of old age.

Fadhma meditates on a troubled household: brave little Mansoor who saved his brother, and Salem, who will feel the pressure of being the eldest in years to come. How will these children survive? Her instincts say they will. Fadhma includes a third candle for Fuad. The children are the easiest ones. It is more difficult to pray for family members who are sinners like herself.

That afternoon the usual worries multiplied with the arrival of Hussein and the sad soldier. Once Abu Za'atar snuck into their house like a cuckoo, her maternal reflexes took over. She wasn't going to allow those she loved to be abused and turned into another of her brother's victims.

But she hasn't come to Theotokos to only complain. "I want to thank you for my granddaughter Muna."

She is grateful that the girl arrived safely, but she and Samira share too many private jokes. Try as she might, Fadhma cannot think of her daughter without a growing uneasiness. If she doesn't trust Samira, "who will, dear Mother of Christ, God and all of creation?" She stares at the statue. Compassion like a worried mother's love shines out of its eyes, as the priest's singing—"Oh, Divine, Great One, do not forsake us entirely..."—envelops them.

Fadhma completes the Orthodox sign of the cross and thinks of her daughter-in-law. She would have preferred a quiet word with Laila, to compare impressions as it were, but Laila is too controlling for her own good. She can handle work, even an unsatisfactory marriage—Fadhma is not blind—but the boys' fight unnerved her. Most days in church Fadhma would revisit the long-standing enmity between the two women, which started with her daughter-in-law, in a fit of rage and insecurity, screaming, "This is *my* house. I'm in charge!" and pushing Fadhma out the front door. Now, as the old woman lights another candle, she prays for the courage to put their antipathies aside. Only combined determination will protect the family.

Undoubtedly the person who has suffered the most is the one closest to her heart. Fadhma handles a seventh candle with the utmost care. Today she saw Hussein challenge her brother. It is a good sign, and she looks to the statue for confirmation, but its expression, leaden and unperturbed, leaves Fadhma alone with her tribulations. The old woman feels determination ebbing away. Where is the Blessed Mother's mercy? Fadhma, conscious of her own frailty, grips the railing before lighting a last candle for her husband. Only his belief in God and the family will strengthen her weakening resolve. Surely his example will illuminate a way.

As the singing for the Ninth Hour Mass continues, she turns away from the statue. Instead of gravitating toward her usual hiding place at the back of the church, for her grandchildren's sake Fadhma is drawn to a central wooden pew. In times of real need she requires the fortitude of her neighbors, and against her better judgment she takes great pains to appeal to every one of them: some she stares at, others she makes a real place in her heart. Their reactions, ranging from patently ignoring her to bestowing a half wink or crinkled smile, make her feel begrudgingly welcomed. Satisfied, she slides into the pew that she and her husband occupied when they pondered the mysteries of the icons together.

At the front on the church's *templon* is a panoply of the holy. In between life-size paintings of the archangels—Mikhail brandishing a sword and messenger Gabriel—are midsize canvases of Enoch in a chariot of fire, a haloed Christ holding the book of alpha and omega, the Annunciation, and an early archbishop wearing a fur stole symbolizing the beard of Haroun. A minute painting, almost as an afterthought, has been placed down in a corner. It depicts the patron saint of Fadhma's family. Clad in a tatty lion's skin, an emaciated Saint Sabas stoops over, his back not yet broken by the heavy cross he bears.

The desert father was one of many in a seething landscape of divination and revelation. From anonymous hermits to the big headliners of the Bible, seers of esoteric knowledge isolated themselves from women in barren wastes, remote caves, or fortified mountain monasteries. Regardless of their persuasion, Christian, Muslim, and Jew consulted them freely, though there were never enough of them to satisfy demand. Like wild dogs, the monotheistic religions became territorial. At the slightest provocation, tensions erupted over a bit of bone or ill-omened prophecy.

From this central pew she also gazes on the place where her husband's most memorable intercession averted a religious war. A party of workmen had removed some rotted floorboards in the oldest part of the church. Beneath nearly a millennium and a half's worth of debris, an ancient mosaic was discovered, and soon after the village became a pilgrimage site for religious fanatics and archaeologists alike.

From Lebanon to the Nile Delta, the Mediterranean Sea to the Eastern Desert, the oldest surviving map of the Holy Land revealed ancient sites in tiny colored stone tiles. There were the porticoed streets of Jerusalem and the Church of the Holy Sepulchre; palms signifying water around Jericho and a wise oak for Hebron. Greek inscriptions identified Bethlehem, Gaza, Beersheba, and Ashkelon. Fish in the blue tiles of the Jordan River had the good sense to swim away from the Dead Sea, where two fishing boats were not having much luck. The fisherman and Jesus walking on water had been defaced, and bridges crossed the water to the West Bank and a church where John the Baptist baptized his lord.

The map reveals a land undivided by man-made boundaries. Its makers lived when the region was the center of the civilized world, circumscribed by the four rivers of Paradise, long before Columbus and Vasco da Gama sailed out of the Bible's sacred geography and filled charts with new continents and enigmatic oceans. Their world eclipsed the old as completely as the church floor once hid the mosaic.

An old shepherdess came down from Jebel Musa to view the curiosity at the church. She entered tranquil enough but, after a few minutes inside, emerged hysterical. When she was finally able to speak she said the waters in the mosaic flowed with blood. As soon as word reached her, Mother Fadhma retrieved Al Jid from the fields, and he joined the priest in an emergency consultation.

For several hours the two men remained sequestered inside the church. They discussed the prevailing light for that time of day and the effects of temperature variation. On their knees, with an oversize magnifying glass supplied by Abu Za'atar, they inspected the map. Then they interviewed the woman who witnessed the apparition. Inevitably they came to different conclusions.

To the waiting crowd outside, the priest was the first to proclaim, "The age of stupendous miracles is over. I don't dispute that it is possible for the home of blessed Birth Giver Theotokos to be preserved from Saracen defilement by flying from Jerusalem and appearing brick by brick in southern Italy. But our world has changed. The best we can hope for now are small wonders, the sick getting well or the reunification of feuding families. These things I myself have witnessed."

Al Jid passionately disagreed. "God still moves in mysterious ways. If He no longer performs prodigious feats, it's because we as people have lost the imagination to appreciate them. Blind faith is one of many solutions. Read the signs around you closely." He refused to believe that the pinkish glow faintly visible in the mosaic waters was necessarily an optical illusion.

Whatever the conclusion, the mosaic ceased to be a mildly interesting archaeological sideshow and took on the distinction of a full-blown religious phenomenon. As news of the shepherdess's vision spread, a steady stream of pilgrims thronged to the village. Some claimed to see the map bleed; others fell into ecstatic trances when they drew near to it. In the charged atmosphere, sectarian fervor accumulated. The question of ownership of the miracle mosaic assumed tremendous importance.

Sporadic acts of violence broke out among the people who gathered at the church. A militant minority began pressing for the exclusion from the church of all non-Christians, whose mystical revelation demanded it should be declared a mosque. This was countered by vague threats to repossess the mosaic by force. The two sides became progressively more entrenched. There were rumors of weapons being stockpiled. The threat to public order was such that the king dispatched a group of suited officials from the capital to adjudicate the dispute.

The villagers and numerous outsiders who assembled before them were invited to state their cases. For the duration of the public meeting members of the various factions maligned one another's God, with calls for ousting all Christians from the country. The crowd was growing ugly. When Al Jid took his turn, the yelling died down. He began by saying he didn't wish to presume on anyone's patience. "However, if any one person is responsible for the abiding existence of Christians in the Islamic world, it is Umar ibn al-Khattab, the second caliph after the Prophet Muhammad, Peace Be upon Him. Caliph Umar decreed that Christians and Jews should be allowed to practice their religions, and so it is until today."

The officials said nothing, which Al Jid took as a sign to continue: "Even after the conquest, the Muslim soldiers left populations of the two other religions alone. They were protected, *ahl al-thima*. They were not required to convert to Islam; their conquerors did not want them to. It was more profitable to tax the vanquished than to make them change religions. Later still, when the Jews were ousted from fifteenth-century Spain, who gave them refuge but Muslim Turkey? They would be still living among us had not Israel claimed them."

Few dared to call the nation across the river by its name. In the newspapers, it was still referred to as the "hijacked country" or, if the official name had to be published, government censors blacked it out. Propaganda considerations required that the proper designation never be used—something nameless was more difficult to empathize with. While shocked voices rose in the crowd, the officials remained indifferent.

Al Jid began again: "History has shown that Islam has embraced non-Muslims, and sometimes the situation has been reversed. The Prophet Himself, may God forgive us all, fled Mecca during the Hijra and lived among the Arab and Jewish tribes of Medina. Certainly the Qur'an recounts subsequent disputes with those same tribes, but wise and all knowing that the Prophet was, never once did he tell his followers, 'Deny *ahl al-kitab*, the People of the Book, the right to live and worship.'"

His voice rose above the tremor of assent running through the crowd. "Islam is a great religion made greater by its tolerance and love of the poor, no matter their religious persuasion." He directed his next words to his community. "Should not our own Christian tribes remember this and graciously return the favor? If our neighbor is threatened, should we not come to their aid? If evil befalls them, surely it is only a matter of time when it knocks on our doors. We have more in common than we think."

Afterward there were congratulations all around. Fifty lambs were slaughtered, and Mother Fadhma and the women of the village cooked and served a feast to which they were not invited. The problem was ignored and that was how it was solved.

As Mother Fadhma sorts through her memories, another mosaic comes to mind. She never saw it herself, but Al Jid's mother, Sabet, spied it as a young widow, after the Christian tribes from the fortress town in the south came and fought for the crumbling Byzantine ruins in the mountains. Near the end of her life, Sabet described it in detail to her second daughter-in-law.

Vividly colored, the mosaic was of a beautiful woman, bare-breasted, with dark flowing hair. She reclined on an opulent bed, with a graceful hand against her forehead. Notwithstanding a long flowing skirt, her *fitna*—sexual danger—was on display. Audaciously her eyes followed anyone in the room looking at her. Sabet had been adamant: there were other mosaics of women with bejewelled breasts that the Christian tribes unearthed in ruined Byzantine palaces and houses. Those images, like that of Christ in the church mosaic, were considered so dangerous that an outraged male hand defaced them, ostensibly to save an innocent world from everlasting damnation.

Sabet also speaks to Fadhma across the threshold of life and death, and her advice is more straightforward than her son's. She often comes to Fadhma in church, and today is no different: "Believe what you like, but every Omar, Abdullah, and Ahmad has a saint on a family tree, where the names of only the men have been recorded for posterity. Where are the mothers, daughters, grandmothers, sisters, aunts, and cousins? Our family history is like so many others. Five Muslim brothers walked out of Egypt. To eat, live, and survive, some of them switched religions. People must be deluded if they think God notices or cares."

Fadhma has never once disagreed with her forthright mother-in-law in this world or the next. But now, with so many troubles of her own, she would prefer to pray for salvation alone by herself.

16

"No way!"

Muna wants to stop sounding like a stupid American, but her trip is turning out stranger than she imagined. She and Samira are deep in conversation on the front terrace, with Fuad playing with a toy car at their feet.

"Okay, sleeveless blouses I get, even if I don't agree. But pigs?" Muna says disbelievingly. "The law dates back to a time when there were no refrigerators. They were not 'unclean'; you could have died from eating them. I mean, what would the Filipinos do without pork?"

She can almost hear her mother laughing contemptuously. "Why do you want to go to Jordan?" She made no effort to hide her disapproval, after her daughter broke the news of her trip over the phone. "For God's sake, don't stand out," her mother stressed. "They hate their own people. Who knows how they will react to a stranger."

"I'm not a stranger, Mamma."

"We can talk about that after you get back."

Muna's mother had never been keen on her husband's large family. Muna never knew of their existence until she was five years old. One day she was arranging the pretty stones near the married students' quarters. A man in a suit and tie approached her and said, "I'm your uncle Boutros."

"I've never had an uncle before." She took his hand and led him to her parents' apartment.

Her father was proud. Later at bedtime, as Muna's hair was being bobby-pinned into tight little curls, her mother threatened to poison the new uncle.

On Sundays when his wife was studying, Abd often borrowed a friend's car and drove his daughter through the flat midwestern landscape, occasionally stopping by the roadside to pick wild tiger lilies. Once they left the car hidden in a lane and made their way into a wheat field. Her father urged her to keep up. Obscured by the tall plants, he gathered up two armfuls and they walked back through the slowly lengthening shadows.

By their car waited an old farmer in denim overalls and a straw hat. He accused Abd of stealing wheat, then calmed down once Muna's father described the arid fields of his youth. He explained, "I just wanted to show my little girl how lucky she is."

The farmer spat out whatever he was chewing. "In America you get more than you bargained for." His voice crackled like the wheat stalks roasting over the fire her father lit in a garbage can at home. While the stalks cooked in aluminum foil, he distracted Muna from the heat by making the leaves sing. The two blades of grass in between his thumbs, laid against his mouth and blown into, made a trumpeting noise. By the time she managed to copy him, the stalks in the fire were blackened. These were rubbed before another puff from her *baba* scattered the chaff. The remaining seeds tasted burned and crunchy in her mouth.

At night, two scratched LPs were stacked under the automatic arm of a secondhand record player. First there was a selection from Fairouz, then Rimsky-Korsakov's *Scheherazade*. The violent crashing cymbals always frightened Muna—it was the same sensation of dread she felt whenever she overheard her parents arguing—but the romantic interlude of the violins that followed never failed to send her off to sleep.

After her father found work with a large plastics company in the next state, the family moved. This house had a porch with a rusted swinging chair and a fence in the shape of a musical scale with notes that ran down to the sidewalk. There was a yard with two plum trees and a garage that backed onto a wall behind a local YMCA, where Muna and her girlfriends spied on teenagers making out after Friday night dances. As more of Abd's brothers and sisters immigrated to Ohio with their spouses and children, they settled in rambling, run-down houses in the same working-class neighborhood. From the homes of her relatives came the sounds of babies crying and the TV on too loud and a strong smell of meat cooking.

It was a rough neighborhood. On the first day of junior high school Muna made friends with the fattest, meanest girl in her class to get through the informal system of segregation enforced by students, who established separate entrances for black and white. By then she had outgrown fairy tales, and her sister became the main beneficiary of her father's bedtime stories. Over the years his focus shifted away from the land to the stern but benevolent figure of Al Jid. Abd regretted that his daughters never met the old man, so he tried to make him alive for them by fashioning a mythical version of his life, one free from hardship. As an awkward preteen, Muna hid in the shadow of her sister's doorway and listened, half entranced, half skeptical. The landscape of her father's imagination was difficult to reconcile with the nastier comments of her mother and the stark images of the Iraq War presented on the TV news. When her father's half sister Hind moved in with them and was placed a grade behind because of her English, Muna refused to walk to school with her.

The families of her aunts and uncles were different from her own. Her aunts spoiled their husbands and sons. Muna suspected that her father would have preferred similar treatment, but her mother, a sociologist, wasn't about to stay at home and bake baklava. At her relatives', the regulation of their daughters, the suspicion of outsiders—including Muna's mother—and the ritual slaughtering of lambs in the garages were at odds with American culture. While this should have united the brothers, misunderstandings over money and feuding spouses kept them apart. During the rare occasions the entire family got together, punches sometimes flew in front of bewildered sisters, wives, and children.

Muna's mother resented Abd's family. All the brothers, bar her husband, married cousins from the old country, a custom she regarded as backward. Since she didn't speak Arabic she was bored in their company. An immigrant herself, she had come to the States to avoid the kind of family commitments her husband seemed intent on embracing. The opportunity to cast off outmoded values was one she was not going to permit herself or her daughters to miss. As she and Abd rose in their respective professions, she participated fully in the American dream, moving from the inner city to suburbia, giving dinner parties, and voting Republican, even after the start of the 2003 Iraq War.

Despite outward appearances, Muna's home life remained turbulent. Caught between the old and the new, her father would have never forced his eldest daughter into an arranged marriage, but there were always distant cousins in the offering. Without her mother's support, Muna would have never made it to New York City. On finding out that she had been accepted to a liberal arts college there, her father threw a chair through a patio window. In a single wink of an eye, Muna's mother showed her daughter that independence was a process of negotiation, one in which her mother had the upper hand. All along she had been standing like barbed wire around Muna and her sister, protecting them from their father's conservatism.

Having escaped the restrictive atmosphere of her family, in New York Muna was more concerned with exploiting her new freedom than with identifying with the past. However, as she made new friends and became more familiar with the city, she was inevitably asked about her background. Much of the anti-Arab bias she encountered was based on what she was perceived to be, and she was quizzed, sometimes unpleasantly, about her Arab family, Islam, and terrorism. This gave her insight into her father. He had idealized his old life because he must have found himself at times unwelcomed in America. His florid descriptions of country and family—part love, part denial—were a way of reclaiming an inheritance that he abandoned. Her father was sentimental—something she promised herself she would not be.

As the Arab Awakening erupted on television screens and Muna watched the news obsessively, she felt ashamed for never believing in the region. She begged her father to let her visit Jordan, but when caution prevailed she began her own tentative investigation, even going so far as attending a meeting of the college's Islamic Students' Union. It didn't matter that they weren't Christians like her family. Her younger cousins who attended the Orthodox Church camp every summer would not have understood, but Muna wanted to go at least once.

During a well-publicized event, a foreign scholar was addressing the Islamic Students' Union on the authority and authenticity of the Hadiths. Muna arrived early and sat on the left side of the auditorium. One by one the seats around her were taken by male students, a few of whom, she noticed, glared in her direction; across the aisle a young woman nodded and smiled, seemingly welcoming her. Only after the lecture began did she realize her blunder: the men and women in the audience were sitting separately, and she was on the wrong side. She should have taken a place among the women, the majority in head-scarves. Muna was dressed in her usual outfit for class—thick purple lipstick and skinny jeans.

Their distinguished guest, an expert in Islamic jurisprudence, explained that the Hadiths were considered secondary to the direct revelation of God in the Qur'an but also formed the basis for Islamic family law. During his lifetime the Prophet had been a man under constant scrutiny. After his death his words and deeds were collected, first orally and then in writing. Each Hadith was authenticated through *isnad*, a chain of transmission, that could be traced over the course of two hundred years to a reliable source, either his wives or companions. As the scholar discussed the different collections of Imam Malik Ibn Anas and Muhammad al-Bukhari, and al-Tabari's *The History of Prophets and Kings*, Muna took notes.

At the end there were questions. After several innocuous exchanges, a Southeast Asian student stated, "When the Prophet Muhammad was asked whether a bowl of soup should be eaten after a fly landed in it, he said yes, because on the fly's one wing is the germ and on the other the cure. That's scientifically untrue."

The scholar was unperturbed. "On the contrary, Muslim scientists have done their own research. The Prophet is correct."

True believers murmured their assent to this vindication; the less committed were unconvinced at such a triumph of faith over logic.

Muna was irresistibly reminded of the old joke—"Waiter, waiter, there's a fly in my soup"—and wondered whether scholar and student missed the point. The Hadith wasn't about insects but hunger in seventh-century Arabia and food waste. As she was leaving, Muna came face-to-face with the bearded scholar, who scowled at her, the woman who had the audacity to sit among men.

Muna, flustered, apologized. "I didn't want to move and disrupt the lecture."

"What does someone like you know about our religion and culture?" His voice was filled with loathing. "Stay among your own people."

"*Khalik maa'na shaabunah*—among my own people?" Muna's minimal Arabic was direct enough. She walked off, disturbed by his suggestion that she didn't fit in and never would.

Outside, the woman who had been trying to get Muna's attention at the lecture was waiting. The two of them ended up laughing about the fly. On learning Muna's background she was insistent: "You must visit Jordan." Muna appreciated her companion's generosity of spirit and mentally started preparing for a trip she had been waiting for since the occupation of Tahrir Square. The trip would prove if her mother was right, that the Middle East was insular and stuck in the past, or if the situation was far more complex. Either way, Muna knew it wasn't going to be easy.

Her doubts increased after her flight landed in Amman and she stepped outside the airport and was met by large groups of watching, waiting men. Some were in uniform, others in T-shirts and jackets, with many more in traditional robes. A few women in abayas were scattered in the crowd. Intimidated, Muna hid behind a pair of wing-tipped sunglasses.

A kindly face detached itself from the crowd and floated toward her. A middle-aged man in a suit and starched white shirt politely shook her hand, introducing himself as Mr. Ibrahim. She was unsure whether she understood him correctly, even though he spoke in flawless, albeit heavily accented, English.

"Muna, I was with your father and mother in Cleveland last week, and I promised to pick you up from the airport and take you to your uncle's house."

In a daze she followed him to a waiting car. Mr. Ibrahim explained that he'd known her father since their school days. They lost touch after Abd emigrated. In time, Mr. Ibrahim began traveling to the United States on business, and a mutual friend put them back in touch. Muna's father never mentioned this man, but his affable manner and familiarity with her family put Muna at ease.

As they drove across the capital, she examined the cramped lanes edged with stores and tea shops through the car window. On some street corners boys hawked lighters and cartons of cigarettes. It was midafternoon, and many people were hurrying home like rush hour in New York. Abruptly the car turned into an area devoid of pedestrians, deathly quiet except for dogs picking through the roadside garbage. The quarter had already closed for lunch and was filled with stalls and garages devoted to car parts and scrap metal. They drove down one lane filled only with headlights, joined the highway, and left the city behind.

As they passed an ancient Roman milestone inscribed with the names of towns and their distances, as accurate today as it had been two thousand years ago, Mr. Ibrahim asked the purpose of her visit.

"I want to see my father's country and meet the family. Anything beyond that, I'm not sure."

"People come here with preconceived notions." He advised her, "Give it time and what you need will find you."

Muna had no idea that one form it would take was of a pig.

"Stupid or not," Samira tells her, "the town is upset with Hussein, but my friends don't care. We have more important things to worry about. Imagine, for some sexual slavery and murder are more acceptable than pigs and the unveiled. Umm al-Muharramat, Mother of All Forbiddens!"

Muna mentions the driver who took her to the airport in New York. "It's curious what causes offense. After I told him I was going to visit family in Jordan, he said he was Afghan, married to his cousin, with two girls in kindergarten. Then he admitted his greatest fear: the day his daughters come home from high school and say they have boyfriends.

"He said he would rather go back to Kabul and raise his daughters in seclusion. For him, his daughters' lives are not as important as their virginity." She makes a V sign with her fingers and taps her forehead. "At least they're safe from a war. You'd think he would be grateful for that."

"And how grateful should he be after the English, the Russians, *and* the Americans wrecked his country?" demands Samira.

"No, you're right. But not everyone has been able to get out of Afghanistan, and this cabbie isn't having difficulty adjusting to the American dream because of his daughters. Every time we passed a blond woman on the street, he looked like he was ready to jump out of the car and eat her alive. When I see this stuff played out in front of me, it makes me think about Baba as a teenager arriving in the US with only five dollars in his pocket and a college scholarship. I really wanted to ask Abu Salih about condoms. But if Mother Fadhma thought I was being rude she would have hit the roof."

"Condoms?!" It is Samira's turn to be surprised.

"After New York, Baba and Abu Salih took this Greyhound bus to Greenville, Illinois." Muna goes on to explain that her eighteen-year-old father needed to urinate, and Salih, who spoke the better English, described his friend's predicament to a traveling salesman sitting nearby. The man gave Abd a rubber, told him to go to the back where no one could see him, relieve himself in it, tie it up, and throw it out the window.

"Baba and Abu Salih had never seen a condom before and didn't know what it was for. The salesman told them and made them repeat the word until they could pronounce it properly. Welcome to America!"

Muna drops another bombshell. "After telling me that story, Baba said if I was still a virgin at twenty-two, then something was wrong. And this came after years of getting at me about boys—like Laila's mom. Culturally my parents are a million miles apart from each other. Mom never cared about having children, much less sons. She was Catholic-lite but that didn't mean she believed in divorce or abortion. However, the one place she and my father did agree was my honor and respectability. So when Dad talked about my virginity, I was pretty speechless."

Samira is beside herself. "You mean my upstanding brother advocates premarital sex?"

"This is from the guy I thought would bury me in the backyard if, God forbid, contraception failed and I came home pregnant." Muna is as baffled as her Jordanian cousin. "What do you think he was telling me?"

"He has a secret life?"

As both women consider the implications, Muna abruptly changes the subject; maybe there are some things that shouldn't be discussed with the relatives. Instead, she asks, "Samira, why didn't you come and live in the US? You must have been tempted."

Her cousin makes a half-hearted joke: "I couldn't leave the loves of my life—my mother and my country." There is another reason, which she never discusses with anyone, but Muna isn't like everyone else. "When Mamma was pregnant with me, Al Jid received a letter from one of the brothers saying it was shameful that Fadhma was still having children at the same time he and his wife were starting their family."

"You mean they objected to an old married couple having sex?" Muna grimaces again. "By their standards, I must be sex crazy. It's the double standards for women I can't stand. We come from such a repressed family."

Whenever Fadhma recounted the story to her daughter, the moral was that Samira should be grateful for her existence. The anecdote also had a more subtle effect. "You can see why I never went to America. My family wasn't going to welcome me." Samira smiles, but she's not happy. It is a subject she doesn't like to dwell on.

Muna is pushing the toy car toward Fuad when "Zourouni" by Fairouz erupts from Samira's cell phone.

"It's a miracle anything gets through!" When Samira doesn't recognize the number she becomes instantly apologetic—"I need to take this"—and hurries into the house. "Hello?"

At the other end a woman asks for her by name. Samira can't place the voice, but once she confirms that she is speaking, the woman gets straight to the point: "A letter is waiting for you to pick up."

The minimum amount of information is conveyed: a designated time and place. It is the arrangements for the letter's delivery afterward that are unusual. Normally Samira meets a member from the women's committee or delivers to a trusted location. Instead the caller tells her that someone, unspecified for now, will contact her this evening. The details are frustratingly vague.

She keeps her reservations to herself. "*Naam*—yes," she understands. "Of course... not a problem," she reaffirms again. After hanging up, she checks her phone; she has time before she needs to leave the house. Because of Fuad she has to wait for her mother or Laila to return. Or she could ask Muna to babysit. Samira rejects the idea outright. Her cousin can be put to better uses. She is the decoy who ensures freedom of movement. When Samira started working for the committee, Zeinab advised her, "Turn left when you want to turn right, double back when you're sure nobody is watching." In Muna's company, Samira can go where she pleases without having to worry or explain. She just needs to make sure that her intuition is not wrong and her cousin can be relied upon.

Samira returns to the terrace. "I have to run a political errand this evening. Want to come?"

"Sure." Muna is game for anything; she doesn't think her Jordanian cousin would be involved in anything too dangerous. "What group are you working for?" Muna asks.

"A women's committee," Samira begins slowly, "that is part of a larger organization operating in Jordan. It's not the most active in terms of the humanitarian crisis, but it is effective politically and helps women. Remember when the Syrian revolution first began? It was a peaceful movement."

Muna is intrigued. "So why did it change?"

"I asked my friend Zeinab that same question," admits Samira. "She said soldiers entering towns and villages were raping women in front of their husbands and sons. In our committee some of the women have been raped or their daughters have been threatened with rape or forced marriage."

She's just getting warmed up. "I don't understand people's reactions to the hundreds of thousands of dead and the millions of Syrians leaving the country. The numbers alone are large enough for the violence to be condemned, but all you get are people like—"

Muna butts in. "Umm Omar."

"Why can't she and others like her understand that Sunni Syrians desperately need help and some of them have turned to the better-armed Islamic fronts. Not every Muslim fighting for their survival is committing Christian genocide. That's what Assad did in the beginning. Those who opposed him, with or without a gun, were labeled terrorists."

Muna raises a critical eyebrow. "It's a mess that won't go away like the others."

"Millions of people," argues Samira, "don't abandon their homes and run from nothing. And if they can't escape, they send their children on a four-thousand-mile hike to Europe. Shouldn't that count for something?"

"It should," agrees Muna. "But people in my part of the world disengage, particularly from the actions of governments in the Middle East. The Internet has turned all of us into isolated consumers. People watch and download what they like and ignore the rest. So there's a refugee crisis—oh, I can buy a bikini."

Her explanation doesn't impress Samira, who scoffs, "At least there are some of us who do care."

"I wonder where someone like me fits in?" Muna surveys the wooden lean-to on the roof next door, which provides shelter for the empty cushions and chairs from the sun. "For most of my life I've been too mixed for the Arabs, and before ethnic diversity became fashionable in the US, I was too odd for them too."

Samira can't believe that she has been talking about the incredibly desperate situation in Syria and Muna's reaction is to think about herself. It is as Zeinab has maintained all along: the privileged are always the ones who feel the most unfairly treated. Samira tries not to show her irritation. "And what do you say to those who don't accept of you?"

After a pause Muna replies, "*Anna mish ghareebeh*—I am not a stranger." She points to herself. "This is the face of the modern Middle East—mixed on the outside and the inside."

"Mixed on the outside and inside? I don't get it."

"I am the Arab who would rather be a daughter than a son," declares Muna. "I refuse to be sacrificed on the altar of family. In short, I am the liberator of myself."

Her words break the tension and Samira joins in. "I'm not mixed on the outside but inside—if the truth be known—I'm upside down." What seems like the first time in ages, the two young women laugh together.

Her usual chores—feeding, grooming, and exercising the children and generally walking about, inspecting perimeters—went without mishap, despite a feeling of unease that grew stronger by the hour.

In the evening, she refused the last feed. Not even the feral cat, which appeared unexpectedly on the farm and stalked Umm al-Khanaazeer's favorite mouse holes, was allowed near her. Usually the two of them communed when she was lying on her side at night. The feline fell onto the pig's enormous bulk and rolled gently against her in an exchange of mutual satisfaction.

Although she had been able to mask her anxiety from her children, it was harder to hide it from Ahmad, who had been observing her moving hay around her pen as though uncertain as to which pile would be more comfortable. With a warm bottle of formula milk, he moved from baby to baby. He knew her well. He was responsible for cleaning and disinfecting her. He assisted her during birth and made sure she took her vitamins and laxatives. Afterward he tried calling Hussein again. "She's not at her best," He had been trying to get through to him since the afternoon. "Maybe tomorrow's better. I might stay on just to make sure."

Human visitors to the farm no longer slept in the barn; there was a pullout cot in the processing block, so Ahmad contented himself by building a small fire outside, drawing a woolen blanket woven by his wife around himself, and periodically checking the barn. Once he saw that Umm al-Khanaazeer had finally settled, he pulled the barn doors shut and went to bed.

She was having another of those dreams; there was no mistaking her own rot and disgust. Before dawn she peered out through the bars of the pen, half expecting to find her old adversary, the crate, waiting. What was making her feel this way? Her anxiety and fear caught a whiff of him before she saw him. As the doors slid open, she crouched down, trying to hide. But when he walked dangerously near a pen of gilts, her heart rate tripled, her bristles stood on end. Squealing, screaming, and charging, she shook the bars of her enclosure. The god-awful racket brought Ahmad running from his chores.

"Strangers aren't allowed in here." Then he took another look. "Why it's Hani, no? Abu Za'atar's friend?"

The two men shook hands.

"That's my girl," said the torturer, pointing at the sow.

The pacing pig kept her poor eyesight on him. When Ahmad opened the hatch to the outdoors, she waited until every one of her babies, even the smallest runt, went into the yard. None of them was going with this killer. Thankfully Hani had business of his own. After the arrival of Hussein and Abu Za'atar, the three of them were absorbed with the equipment on his truck. To celebrate his long-standing friendship with the old man, Hani had brought new technology for the farm. Periodically during the installation and testing of the sausage-making Wurstmeister machine, Hani showed up at the fence, and Umm al-Khanaazeer was forced to round up her piglets and get them behind her. Not one was she giving up. After payments were made and he drove off down the mountain, she celebrated by strutting with the family in the yard. It would be a short-lived victory parade.

A mother knows her children by smell no matter their numbers. She was growing them around her and she loved each and every one of them. Some were more needy than others, and others raged out of control. The larger the boars grew, the more aggressive they became, before castration. These ill-tempered progeny could no longer be in the company of their brothers, and if they were housed with her or the girls, they became a terrible nuisance, with one thing—copulation—on their minds. So she and her daughters lived by themselves, sometimes with the smaller piglets, in the other pens, which kept multiplying. The barn had grown into a small city. Before the arrival of Hani and his machine, a few went missing, but usually this happened in the run-up to giving birth, when hormones forced her attention inward. Now there was no mistaking the empty pens in the barn where many of the older boars, her boys, had once been kept.

Ahmad's eldest son had started coming regularly to the farm. His work, it seemed, was confined to the buildings around back, and whenever he came into the barn for tools he paid her scant attention. He was interested only in the boars and was too free with the electric prod for Umm al-Khanaazeer's liking. It was then she noticed the body-length rubber apron he wore and the sharp long knives in his pocket. He took out boars that never returned. The rancid smell of his bloodstained apron made her retch. Her suspicions were aroused but she was still unsure why.

She didn't pay any attention to the cluster of low buildings behind the barn; they were too far away for her to see and a wall was being built around them. But Abu Za'atar, the architect of the wall's placement and design, had been in the barn, reading from a raft of Internet printouts when he glanced down at her.

"Now I understand why pork, as tender as it is sweet, never became a popular meat," he announced to Umm al-Khanaazeer. "When the early Arabs slaughtered your ancestors, they thought the animals dumb. But pigs are smart: the stress of seeing one of your own kind killed releases a hormone that poisons the meat." He teased her, "People don't mind eating something cleverer than they are, but it has to taste nice."

The wall, which was supposed to shield her from a terrible knowledge, made matters worse.

Eventually the stress of her murdered sons entered Umm al-Khanaazeer's heart and the infection spread to her brain, until all she could smell were bespoke hams, spiced sausages, and the bloody corpses of murdered children. A loving pig became moody and belligerent. Suddenly the demands on her body were too great. With so many babies underfoot, needing her attention, sucking up her life's blood, there was not one she trusted to survive Ahmad's son and the electric prod. She turned nasty before feeding, and the cleanli-

ness she prided herself on started to slip. Nothing gave her pleasure or rest. During the day or night, waking or sleeping, she was gripped by horrific nightmares. Only Hussein, who artificially impregnated her, and Ahmad, devoted to her care, wondered about this change in her behavior.

17

The final piece of Al Jid's legacy lies at the end of a dirt track in a fold between three hills. The secluded location makes it ideal for pig rearing. Nobody is likely to come up here, but that's not the reason Hussein chose to keep this part of his father's land. What makes it special is the tiny spring, which collects in a cleft at the base of the hills.

The spring was always there, only Hussein didn't know about it. Shortly after leaving the army, he engaged the services of a water diviner. He had not yet decided to sell his father's farmland and was desperate to find ways to make it more profitable. For five days he trailed behind a wizened old fellow who methodically walked over every inch of ground, holding the two ends of a Y-shaped branch. Several times the stick twitched, but these were false alarms. On the last day they went up to Al Jid's most inhospitable parcel. As soon as they arrived, the diviner's eyes lit up. Without even using his implement, he marched purposefully over to a low pile of rock and rubble. "Dig here," he commanded, and withdrew to the shade of a bush where he sat with his arms folded.

Hussein removed the boulders. Only a few inches below the surface, water began to seep into a shallow depression, and by the time he excavated a basin three feet deep it was filling rapidly. He carefully lined the hole with stones and came to regard it as a shrine to his father's memory. When he sold off most of Al Jid's property, he never once thought of getting rid of the seventy dunams surrounding the spring.

"My father would have thought this nothing short of a miracle."

Hussein is standing with Mustafa by the stones and a trickle of water. Taking the soldier's bags between them, they have taken the path opposite the farm buildings toward an outlying rocky crop. Mustafa doesn't look entirely at home in civvies, but he will no doubt grow into them, notes Hussein, as they start negotiating an ever-steepening track. They eventually stop at the lone terebinth tree, beneath whose spindly boughs Hussein's father once kept a vigil during a rainless season. Family and friends begged Al Jid to quit his fasting and take at the very least some water, but his answer was always the same. The parched land was a test sent by God alone. He cited the irascible Saint Sabas, who put his hands against heaven and each finger burst into a miraculous flame.

"My father really did believe it was a matter of conviction. Water would come if he prayed hard enough. And it did." No matter how many times Hussein turns it over in his mind, he is not so much surprised by the event but by the maliciousness of nature. "Thunder broke over Jebel Musa and turned into a deluge. Al Jid danced for joy but was humiliated by the ensuing flash floods." Hussein is momentarily lost. The story always leaves him with no resolution.

He and Mustafa gaze down on the terraced fields Al Jid once plowed, now scraggly and underutilized; his hectares on the town's edge lying fallow will in time fall to developers' bulldozers. Near and far, the arid steppe and the mountains running alongside the river valley change color from brown to gray, purple, and gold in the bright sunlight and shadows. Mustafa takes in the tranquil scene with a deep breath. "He sounds like a man of deep and abiding belief."

But that, Hussein feels, is never enough. "You could say he spent his whole life battling injustice. My father was convinced if there was a Promised Land, then there was also a land denied."

Hussein doesn't have to spell it out. The contrast between the mountainous scrub and patched greenery on the east bank and the pastures of plenty on the other side is like an insult or a dare. Faced with such an obstacle, most men would have submitted to nature. However, Al Jid was a realist who was in many ways a fool.

"It had been my father's mission to make this side of the river remember."

Every day without fail, Al Jid left home hours before dawn and returned after dark. Fatigued oftentimes to the breaking point, he never completely gave up. The year his fortunes finally changed, the rains arrived early. He had seen other promising starts end in disaster, so he carried on as usual, expecting the worst. Throughout the season the weather continued to be clement, and the fields turned green, but still he did not allow himself to rest. When harvest came he found that, after a lifetime of clinging to a precarious subsistence, he finally had enough to feed his family, with a small surplus left over to sell. There were plenty of things to spend the money on—the children's clothes were threadbare and their old house of mud brick and stone in desperate need of repair—but Al Jid had plans of his own.

Education had been a lifelong passion. In a fit of self-improvement, he taught himself to read and write. He came to believe that all roads, whether that of the caravan or the colonizer, passed through the Middle East. The region nurtured the earliest stirrings of civilization and had given rise to religions that ruled the world. People carried faith in their hearts, and this was the basis for morality, which survived only because of farming that began thousands of years ago in the fields and plains all around them, when animals were herded and the first seeds were sown.

Al Jid prided himself on an erudite knowledge of religion and history, although he realized that if his sons were ever to be free from the tyranny of the land they needed a more pragmatic wisdom. The European powers, which had dominated since the fall of the Ottoman Empire, were withdrawing, and the consequent reshaping of the political map could not be predicted with any accuracy. The educated might survive, while the ignorant would only continue suffering. The family's lifeline wasn't the land the old man fought and tamed but the children he educated and insisted on sending overseas.

Hussein never analyzed his father's motives too deeply; he had been too preoccupied with rebelling against them. Now, in the company of the fatherless soldier, he feels compelled to talk about Al Jid and his life.

"He was determined that all his sons would do well. When my brothers and I came of age, he picked our respective fields—science, business, engineering, medicine, the military, commerce, property and retail. To be honest, I wasn't keen on the army, but good men like you and your brother made my time there worthwhile." Sweating, he puts down the soldier's duffel bag; he is that out of shape. "And when I retired I vowed not to take on any of my father's battles."

The natural trajectory of the path descends to a distant ravine, and then it's a steep few miles to the bottom and the town. Instead, Hussein lifts Mustafa's duffel bag, shoves it onto a ledge above them, and then scrambles up after it. A few feet away he climbs through a tight opening in the rock and waits for Mustafa to push his bags through to him. Once these are on the other side, Mustafa comes through the gap, which widens onto another rocky promontory. Hussein has his own reason for familiarizing the soldier with the terrain around the farm, which he hints at: "You already know from your time in the field, preparation is the first line of defense."

The bags are left beside a series of irregularly shaped openings in the rock, some rabbit-size, others large enough for four men. They enter one of the larger ones where the air is motionless and dry. Hussein lights a cigarette. "We're not so far away from Jebel Musa and the monastery. When the number of hermits overran their cells, they migrated to some of the caves around here. In one, I discovered a wooden cup and bowl, not much of a reward for a life spent on your knees in prayer."

He gestures toward the dark heart of the cave. "If you follow it around, always heading downward, there is a way of coming back out on the path we just left, which doubles back toward the ravine. If you don't lose your way, after eight miles you'll reach the town. It's not a walk I'd do in the dark, but it's not impossible."

Hussein makes one of his sad jokes again. "The trouble with the army, it gets you ready or gets you scared. I keep a few things here just in case." He pulls back a rock near the entrance and shows Mustafa a cloth sack and its contents: a working flashlight, a rope, a lighter, a candle, and a plastic bottle of water. "And I'm not the only one," he points out. "I found a pile of women's robes in one of the other caves and I put them in here too." He shines the flashlight into the interior. The light glances off the side onto a pile of rocks, behind which is another bundle.

The soldier nods. "You never know what comes in handy."

They understand each other. Working together, they stow the bags again out of sight behind the rocks, bathed in the glow of afternoon light coming in through the cave's entrance. Outside, a sweep of rock hits a blunt blue sky. It is a majestic view that once inspired prophets and desert fathers.

"You can feel God," says Mustafa.

"Sure," Hussein is non-committal, although he wonders what is more phantasmagorical, the fingers of a saint catching fire or a diviner's rod that uncovers water by default. He throws his cigarette on the ground and maneuvers himself through the opening in the rocks, then along the ledge and down. As they retrace their steps, Hussein formulates a plan: he will take the soldier to the barn and show him what will alienate him forever or provide another colorful anecdote for his travels home.

At the spring on the path to the farm, Hussein picks up the sound of a car engine straining on the mountain. He can tell almost to the second when it leaves the smooth asphalt and turns onto the rough dirt track toward the farm. Around the second bend, by the low buildings crammed into the narrow valley between the steep hillsides, one of the dilapidated taxis from town pulls into view.

Ahmad is already outside the barn, calling to him. Glimpsing the car's unlikely occupants, Hussein quickens his step. "Take Mustafa inside," he instructs his farm manager. The soldier will have to make up his own mind. His ex-commander is required elsewhere.

"Mikhail, welcome!" Hussein reaches in through the open window of the cab to shake the driver's hand. He doesn't have to ask;

he can tell something's up. Laila rarely comes to the farm these days. He expects her and the boys to tell him, but the three sit perfectly still. When he opens the front door, his dishevelled sons tumble into his arms. He regards his wife.

"They were in a fight," she says.

Hussein inspects Mansoor's black eye. "Fair assessment."

At the sound of their father's voice, the children start sobbing, and as Hussein consoles them, Laila gets out of the taxi and pays Mikhail. But before the driver leaves, Hussein motions over his sons' heads for him to wait. After he disengages himself from the boys, he goes into the processing block, where Ahmad and Mustafa are taking tea together. The soldier looks fine. Jihad is more treacherous than the whirring Wurstmeister. Hussein returns to the service taxi, carrying a string of sausages wrapped in wax paper. "For your wife, Mikhail. I know she is fond of them."

The driver, clearly pleased, bids Hussein and his family goodbye: *"Ma' al-salameh."*

Hussein regards his sons sternly. He expects the appropriate polite response no matter how badly they feel. "And what do you say?"

"Bi salam Allah," the boys answer respectfully through their sniffles.

As the car reverses along the track that eventually leads to the road, Hussein stands with his children and waves. He then takes them over to a large, flat rock, where they sit down. Gently he probes Mansoor's face where the skin is soft and tender. "Was it about the farm?"

They don't answer. He repeats his question but Mansoor and Salem avoid his eye. Hussein pleads with wife. "Honestly, Laila, tell them it's not worth fighting over pigs."

She throws up her hands. "Why not? Everybody wants to!"

There is an edge of panic in her voice that worries Hussein. He puts his hand on his sons' shoulders and says, "Boys, go and find Ahmad—he's in the processing block by the sausage machine. Ask him if Umm al-Khanaazeer has had her new piglets."

The hesitant children start off slowly but are running and laughing by the time they reach the processing block. Laila sits down on

the rock beside her husband and opens the food bag. There is tabbouleh and sliced meat in a plastic container, bread wrapped in a
napkin, and a quantity of fruit. She offers it to Hussein. "Your mother is better equipped to deal with a crisis than I am. If you relied on
me, there would be nothing to eat but grass. Then," she adds glumly,
"we'd all be as dumb as sheep, if we're not already."

Hussein, a little perplexed by her words, takes an apple, but after
rolling it around in his fingers for a few seconds, he returns it to the
bag. "I'm not hungry. This business with the boys is not the only occurrence of the day." He describes his past couple of hours at length,
including the appearance of the soldier Mustafa. He even makes
Laila laugh when he describes Abu Za'atar's crazy antics. "All in
all"—he shakes his head—"it's been most illuminating."

"That's not a word you normally use." Laila is scrutinizing him
closely, but he knows his eyes are clear and his breath doesn't smell
as strongly as it normally does by late afternoon.

"I feel like someone, and not Mrs. Habash, is trying to tell me
something," he jokes. He wants to lighten the mood as much for his
sake as hers.

She responds sarcastically, "Husband, I can tell you exactly who
it is. Guess if you can." Stroking movements with one hand under
her chin represents a beard, while the other sweeping across her
forehead indicates a turban. "He gave the khutbah at the mosque
today."

Despite their problems, Hussein finds himself smiling. "No,
that's not what I mean. There have been too many signs of late. It's
clear to me now that if I carry on the way I have been it will lead
to disaster, but it's not just me: the family, the farm, all of us must
change."

Intrigued by her husband's seriousness and sobriety, Laila nods
in agreement. "Separately the two of us have come to the same conclusion. What are we going to do, Hussein?" She lays her hand on
top of his, but he makes no move to take it.

"I don't know. I have to think more about it, but sooner or later
I will be forced into a decision. I only hope there is enough time to
make the right one for us." He takes his wife's hand and caresses the

soft skin with his thumb. "Tell me truthfully, Laila, have we all that we need? Are we lacking in anything? The house is filled, the children well fed. Many people could not say the same. Look at Mikhail." Hussein hopes she will immediately understand that many of the town's families survive on little. "Can you be happy with what we have and expect nothing more?"

He has never before spoken to her so honestly, and she is touched by the genuine nature of his concern. In the past she took it for granted that his motives were as selfish as hers. Now she realizes he has been thinking about her and the family all along. He has even placed them above his own happiness. She cannot believe that through her neglect she has acted so badly toward the only man who has treated her well. Everything, even the putrid stink of the farm, melts away. All she can see is Hussein's face. For the first time in many months she feels a stirring of desire for her husband and, leaning forward, she kisses him tenderly on the lips.

He puts his arm around her and she leans against him. "We have our health and our children," he says. "What more can we expect?"

It occurs to Laila that despite all they have been through, they might actually learn to love each other again. They sit together in silence. The sun is edging slowly behind one of the hilltops. There will be light in the town and on parts of the mountaintop for a few more hours, but because of the farm's location, dusk comes early. Laila hasn't been here in a long time. After the first profits came in, she lost interest. Whenever the rest of the family went, she purposely stayed at home as another way of punishing her husband. Periodically she asked after the health of Umm al-Khanaazeer but never showed much interest.

Hussein breaks the silence. "I plan to ask Mustafa to help out on the farm until he feels ready to go home. He will have the time he needs to adjust to life before he returns to his own family. It's God's will that he comes to us now. With all the pressure, I don't know how much longer we can expect Ahmad to carry on."

The farm manager has gone against the wishes of the younger, more radical elements of his community by continuing to work with the pigs. That he has carried on for so long is a tribute to his loyalty to

Hussein. Whenever the old man is confronted about his employer, he responds by saying: "I submit myself to Allah just as you do. If He wants me to provide for my family and sick wife by working for an unbeliever, then so be it. Like all devout Muslims, I give ten percent of what I earn to charity. Do not criticize me for doing what I must." Until now this has been enough, but with tensions growing each passing day, in the end he knows that he and his sons will have no choice but to leave.

Loud shouting rouses Laila from her thoughts. Ahmad runs out of the farrowing shed, his arms waving, evidently disturbed.

Inside the shed, Mustafa and Ahmad's sons are standing in front of Umm al-Khanaazeer's pen. When Hussein enters, Mansoor and Salem rush to him. He pushes through. Once Laila reaches her husband's side, she gasps, "My God, the size..."

The repeated pregnancies have had the same effect on the animal as it would a woman, except few women grow to more than six hundred pounds. Blood drips down the pig's forelegs onto the straw. Around her hooves, like trampled flowers, are the remnants of her latest litter. Within hours of their birth they were crushed beneath their mother's gargantuan weight. She simply rolled over them as though they never existed.

But that doesn't explain the blood streaming from the sow's mouth. Then with sinking disgust, Hussein understands. Nothing on this earth should be forced to breed indefinitely. The stress has been too much and it was, as he repeatedly warned his uncle, only a matter of time before his worst fears were realized. Umm al-Khanaazeer, eating the remains of a piglet's hindquarter, crunches it in huge, powerful jaws like an apple. She appears to be relishing it. Smeared blood and bits of bone cover a once inquiring snout. Mortified, Hussein shoves past his wife and sons and strides quickly outside. Within seconds the sound of the butcher's van can be heard driving away from the farm.

18

An intense disembodied voice cracks the clear blue dome of the sky: "*Allahu akbar, Allahu akbar!*" "God is great!" The words bounce back and forth between the mountains, fusing with the succeeding lines of prayer. "There is no god but God." "I bear witness that Muhammad is God's messenger." "Come to prayer." "Come to success." "God is most great." "There is no god but God." The message falls like rain over the town.

Some people in the Eastern Quarter immediately stop working and kneel facing Mecca. Others accept the invitation and head in the direction of the mosque. In the town's Christian community, the six o'clock call to prayer has a different meaning. For those who religiously avoid the heat of the day, it is a call to life. In walled gardens elderly grandmothers, their hair and skin whitened from old age and self-imposed seclusion, emerge to sweep walks. Roads and alleys fill with visiting relatives and friends. Farmers greet each other on their way to the fields for one last look before retiring to the Rest House and Internet Café for coffee, backgammon, and gossip. The stifling oppressiveness that has hung over them all day begins a slow retreat.

Across the road from the Sabas house, a neighbor comes out into a yard, as if recently awakened from a long sleep. Samira and Muna have whiled away the late afternoon on the front terrace. If they are going to take what should appear as a leisurely walk, Samira realizes, they should leave soon. She needs to be at the appointed place before the streetlamps come on. On the floor Fuad carefully stacks wooden blocks. With a capricious flick of his wrist, he knocks them over. Missed appointments are as easy as that. Samira scans the road again. Three figures appear. It is Laila and the boys.

"Let's go," she urges Muna. With Fuad in her arms, she hurries down the front steps of the house. In the dirt street, she hands the toddler to Laila and explains that Muna wants a stroll in the town. "It would be nice to show her a few things before dark. We've been cooped up all day."

If Samira had been by herself, Laila would have given her grief. Instead her sister-in-law silently gathers her youngest son in her arms. Mansoor and Salem are also subdued, their faces smudged and dirty; it has obviously been a trying afternoon.

The last stone house along the dirt track—the one with a garden—belongs to the widow who monitors the street. As the two young women pass, a voice calls from an open window: "Up and down, where are you going, my child?"

Samira reaches in through a gap, grabs hold of fingers laden with gold rings, and jokes, "Auntie, I'm always at home, watching you from my window. I promise to visit soon." She and Muna continue down other dirt tracks and across unfenced yards. In fifteen minutes they join a partially paved main road and groups of teenage girls walking in twos and threes. Something about their mood suggests that they are not simply taking the air.

At the far end, by the roundabout, teenage boys wait. A battered Mustang drives past, and the driver shouts out, "Hey, Wafiqa!" followed by several short stabs on the horn. The opposite sexes seemingly keep to their own side of the street.

Samira checks her phone and reduces her pace. Because of the time she isn't worried. Also, other girls are out, another clear indication that she and Muna don't have to rush. When she sees the twins heading toward them, she realizes there is no way to avoid her friends without being rude.

"Welcome to Lovers' Lane," Yvette greets Muna. In front of them, a boy breaks away from his crowd of friends. Hands in his pockets,

whistling, he darts across the roundabout and casually falls in behind a group of girls. He keeps at a discreet distance but moderates
his walking speed and follows behind them.

"He's got some nerve!" Yvette's tone is more admiring than ac-
cusatory.

Samira would like to get going, but unable to offer a good excuse
to the twins, she meekly suggests, "I don't think Muna is interested
in this."

Yvette loops her arm through Muna's and nods at the boy. "Not
interested in love Arab style? Come on. He's making his intentions
perfectly clear."

"What intentions?" To Muna, someone crossed the street.

The twins nod at each other. "I can see we're going to have to take
her through this step by step." Yvette expands, "For those who can't
pick out the finer nuances, looks can be deceiving."

Gigi whispers to Muna, "He walks behind the girl he likes."

When the group cuts in front of them, she stops talking. The boy
is still whistling as he passes.

Yvette giggles and sings a few bars of the same song: *"Your eyes
make me hungry. I am weak from lack of food."*

Despite herself, Samira laughs out loud. Yvette is perfect. Occasionally, when Samira is attending political meetings, her thoughts
meander back to Lovers' Lane. In the capital, they take themselves
too seriously. She misses the antics of her friends. At the roundabout with the twins, she is suddenly reminded of Walid. He once
stood watching her from the other side. She shakes her long, dark
hair to expel him from her thoughts. She was so unsophisticated
then. There is no reason to feel sentimental about acting stupid
now.

"Come on!" Yvette stamps her foot, encouraging her to keep up.

One of the teenage girls waits behind her friends until the boy
catches up to her. Yvette brings her small group to a standstill as the
couple exchange a few words. Then, as the boy runs back across the
street, the girl catches up to her group.

"They've made a date to meet," Yvette deciphers.

"Dania," Samira calls out, "wait till I tell your mother."

The teenager turns around, alarmed. When she sees Samira, she skips over and gives her a big hug.

Looking over her spectacles, Samira rolls her eyes. "That's the trouble with girls in love—they hug anybody."

Dania places her head on Samira's shoulder and takes her hand. They walk together. "My mother doesn't like him," she admits.

"So what else is new?" says Yvette, overlooking the proceedings.

"I don't want to disappoint her."

The twin is sympathetic but stern: "Nobody should be disappointed."

"Least of all you," adds Samira soothingly. "You must follow your heart."

"You think so?"

Samira nods sagely.

The younger girl skips back to her friends.

"The voice of experience," Yvette squeezes Samira's arm. "Sounds like your heart has been broken."

Even though Yvette is teasing, Samira knows she is curious. Walid has not been mentioned since he found a job in the Gulf and is no longer a fixture on Lovers' Lane. In the not so distant past Samira claimed that they were e-mailing each other, but she can no longer bother with the pretense.

"Whatever Dania does, her life will not change. She will still yearn to walk out in the evening, like we old women do. You know"—Samira links arms with Yvette and Gigi—"there will be a time when we won't be welcomed. Instead of agony aunties we will be..." she whispers naughtily, "...spies."

She has managed to get the twins and Muna striding along at a reasonable pace and they reach the line of shops. As they pass the butcher's, Samira waves to Khaled behind the counter serving customers and wonders where Hussein is. Her chattering friends push the thought away.

"When we're old we'll wear scarves," promises Gigi, shaking her long, curly hair.

"And we'll go to church every day. But until then we might as well"—Yvette stands by the opened door of a small music shop—"enjoy ourselves."

Samira hesitates and checks her phone. There's still time. She would like to arrive early, but Yvette blocks her path. "What's going on? Come in for a few minutes, Laila won't mind. Also, Muna needs to see and hear our one guilty pleasure."

Meekly Samira follows her in. Everywhere on tables, cassette tapes, old vinyl records, and CDs have been stacked up against walls, in shelves and boxes. Some have pictures on their cases and sleeves, but most are unadorned except for a single line of Arabic writing. The hole-in-the-wall shop belongs to Abu Za'atar's youngest son, Sammy, who built it up from a cardboard box of cassettes outside the Marvellous Emporium. His father, not much of a music lover except when he thought that Sammy was going to make a fortune writing ringtones, was unsympathetic to his son's obsession. This changed dramatically with the growing crowd of youngsters hanging around Sammy and his CD/cassette player. The Featherer lost no time in securing a tiny storefront for his son's business. Sammy, more interested in collecting music than selling it, had other ideas and procured a used DJ mixer and two turntables from the Beirut Craigslist. To subsidize the shop, he does odd jobs for the Marvellous Emporium and keeps the music store open late into the night. Whenever he is asked about closing, his answer's the same: "We never shut. Where would the broken hearted go after Lovers' Lane?"

In a hoodie, with a face scarred by acne and bad food, Sammy displays his father's hunting instincts as soon as Muna is introduced to him.

"I could use an American connection." He outlines his preferences: "Rap, hip-hop, dub, and grime. Anything you get to me would be appreciated." He closes with a short but effective bow. Tacked on a shelf behind him is an article about Michael Jackson torn from a magazine. The headline speaks of pharmaceuticals and the singer's last tour.

Noting Muna's curiosity, Sammy observes, "The one story that never fails to entertain across the generations is tragic fame."

"You know what tragedy is?" interrupts Yvette. Crinkling her nose, she describes the attack on the music shop by vandals who tore down its collection of vintage posters.

"Except for Michael. He so saved us!" Sammy gives Yvette a high five. "If it had been Liberace, Sylvester, or the Village People, the shop would have been burned to the ground."

"And the posters were of who exactly?" asks Muna.

"Glamorous singers and belly dancers showing too much..." Sammy whips his finger down the front of his shirt to indicate cleavage, then holding his hands in the air, he shakes a bony DJ ass. "Imagine being hot and bothered by a woman old enough to be your grandma. But in business, the customer is always right."

"You sound like Abu Za'atar." Gigi, browsing through a box of recently arrived tapes, has been nominally following the conversation. "How come there's never any new music, Sammy? Some of this stuff is ancient." She moans, "My mom's collection of seventies LPs are more up to date than this!"

"The problem with bootleggers is their small-mindedness," the youthful proprietor explains to Muna. "They pirate nothing that isn't a worldwide smash. Why should I carry the same trash as the next guy?" He turns to Gigi. "If you don't find what you want, with my blessings, go elsewhere."

"There is no other place." Gigi hands him a cassette tape with a picture of a stylish middle-aged woman with perfectly coiffed hair and a pair of large sunglasses. It is a singer Muna recognizes: "Umm Kulthum!"

Yvette joins them and sighs, "When she sang even the nightingales stopped to listen. Four million people attended her funeral in Cairo. Sure, a million more attended Abdel Nasser's, but unlike his, none of her mourners was shot dead by the Egyptian army."

Sammy, yawning, slides the cassette into the player and hits play. A mass of soaring glissandi rises dirgelike. Bored, the frustrated enthusiast supports his hoodie-covered head in his hands, with his elbows on the counter.

Yvette tells Muna, "Unrequited love and brutality are the themes of our lives. It was true then and it's true now." She reaches behind Sammy and turns up the volume. The ear-splitting violins strain against the speakers.

Mesmerized, everyone stands perfectly still before mournful singing begins: "*My darling, don't ask where the ecstasy has gone. The citadel of my sensual imagination has collapsed. Quench my desire and drink on its ruins...*" The song bounces against the walls of the shop and swells out onto the main street. Evening shoppers outside stare in through the open door. It is too much attention.

"We have to go," Samira says to Yvette, who can't hear her above the music. She takes Muna forcibly by the arm and the two of them slip out with sadness and betrayal trailing after them: *"Tell my story as long as the tears are flowing..."*

Down the road from the shops, through an alleyway below the air-conditioning ducts of the Holy Land Hotel, the singing dissipates in the steady whirl of plant machinery. When they emerge, a strand of melody and disembodied lyric—*"Set my hands... free..."*—float toward them on the wind. Samira takes a track that leads behind the Rest House and Internet Café to an old garden. Surrounded by a tangle of flowering jasmine and honeysuckle, the two are obscured from view behind an unfinished wall. Through the windows, a bluish glow from a line of monitors illuminates the back of the building, as voices intermingle with the slap of backgammon tiles, the tinkling of glassware, and the sound of computer games. Where Samira and Muna stand the air thickens with the evening perfume of flowers. In the garden, someone lingers.

The shadowy figure doesn't look like one of Samira's usual contacts. He is young, with some facial hair, but from what she can tell in the light, not an awful lot. In a loose tunic and light-colored trousers, he's also wearing a woven prayer cap on his head. She thinks she has seen him before, maybe with the sheikh. Some of the people she has dealt with in the past are religious but by their own admission not fundamentalist. To her knowledge, the women's committee and its umbrella group do not associate with extremists. It goes against everything Zeinab, observant and moderate, believes in. For a split second Samira again worries about her involvement with the Syrian women. Maybe the youth is not whom she is supposed to meet, but he is the only one here. From the look of impatience on his smooth face, she thinks he is expecting her. Samira emerges from behind the wall with Muna. They walk toward him.

"I was told you were coming alone." He studies Samira.

"This is my cousin," she says, stepping forward. "I can vouch for her."

The youth doesn't appear convinced. Nevertheless he reaches inside his tunic and pulls out a crisp brown envelope. He sneers, "Don't lose it."

Samira slips the envelope into the pocket of her skirt. It is almost dark. A young couple holding hands enters the abandoned garden but, upon seeing people already there, leave quickly. Samira's contact looks at her as though she's the one to blame, but she stares back at him, refusing to be intimidated.

"If you picked the meeting place, you must have known." Her tone is matter-of-fact: those in the town her age and younger are aware that the garden serves as an unofficial annex of Lovers' Lane. The romantically inclined arrange their assignations in public view. Only the determined find their way to the bushes. It is her turn to sound irritated. However, when she emphasizes, "So don't be surprised," she thinks she sounds shrill. His unwarranted stridency has really gotten on her nerves.

A streetlamp on the other side of the garden wall starts to buzz. In a moment, it will turn on. Then the loved and the unloved, the loners and the thieves, will consider the time and return home. The unofficial curfew for the young at heart is to be respected at all times.

"When will the letter be delivered?" demands the youth.

"Tonight." Samira can tell he has no confidence in her whatsoever. The streetlamp flickers into a weak yellow light.

Out of provocation, she thrusts her right hand forward to shake his. With his arms rigidly at his side, he abruptly walks away.

"Chilling" is Muna's verdict.

Samira, exasperated by the encounter, makes light of it. "Remember, we're improperly dressed. No headscarf means we might as well be standing naked in front of him. Imagine if we said you just arrived from America—he would have lectured us on war crimes!"

Although she probably would agree with his assessment of US foreign policy, it is his attitude toward her that she finds unacceptable. As her fingers nervously skim the surface of her pocket, feeling the contours of the letter inside, she wonders what is so important that it couldn't be e-mailed. Samira rarely knows the contents of the messages and parcels she carries and as a rule doesn't want to. However, her previous errands never involved someone so dubious and close to home. She suppresses her nervousness by thinking about Zeinab. What would she have done under similar circumstances? How would she have avoided an unnecessary confrontation? She is cool under pressure, a trait Samira is attempting to master. With practice, in time she expects it will come naturally. The woman who called her promised she would be approached later that night. She didn't know when it would happen, but she warned Samira not to change her plans and to go to the wedding feast. Whoever has been assigned to find her will know where to look; it's such a small town. All she needs to do is keep watch and be on her guard.

19

Hussein, crushed inside the van, is panting heavily. He bolted away from the disaster like a man spooked by his own shadow. At the turnoff to the farm, instead of heading downward toward the town, he veered in the opposite direction, leaving black skid marks on the smooth road maintained for the Holy Land sightseeing tour buses. By a cross, he pulls into the entrance leading to a church, monastery, and museum. The van jerks to a stop in a car park, inches away from a stone embankment with nothing beyond it but sky.

All around the air radiates with the last vestiges of the golden light, but Hussein is oblivious. He should have stayed and consoled Laila and the boys, but the sheikh's threats combined with Umm al-Khanaazeer's filicide set off a chain of violent jolts as his brain exploded with images of his wife and children on the rack. He thought he was making sacrifices for their sake when in fact he was only placing them in the line of fire. The realization is electrifying. His shaking hand gropes for the steering wheel; he feels nothing but shame and self-loathing.

Nothing good comes from religion. Hussein doesn't feel God nor does he blame Him. If God does exist, He must be malicious. Hussein wearily climbs out of the van. Coming to Jebel Musa, the very place his father loved, is the cruelest of jokes. Tourists finished praying in the church can pick their way through the ruined monastery to the museum, where they can add their names to a mosaic for the world.

For Hussein's father, Musa taught the word of God by teaching people about themselves. According to the philosopher Ibn Sina, the prophets were not only mirrors of the divine, they embodied God's greatness. One could not narrate a point of understanding between the worldly and the celestial without their intercession.

There was a Qur'anic verse that Al Jid, as a Christian, held dear: "He is Allah; there is no god but He; all the excellent names are for him." Some names, he explained to anyone who cared to listen, were well known, such as All-Preserving, Time, Eternal, Proud, and Watchful. Others were distinct aspects of the Godhead, and then there were the secret names. Al Jid celebrated what he considered two facts of creation: there was not one truth for all but many paths to enlightenment, and God's mystical powers were not His alone; these too were manifest in exceptional men and women. Whenever Hussein searched for signs he came up short. However, for his father, they were everywhere, in the landscape around them and the air they breathed.

Al Jid told his son that Musa learned his ancient arts of healing in the desert. Medieval Islamic scholars believed the prophet cured the afflicted by serenading them with a magic flute. Faith, like storytelling, requires a suspension of disbelief. Musa could have easily parted the Red Sea and saved his people with a pop song of his day.

Pilgrims on Jebel Musa found Al Jid after he had fallen off his horse and suffered a stroke. With most of his children gone, his once busy home was deathly still except for the singing of his small daughter Samira, who puttered through empty rooms like Zenobia of Palmyra. Hussein, his only son in the country, was off on a secret assignment for the army, or so the family had been informed, when in truth he was on a terrific bender. By the time Hussein resurfaced, it was too late. The old man was gone and buried.

Mother Fadhma is a woman who rarely takes advantage, but this time she did. Because of her stepson's remorse, she extracted from him an irrevocable promise. It was an onerous task but one she would insist on from beyond the grave. Al Jid and his second wife had presided over an extended family, even after nearly all their children and her sister's disappeared into exile. In death as in life, the two of them never once turned anyone away, and as a consequence the family grave became overpopulated with distant cousins and upstart relatives.

"When my time comes," she instructed Hussein, "retrieve the bones belonging to Al Jid and the great loves of his life, Grandmother Sabet and Mamma-Sister Najla. Bury them with me. Let us be a family once more so the women are not left among strangers with our honor compromised."

Whenever Hussein considers his promise, he can almost taste the dirt and dust rising from calcified bones, wrapped in shredded muslin, deep in a sandy grave. It is a job he will not like and will resent. Memory and death have made him conscious of feeling one thing: parched. His thirst for oblivion like his father's goodness is deep and abiding. Fed up with communing with other people's deities, he plans to seek solace in the company of his own.

20

With curtains drawn and no lights, the new house appears forlorn and unloved. Mother Fadhma inches up the front steps one at a time. The locked front door only confirms her suspicions that no one is home, and she resorts to her latchkey. Inside she can just about make out her grandsons' whispering in the gloom. They are usually this mindful only when their mother is suffering from a bad migraine. Fadhma ventures past the living and reception rooms down the hall to a partially opened door and peers inside. In the bedroom Salem and Mansoor regard her despondently. When Fuad crawls toward her, his brothers gently grab hold of him, and the three return to a quiet game. Mother Fadhma, keeping her own counsel, moves farther down the hallway.

Samira's bedroom is empty, as is Laila's, although the old woman expected to find her daughter-in-law's door shut. Still, it is uncommon for the boys to be left alone in the house. She could have missed a note on the table by the front door and goes to check, but nothing's there. In her own room she sinks into the softness of her bed and pulls off her scarf. She is relieved to have reached home without falling down. Leaning forward, she barely manages to unlace her shoes. She knows she is not far from when this simple task will elude her but not yet. She feels with her toes across the tile floor for her slippers, ignoring the pain in her ankles. The mattress creaks as she tries to stand up. Eventually successful, she continues her investigations into the rest of the house.

She only has to reach the kitchen. Laila is slumped over the table. When Fadhma places a firm but consoling hand on her shoulder, the younger woman whimpers, "It was horrible."

Fadhma draws near. "Never mind," she whispers. Emboldened by church, she wants to channel her strength of faith into the younger woman, but Laila dispiritedly shakes her head.

"Umm al-Khanaazer as big as a house, and she was devouring her babies... Hussein was so upset. He left us at the farm and disappeared. I don't know where he is or..." Uncertainty hangs in the air.

"How did you and the boys get home?" Mother Fadhma masks her disappointment with a question. Whatever happened, this is a new low for her stepson who in the past would never have abandoned his wife and children. But it is not totally out of character either. Sometimes at his drunkest, Hussein has difficulty remembering who any of them are. It is Laila's mention of the pig that Fadhma can't let go of, but Laila continues.

"Ahmad couldn't take us. He was already behind for the weekend, so we phoned Mikhail and started walking on the road down toward town with one of Hussein's men. A soldier—Mustafa?"

Mother Fadhma is immediately grateful; the young man returned her hospitality and safeguarded her family.

"I couldn't have done it without him." Laila is breathing slowly. "He seemed to carry the boys off the mountain. As we walked down together, he told them not to dwell on the bad. They needed only to remember that their father loves them and will do anything for them. He said he knows this to be true because Hussein was like a father to him and his brother in the army. The soldier told us of his travels. The boys enjoyed his company, but still I worried about Hussein..." Her voice weakens again. "Then Mustafa cried out. He was cowering on the ground, initially, I thought, from some kind of attack. I've never seen anything like it. When the boys rushed to help him he yelled at them to leave him alone. He told us to get away while we could."

The wild, disbelieving look in her eyes suggests that Laila has her own doubts about what happened next.

"But he wasn't shouting just at us. He was talking to people who weren't there—as real to him as I am to you." Her eyes grow wide. "That's when the boys and I ran away. Soon after, Mikhail came and got us. When the taxi turned around, the soldier was standing where we left him. Oh, Fadhma, what's happening?"

"I don't know." Because Mustafa assured her grandsons of Hussein's love, Mother Fadhma feels a growing responsibility toward the soldier. Along with those she loves, she has already included him in a protective ring of candlelight. She also glimpses another shape in the shadows, rotund and snuffling. Fadhma has never been into speciesism, so she prays that all of them will survive the rising tide of terror.

21

Samira feels too wired to go home. She doesn't want to say anything that would unduly worry her mother or, worse yet, rouse Laila's suspicions. "Let's go to the Internet café," she suggests to Muna. "You were complaining about not being netted up. Here's your chance."

"Great." Her cousin nods appreciatively. "Can't wait to check my e-mail and tell friends where I am."

The two of them cross the garden to a squat annex housing the Internet café, part of the larger building belonging to the Rest House. In an open-plan room with fluorescent lighting overhead, computers are arranged to make optimum use of the space, some facing each other or the walls, others with their monitors back to back. After the early-evening rush, many machines have been vacated. A few refugees from Syria and Yemen occupy those in use. In the café Samira purposely avoids scrutinizing other customers' monitors. It is a simple courtesy on her part that she expects from others.

She talks to the kid in charge. She knows Salameh's family. He has been running the café since it opened. "We want fifteen minutes on two separate computers," she tells him. As she waits for the codes, she inquires, "Anyplace you want us to sit?" The café's variable access to cyberspace depended on the wind and the proclivities of the secret police. Salameh answers with a gruff jerk of his head and two paper slips. Samira leads Muna to the back, and as soon as a code is in her possession, she happily types away.

Samira checks her e-mails but there is nothing except spam. Because she has been reading the Arab press and perusing political tracts, the websites she visits display banner ads for Syrian charities and the documentary about Edward Snowden.

Muna eyes Samira's screen, suitably impressed. "And all I get offered are sale T-shirts with ugly rhinos on them."

Samira goes to Facebook. "Nowadays you can tell who's religious and who's not, even when people don't declare themselves outright."

"How's that?" Muna is back again, perusing her cousin's monitor.

"By their reactions. Some Sunnis like L+U+V+Surie." Samira shows Muna a Facebook page with a picture of Astro Boy in a keffiyeh and with an Islamic beard. "He is against the Syrian regime but a staunch supporter of the Bahraini royal family."

"Oh yeah," says her cousin, who seems a little distracted but then focuses. "I read an article about the new housing constructed for Bahrain's latest recruits, South Asian Sunnis hired to police the dissidents."

"Then there are Shias," points out Samira. "On Twitter Iranians express regret over their country's involvement in regional wars—Syria, Iraq, and Yemen—but Tehranis don't care that their government is on a war footing. More Revolutionary Guards abroad means less at home to control 'bad hijab' women. It seems the religiously righteous are always behind violence. The real revolution should be one of tolerance and compassion, not in defense of the faithful but the rest of us."

"I keep asking myself," Muna says as she goes back to her keyboard, "what happened to old-fashioned secularism? Less than a generation ago people thought there could be a political solution."

Samira, casting an eye over the room, is no longer listening. "One second." She maneuvers through the café and wonders if she's right. She stops alongside a computer. "You're not supposed to be here."

Mustafa peers up at her. He looks more unsettled than the last time they met, and that was only a few hours ago.

"Hey," he replies softly. On the screen in front of him is a lurid website on the dark web filled with bold Arabic script and hundreds of photos.

"I thought you were with Hussein." Samira is trying to sound and look casual.

"I was."

He returns to the screen, and she notices the cotton jersey, the one he put on in their house, is soaked through with sweat. The soldier has been going through a rough patch.

"What are you looking at?"

After a long pause, Mustafa gestures at a picture in the corner of the page and hits the maximize button to enlarge the image. "My brother."

Samira leans in closer. The photograph shows a group of bearded men and boys in traditional clothing in the mountains of Afghanistan. They look at the camera like it is an imposition. More striking is that all of them, even the smallest, are armed to the teeth.

"There's Sayeed." A young man with a slightly smaller build than Mustafa's holds an old-fashioned Lee-Enfield. The person on his right clutches a ground-to-air rocket launcher.

Samira's finger lightly grazes the screen. "That you?"

Before he can answer, there is a loud scraping of a chair, and a brash, jocular voice calls out, "My favorite..." Samira reaches down and strikes the quit function on the computer keyboard, and the webpage instantaneously disappears into the blue oblivion of the desktop. Composed, with a broad friendly grin, she turns and faces her uncle Abu Za'atar.

"Amo, you're the last person I expected to see. What brings you here?"

"Research." He darts about her, trying to get a better look at the computer screen. "And your friend?" He smiles at Mustafa. "Don't think we've met."

Mustafa stands as Samira makes the introduction. "Ali and I know each other from college."

"So you were training to be a teacher too, at the women's college?"

Another hand is vigorously thrusted toward Mustafa's. Muna gate-crashes the small group. "Hi! Don't believe we've met." She winks at him. "I'm Samira's cousin from America. Just arrived from the land of the Great Satan!"

Then shining her goodwill onto Abu Za'atar, she takes his arm and begs him, "Come and join me." On the way back to her seat they begin an animated discussion on the dark arts of Internet bidding.

Alone once more, Samira confronts Mustafa. "According to my brother, you need to keep out of sight. You should get out of here." When he doesn't react, she promises, "You leave first. Muna and I will catch up."

She coolly rejoins her cousin and her uncle. "Don't mean to interrupt, Amo, but Mamma and Laila are waiting for us. See you at the wedding feast tonight."

Both girls give Abu Za'atar an affectionate peck on the cheek and depart quickly. Beyond the windows of the Internet café, they find Mustafa in the garden in the back. No one speaks until the café is out of sight and the streets empty.

Samira addresses Muna: "What made you come to our rescue?"

"I could see you needed help," Muna replies. She turns to Mustafa. "What's happened to you?"

With downcast eyes the soldier admits, "I must be suffering from..." He doesn't continue.

"PTSD." Muna recites the letters as though quoting from a medical journal, then catches herself. "Oh, sorry," she apologizes. "American soldiers who served in Afghanistan and Iraq suffer from post-traumatic stress disorder. It's all over the US news."

With his gaze still lowered he describes to Samira and Muna the walk he took with Laila and her two children. "I had a..." His voice trails off again.

Muna, who has been watching him closely, finishes his thought: "An episode?"

Samira understands now the reason for Laila and the boys' upset.

"I'm leaving." He takes Samira's hand and holds it gently—his warmth against her natural coolness. "Thank you. Good-bye."

"I thought you were staying around a little longer." She peers over her glasses up at him.

"I don't think that's a good idea."

"Well, good-bye. Again." She looks long and hard at him. She will remember his intensity. But she doesn't want his memory of her to be meaningless; she does care. "Listen, stay," she won't let his shy smile derail her. "Stay out of sight. Take the most direct route home. Talk to no one."

It takes everything in her to turn away and go with Muna in the opposite direction. Once the two women are beyond earshot, Samira sighs sadly and pushes the soldier from her mind.

As they pass Sammy's music store, Syrian rap blares from the loudspeakers: *"Outside the tent there was talk about honor... about haram... I'm a woman not a slave..."* Samira and Muna keep to the shadows away from the flashing signs of the Marvellous Emporium and skirt the deserted roundabout of Lovers' Lane. Walking briskly through unfenced yards, the women emerge fifteen minutes later onto the unnamed dirt road. From the new house they can hear the TV before they see light flickering through the living room curtains. Samira pauses before the front steps. In all the excitement she almost forgot the letter. She checks that it is secure before running after Muna.

In the living room the boys are engrossed in an episode of *CSI*. Mother Fadhma, lightly snoring, is napping in a chair with her swollen feet, in stockings, propped up on a stool. Everything appears as it should be, nothing untoward. Relieved, Samira offers Muna a seat on the sofa. Looking a little tired, Laila enters the living room and announces, "If we don't get ready now, we'll never go," although she doesn't seem to be in much of a hurry herself and stares vacantly off into space.

Mother Fadhma rubs her eyes and yawns. Muna helps her out of the chair and she leans on her granddaughter's arm as they navigate the hallway.

Alone in her room, Samira takes out the envelope and holds it against the light. She can't make out anything, but then she's not supposed to. Placing it carefully on the table, she changes clothes.

Folded, it fits snugly into another convenient pocket. Once Muna joins her, they dismiss the unsuitable clothing in the suitcase and choose again from Samira's closet. As the two of them wait for the rest of the family, Samira repeatedly touches the letter as though it's a religious relic or lucky charm.

22

Abu Za'atar fingers the magnifying glass around his neck. He usually avoids screen-work after dark; it makes his good eye wonky. After the departure of his nieces, he upbraids himself in the Internet café. He should have paid closer attention to where Samira had been standing with her friend. Physically Ali doesn't look related to any of the town's prominent families, with none of their extravagant hooked noses and acute bowlegged-ness. The Featherer's brain whirls like a Rolodex of local genealogy, recalling births, deaths, and body types.

Truly there was nothing outstanding about the young man, not even the shirt on his back. Still, this small detail won't leave Abu Za'atar alone. The blue cotton jersey, a jumped up tee with a white collar, could have been procured from any number of clothing outlets. The shirt's leaping camel logo appears on casual clothing that camouflages rich and poor alike. He keeps turning it over in his mind. A similar consignment arrived in the Marvellous Emporium from Aleppo with frayed or falling-off collars—the last of the great Syrian cotton manufacturing industry fleeing the war. Never one to shirk from duty, Abu Za'atar redressed the damage, but his needlework around the affected necklines was remedial at best. He had been forced to use chartreuse-colored thread instead of brilliant white because of a run on cotton goods by Uzbek pilgrims. Preparing for the hottest and holiest journey of their lives, they ransacked the emporium for micro-thin robes and paper-thin terry cloth towels for the Hajj to Mecca.

Revisiting the shirt, Abu Za'atar realizes it is his own crude handiwork calling out to him. The consignment of jerseys arrived in every color of the rainbow. The pastel pinks and lavenders were quickly disposed of, sold to the restaurant staff of the Holy Land. He held back the manly blues and sold one with a not so modest markup to Hussein.

"I require more time than the usual." He leers confidently at Salameh over the counter. "Any discounts?"

Entrepreneurs should stick together, but the kid conjuring codes dismisses him with a paper slip.

The winged proprietor snoops between the computers before unceremoniously taking a seat and typing. Screwing up his good eye, he clicks on Internet Explorer and drags the cursor along the top toolbar to favorites. Beneath that, he finds and selects history, and a list of arcane links appears for the Dead Sea scrolls and YouTube videos by Beyoncé. Although it seems highly unlikely that any of these, except for "Single Ladies," would be pressing topics for his unmarried niece, Abu Za'atar feels his overarching stratagem is not without merit.

He logs out and moves sideways—new seat, new machine. This time the history reveals endless links for video games. Abu Za'atar doesn't quite understand on-screen violence. Why playact murder and decapitation, when the real gore takes place daily just over the border? He dismisses these links too. Ali is too sunburned and muscular to be a couch potato. Not even a chin as raw and tender as a baby's diaper-rashed bottom can disguise that.

Abu Za'atar exits this terminal. Ideally he would like to go phishing in the next one beside it. But a headscarfed young woman, deep in conversation via a headset with a mouthpiece, blocks his access. He doesn't wish to pry, but from his limited experience, social networking leads only to trauma and disillusionment. He can see that she is already exhibiting the telltale sign: excitable irritability. So he avails himself of the computer on her other side. Before he fully settles, Salameh beckons him to the front. With his magnifying glass and code in hand, Abu Za'atar cheerfully complies.

"Every computer is the same," the kid carefully enunciates as though speaking to a moron. "No need for musical chairs."

"Of course!" Abu Za'atar is thoroughly enjoying the novelty of conversing with an IT guru. A regular since the launch of the Internet café, the Featherer spends as much time there as his wandering eye and business commitments allow. Usually the under-eighteens scrupulously avoid him, let alone surrender valuable tech tips. "I appreciate your concern."

He really means it. The older man recognizes something green and good in the boy, a mistaken arrogance perhaps. Heartened by the healing powers of commerce, Abu Za'atar strides toward the next site of intended excavation, only to find a young buck in situ.

"Age before beauty!" he squawks, slamming down the magnifying glass on the monitor. Startled, his adversary slinks away.

Abu Za'atar peers into a past of online shopping sites that, hand on heart, he will return to. In a fit of pique he pops his head over the monitor. He is going to be forced into the unenviable task of taking matters into his own hands. The situation isn't right and, if misunderstood, could turn downright ugly. "Wonder," as he has nicknamed the young woman in the headscarf beside him—not unkindly—has to get out of her seat and give him her computer.

Once a proprietor always a proprietor; he can draw only from past experiences. There was a time in the Marvellous Emporium when the aisles of Islamic prêt-à-porter—abaya robes and cloaks, shawls, cowls, gloves, stockings, and veils—were entirely in black. Periodically the odd high-necked, long-sleeved, and ground-length sharia coat broke the monotony with dark gray or navy blue: serious colors for a serious religion. In a separate area, unofficially marked, shelves and drawers were stuffed with garishly colored tops and leggings, some adorned with bling or costume jewelry. The rule of thumb was thus: the drabber the outerwear, the greater the possibility of flamboyant garmenting concealed beneath.

Then seemingly overnight the emporium started doing a brisk trade in lurid fluorescent scarves, tight shirts, cigarette jeans, and *big* sunglasses. A younger, more determined generation was stepping out, and Abu Za'atar began noting their progress on the high street. The brashness of their hip-hugging clothes, a withering no-nonsense approach, particularly toward the men of the town like himself, and the happenchance of a long-sleeved T-shirt with the letter "W" written in glitter across the front all combined to be—he realized in a lightbulb moment—the Wonder of Fashion. In some circles these modern hipsterettes were called "hijabis" or "muhajababes," but those names were derisory and, to his mind, didn't capture a socially transformative new look. Abu Za'atar has always championed independent clothing in the marketplace, but tonight's different.

"That's no way to snare him, dear." The Featherer's magnifying glass is such a breech of personal space that the appalled young woman logs off, grabs a purse the size of a small pony, and flees.

Abu Za'atar knows he has half a minute, if that. He slips into the seat, slams in the code, and opens the browser's history. He soon understands how badly he misread Wonder. She wasn't in love. She had been reading news leads about the bodies of dead Muslim Brotherhood regularly dumped on the Egyptian side of the Sinai border. Abu Za'atar hates it when his assessment of people and situations are so off the mark, but his need outweighs social niceties. One link with an unusual configuration stands out from those before and after. He ignores the nervous tingle of anticipation across his shoulder blades and remains in the zone, with his magnified eye fixed on the screen and his unmagnified one on Wonder complaining in no uncertain terms to Salameh up front.

The Featherer clicks on a URL from the badlands of Afghanistan—finally a page in celebration of holy war, an Instagram for jihadists. He ignores the lurid religiosity and scrolls through the posted pictures until he finally finds the one of men and guns that burned themselves onto his retina. He glimpsed it for only a second behind Samira and then it was gone as fast as she could make it disappear. "Oh, Ali," Za'atar is tutting to himself as Salameh pushes through the rows with the young woman in tow. In the time it takes them to reach the disputed computer, the desktop has been tidied up and all is well in the world of information technology.

"You were warned!" The kid sounds exasperated. "What's going on?"

"He insulted me," says Wonder. "Men who do not respect women should be barred from the Internet café!"

Abu Za'atar peers up through his magnifying glass as he strokes the machine. "The Internet means universes to me." He's not telling an untruth. He has come to regard cyberspace as a virtual Marvellous Emporium. His looming magnified eye follows the tender curves of the keyboard and monitor.

"You love and respect it too?" He directs his question to his adversary. She has no idea what he's talking about. Nonetheless he is completely sympathetic. Declaring, "Borrowed but not stolen," he vacates the seat with a flourish.

After escorting him to the front of the shop, Salameh accepts Abu Za'atar's extra piastres and his explanation for the "misunderstanding incurred, accidentally or otherwise." Then the Featherer takes off through the streets like a maniacal homing pigeon.

He feels topflight. The afternoon excursion left him listless and low. Instead of moping around the emporium he had coffee at the Rest House and went to console himself in the Internet café—time excellently spent. What flew out of Hussein's house fell from the sky and hit Abu Za'atar on the head. Crossing the asphalted part of the main street, he really does feel like crowing. If it weren't for the come-hither neon array of the Marvellous Emporium and everything it promises, this town would have been run into the ground long ago.

Inside he doesn't have time to switch on the lights. The outdoor signage strobes in thousands of complex color combinations. The effect amplifies the tangled excesses of the emporium, which tower above and all around him. In the intermittent darkness and light, he throws open his booty nest. No need to search; it had been prepared beforehand. With the magnifying glass in one hand and a cell phone in the other, he dials the number on the business card.

He is expected. The Marvellous Emporium, its proprietor, and love of the oddball are renowned. He conveys the minimum amount of information in the language of security he and his listener understand, with the usual buzzwords: "terrorist," "fundamentalist," "algorithm."

Even though he holds back a detail or two, a secret plan is so easily slotted into place that the Featherer can hardly believe his munificent luck. No one will know about the call and he alone will reap its benefits. Only the frenetic stabs of color and light bear witness to his greed.

23

At her dressing table, Laila doesn't feel like going out. The wedding feast will be a stark reminder of her own broken marriage. She would rather wait for Hussein at home. They need to talk. At this time of crisis, she knows she should be grateful for the little she has and focus on her children. Instead another question crowds her thoughts: Could her life have been different?

Absentmindedly she takes a pair of black star sapphire earrings from her jewelry box and inspects them in the palm of her hand. A long time ago a man expressed an interest in her but not through the official channels of her family. Because she was young and impressionable, she arranged to meet him clandestinely but never for too long. The very walls of the fortress town where she lived in the country's south festered with the many eyes and ears of the Sabas tribe.

Constructed during the Crusades, ancient structures within citadel walls had been extended and divided by an ever-increasing population. Its labyrinth of narrowing stone streets, compacted courtyards, concealed entrances, and barred doors constituted a place of mystery that should have revealed its secrets slowly. With everyone living at such close quarters and more than half the families able to trace some kind of blood relation, the opposite was true. At one baptism Laila counted twenty-seven cousins. The extended family represented a mere fraction of the second-largest Christian tribe in Jordan.

Beyond the *wadi* and desert, in the mountains, Al Jid presided over a smaller branch of the family, and from there, the Sabases spread throughout the country in a web of complex relationships. Not even national borders confined them. Many traveled to work in the oil-rich Gulf States, and when they returned their showy material wealth enticed others to leave. The more adventurous sought variety in the world at large. Laila's most treasured possessions were not traditional embroideries or carvings but scarves and perfumes from duty-free shops. Although the men of the family spent years abroad, when they married, they *idhan wijhak biteyn ardak*—"painted the mud of their own land on their face"—and sought a partner from within the family.

The forbidden nature of Laila's new friendship made it exciting. How happy she had been the day he placed the earrings in her hand. "Stars to match those that are your eyes," he said.

Even now she can hear his voice. Laila admonishes herself. It is Hussein or the disturbed soldier who should fill her thoughts, not an illicit love affair. She hesitates before giving in completely. She puts on the earrings. Her reflection in the mirror reminds her that she never once wore them in public, although at the time she kept them close, in a pocket or a change purse. That year, there had been a scandal. A girl in her class seen with a Muslim boy on the street disappeared. Her mother wept openly, but the girl's brothers were taciturn. When her body was discovered in a ravine, all her father said was "At least our honor is secured." The death was recorded as an accident, but the news whispered from house to house might as well have been broadcast over a loudspeaker. For the young women living in the fortress town, it was another reminder of the no-go areas in their lives.

Eventually Laila's earrings were discovered and she was forced to reveal her friendship to her mother, who displayed real anger for the first and last time. "How can you be so stupid? You know the dangers." She kept her voice low so the brother, who had taken in mother and daughter after the death of Laila's father, would not hear. The earrings were confiscated and Laila was forced to stop seeing the only man, apart from her husband, who gave her jewelry. For years she believed they had been destroyed, but after her mother's death, she found them hidden among her old stockings.

Soon after she received the earrings came her engagement. Laila returned home one afternoon from the government-sponsored teacher training course and found the women of her immediate household in a state of excitement. She realized a momentous decision was being made on her behalf. Her aunt called her mother "Mother of Pearl," a family nickname used only at times of great happiness.

"Saduhf, it is your daughter they are asking for."

Flushed with pleasure, Saduhf meekly joined her elder brother in the front room. He was drinking tea with a handsome army officer and a self-obsessed chatterbox of a man bragging incessantly about his business and their town. Her aunt, holding Laila's hand, pulled the curtain partition open slightly so the girl could watch the negotiations unobserved.

Her uncle's mood was expansive, although good manners prevented him from appearing too eager. He told his visitors that in addition to being pretty, his niece was *thakiya wa shaatra*—"clever and good." Then he confided in hushed tones, "She can be headstrong."

Laila had been so shocked she barely took in her aunt's running commentary. The officer, ten years her senior, recently lost his father. With most of the family abroad, except for his mother and youngest sister, Laila would govern unchallenged in his household. After the two men left, her mother kissed and hugged her, saying, "God willing, he looks healthy."

Saduhf had never gotten over losing her own husband, who died before her daughter was born. The brokenhearted widow with the beautiful name was treated as a pariah in her own family. Without a husband and provider, mother and daughter were shunted among uncaring relations until Saduhf's fifth brother took pity on them. Under his roof, Saduhf endlessly and gratefully cleaned, cooked, and sewed. It was her mother's fingers that Laila keenly recollects: craggy, misshapen, bone under translucent flesh, polished smooth by toil. When she massaged them at night Saduhf frequently repeated one piece of advice: "Guard yourself, daughter: marry strong, not weak."

The situation in her uncle's house made Laila only more determined. Studying came easily, and she worked hard. Initially her uncle had been pleased by his niece's achievements, but as she began to mature, tensions rose. Once her breasts developed, he stopped talking to her altogether. As an outspoken, precocious child, she had been treasured and accepted. As a young woman with a mind and body of her own, she was always made to feel awkward, like someone who ought to be constrained.

Saduhf's brother, pleased by the proposed union, told his sister, "There is no better match," as though the teenager were not in the same room. The limited freedom she hoped for seemed permanently marred by those five words from her obdurate relative.

Television arrived in the citadel, and Laila often accompanied her mother to the house of a cousin who had purchased a set. In a living room crowded with relatives, she glimpsed conflicting images of life outside: Hollywood matinee idols and, by the standards of the fortress town, scantily clad presenters on Italian game shows. These women weren't traded or bartered like animals; they were free to do as they liked—while she was not allowed to make the most basic decisions. Laila considered herself an obedient and caring daughter, but something in her rebeled against yielding to feudal custom. After Hussein and Abu Za'atar appeared at her uncle's house, Laila's dreams—unformed but shimmering like the salmon-filled streams she watched in nature programs—ended as abruptly as someone switching off the TV. Whatever her own feelings on the matter, she was to be married. Her uncle's only concession, one that her husband insisted on, was that she be allowed to finish the teacher training course and earn the certificate that would guarantee her employment. That's what made Hussein different: he wanted her to have a professional life when the majority of her male relatives would have kept her at home.

Within months, marriage plans were finalized, and gradually the hazy shape of her first love was absorbed into Hussein's. As a newlywed, she might have pined for her husband even when he was in the same room, but that was long ago. The both of them have been at odds with each other since the birth of Fuad. But the argument—like their passion—has been neglected. She thinks about those few minutes together on the farm. It was supposed to be a fresh start. The new house, which she feels is entirely her own, has in many ways blotted out the deprivation and shame of her upbringing. Now that it is threatened, the past floods back. Frustrated, she pulls off the earrings so violently that one of the gold posts scratches her earlobe. Out of disgust, mainly with herself, she buries them in the jewelry box and dresses.

Under the festive twinkling lights around a tall metal gate, the father of the bride greets an elderly patrician of the town: "You are welcome, a thousand times."

The old man in an oversize suit does not release his hold of Matroub's arm, while emphasizing, "No, the pleasure is mine."

The host graciously answers him again. "Our house is blessed on your arrival."

The old man bows and refuses to let him have the last word. "I am the one who is blessed."

After a traumatic day, Laila finds herself unaccountably charmed by the exchange of traditional greetings. She surprises herself by joking to Mother Fadhma, "If these two don't hurry up, Anna will be married and bearing children by the time we get in there." Maybe it is the fairy lights, or the anticipation of seeing her friend, but Laila feels she is recovering.

With a wave of his hand, Matroub calls the Sabases forward. "Welcome, ladies and young gentlemen. Please, make yourselves comfortable in our home. Laila"—he presses her hand into his— "Warda has been asking after you all day. She's waiting upstairs." He returns to the old man.

A large tent, decorated with more lights and flags, has been set up in the garden. With the money from the Gulf, Matroub opened a successful electrical business in the capital and built a spectacular family home. Since they are from one of the town's oldest Muslim families when the town was mainly Christian, everyone of standing has been invited to the wedding. The lavish celebration is not only for his eldest, Anna, the first of his three daughters to marry. It is an opportunity to impress on prospective suitors for the others the family's status and generosity. From inside the tent, which opens on one side, chairs exclusively occupied by the male guests spill out onto the patio and garden. A bartender in a white waistcoat is serving whisky and short glasses of milky *arak*. For those who don't partake, there are fresh juices. As a group of musicians tune their instruments, Salem and Mansoor run off to play hide-and-seek in the crush.

Fuad, desperate to join his brothers, cries as Samira carries him upstairs. In an upper hallway where the sharia coats and outer coverings have been hung, Laila retrieves her son and plants loud kisses on his flushed cheeks. "Now you'll have fun with Mamma," she promises.

The interior of the house is decorated in a way that, though tastefully restrained, leaves no doubt as to the wealth of its inhabitants. Enormous brass trays decorate the walls, and elaborate *arghilehs* and antique urns stand in corners. Because it is summer, the Oriental carpets and runners have been put away and the tile floors gleam. The Sabas women pass through a series of rooms, each more comfortable than the last, until they reach the party in an amply proportioned reception room. The bride's female relations squeeze through the crowd, distributing trays of juice, mint tea, and bowls of assorted snacks.

All the chairs have been pushed back against the walls except for one on a wooden dais in the center of the room. In a bridal gown, Anna waits with a sheer red scarf obscuring her face. Almost immediately a tall, gracious woman grabs Laila.

"Where were you this afternoon? I missed you. Mrs. Salwa said you were on your way." Warda Matroub screws up her face. "You should have been with us!" She folds Laila and Fuad in her arms.

Laila can instantly tell that the festivities have been a lot for a friend who could have used her help. Warda didn't invite her to the women's gathering because she assumed Laila would know to come. If the two of them were alone by themselves, Laila would have described her day. Instead she smiles.

Her friend is discretion personified. "If you saw the Syrian lingerie gift sets my cousins brought Anna! I nearly died—thongs with cell phones that light up and blink, a bra and pantie set, when you"—Warda claps once, loudly—"it falls right off! Can you believe it? Afterward Anna asked me, 'Am I really expected to wear these things and *dance* for my husband?' She looked as though she was about to cry." The bride's mother laughs. "Why pretend? I told Anna she would have to do that and much more. I think she was ready to tell her *baba* to call the whole thing off. And who could blame her?"

Laila gratefully appraises her friend. Being in her company is always a pleasure. There will be plenty of time for crying, but tonight she and Warda are going to laugh at life's ridiculousness. Every woman there knows all too well what is good deteriorates and the bad at least has a slight chance of getting better. Women need to dance—not for their husbands but for themselves, to face down adversity.

Four female musicians equipped with an oud, a *ney*, and two hand drums—a counterpoint to the male troupe downstairs—warm up in a corner. Warda raises her voice to make herself heard: "Why weren't you there? Anna needed pragmatic advice, not nonsense about cucumbers and carrots! It was enough to scare me and I've been married for a long time."

Laila allows Fuad to clamber onto his grandmother's lap. Although she is smiling, her eyes are sad. "I would have been..." She is about to make some excuse, then changes tack. "Anna looks radiant," she exclaims.

The bride, sitting erect, appears lifeless, like a painted doll.

Warda raises her hand to her brow. "How neglectful of me." She moves a side table with bowls of olives and nuts nearer. "Please, help yourself," she invites Mother Fadhma. "Laila and I have known each other for so long. Still, that's no excuse for me to forget my manners." She passes around a bowl, then returns to Laila. "We are fortunate. Everything is going well. Asaf will make a fine husband for Anna. As you know we chose him carefully. There were other candidates but his family is respectable. The two of them may not yet love each other madly, but they might."

Warda bursts out laughing. "You know what Matroub told me? He said that his most difficult business deal was easy compared with the negotiations with Asaf's family. Remember the saying 'Daughters, easy to have, hard to give away'?"

Laila won't hear of it. "Nonsense. An attractive, intelligent girl like Anna? Asaf is the one who should be pleased. Warda, you and your daughters are like pearls."

"If only mothers believed that," whispers Warda. "All of us are extremely pleased and relieved." She beams at Mrs. Habash waving from across the room. Patting Laila's knee as a signal for her to stay put, Warda goes to the mayor's wife. Laila can feel Mrs. Habash's eyes on her, but she is soon forgotten in the swell of guests: Laila's colleagues from school, Hussein's customers, and neighbors all shaking hands and saying hello. While some are the very ladies whom Laila and Warda would avoid socializing with, the exchanges are friendly and well intentioned. The wedding feast, like a funeral, is an opportunity to make amends. In such beautiful surroundings everyone pretends she can't remember whether there were any disagreements at all.

On returning to Laila, Warda collapses into a seat and fans herself with her hands. "Let me tell you, no more next times. I've told the rest of my girls to forget these big parties, do us all a favor—elope!" When she realizes Samira has also been listening to her, she apologizes: "Don't pay the least bit of attention to anything I say or do tonight, dear." She stands again. "I must check on the food. By the way, Laila, I wanted to thank Hussein, the meat is excellent. Is he downstairs with the men?"

The words catch in Laila's throat as Mother Fadhma replies for her. "We expect him later."

Laila takes the moment and tries to compose herself. A steely exterior, second nature to her in most company, is useless in Warda's; with her dear friend Laila is only herself. Smiling weakly, she rises from her seat as Warda tells Fadhma, "I'm going to steal her for a while."

The two women vanish into the crowd.

24

Samira has never attended such a grand wedding feast. Separate musicians for men and women are a great extravagance. As a stocky tabla player prepares the female troupe of musicians with an imperious wave of her hand, snatches of conversation drift toward Samira.

"They are remembering their own weddings," Mother Fadhma whispers to her daughter, "or yearning for one like this for someone in their family."

Samira detects a hint of regret in her mother's voice. At one time she too would have been envious of Anna Matroub's good fortune. Her marriage to a boy from a respected family is an aspiration shared by many of the town's young women. Samira watches Anna's friend offer the bride a glass of tea and help with the red veil. Anna is in many ways the perfect daughter. Well-liked, always well presented, she never once frequented Lovers' Lane. The lavish feast will be the biggest event of her life. Except for giving her husband plenty of sons, nothing will provide her greater satisfaction. She is a credit to her parents and a role model to her peers. Anna is all these things and one more, Samira thinks: dull.

Young women like her follow a safe path. It never occurs to them that the ground beneath their privileged feet might give away. Samira doesn't allow herself to believe in the certainties they take for granted. "Oh, Mamma, you know I will die a spinster," she jokes, and touches Fadhma's elbow playfully.

The old woman assesses her daughter. "I thought as much." She kisses her tenderly on the cheek. "And what's the harm in that? As long as you love and are loved."

Samira wants to ask her mother her meaning, but the musicians have started playing and she helps Fadhma and Fuad move closer. Afterward Samira takes a place among her friends on the floor cushions.

"What happened to you in the music shop?" Yvette's voice is drowned out by the older women clapping and singing all around them.

"*Your anklet, O beautiful one, resounds and gives voice.*"

The women of marriageable age, including Samira and the twins, respond loudly: "*Your skirt, the color of peppers, has in it the hue of life and death.*"

Shrieking ululation pierces the air. The time for advice has passed. The women have gathered to show solidarity with the new bride and give her courage. The wedding bed, only a few hours away, could contain a lifetime of woe if blood isn't found on white sheets in the morning.

Samira has attended enough meetings and study sessions under Zeinab's tutelage to feel nothing but disdain for weddings. They have thoroughly discussed the shackles of marriage. A woman's chance for happiness is determined by how vigorously she suppresses her opinions. Samira understands the theory, has even experienced this in her relationship with Walid, yet despite the consciousness raising, something in her still responds to the dream of the bride. She wants to blame the excitement or the music, but she's wrong. She cannot completely distance herself emotionally. On this occasion the women have segregated themselves by their own volition, to celebrate their experiences beyond men's reach and empower one of their own.

The tabla player carries her drum into the center of the room. From the back, a voice suddenly calls out: "Mother Fadhma!"

Surprised, Samira's mother freezes in her seat until many other women take up the call. Samira helps her mother stand up. Only the truly honored are asked to lead the dance. A belt of metal coins is loosely tied around her ample hips as she faces the roomful of women, some at the beginning of their adult lives, others like herself closer to the end, and, at the heart, innocent Anna, on the threshold of womanhood.

Samira can see that her mother is losing her nerve, but the tabla player's beat is infectious and Fadhma begins moving in spite of herself. After an awkward beginning she is instantly transformed. It is scarcely credible that someone her age dances so gracefully. She glides in short steps, spinning in small slow circles. Her hands perform the ritual gestures, evoking the moon and its little sister, Sirius, the Dog Star, the celestial guardians of women since the dawn of time. She stamps the floor, drawing fertility from the fields. As the tempo of the music increases, some of the women can no longer resist and they propel themselves into the center of the room, elegantly waving hands held high. The drums grow louder and they move with wild abandon around the throne of the bride.

The constraints of good manners and stiff bridal taffeta keep the veiled figure on the dais from responding to the music. Every once in a while she trembles. The dance awakes in her forces that have lain dormant. All that she wants whirls like a promise around her; in an instant, the past, the present, and the future collide.

The song, reaching its peak, unfurls like a banner drifting back to earth. Some women fall, as though entranced, back into the arms of chairs or onto floor cushions; the rest stand, sweating and disorientated. Water is passed around and for several minutes nobody speaks. The only sound that can be heard is the slow, monotonous beating of a single drum.

During the dance Samira lost track of her family and the twins. Looking to cool off, she lets herself out through a closed door and walks along an empty corridor and, on impulse, up a flight of stairs. At the top in a window alcove overlooking the garden sits Dania, from Lovers' Lane. Instead of being with the women she has been watching the men. She makes room for Samira. "Look" is all she says.

Below, the men too are dancing. A fellow at the front entices the groom with a fluttering white handkerchief. His other hand, outstretched, keeps time to the music. The men sway in a line behind him, their arms interlocked. As the beat rises, they leap forward and backward, stamping hard and loud, over and over again, their strong, agile bodies in a display of male prowess.

"He's so handsome," Dania whispers.

Samira picks him out. A few feet away watching and enjoying the dance is another man Samira vaguely knows. She nearly overlooked him in the crowd, but for some reason she keeps coming back until the reason becomes clear. Mr. Ammar, the front's political officer who knew about Hussein, is with another activist she might have met at their office. Apparently the two slipped into the house once Matroub finished his formal greetings of guests by the gate. Instinctively Samira reaches for the letter and relives the upset she experienced with the courier in the garden. She's not a fan of Mr. Ammar's either; she tried telling Zeinab, but none of this matters now. Samira makes her excuses to Dania and goes downstairs. On the way, she runs into Laila, who tells her to come and help with the food.

The kitchen is a swarm of activity. At the center, Matroub gingerly places the tastiest pieces of lamb, which have simmered all day in a sauce of dried *mansaf* yogurt, onto trays piled high with rice and roasted pine nuts. One is handed to Samira, and she carries it to the long tables in the garden beside the tent. Here the men stand and eat communally. The musicians, by now a little tipsy, are playing a jolly folk tune.

After setting down the tray Samira looks for Mr. Ammar but doesn't find him or the other man. On her way to the house she runs into Yvette, also conscripted into kitchen duty. The twin, attempting to balance one too many dishes on top of one another, is in danger of dropping the lot. Her face is flushed around the edges.

"At the *arak* again?" Samira helps her friend and takes a few dishes to a table. She is rewarded for her efforts. Standing near the tent is Mr. Ammar, who nods imperceptibly. He knows that she knows. There are too many people around to make the delivery. Samira follows Yvette inside. She will meet Mr. Ammar secretly soon enough.

The friends carry their plates of rice and lamb upstairs and join the others who have started eating. Mother Fadhma attempts to coax Fuad with a tasty tidbit; the excited toddler pushes her hand away.

Samira picks at her food. It's one thing for her to decide, but quite another to involve her family. She knows Hussein, Laila, and her nephews will be all right in the end; it is her mother who will suffer. As Fadhma's youngest unmarried daughter, Samira is expected to care for her aging mother. She never considered herself ambitious; any plans she has remain unformed. However, since joining the women's committee, she wants her life to have meaning. In her mind Zeinab, Syria, and Palestine have become intertwined, and she feels she must steel her resolve for what comes next—be it tonight, tomorrow, or in a year from now—even if it means one day leaving home. She is so lost in her thoughts that she doesn't hear Warda above the hubbub calling the women downstairs.

In no time long-sleeved coats and robes cover glittering party dresses. Some of the women Samira saw dancing put on their niqabs. She follows them. Near the dining room, her uncle lies in wait.

"You, my dear, are a contortionist!"

He is in fine form, his good and bad eyes glinting. Obviously something's going on.

Abu Za'atar reprimands her. "I don't know why you don't confide in me. I'm the only one in a position to help. Your mother won't understand and Hussein is"—he gestures toward the garden—"a fool."

Samira is having trouble following him.

"And if you do," he promises, "the both of us will benefit enormously—you for your causes and me for me!"

Samira finally understands her uncle's strategy: first enticement, then the stick. "And what is it you want?" She is actually curious.

"Your interesting friend—"

"Is gone." Even if she knew where Mustafa was, she wouldn't give him up. "He was just passing through," she comments, "so I'm afraid you're too late." However, because Abu Za'atar has declared an unqualified self-interest, she doesn't hide her own: "And I didn't get the chance to tell him how much I cared."

Abu Za'atar is crestfallen, amused, shocked, and guilty all at once. It occurs to Samira that perhaps the damage he intended to do has already been done. Once Mother Fadhma appears, perturbed by the sight of her daughter and brother in earnest conversation, he slips away.

In the dining room waits an elaborate six-tier wedding cake from the European bakery in the capital. With all the guests assembled, Asaf lifts Anna's veil and a cry fills the air.

"Yabayeh! Yabayeh!"

A low, gravelly voice that could have been mistaken for a man's belongs to Umm Omar, who sings, *"I put bracelets upon thy hands and a chain on thy neck."* The song is reminiscent of desert wastes and the lamentations that follow the birth of girls. Holding the knife, together the bride and groom are poised to cut the first ceremonial slice.

With all the attention in the room on them, Samira takes the opportunity and sneaks outside, followed by Muna, waiting on the fringes of the party. The garden is empty; even the bartender is indoors. A man, slumped against a table inside the tent, casts a forlorn shadow against the canvas. Samira points out the silhouette to her cousin. Then, reminded of her uncle's words, she investigates and discovers Hussein inside. Near his sagging head, on a side table, is a near-empty bottle of whisky. When his eyes momentarily clear and he tries standing up, he staggers as though the ground is moving beneath him. His chair becomes a raft.

"Relax, brother." Samira has seen him out of it before, but tonight he's in really bad shape. Her hopes from the afternoon vanish.

He regards Muna behind his sister. "Don't you think our way of life is peculiar?" his sad voice slurs.

"La amo, la, I'm fine." Muna means it. "I'm glad I'm here."

"How different we are from you." He draws his words out slowly. "I have seen the world and loved, but love is unpredictable. The more you love, the more you know, and knowing more leaves less room for respect. Here, we marry strangers and learn to respect them. The family sees to that. And love? Keep your loves for yourself."

A thin line of saliva trickles from the corner of his mouth, and his eyes glaze over as he slips into his private world of pain. Samira pulls her cousin away. She would prefer Muna not see Hussein like this, but he can't be her priority at the moment. Outside the tent she tells Muna to join the party and promises to come soon, she needs a few moments to compose her thoughts. Alone, she surveys the garden and spies Mr. Ammar and his accomplice near the house. Samira walks over and thrusts the letter into his hand. Without looking, he places it in his coat jacket. He doesn't thank her.

"We've expanded our activities to include new people," he states.

"Like the contact I met this evening?"

Mr. Ammar is noncommittal. As his friend moves off to keep watch, he says, "We need to talk. Is there somewhere private we can go? We have a car."

Samira chooses her words carefully. "This isn't a good time. Can it wait?"

He is either unsympathetic to her situation or doesn't care. "No, tonight," he insists.

Begrudgingly Samira points to the hills above them that grow into Jebel Musa. "My brother's farm is up there, a half hour by car." She isn't sure whether this is a good idea. If they do need to talk it will have to be out of sight. She will also have to be back before anyone misses her. Then she remembers Muna and demands, "My cousin has to come too." She sees that her demand is not one Mr. Ammar expects, so she explains, "My mother won't worry if we're together." Certainly the man is no fool and can understand the importance of a girl's reputation in a small town.

"All right," he agrees. "We'll meet you among the parked cars. We came late; the blue Nissan in the field is ours."

Samira reenters the Matroub house and collects Muna. Samira tries to make it sound like an adventure: "We're going for a ride." As they cross the front garden, she isn't sure why she feels it but she does: the two of them are being watched. She doesn't remember Hussein as they pass the tent. Outside the gate she gestures for Muna to slow down and Samira takes another good look around. A woman in a niqab and abaya loiters behind them at a respectful distance. Samira and Muna start off again. In the darkness, they nearly stumble into a couple lost in each other's embrace. It is Dania and the boy.

Parked cars line the driveway and spill into an adjacent field. As Samira attempts to pick out the car in the dark, the woman in the niqab brushes past and says in a barely audible voice, "Over there."

Samira takes in a sharp breath. Does she know this woman? The robed figure, complete with keys, unlocks the Nissan and issues a rebuke under her breath. "You should know better than to get into a car with a strange woman."

There's no doubt in Samira's mind. "Zeinab!" She doesn't speak too loudly.

"Took you long enough." The sly voice belongs to the mischievous moonfaced woman, who furtively unhooks her face mask. Samira's political mentor climbs into the driver's seat and invites Muna to sit in the middle between them.

"This is my American cousin," says Samira, closing the passenger-side door.

A small, delicate gloved hand reaches for Muna's. "Welcome, cousin. Has Samira told you about us?"

"Not much."

Once the car maneuvers onto the main road, Samira can no longer contain her excitement. "What are you doing here?"

"I wanted to come and tell you myself."

"Tell me what?"

"I'm going back to Syria."

Her news doesn't surprise Samira. This has probably been in the works long before she joined the women's committee.

"Why now?" Samira wants to know.

"I feel I might be too late."

"Too late?" Muna inquires.

Zeinab glances at them from the road. "I watched a news report about the last garden in Aleppo. A ten-year-old boy stopped going to school so he could help his father grow flowers and plants—there were roses—that they planted in the city's roundabouts. It almost seemed normal except for the shelling, but the father was not afraid. He said it was like listening to Beethoven. Then a bomb killed him—a tragedy like so many others that left another child alone in a destroyed city.

"Then my aunt phoned me from Syria. She was watching the evacuation of Daraya on the TV with two friends, a man and his wife, who left the district after a massacre by government troops in 2012. They were hoping to see the son they left behind in the fleeing crowds. In Daraya, the activists are unable to return to government-controlled areas. They'll be imprisoned, so they're fleeing to Idlib, Daesh's stronghold in the northwest. Torture by the regime or enslavement by the jihadists, how can it be that these are the only two choices left for the Syrian people?"

Zeinab's smooth, open face fills with anger. "I can no longer stand on the sidelines. In my worst moments I believe there's no difference between me and the Palestinian delegation, which broke Ramadan fast with members of the regime in Damascus. They ate a lavish *iftar* while a few miles away my family and friends were starving, and still are, in Yarmouk Camp." Her tone becomes defiant. "It's time for me to dirty my hands or those brave people will have died for nothing. Their blood cannot be wasted."

Samira knows Zeinab is referring to the human rights lawyer Razan Zaitouneh and her colleagues from the Violations Documentation Center: Wael Hamada, Samira al-Khalil, and Nazem Hamadi. They had been verifying the identities of the dead, until they were kidnapped by a splinter Islamic faction in Douma. Zeinab was always trying to find out about them, asking people who had just come from Syria. Over a year ago she heard that the Douma Four had been sold to another front more extremist than the previous one. Then the trail went cold.

"What are you going to do?" Samira asks her.

"Whatever I can. We Palestinians have a history of woe, but we're not the only ones at the bottom to be kicked."

Zeinab pulls the car abruptly to the side of the road, and Mr. Ammar and his companion get in. They had found a way from behind Matroub's house and scrambled up the rocks.

"Okay?" Zeinab peers through the rearview mirror, then checks with Samira for directions.

"Follow the road. Near the top there's a turnoff," she tells her.

Zeinab starts driving again. "There's something I want to ask you—"

"Not now," objects Mr. Ammar, "wait until we get there."

Ignoring him, Samira whispers to her friend, "When do you go?"

"Tonight."

Samira is stunned. "It's too soon." She tries not to sound upset, but her tone is terse; she is becoming increasingly anxious for Zeinab and for herself. She understands that it is selfish, but she relies on Zeinab and the other women in the committee. Without them she would be lost.

The car ascends the hills above the Matroub villa. From the road's edge, Samira can clearly make out the lights, the house, and the tent. She imagines the bride feeding cake into the mouth of her new husband, an experience she will never know. Her involvement with the women's committee ushered in a new era of realism in her life, which banished romantic illusion forever. But the evening showed how easy it was to become enthralled once again with the dream of the bride.

If their time together is short she has to tell Zeinab. Only she and the other women from the committee would understand. Leaning across her cousin, Samira admits quietly, so the men in the back won't hear, "Tonight I came face-to-face with the 'enemy within.'"

Zeinab keeps her eyes firmly on the road. "I don't know about your cousin, but you and I are susceptible to weddings."

From where Samira is sitting, she can see her leader smiling. It is a small consolation. Samira leans back, distraught. She glances out the window at the fairy lights from the Matroubs' garden but she doesn't see them. Her anxiety over Zeinab's imminent departure clouds her vision. She also doesn't notice a group of uninvited guests or the man they drag away between them.

25

The car leaves the road and heads down a dirt track toward a barn illuminated by a single bare lightbulb. Zeinab parks in a clearing, near a cluster of small buildings. The night is intensified by the singing of the mountain cicadas.

Holding the door, Samira whispers as Muna gets out, "At least you'll see the pigs."

Muna doesn't think it's funny. Wide-eyed, she is unsure of the darkness and Samira's friends. She would like her cousin to tell her why they're here. Or perhaps she hasn't a clue, which makes Muna more apprehensive.

Meanwhile Samira refuses to make any excuses for the farm. There is an awful rancid smell that cannot be concealed by any number of cigarettes Mr. Ammar and the bodyguard, who introduced himself as Uthman, smoke by the car.

Mr. Ammar apologizes and leads Samira and Zeinab to the side of the barn and the light, where they settle on a pile of plastic crates. Mosquitoes mass in the yellow haze above their heads.

Alone in the dark, Muna and Uthman stand awkwardly together. Aside from the fact that the man is no stranger to weightlifting, all Muna knows about him is his name. They could discuss his namesake: Uthman ibn Affan, the third caliph to rule after the Prophet's death, collected Qur'anic revelations and inscribed them on camel bone and pottery shards. Vellum manuscripts did not appear until a century later. She would prefer talking about that than her anxieties. She has just met the bodyguard and she doesn't feel she can trust him.

The big man might have the same impression of her. Throwing down his cigarette, he moves toward the other end of the barn. In the gloom, Muna hears what sounds like a large wooden door sliding open. "Let's look inside," he calls to her, then vanishes.

Muna stubbornly stays put until the electric generator has been located and fluorescent lighting reveals the open expanse of a barn crisscrossed and subdivided by all manner of pens.

As she joins him, he whistles under his breath. "So this is the place!"

Hussein's business is not factory farming, although it is on a grander scale than Samira led Muna to believe. To the untutored eye, everything appears ramshackle. Some of the pens or stalls are blocked off with railings, others with wooden planks and strips of corrugated tin, but on closer inspection she sees that the enclosures are clean and well maintained. The feed is kept in burlap sacks stacked against the wall, and there is a dedicated soiling area. Uthman considers the pigs stirring in their pens.

"I would have never believed it," Muna says, astonished, as she takes in the animals and then Uthman. A man named after a caliph might have another opinion. His expression is one of amusement rather than outrage.

"Personally I don't care for them, but there are cousins on the other side of the river waiting for a shipment of pork. On this side we always wait—always—for guns."

"You mean *your* cousins?" says Muna, a little confused. He's talking about his family?

"*Our* cousins," Uthman roguishly replies. "All Semites are related whether we love them or not."

The big man continues with his thoughts. "Some of the money from the pork sold there is siphoned off to purchase guns that are sold at even higher prices. It is the cycle of ever-increasing profit."

When Muna, mortified, doesn't comment, he observes, "Now, I know you're American."

"How can you tell?" This guy is getting on her nerves. Surely pig rearing is an unlikely setting for gun smuggling.

"Naive and simplistic," he informs her. "Americans are all the same. To them it's always a binary equation: us against them. You feel better if one side's good and the other is bad. Life is more complicated than that."

He isn't finished. "My mother's brother in Florida told me that every time a bomb goes off in the US, Americans assume that Arab terrorists are to blame. There's violence on your streets, in your homes, in your schools and churches, and each time it's *our* fault? The warm wind blows in from Mexico, the cold comes down from Canada, and there is nothing good in between."

"We suffer from the same thing," Muna comments drily. "You don't know my country and I am not familiar enough with yours." She motions in the direction of the pigs sleeping huddled up against one another. "If anyone is living constantly under the threat of death, it's them."

When one of the tiny bodies rolls over, the next one adjusts itself ever so slightly to optimize the use of space. Little mouths curve into tiny, toothless grins, the very picture of innocence and contentment. In the next pen, a heat lamp is attached to one wall. Tiny piglets, no bigger than her fist, press against it in an untidy pile of snouts and tails.

She and Uthman stop in front of a subdivided pen holding five stretching and yawning boars, each in its own cell. The light woke them and they mill about, scratching themselves against the railings. As Uthman approaches they press forward, competing for the best spot. He touches a bristly forehead. "They're hungry," he calls out.

Muna doesn't reply, transfixed by a corpulent backside of black-and-tan fur, covered in sharp ginger bristles, dominating the largest pen in the barn. Closer inspection reveals the shape and dimensions of an enormous sow with a snout as big as a bear's. Over five feet long, with broad muscular shoulders, its tremendous bulk nearly fills the sty. On its side, the pig lays in imperious splendor. A milky liquid oozes from teats that cover a massive swollen underbelly; the same sticky substance has been smeared all over the pig, the straw, and the pen. The sight, combined with the smell, nearly makes Muna retch, but she doesn't look away. The animal's mouth is open, its eyes rolled back. A rippling movement in the blubber caused by shallow breathing indicates that it is alive.

Muna murmurs out loud, "How disgusting!"

Uthman comes up beside her. "So this is the famous beauty!" The mocking of Muna's country has been replaced by curious admiration for a pig.

As though on cue, a wave undulates through the humongous body and the head slowly lifts. Once the animal's eyes turn, the stare is fixed and rigid. The pig groans. Low and menacing, part animal, part human, it sounds like someone being tortured or out of their mind. Wheezing and grunting, it strains to shift its weight in an effort to stand up, but the necessary equilibrium is, at first, beyond its control. With each attempt, the groans become louder. The piglets in the other pens, now fully awake, fidget. The larger ones paw the ground. The sow's discomfort is having a visceral effect on the rest of the animals. Finally it pulls itself upright. Muna can't tell which is worse, the pig's terrible smell or its incredible ugliness. "What's up with this one?"

"You don't know?" Uthman becomes effusive. "Let me introduce you. Umm al-Khanaazeer, Mother of All Pigs, queen of the sty, meet your cousin from America!"

Muna, wrinkling her nose, turns away as loud voices breach the barn walls. Not everyone is in agreement outside. Muna can easily pick out Samira's angry voice while the others attempt to calm her down. Peering at Uthman, Muna wants to gauge his reaction, but he appears uninterested; opposing viewpoints among comrades are nothing new.

He is pointing at the adjacent pens. "The little ones belong to her or her daughters. She has been, in effect, a one-pig population explosion, a fertility goddess." He bends down and peers into the sow's beady eyes. "Don't be humble, missy, your reputation precedes you."

As he reaches into the pen, the massive sow lunges at him without warning. Uthman plucks his hand out just in time and holds it warily against a broad chest strengthened by steroids. Disbelief mingles with alarm on his face.

Muna is unsympathetic. "If I was a factory birth-giving machine, I probably would have attacked and maimed humans long ago."

The animal, bloated beyond belief, snorts in short, loud bursts. It kicks the ground with its front hoof, then throws itself headlong into the wooden planks of the pen, which shake under the strain of the impact but hold firm. Caught off guard, Uthman and Muna move off quickly, as the rest of the barn's inhabitants, in a malign chorus, squeal loudly.

"Let's get out of here!" She retraces her steps through the labyrinth of pens to the door and flees into the night.

Once Uthman shuts down the generator, her vision is filled with a bright afterglow before everything fades to near black. She is still adjusting to the darkness as the two of them make their way toward a rocky outcrop. Muna, in the wrong kind of shoes, snags a heel on uneven ground. She almost loses her step a second time, but Uthman catches her by the arm. She is going to thank him when she hears a sudden commotion and feels a rush of air; someone or something scuttled past her. It was close, whatever it was. The big man too is standing perfectly still, waiting, watching, and listening.

Muna breaks the tension by quietly asking, "What was that?" She can't hide the fear in her voice.

Still scanning the murky shapes of rocks and scrub, the bodyguard doesn't answer right away. When he does, he mumbles, "Maybe man, maybe pig, can't tell."

They start walking again—this time Muna treading more cautiously over the rutted earth and Uthman less attentive to the woman by his side. The both of them are attuned to the noises of the night. When nothing else happens they both think they must have been mistaken. Despite their political differences, the brush with the unknown has brought them closer and Muna finds herself not minding the bodyguard as much.

They stop near where the ground slopes downward and rolls off into the distance, with the lights of the town far below. The blazing neon sign advertising Abu Za'atar's Marvellous Emporium blinks on, off, on, on, on, with menacing irregularity like search lamps. Even the outlines of the service square are still visible with the headlights of the taxis and the fires from the outdoor barbecues. Towering over the town are the two domes, one belonging to the mosque, the other to the Church of the Mosaic. At the very bottom, where the dimmest outline of the road runs like a ribbon through the hills, are the twinkling lights of the wedding party. Above, a waning moon hangs in a vault of stars.

"See that?" Uthman, his gaze turned upward, picks out the Pleiades. His tone is wistful. "Radiation that has been traveling since the world was nothing but a chunk of molten rock hurtling through space, and this second now it reaches us tonight. They should remind us of our insignificance." He is interrupted by gunfire coming from the Matroub villa. "Hey, they're celebrating the wedding."

The firing, followed by shouting or singing—Muna can't tell which—catches the wind and is carried up to the farm.

"Ever handle a gun?" Uthman asks her.

Her reply, a shake of her head, sends him in long strides toward the car. Muna hears the trunk opened and then slammed shut. When he returns, there is pride in his voice as he hands an automatic weapon to Muna.

"Kalashnikov!" he declares.

"No, that's all right." She wants to give it back to him, but he presses it into her hands until she has to take it.

"No worries," he insists, "I will help you."

The steel is cold and heavy. Before Muna can stop him, Uthman has reached in from behind her. In another time or place she would have been a young woman cradled in the arms of a capable man. Uncomfortable, Muna doesn't want to give in but she does. "Okay."

Resting the Kalashnikov's butt in the crook of her shoulder, he guides her left hand beneath the barrel and pushes it upward so that she aims at the stars he says he loves. Undoing the safety catch, he steps back and orders, "Now!" As a volley of bullets explodes into the air, Muna isn't prepared either for the force or the shock of the sound—loud, sharp, resentful—like an angry Old Testament God.

26

Abu Za'atar peers blurry-eyed at a night filled with clandestine pursuits. In the dark with his magnifying glass rendered useless, his other senses intensify. Around him the air is suffused with the sounds of laughter, crying, moaning—the pleasure and pain. Weddings are like carnivals. With the rustling in the bushes, someone somewhere is getting kissed, smacked, or kidnapped. Outside the Matroub villa, the men who were shooting into the air have lowered their guns and are returning to their whiskys. At one time he would have joined in the carousing. Looking toward the mountain, Abu Za'atar deeply inhales the aroma of grime and dirt laced with petrochemicals before he starts stretching. He feels remarkably limber after his physical exertions. Muscle strain doesn't bother him as much as the inexplicable behavior of his nieces.

His pursuit of them was no mean feat. He maneuvered though the parked cars until he was forced to insinuate himself into all manner of tight spots. He tucked himself behind wheels, lay over trunks, and even surprised himself with a gravity-defying sideways stork pose in the cavity beneath a passenger-side door, secured by a deftly placed foot. This Wonder was worth it. Because of her garb, she could have been easily overlooked, except for her shoes, a knockoff pair of Converse, which gave her away. It was a red rag to a falcon. Of course he recognized them; he had even tried to sell them in the emporium, but the distributor ran out. More than them, he admired her spunk and initial approach to Samira. It was so discreet that even at his close range he was unable to pick out a word between them.

He didn't need to hear them because the unpinning of the niqab plays over and over in his head like a scratched record on Sammy's turntables. Abu Za'atar is pulled away from the image of this improbable scenario by his vibrating phone. His son, sounding disturbed and breathless, is on the line: "I don't know—men—" His voice keeps cutting out due to bad reception. "—watch out!"

Abu Za'atar scratches his back against a side mirror of a transit van and goes to where he can see the town. He follows two sedan-loads of *mukhabarat* cutting a swathe through the streets. Corrosive suspicion is like that, it permeates every crack like flammable exploding grease.

Sammy is yelling, "Everybody in the shop was rounded up and taken outside—I escaped—but before I did I overheard one of the men saying they're looking for a secret cache of weapons. Dad, do they mean yours?" The phone goes dead.

When it vibrates again Abu Za'atar assumes it is his son. This time the call sounds like it is coming from the center of viciousness: yelling, thumping, and cursing are all he hears in between seconds of deadly silence. A mental picture forms in Abu Za'atar's mind of big men in ill-fitting leather jackets, a bulk buy from Irbil, not Istanbul.

"We're in the alleyways and the *arghileh* bars of the Eastern Quarter," a man shouts above the cacophony. "Haven't found him yet. We need to dig deep. What about your store?"

Before Abu Za'atar can put him off, the man bellows, "We're coming to get you!" then hangs up.

This is not Abu Za'atar's idea of a fun night out, but he knows better than to argue. They have his GPS coordinates. More disturbing is his house of cards, the Marvellous Emporium, tottering before him. One gasp and it's gone.

As he waits another pair of glowing headlamps loses itself in the angular shadows of Jebel Musa. A volley of bullets inexplicably exploding from on high gets the Featherer's synapses firing. Only one place can offer the level of intrigue, not to mention exotic animal husbandry, needed to distract and impress his new friends.

His cell phone vibrates and then is silent. Abu Za'atar touches his nose to his knees one last time. Mean, lean, and ready for action, he scurries through and around the dead metal of parked cars to a fate unknown on the other side.

27

Outside the barn, under a bare lightbulb, Zeinab and Mr. Ammar have been endeavoring to allay Samira's fears, but she will not be persuaded. Frustrated, she raises her voice: "They're against everything the women's committee believes in—what you taught me to believe in." She scowls at Zeinab. "Why change now?"

Samira gets up from the crate and walks away. Her friend, following, guides her back to where they stand glumly together, staring at the ground.

Mr. Ammar lowers his voice. "That's why Zeinab and I need to talk to you."

Samira peers at the both of them over her glasses and sits down. Mr. Ammar moves to the nearest crate beside her. Hunched over, he talks with his hands. "When I said the front is widening its scope, I wasn't just referring to them." He motions toward the town. "As you know, Zeinab leaves tonight. We take her as far as the Nasib/Jabir crossing in the west, or if she can't leave from there, then to one of the unofficial places in the east of Jordan, where the smugglers bring people in. Those areas are heavily patrolled by the Jordanian army and there are rumors that the US will be giving Jordan the same heat-seeking surveillance equipment used on the Mexican border. The time is right now. She will be met and taken across the desert into Syria. It's nearly impossible to enter Daesh-controlled As-Sweida, but it can be done.

"If that fails we take Zeinab to Iraq and she crosses the border there. Too many factions are fighting inside. However, rebels we know supervise a stretch. She has to avoid populated districts where the regime or the Russians are bombing."

As the contours of Zeinab's journey take shape, Samira's anger about the youth in the garden subsides. She has heard stories about comrades disappearing in the middle of the night from members of the women's committee, employed as secretaries in one of the front's dummy offices. Normally it was the men who vanished across borders. This time Zeinab has made the decision herself. Samira feels a twinge of satisfaction.

"I wanted to ask you," Zeinab begins quietly again.

Samira is listening carefully.

"If you'll consider coming with me. We work well together. The toughest part will be the desert crossing. Once inside, our real work can begin."

Samira is secretly thrilled. But before she can react, feelings of regret suffocate her. "M-my mother?" she stammers.

"We're your family now," says Zeinab soothingly. "You will visit them from time to time. Remember, you will be among those who believe enough in you to entrust you with their lives."

Her words return Samira to the disagreeable encounter among the sickly-sweet honeysuckle and jasmine in the garden. "And the sheikh and his followers, are they trustworthy too?"

Zeinab becomes exasperated. "You're not being realistic. Tell her, Ammar. We survive on the grace of others. The same forces that nurtured us in the past invest in others. It's the old story—divide and rule. Everyone wants to drug the masses. Why not with religion? The loyalty of people can be bought, some believe, with little effort. Whoever organizes the militias, buys the guns, runs the hospitals and schools, cleans the streets, generates a thriving underground economy, has the power. Whoever digs the tunnels and runs the blockades are kings in the land of the brutalized. But it doesn't have to be that way. If the Americans and the Peshmerga fight Daesh in Iraq and the only fighters left in Syria are Assad's assassins, the Russians, al-Nusra Front, and Jaysh al-Islam, what's to become of us? I have no choice but return." She is silent after her outburst.

"Believe me," Mr. Ammar stresses, "none of us wants anything to do with the Islamists, but they have unlimited resources and a formidable network through their charities and religious madrassas. Who else is strong enough to support us and give us arms?"

His argument gives way to anger. "If we are weak and do nothing, it means death. If we stop moving, even sleep, we die. We need them now, not forever."

Samira feels dejected. Where they sit, against the barn, Hussein erected an old plaque of their father's, a faded handprint in the blood of a sacrificed goat. It was a sign of Al Jid's belief that God Himself protected the grain and animals. Samira prays that she too will share in its provision and that against the odds her life will not be wasted.

A burst of close gunfire rouses her from the crate and she abandons Zeinab and Mr. Ammar without a word, rushing toward the car. "What happened?" she asks Uthman, who is returning the Kalashnikov to the trunk. Zeinab, Mr. Ammar, and Muna join them.

Uthman brags, "Your cousin is a *feedayeen*—a freedom fighter. *Mabrouk*, congratulations!"

Samira is more excited than relieved. Smiling, she turns to Muna and announces, "I'm going to work for Syria whatever way I can." A decision has been made in the short distance from the barn.

She continues speaking, even though she knows Mr. Ammar would prefer her to say nothing of their plans. "I leave tonight."

Samira, hugging her cousin, feels her flinch. She would like to talk with her more so she won't worry. Instead Samira stops and listens to a whining car engine straining on the hills. It's not as faint as it should be, which means it's closer than she thinks. Once the car is on the turnoff and the long reach of its lights reflects off the dirt track, Uthman takes charge. Quickly gathering the small group behind rocks, he signals for them to keep out of sight and remain absolutely still, as a battered station wagon pulls near them.

The elderly turbaned sheikh with a walking stick is the first out, followed by two younger men dressed in loose tunics and trousers.

One of them brandishes a handgun. Samira can't be sure in the dark, but she thinks she sees the youth from the garden. Two more men emerge, supporting a third incapable of walking by himself. Badly beaten up, his body hangs limply forward. Although his face is hidden, Samira immediately recognizes Hussein. Biting her knuckles, she clutches at Muna.

The men drag Hussein around to the front of the car and drop him. He moves fitfully in the headlights. His captors have apparently been having their own heated discussion on the drive up. A large man wearing a prayer cap speaks first: "This place is an abomination. Behead him now. Be done with it. Why care about an infidel? He will burn in hell anyway."

Another man calls for calm: "Do we kill everyone in our path?"

The youth from the garden is impatient. "We've debated enough. Haven't we warned him? Each day that goes by we are abused by his vile presence, and all of this"—he dismisses everything around them—"just by breathing in this stench we endanger our souls." He grabs Hussein by the collar and lifts him off the ground. "*Ya kalb*—dog—we'll show you what we do to people who disrespect our religion!"

Behind the rocks, Samira hisses at Mr. Ammar, pleading, "Do something!" Tears of mascara form in deep pools beneath her glasses. "I warned you not to trust them, but you wouldn't listen—"

"Your brother will be all right," Zeinab whispers. Her dark beautiful eyes are frightened but her demeanor cool. She looks to Mr. Ammar for confirmation.

"We'll do everything for him, but not now," he promises Samira. "One man can't destroy something that has taken a year to build."

Samira whimpers, "And when will you do it, after he's dead? After I'm dead?" *How many have been tricked by this political fraudster?*

He attempts to calm her by taking her hands in his.

"Don't touch me!" she screams, and stands up. Muna pulls her back, but it's too late. Before Samira walks into the light, Mr. Ammar steps decisively in front of her, followed by Uthman and Zeinab. The sheikh and his men are so astonished, they let go of Hussein and he falls with a thud to the ground.

The political officer wastes no time. "I am Mr. Ammar." He speaks as though there is nothing out of the ordinary about his appearance in the middle of the night on a disreputable farm. He nods respectfully to the sheikh. "The two of us have been in correspondence. Tonight I received your final terms and conditions." He raises his voice to emphasize the seriousness of his commitment. "I never thought we would conclude our negotiations here."

"There is no place my followers and I do not go—"

"What are you doing to my brother?" Samira goes to Hussein, but the youth from the garden blocks her way.

The sheikh addresses Mr. Ammar. "I know you have connections to this family. A courier is one thing," he admits brusquely, "but I did not realize the extent of your relations. Political officer, it makes me think twice about our plans. The price of our cooperation is a willingness on both of our parts to fight a common enemy." He dispassionately points his stick at Hussein on the ground. "Some actions demand a response. We tried reasoning. For this man, words were not enough."

Samira interrupts him by screaming, "Leave my brother alone!"

The sheikh turns and regards her. His voice is colorless and flat. "Have you ever considered, little sister, that we both fight on the same side? Everywhere our people suffer. At this very moment some are bombed or tortured or live starving under siege. Life without fear is the preserve of the wealthy, never the poor. In this world, an individual is powerless. Only sharia will restore the balance. But how can we hope for His guidance with corruption and pollution all around us."

"Yes, we must take our decision." It is the youth from the garden again, contemptuous of Samira and her friends. "They are with or against us. There is no middle way."

"Show them who we are!" another of the sheikh's followers shouts out, and kicks Hussein, who covers his head with his hands.

As the others taunt, "Kill him!" the sheikh pronounces, "The Qur'an is clear. For His survival alone, enemies of the faith must fall. Our actions will breed terror in the hearts of the kaffirs."

"Before you kill him, you will have to kill me first." A disembodied voice, weary and indifferent, floats to them from out of nowhere.

Mustafa steps in front of the sheikh's car with no shirt, in his boots. He holds one of his travel souvenirs, America's finest for CQB—close quarters battle—an M4 carbine assault rifle.

"I am the only person here truly qualified for the job. My credentials are"—he wets his lips—"impeccable." His quiet deliberation gives the impression of a man talking to himself. Then raising his voice, he growls at the men standing over Hussein, "Move!"

The sheikh's followers step closer together, forming a tight circle around the heaped body on the ground.

"Should I demonstrate?" Mustafa is seconds away from firing.

Even in the poor light, the henna prayer etched across the young man's chest is visible. "But you," the sheikh is staring at him, "are one of us. You are marked, a soldier of Allah." He leans on his stick. "*Mujahid*, remember your instruction; put down your weapon."

"Move!" Mustafa shouts again. "Or everyone will die, except the lieutenant. He's suffered enough. All of us have suffered enough."

The sheikh's words sound honey-coated. "Why threaten us? As true believers, we are only doing our duty." When the soldier doesn't reply, the sheikh becomes aggressive. "I demand the truth. You have dedicated your life to Allah—what are you doing in this hellhole?"

Mustafa answers thoughtfully. "Only what I have been taught, master: bide my time, surprise the enemy, then be quick, be brutal. Jihad is only satisfied with human blood. And these revolutionaries," he jeers at Mr. Ammar, although his eyes won't leave Samira, "look at me for your lost innocence."

Muna stifles a scream as the young man from the garden throws himself at the soldier, but the *mujahid* is quick. He swings the rifle hard into the boy's stomach and, as he doubles over, once more across the forehead.

"Such foolishness," Mustafa sounds coldly detached. With a faint jerk of his chin, he glowers at the man with the handgun, daring him to act. The sheikh's follower throws it to the ground.

Hussein staggers to his feet, and Samira, rushing to his side, leads him away from his attackers. A low rumble of engines belonging to at least two vehicles—now on the mountain, are making the turnoff. Hussein, leaning on his baby sister, whispers the only

real advice he has ever given her: "Take who you love, travel lightly. Leave now!"

She thinks he must be delirious until he promises her, "I will tell
Mother Fadhma and she will understand. Send word when you
can, return if it's safe; we will wait for you." When she hesitates
again, he stresses, "Go before it's too late. Those who come now are
truly dangerous. Listen to a brother who has witnessed too much."
Despite his weakened condition he gives her a last piece of useful
advice—"The soldier knows the way"—before forcibly pushing her
aside and stumbling off into the darkness.

The sheikh is berating Mustafa again. "Believer, among us, your
brothers, you are not an outcast. Among them"—he points at Samira—"a hired hand, a murderer, condemned to run for the rest of
your days."

The soldier takes aim. "Before you drown in your own blood,
drink from mine."

In the split second between threat and action, the assault
weapon wavers. Samira, recognizing the signs, positions herself
beside him to do whatever she must, as two sedans barrel down
the dirt tract toward the farm. Headlights akimbo, they screech to
a halt. Heavily armed men rush the sheikh and his followers. In
the confusion Samira seizes her chance and she is not alone. At
that moment the heavy barn doors slide open and a cascade of
fluorescent light fills the yard. The roar of grunts, howls, thrashing, and cussing dies down. All eyes are drawn to Hussein, beat-
en and weak, standing perfectly still. In his hand is an enormous
meat cleaver. He gazes at the assembled and walks around the
enclosures housing the pigs. Each time his step falters, he supports himself against a railing. It is the arduous journey of a man
in pain, but his purpose is clear.

At the largest pen, he places one leg over the bars, summons his
remaining strength, and climbs into the minuscule space not tak-
en by Umm al-Khanaazeer. Shocked by the unexpected visitor, the
pig's gargantuan body rears onto her hind legs. Hussein is nearly
dwarfed, but his weapon is well placed. Treachery from the hand that
once cared and nourished it is the cruelest blow. The pig's bellowing

cries intermingle with whimpering groans that Hussein identifies as human and belonging to Abu Za'atar. His corporeal body or astral spirit—Hussein isn't sure which—has ascended Musa's mountain to bid his lucrative IVF experiment good-bye.

But nothing distracts Hussein from his errand. A lifeless face squeezes words out through clenched teeth. Every third one is emphasized as the cleaver hacks into flesh. "I will *not* let a *pig* stand between *you* and your *maker*. If you *believe* that Umm al-Khanaazeer's *death* means our *resurrection*, it's *my pleasure* to help *you*."

The sharp blade comes down hard on the sow again and again. Crouching, she endeavours to crawl into the four corners of the pen, but Hussein is relentless.

"How we all yearn for greatness."

Blood rises in fountains and falls like rain.

"And all the while it is here, in the belly of a pig. God knows we are all tired of being last, stupid, corrupt, attacked."

As Hussein works on, the animal stops moving and the mass of flesh accepts the blows as easily as a pillow. He hauls himself up on the side of the pen, holding what's left of the big pig by one ear. Her half-open eyes peer haughtily out.

"This is my sacrifice so the killings will end. No more wars over useless land. No more feuding between the godless and the godly, one bloated with hunger and thirst, the other with righteous greed. What benevolent ruler kills hundreds of thousands for a Swiss bank account? Who considers rape of little girls religious ecstasy? Any excuse is convenient when you want to destroy countries and steal lives."

Abu Za'atar has been watching Hussein with mounting revulsion. When he can no longer restrain himself and is about to fly into the barn, a hand reaches out from the darkness and holds him firm. Squinting with his good eye, he can just make out the charm against the evil eye around Samira's neck. Its dull gleam catches the light before it fades away into nothingness. He could have easily imagined it but will brag about this detail for years to come. Muna stands at his side as Samira blows both of them a kiss before disappearing behind a ridge for good. Following her are two unlikely companions:

one wonderful and the other an unknown quantity but more than likely useful in a pinch.

Sometimes when his good and bad eyes cross each other, they prevent him from seeing clearly, or rather that will be his excuse if called to the witness stand. He could alert the *mukhabarat* that the fugitive they seek is getting away, but with so many suspects to choose from, he won't be missed. Abu Za'atar has been in the company of the secret police long enough to appreciate their particular brand of deterrence: men intent on doing so much good they cut down everybody in their way. Abu Za'atar removes his never-without, woven from five hundred thousand of the finest Egyptian cotton threads, and derives much-needed comfort from its softness. No matter the situation, Samira wouldn't want it otherwise, and he won't allow her impeccable standards to slide.

"Hope is something with wings" is his final comment on the whole sorry ordeal, which he imparts to Muna.

In the barn Hussein has sunk to his knees and plunged his hands into the massive dead pig. "God Almighty," he sobs in great gasps, "let this *khanzir* wash away its sins and ours."

His clothes are bathed in blood. He lays down the meat cleaver and steadies himself enough to climb out of the pen. Something else is on his mind.

"My father taught me to give in order to receive. Wild boar ran in the Yarmouk Valley before man sowed the first seeds in 5500 B.C. They will thrive there once again," he vows. As he regards his blood-soaked fingers, he is astonished to find that, for once, they are not trembling. The pain of the beating and the sorrow of killing his pig have been pushed aside by a curious elation. At last, he feels responsible for himself.

As he walks the length of the barn, flicking open the latches on the pens, his mind is racing. It will be impossible for his rapacious uncle to understand, but Hussein and his family will manage. Any material deficiencies will be compensated for with love and attention. Laila will learn to trust him. So will Mother Fadhma—if she can fight her natural tendency of living in regret. There will be the initial shock about Samira, but he and the old woman will cope. For too long each and every one of them has been engulfed by memories more vivid than the reality of their lives.

Hussein's hands begin to pulsate and expand, filling his field of vision. He can clearly distinguish every fold of skin in sharp, unnatural detail. Each is a tiny river of blood, and in the rivers a thousand futures are flowing. He cannot be sure what will be unleashed. His sons will either end up as doctors or killers. He doesn't know which. His sister was the one person in the family who could have benefited from his experiences. Tonight was the first time he tried to help her. If they meet again, and this too is an uncertainty, he will explain that many roads lead to redemption. Temporarily, his burden feels lighter. As the barn starts spinning fast and then very, very slowly, with great difficulty Hussein raises his head and sees the specter of his father. Al Jid is no longer angry or ashamed of his son.

Pigs of every conceivable shape and size run amok—speckled, tan, black, and brown, hairy and smooth, the beauties and the ginger beasts, piglets with the good fortune to evade their mother's digestive tract but who will not survive the cruel night alone, the castrated six-month-olds ready for slaughter, the crippled and the runts. Caught in the teeming animals, the sheikh and his followers, the *mukhabarat* strongmen, and the front's political wing fall angrily over one another. Wordlessly, Muna and Abu Za'atar detach themselves and go to Hussein while all around them porcine mouths, from which milk teeth have been lovingly plucked or filed, issue an unearthly cry of liberation.

A handful of male animals, their instincts dulled by captivity and testosterone growth hormone, turn northwards and ascend the barren higher slopes towards the church and ruined monastery on Jebel Musa. The rest, as through drawn by gravity, move downhill. Suddenly mountainside rocks and shrubs are alive with hoof, snout and twisted tail. Faster than anyone can drive, for the road is far from being the most direct route, the pigs flee through the lower pastures and fields. Some, sensing the long journey ahead, stop for water at the prophet's springs and drink before trotting off to catch up with their friends. When older sows start slowing down and losing their way, brazen younger pigs take over and, at the bottom of the small hills, avail themselves of the pleasant respite offered by the lilies and oleander in Matroub's fragrantly cool and fairy-lit garden.

By the forked crossroads, siblings who have not been separated since birth gamble on the final destination of the main arteries through the town and take off in different directions. Some head into the Eastern Quarter, and the thin streets and contorted alleys become a racetrack, from which the animals emerge at the other end, dizzy but amused. Others are waylaid by roadside garbage near the covered market but not for long. Soon every corner of the town is filled with snuffling rooting pigs.

In the grey before dawn, as the rich dew forms, the dogs yield their accustomed haunts to an unseen threat. Glimpsing the cause from the front terrace, Mother Fadhma carefully disengages herself from sleeping Laila and the boys so as not to disturb them. The old woman walks slowly through the new house and doesn't stop to consult her dead husband. In the kitchen she starts her preparations for the family's comfort food, hot mint tea and toasted *za'atar* bread. Samira and Hussein have been out all night and they still might not be on their way home. Fadhma realizes she will have to face whatever comes calmly, rationally and without fear. It is no good preparing all the while for disaster; sometimes you have to be ready for what might have a passing resemblance to success.

At that hour the only person on the streets of the town is the butcher's assistant Khaled. The juvenile favours the wee hours of the morning and often sneaks out of his father's house for a relaxing stroll. Initially the odd pig or two doesn't make much of an impression on him but as their numbers grow he stands out of their way on the steps of the mosaic church and observes. He is well versed in Biblical stories about plagues of frogs, locust and vermin but *khanaazeer* has never been mentioned. He doesn't mind. The animals are in too much of a hurry to cause him trouble. When an adorable bone-tired runt collapses, Khaled picks it up and strokes the soft downy fur beneath its belly. He thinks about keeping it under his bed but he's never been good with pets. He might be slow but he isn't stupid.

As he leaves it snoring on the steps three veiled women pass in front of the church. He thinks he catches his name on the wind. Only then he notices that one is wearing heavy boots and has feet like a man's.

For the pigs, the unpaved streets seem to hold little fascination, except for the smell of food from the falafel stand. Two, which don't have the good sense to follow their noses to the service square and frolic in the rubbish heaps of the barbecues and restaurants, find themselves listlessly sniffing around Abu Za'atar's Marvellous Emporium, where the scent belonging to their great-great-great-great-great-great-great-great-great-great-grandmother is vague but unmistakably pungent. On Lovers' Lane, a large rust-colored boar releases his pheromones and urinates under a lamppost.

Most of the pigs converge on the track between the boys' and girls' schools, which leads to the fields and open countryside of the surrounding plateau, eventually down the desert steppes to the valley, and finally to the jungle wilderness of the *zur* along the banks of the Jordan River. They have been given a chance they cannot afford to squander. Only the most ignorant would choose to be in the town after the first glimmer of light in the east signals the beginning of another hot bothered day.

ACKNOWLEDGMENTS

We are daughters of the morning star poem from Mohammad, sceau des prophètes: Extraite de la Chronique de Tabari, trans. by Hermann Zotenberg, was translated into English by Olivia and Bassem Snaije, 2017. *Outside the tent there was talk about honor... about haram...I'm a woman not a slave...* from the rap song Female Refugees by Monma, Al-Raas and Al-Sayyed Darwish was translated by Ghias Aljundi, 2014. *The mud of their own land on their face* appeared in Land Without Honour by Kitty Warnock, 1990.

Malu Halasa thanks Marina Penalva and the Pontas Literary and Film Agency; Olivia Taylor Smith, C.P. Heiser, Jaya Nicely and Nancy Tan at Unnamed Press, Majd Masri, Lawrence Joffe, Mitch Albert and Rebecca Carter.

@unnamedpress

facebook.com/theunnamedpress

unnamedpress.tumblr.com

www.unnamedpress.com

@unnamedpress